Charles M. Schulz

PEANUTS™

Special thanks to the Schulz family, everyone at Charles M. Schulz Creative Associates, and to Charles M. Schulz for his singular achievement in shaping these beloved characters.

Cover
Pencils by **Bob Scott**
Inks and Colors by **Justin Thompson**
Design by **Iain R. Morris**

Editors: **Matt Gagnon & Shannon Watters**
Asst. Editor: **Adam Staffaroni**
Trade Designer: **Stephanie Gonzaga**

For Charles M. Schulz Creative Associates
Creative Director: **Paige Braddock**
Managing Editor: **Alexis E. Fajardo**

ROSS RICHIE Chief Executive Officer • **MATT GAGNON** Editor-in-Chief • **FILIP SABLIK** VP-Publishing & Marketing • **LANCE KREITER** VP-Licensing & Merchandising
PHIL BARBARO Director of Finance • **BRYCE CARLSON** Managing Editor • **DAFNA PLEBAN** Editor • **SHANNON WATTERS** Editor • **ERIC HARBURN** Editor • **CHRIS ROSA** Assistant Editor
STEPHANIE GONZAGA Graphic Designer • **JASMINE AMIRI** Operations Coordinator • **DEVIN FUNCHES** E-Commerce & Inventory Coordinator • **BRIANNA HART** Executive Assistant

PEANUTS Volume Two — February 2013. Published by KaBOOM!, a division of Boom Entertainment, Inc. All contents, unless otherwise specified, Copyright © 2013 Peanuts Worldwide, LLC. Originally published in single magazine form as PEANUTS Volume 2 1-4. Copyright © 2012 Peanuts Worldwide, LLC. All rights reserved. KaBOOM!™ and the KaBOOM! logo are trademarks of Boom Entertainment, Inc., registered in various countries and categories. All characters, events, and institutions depicted herein are fictional. Any similarity between any of the names, characters, persons, events, and/or institutions in this publication to actual names, characters, and persons, whether living or dead, events, and/or institutions is unintended and purely coincidental. KaBOOM! does not read or accept unsolicited submissions of ideas, stories, or artwork.

A catalog record of this book is available from OCLC and from the BOOM! Studios website, www.boom-studios.com, on the Librarians Page.

BOOM! Studios, 5670 Wilshire Boulevard, Suite 450, Los Angeles, CA 90036-5679. Printed in China. First Printing.
ISBN: 978-1-60886-299-3

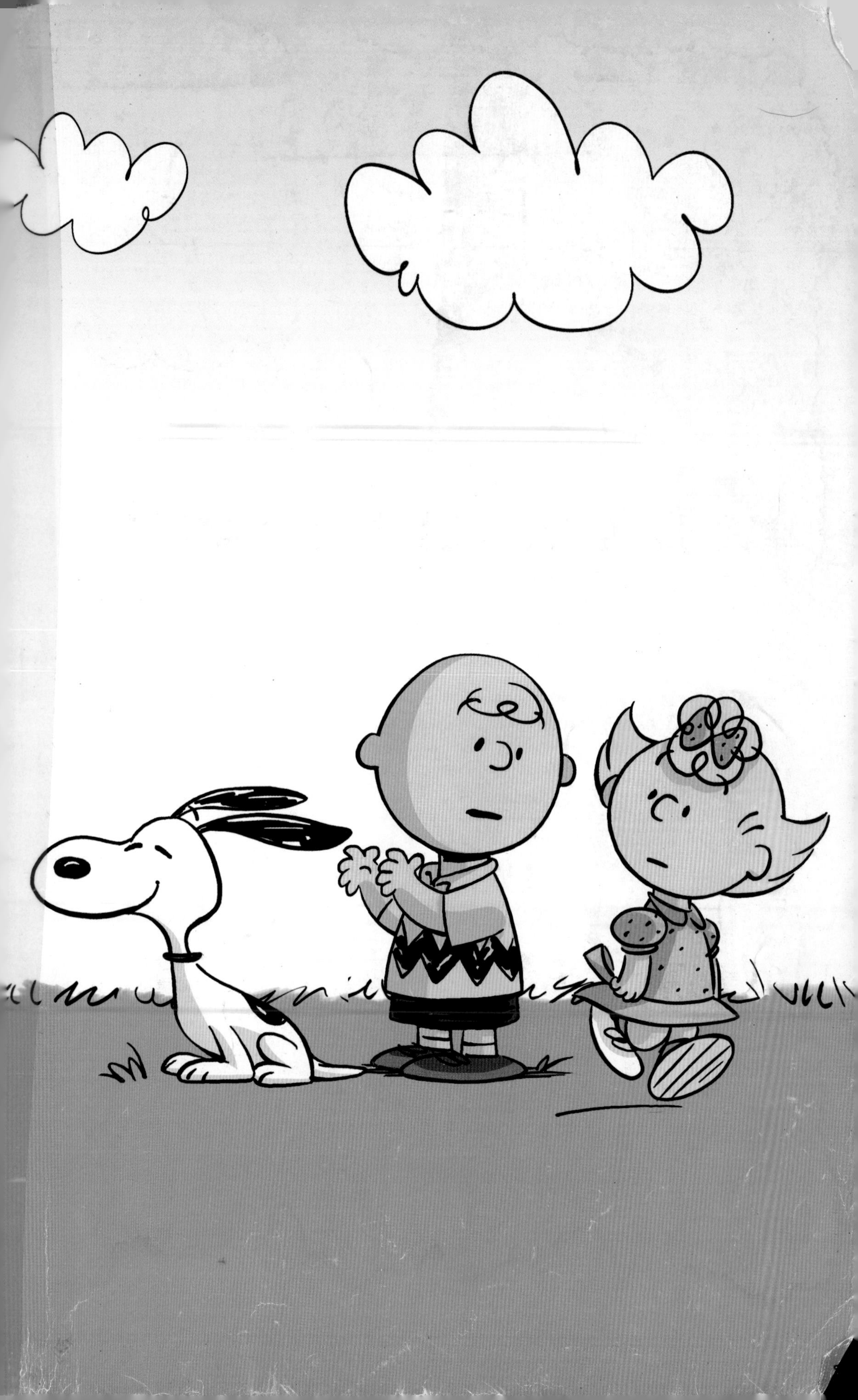

TABLE OF CONTENTS

Classic Peanuts Strips by
Charles M. Schulz
Colors by **Justin Thompson**, **Alexis E. Fajardo**, and **Nina Kester**

From The Drawing Board
Composed by **Justin Thompson**
Designed by **Iain R. Morris**

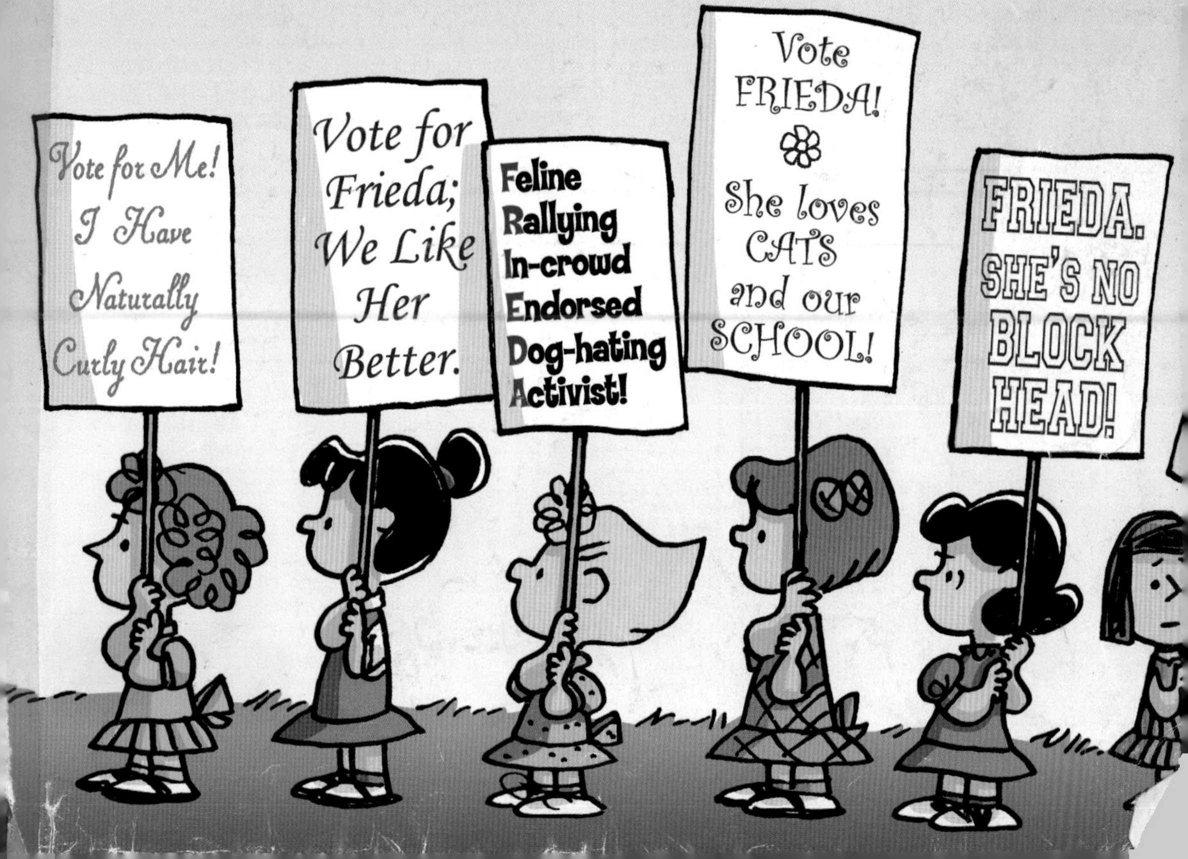
Vote for Me! I Have Naturally Curly Hair!
Vote for Frieda; We Like Her Better.
Feline Rallying In-crowd Endorsed Dog-hating Activist!
Vote FRIEDA! She loves CATS and our SCHOOL!
FRIEDA. SHE'S NO BLOCK HEAD!

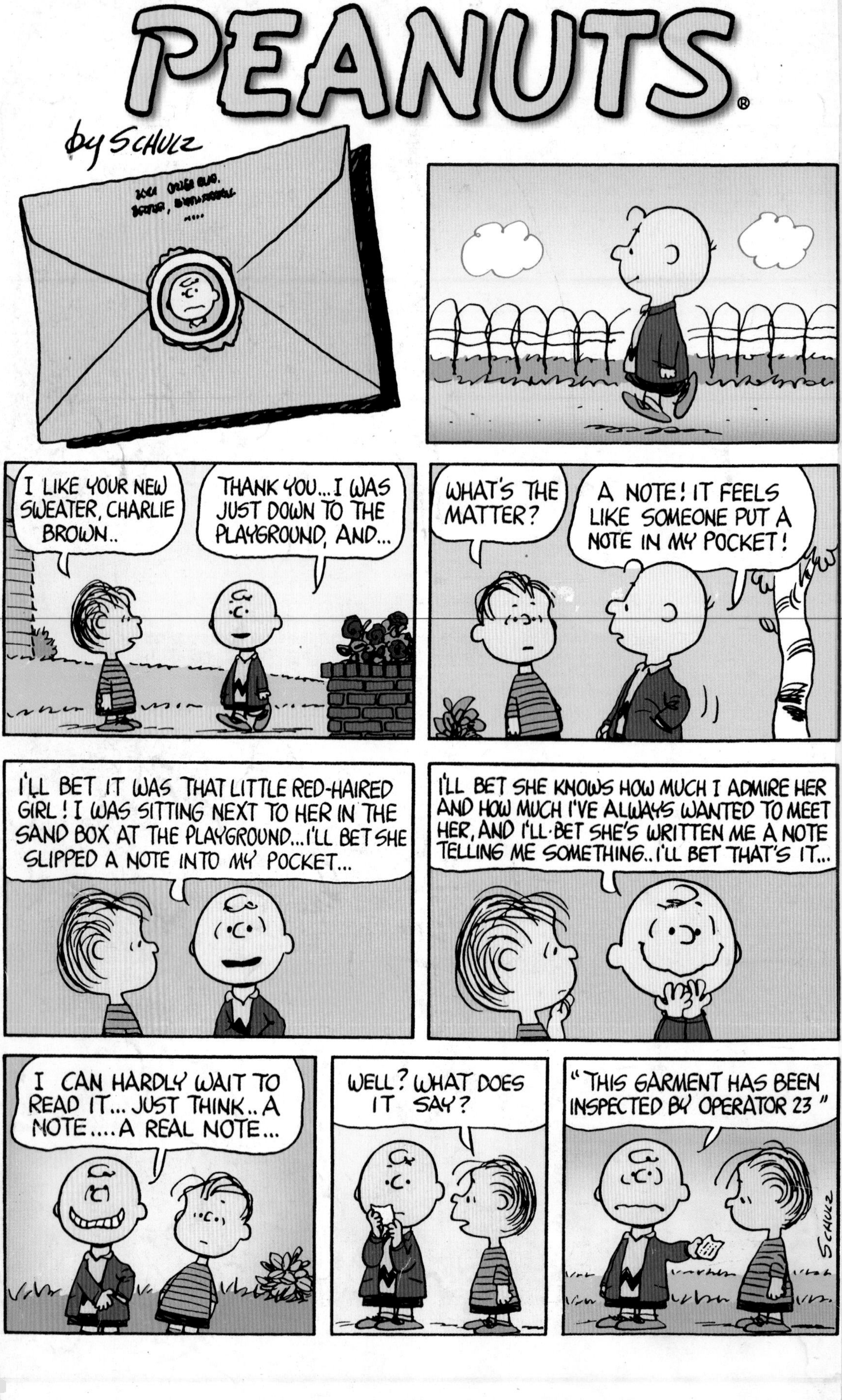
PEANUTS®
by SCHULZ
I LIKE YOUR NEW SWEATER, CHARLIE BROWN..
THANK YOU...I WAS JUST DOWN TO THE PLAYGROUND, AND...
WHAT'S THE MATTER?
A NOTE! IT FEELS LIKE SOMEONE PUT A NOTE IN MY POCKET!
I'LL BET IT WAS THAT LITTLE RED-HAIRED GIRL! I WAS SITTING NEXT TO HER IN THE SAND BOX AT THE PLAYGROUND...I'LL BET SHE SLIPPED A NOTE INTO MY POCKET...
I'LL BET SHE KNOWS HOW MUCH I ADMIRE HER AND HOW MUCH I'VE ALWAYS WANTED TO MEET HER, AND I'LL BET SHE'S WRITTEN ME A NOTE TELLING ME SOMETHING..I'LL BET THAT'S IT...
I CAN HARDLY WAIT TO READ IT... JUST THINK.. A NOTE....A REAL NOTE...
WELL? WHAT DOES IT SAY?
"THIS GARMENT HAS BEEN INSPECTED BY OPERATOR 23"
SCHULZ

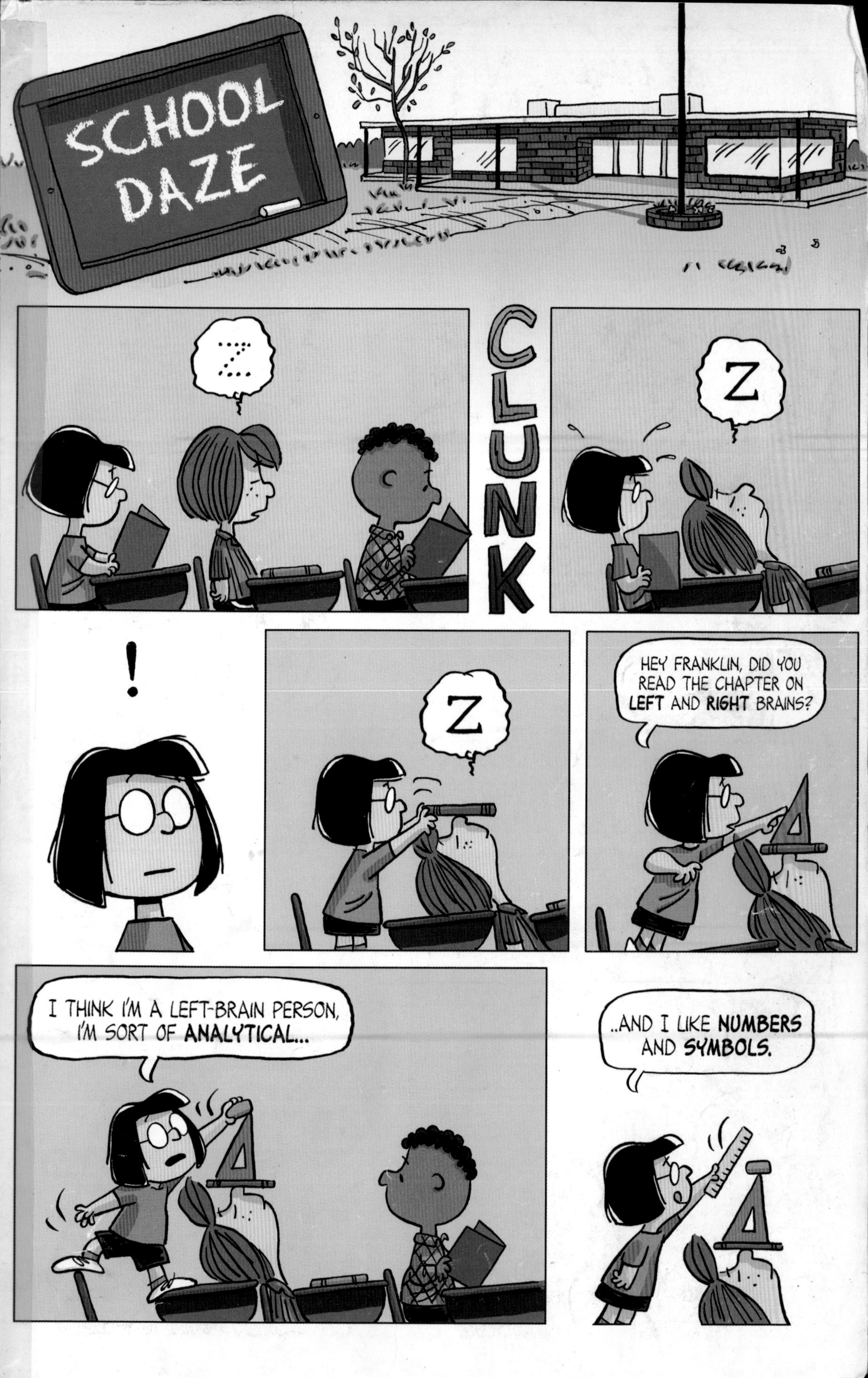
SCHOOL DAZE
Z
CLUNK
Z
!
Z
HEY FRANKLIN, DID YOU READ THE CHAPTER ON LEFT AND RIGHT BRAINS?
I THINK I'M A LEFT-BRAIN PERSON, I'M SORT OF ANALYTICAL...
..AND I LIKE NUMBERS AND SYMBOLS.

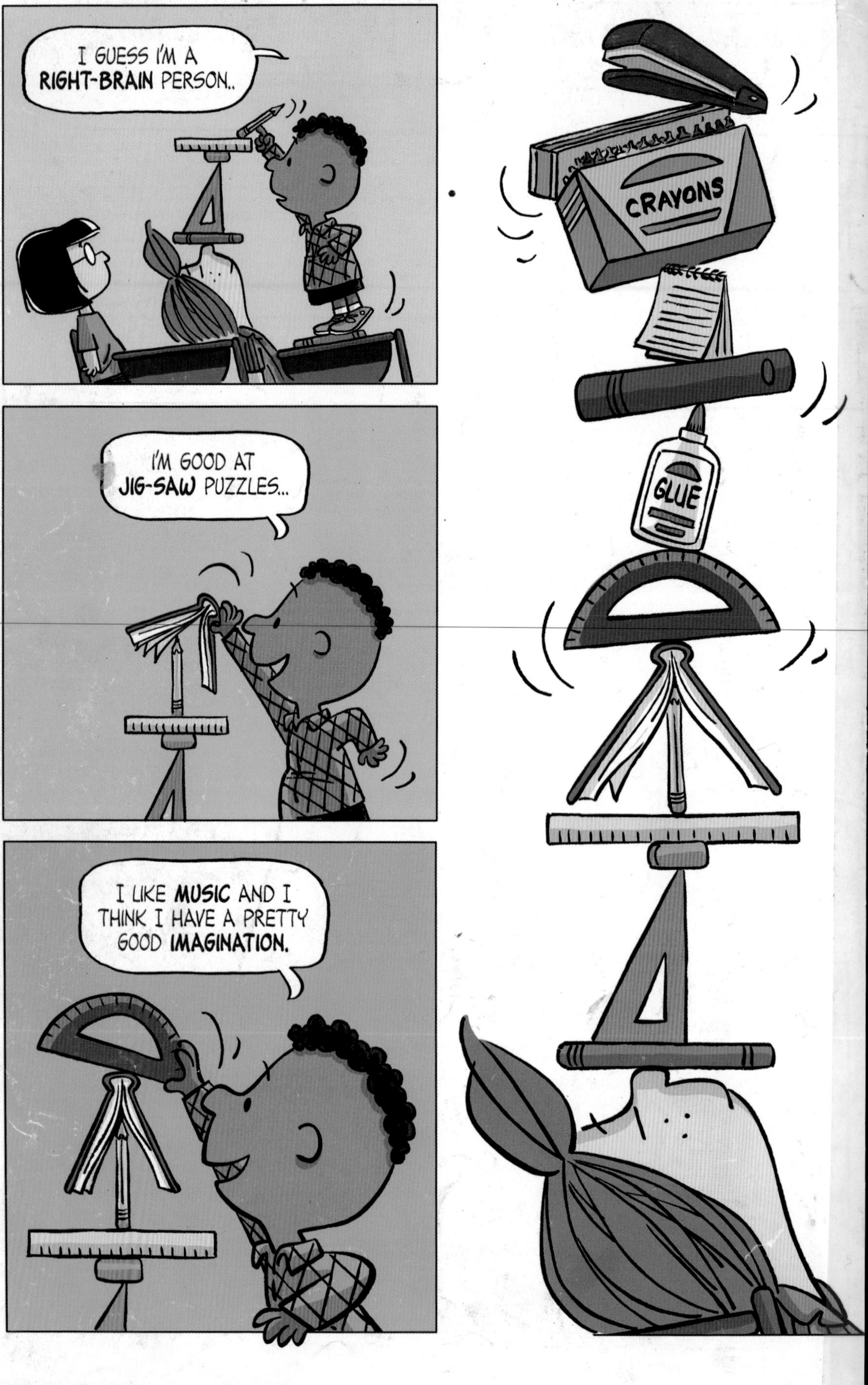
I GUESS I'M A RIGHT-BRAIN PERSON..
I'M GOOD AT JIG-SAW PUZZLES...
I LIKE MUSIC AND I THINK I HAVE A PRETTY GOOD IMAGINATION.
CRAYONS
GLUE

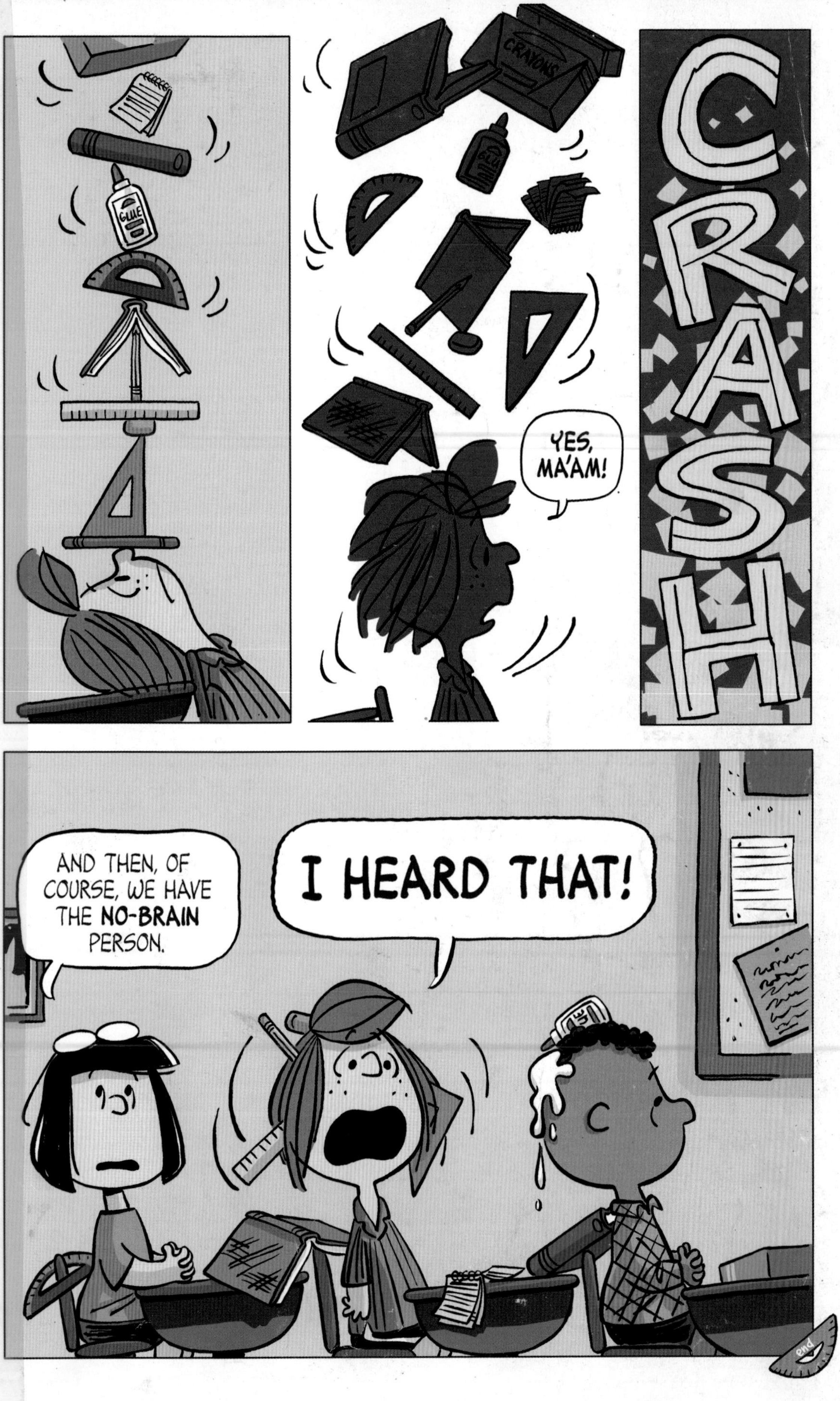

CRAYONS
GLUE
YES, MA'AM!
CRASH
AND THEN, OF COURSE, WE HAVE THE **NO-BRAIN** PERSON.
I HEARD THAT!
end

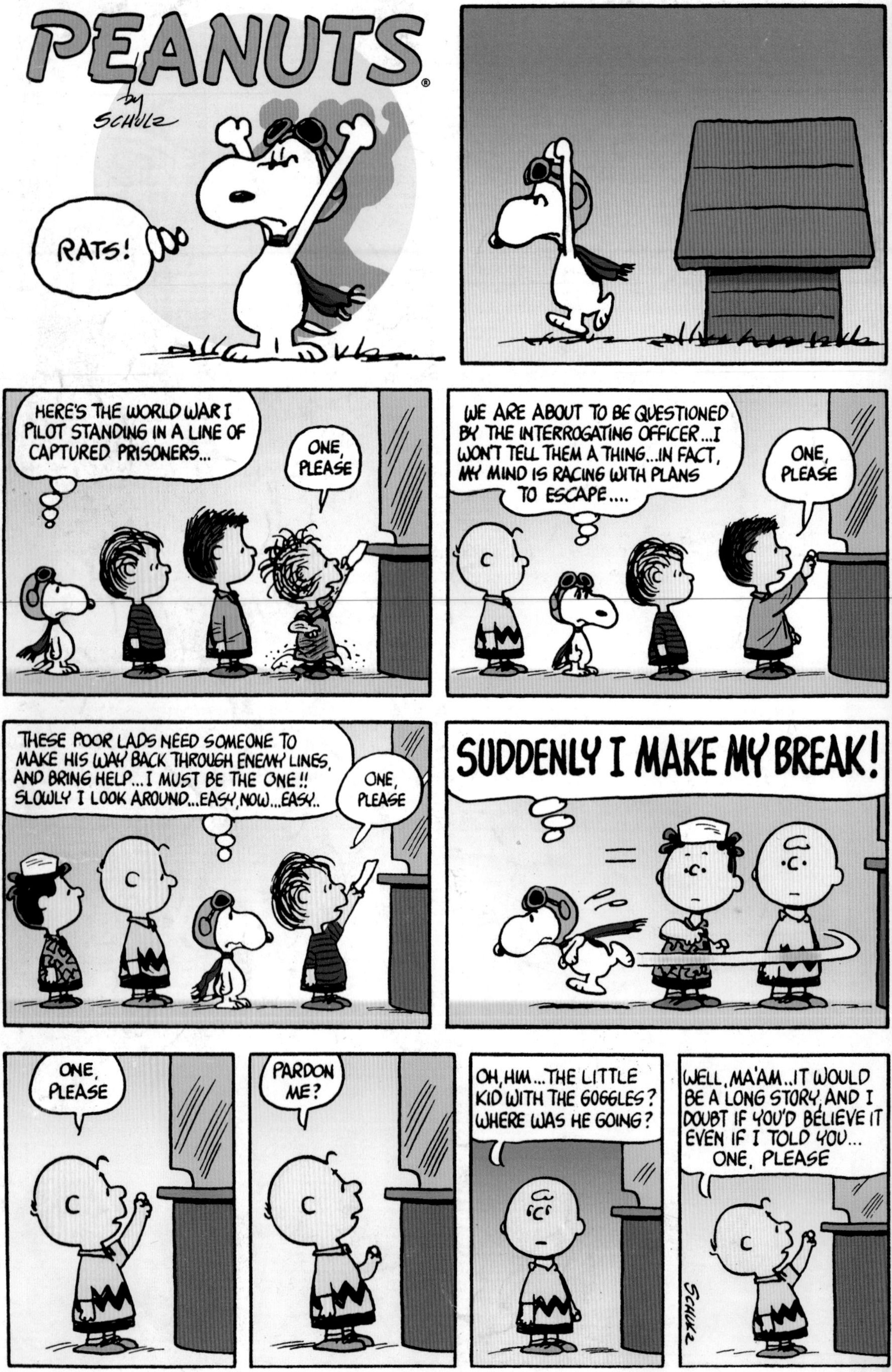
PEANUTS
by SCHULZ
RATS!
HERE'S THE WORLD WAR I PILOT STANDING IN A LINE OF CAPTURED PRISONERS...
ONE, PLEASE
WE ARE ABOUT TO BE QUESTIONED BY THE INTERROGATING OFFICER...I WON'T TELL THEM A THING...IN FACT, MY MIND IS RACING WITH PLANS TO ESCAPE....
ONE, PLEASE
THESE POOR LADS NEED SOMEONE TO MAKE HIS WAY BACK THROUGH ENEMY LINES, AND BRING HELP...I MUST BE THE ONE!! SLOWLY I LOOK AROUND...EASY, NOW...EASY..
ONE, PLEASE
SUDDENLY I MAKE MY BREAK!
ONE, PLEASE
PARDON ME?
OH, HIM...THE LITTLE KID WITH THE GOGGLES? WHERE WAS HE GOING?
WELL, MA'AM..IT WOULD BE A LONG STORY, AND I DOUBT IF YOU'D BELIEVE IT EVEN IF I TOLD YOU...
ONE, PLEASE
SCHULZ

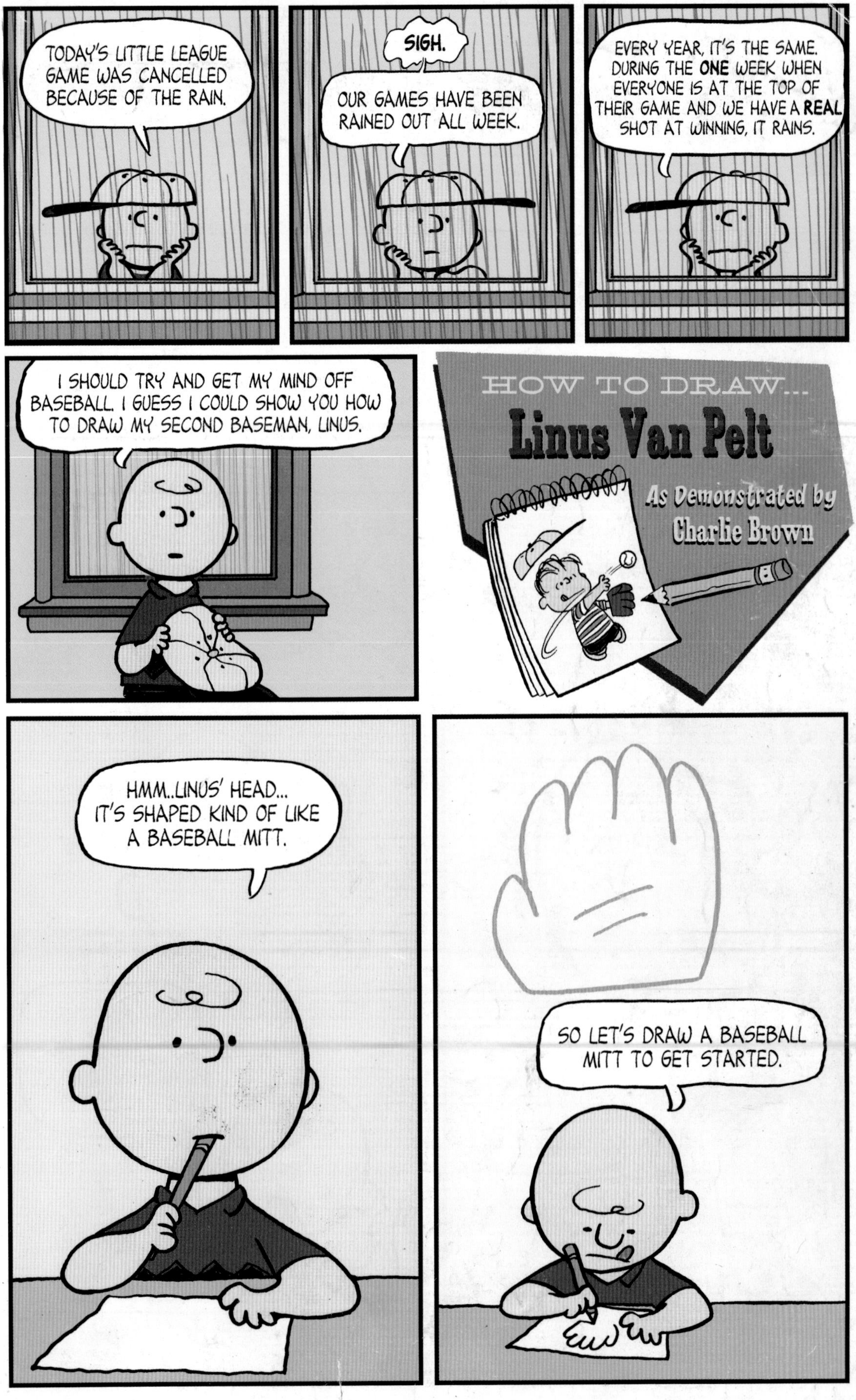
TODAY'S LITTLE LEAGUE GAME WAS CANCELLED BECAUSE OF THE RAIN.
SIGH.
OUR GAMES HAVE BEEN RAINED OUT ALL WEEK.
EVERY YEAR, IT'S THE SAME. DURING THE **ONE** WEEK WHEN EVERYONE IS AT THE TOP OF THEIR GAME AND WE HAVE A **REAL** SHOT AT WINNING, IT RAINS.
I SHOULD TRY AND GET MY MIND OFF BASEBALL. I GUESS I COULD SHOW YOU HOW TO DRAW MY SECOND BASEMAN, LINUS.
HOW TO DRAW...
Linus Van Pelt
As Demonstrated by
Charlie Brown
HMM..LINUS' HEAD... IT'S SHAPED KIND OF LIKE A BASEBALL MITT.
SO LET'S DRAW A BASEBALL MITT TO GET STARTED.

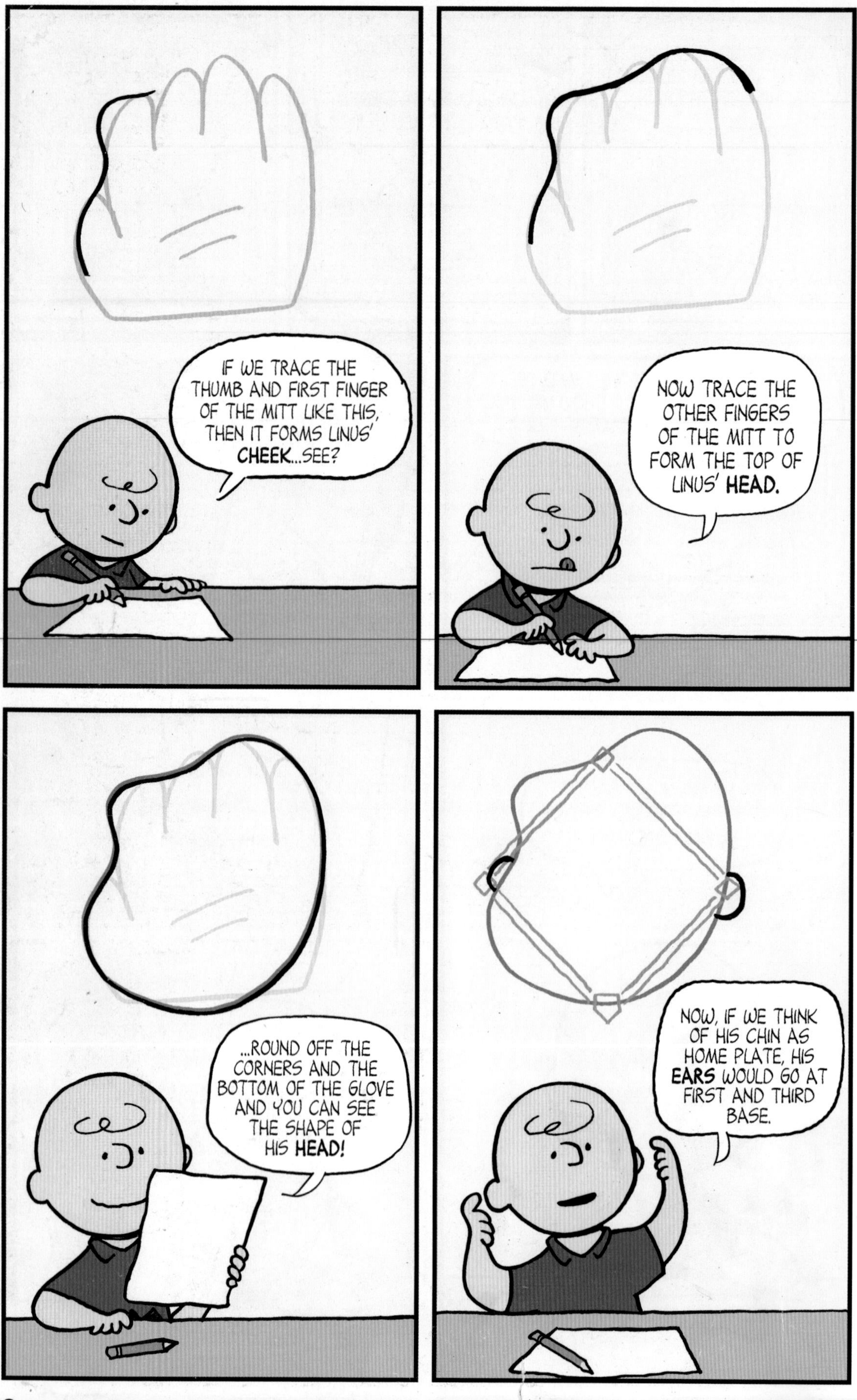
IF WE TRACE THE THUMB AND FIRST FINGER OF THE MITT LIKE THIS, THEN IT FORMS LINUS' **CHEEK**...SEE?
NOW TRACE THE OTHER FINGERS OF THE MITT TO FORM THE TOP OF LINUS' **HEAD.**
...ROUND OFF THE CORNERS AND THE BOTTOM OF THE GLOVE AND YOU CAN SEE THE SHAPE OF HIS **HEAD!**
NOW, IF WE THINK OF HIS CHIN AS HOME PLATE, HIS **EARS** WOULD GO AT FIRST AND THIRD BASE.

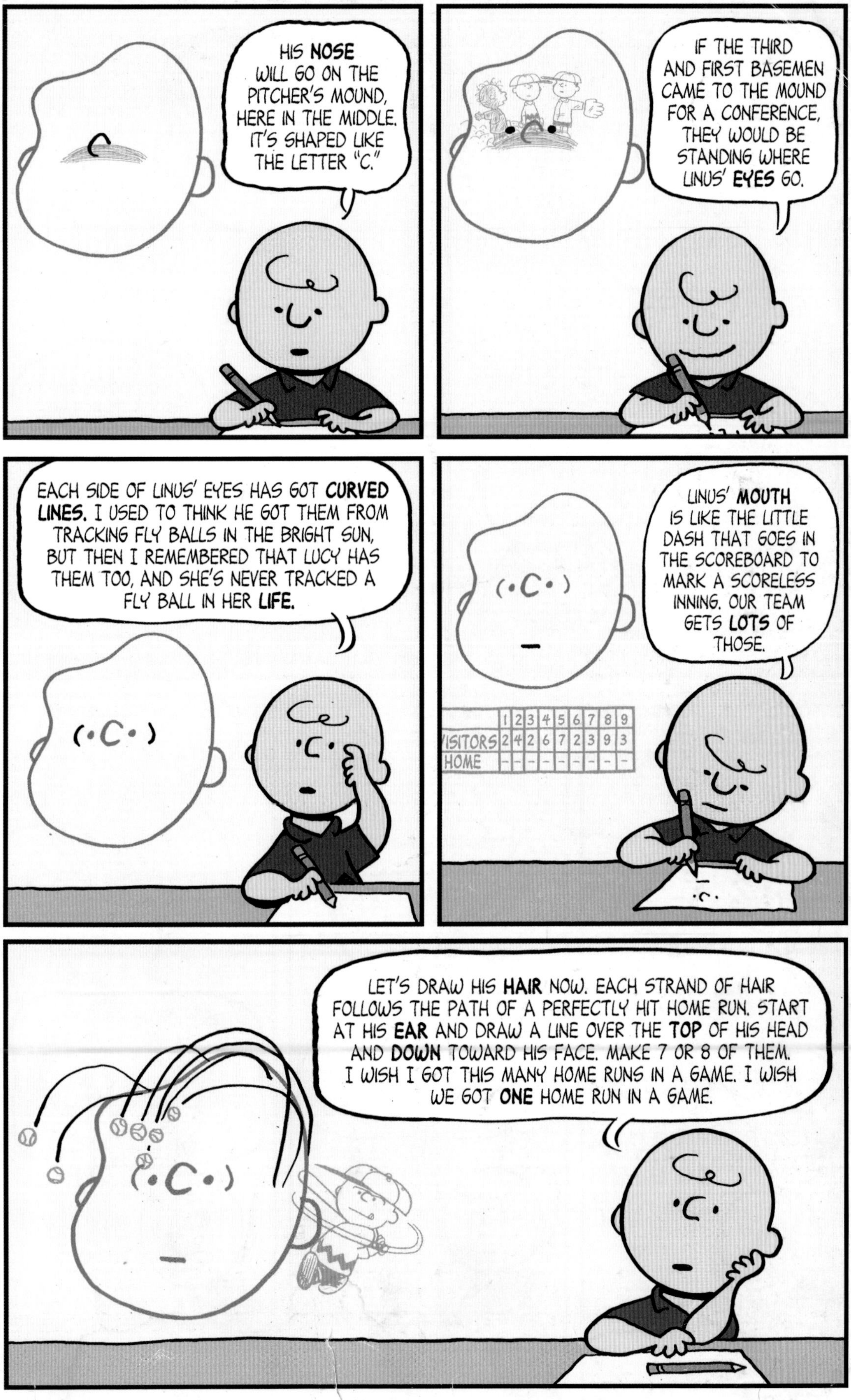

HIS **NOSE** WILL GO ON THE PITCHER'S MOUND, HERE IN THE MIDDLE. IT'S SHAPED LIKE THE LETTER "C."
IF THE THIRD AND FIRST BASEMEN CAME TO THE MOUND FOR A CONFERENCE, THEY WOULD BE STANDING WHERE LINUS' **EYES** GO.
EACH SIDE OF LINUS' EYES HAS GOT **CURVED LINES.** I USED TO THINK HE GOT THEM FROM TRACKING FLY BALLS IN THE BRIGHT SUN, BUT THEN I REMEMBERED THAT LUCY HAS THEM TOO, AND SHE'S NEVER TRACKED A FLY BALL IN HER **LIFE.**
LINUS' **MOUTH** IS LIKE THE LITTLE DASH THAT GOES IN THE SCOREBOARD TO MARK A SCORELESS INNING. OUR TEAM GETS **LOTS** OF THOSE.
1 2 3 4 5 6 7 8 9
VISITORS 2 4 2 6 7 2 3 9 3
HOME - - - - - - - - -
LET'S DRAW HIS **HAIR** NOW. EACH STRAND OF HAIR FOLLOWS THE PATH OF A PERFECTLY HIT HOME RUN. START AT HIS **EAR** AND DRAW A LINE OVER THE **TOP** OF HIS HEAD AND **DOWN** TOWARD HIS FACE. MAKE 7 OR 8 OF THEM. I WISH I GOT THIS MANY HOME RUNS IN A GAME. I WISH WE GOT **ONE** HOME RUN IN A GAME.

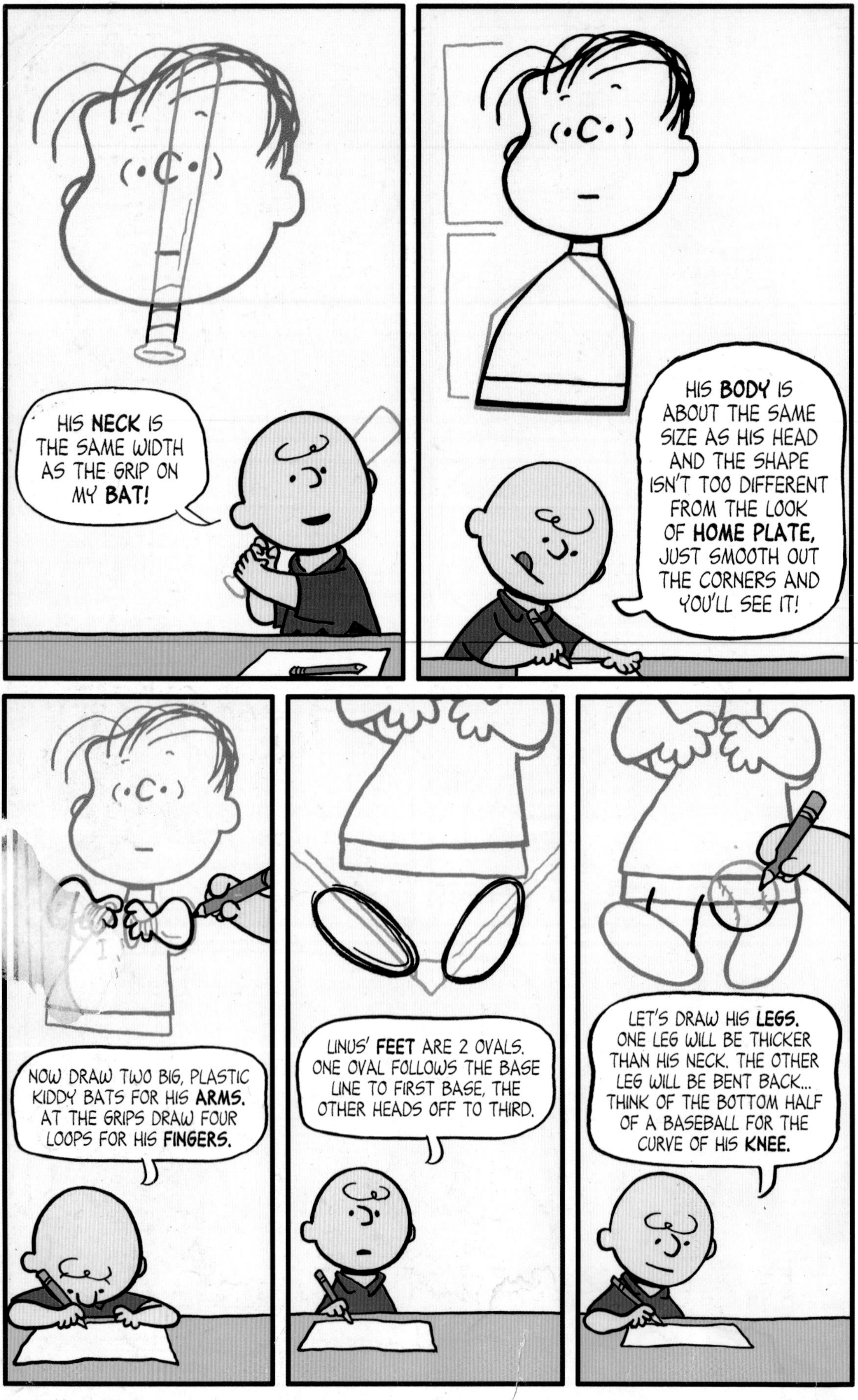

HIS NECK IS THE SAME WIDTH AS THE GRIP ON MY BAT!
HIS BODY IS ABOUT THE SAME SIZE AS HIS HEAD AND THE SHAPE ISN'T TOO DIFFERENT FROM THE LOOK OF HOME PLATE, JUST SMOOTH OUT THE CORNERS AND YOU'LL SEE IT!
NOW DRAW TWO BIG, PLASTIC KIDDY BATS FOR HIS ARMS. AT THE GRIPS DRAW FOUR LOOPS FOR HIS FINGERS.
LINUS' FEET ARE 2 OVALS. ONE OVAL FOLLOWS THE BASE LINE TO FIRST BASE, THE OTHER HEADS OFF TO THIRD.
LET'S DRAW HIS LEGS. ONE LEG WILL BE THICKER THAN HIS NECK. THE OTHER LEG WILL BE BENT BACK... THINK OF THE BOTTOM HALF OF A BASEBALL FOR THE CURVE OF HIS KNEE.

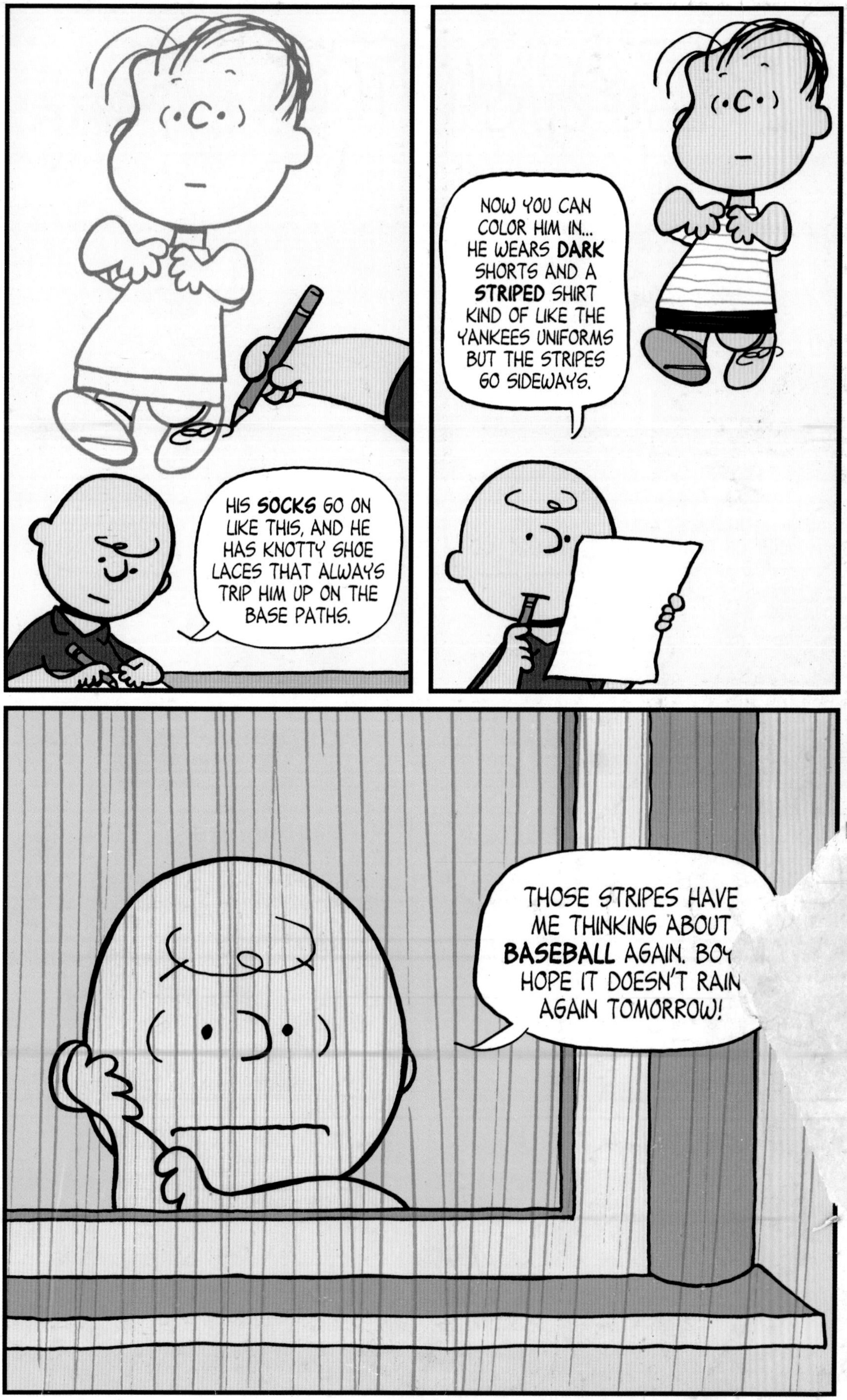
HIS **SOCKS** GO ON LIKE THIS, AND HE HAS KNOTTY SHOE LACES THAT ALWAYS TRIP HIM UP ON THE BASE PATHS.
NOW YOU CAN COLOR HIM IN... HE WEARS **DARK** SHORTS AND A **STRIPED** SHIRT KIND OF LIKE THE YANKEES UNIFORMS BUT THE STRIPES GO SIDEWAYS.
THOSE STRIPES HAVE ME THINKING ABOUT **BASEBALL** AGAIN. BOY HOPE IT DOESN'T RAIN AGAIN TOMORROW!

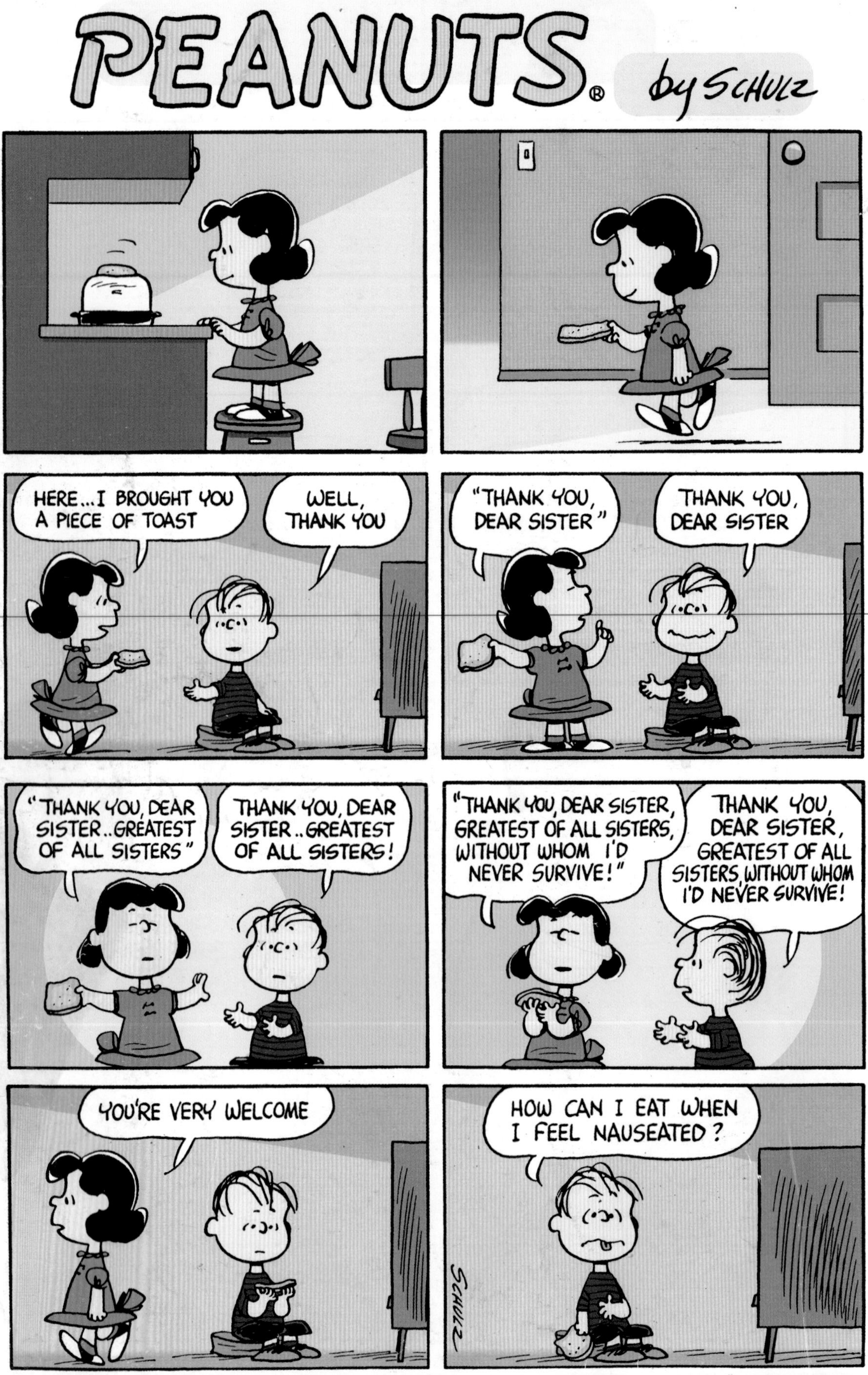
PEANUTS®
by SCHULZ
HERE...I BROUGHT YOU A PIECE OF TOAST
WELL, THANK YOU
"THANK YOU, DEAR SISTER"
THANK YOU, DEAR SISTER
"THANK YOU, DEAR SISTER..GREATEST OF ALL SISTERS"
THANK YOU, DEAR SISTER..GREATEST OF ALL SISTERS!
"THANK YOU, DEAR SISTER, GREATEST OF ALL SISTERS, WITHOUT WHOM I'D NEVER SURVIVE!"
THANK YOU, DEAR SISTER, GREATEST OF ALL SISTERS, WITHOUT WHOM I'D NEVER SURVIVE!
YOU'RE VERY WELCOME
SCHULZ
HOW CAN I EAT WHEN I FEEL NAUSEATED?

SUN TAN HERO

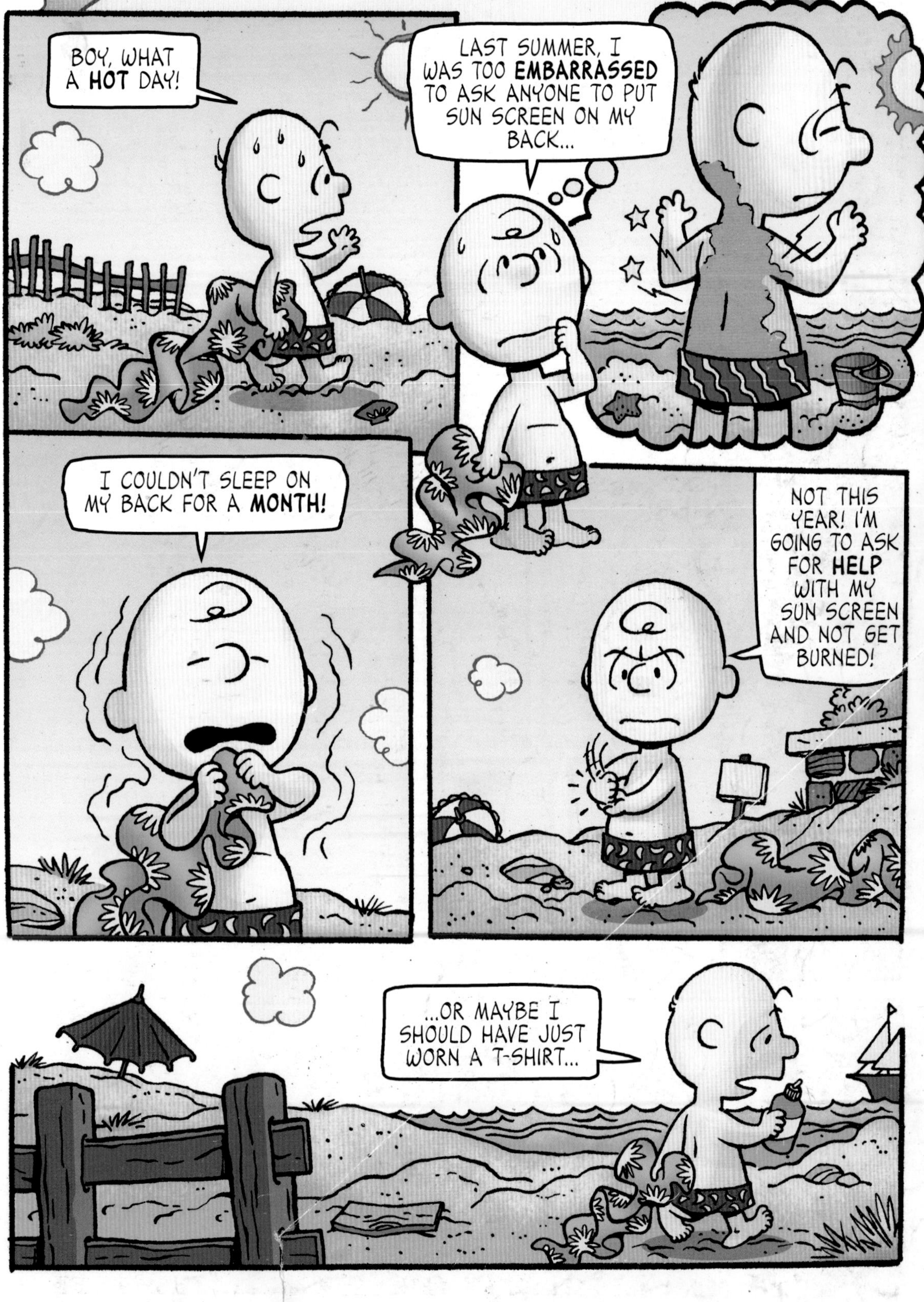

BOY, WHAT A **HOT** DAY!
LAST SUMMER, I WAS TOO **EMBARRASSED** TO ASK ANYONE TO PUT SUN SCREEN ON MY BACK...
I COULDN'T SLEEP ON MY BACK FOR A **MONTH!**
NOT THIS YEAR! I'M GOING TO ASK FOR **HELP** WITH MY SUN SCREEN AND NOT GET BURNED!
...OR MAYBE I SHOULD HAVE JUST WORN A T-SHIRT...

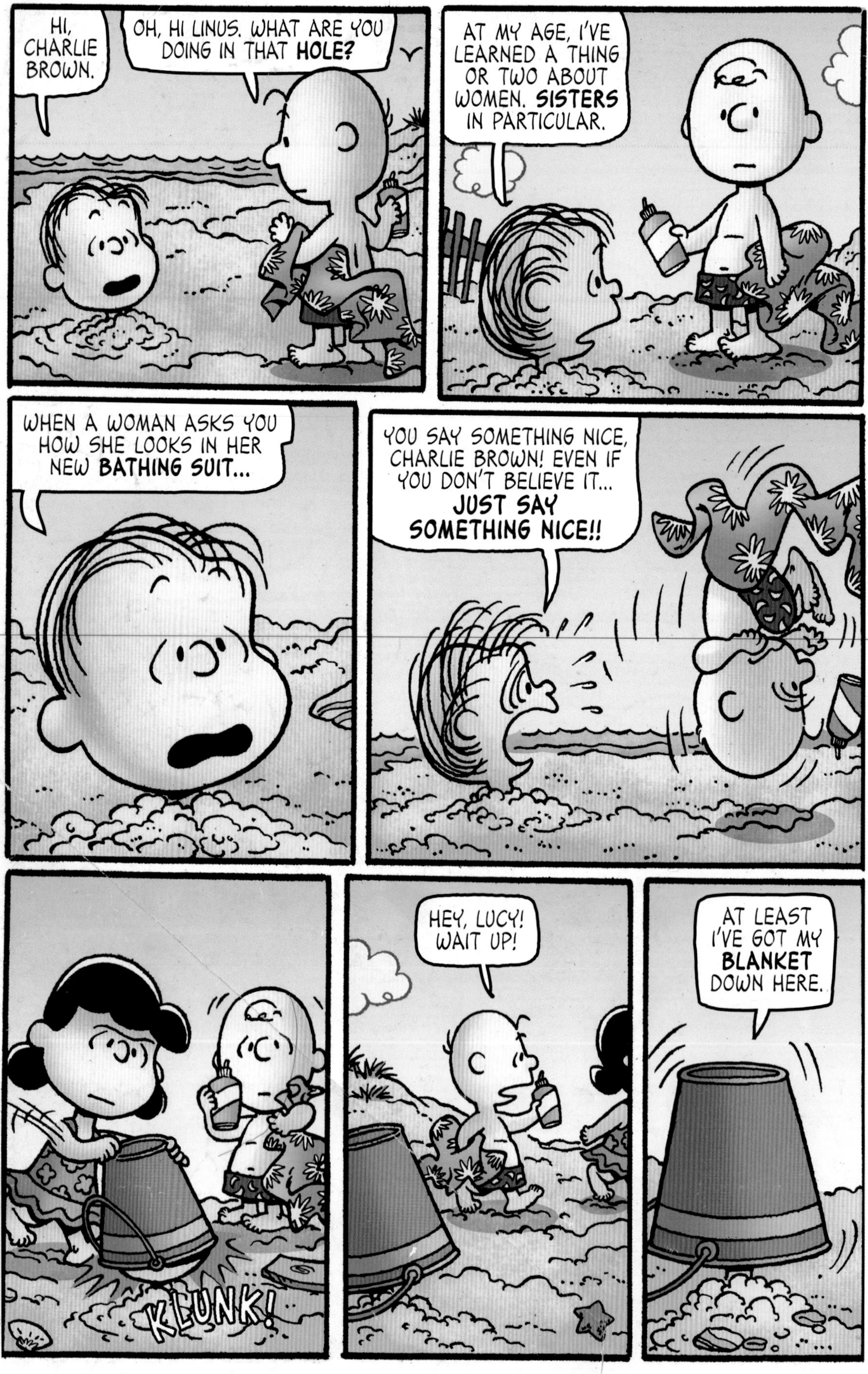
HI, CHARLIE BROWN.
OH, HI LINUS. WHAT ARE YOU DOING IN THAT HOLE?
AT MY AGE, I'VE LEARNED A THING OR TWO ABOUT WOMEN. SISTERS IN PARTICULAR.
WHEN A WOMAN ASKS YOU HOW SHE LOOKS IN HER NEW BATHING SUIT...
YOU SAY SOMETHING NICE, CHARLIE BROWN! EVEN IF YOU DON'T BELIEVE IT... JUST SAY SOMETHING NICE!!
KLUNK!
HEY, LUCY! WAIT UP!
AT LEAST I'VE GOT MY BLANKET DOWN HERE.

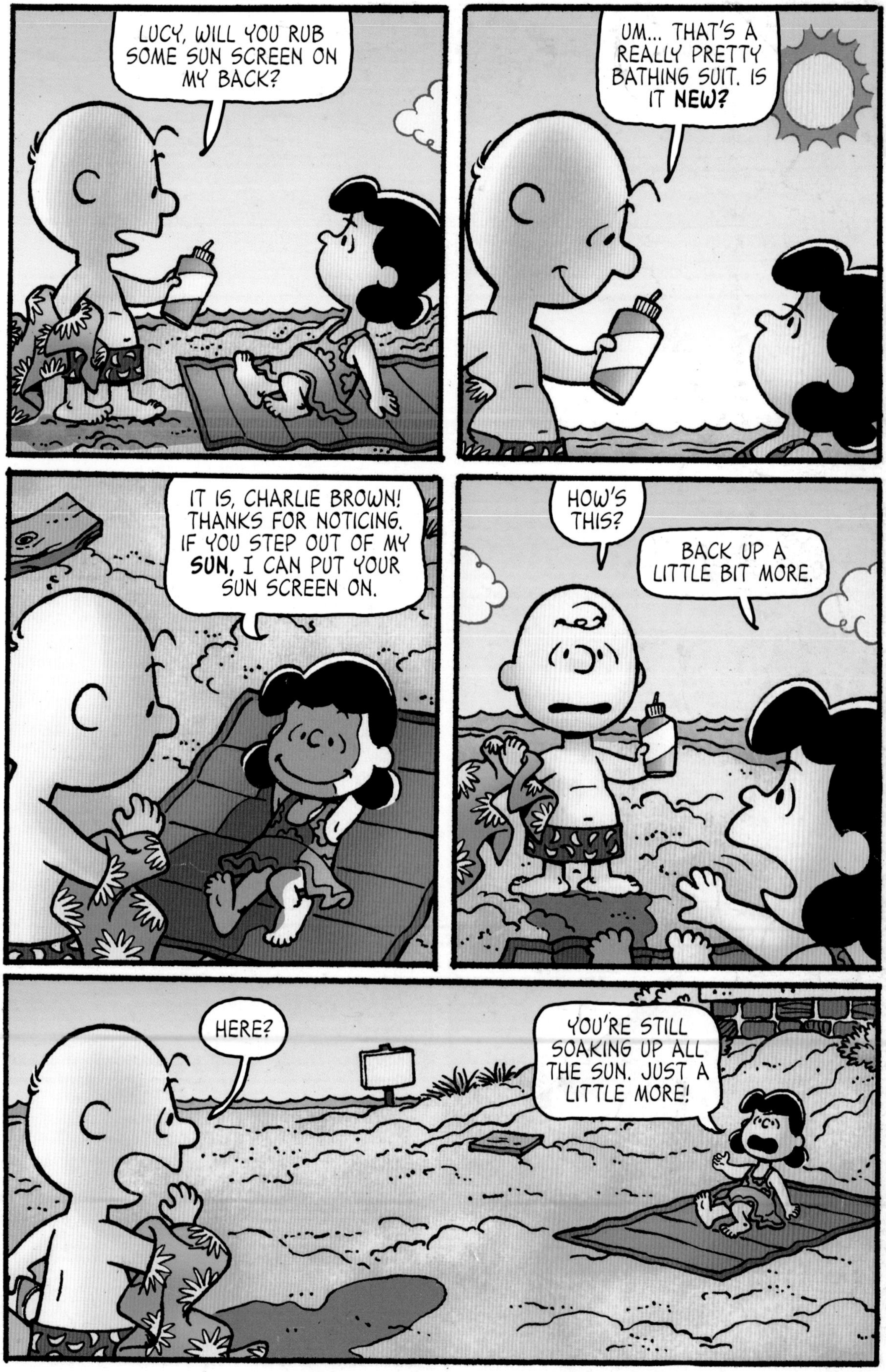
LUCY, WILL YOU RUB SOME SUN SCREEN ON MY BACK?
UM... THAT'S A REALLY PRETTY BATHING SUIT. IS IT **NEW?**
IT IS, CHARLIE BROWN! THANKS FOR NOTICING. IF YOU STEP OUT OF MY **SUN,** I CAN PUT YOUR SUN SCREEN ON.
HOW'S THIS?
BACK UP A LITTLE BIT MORE.
HERE?
YOU'RE STILL SOAKING UP ALL THE SUN. JUST A LITTLE MORE!

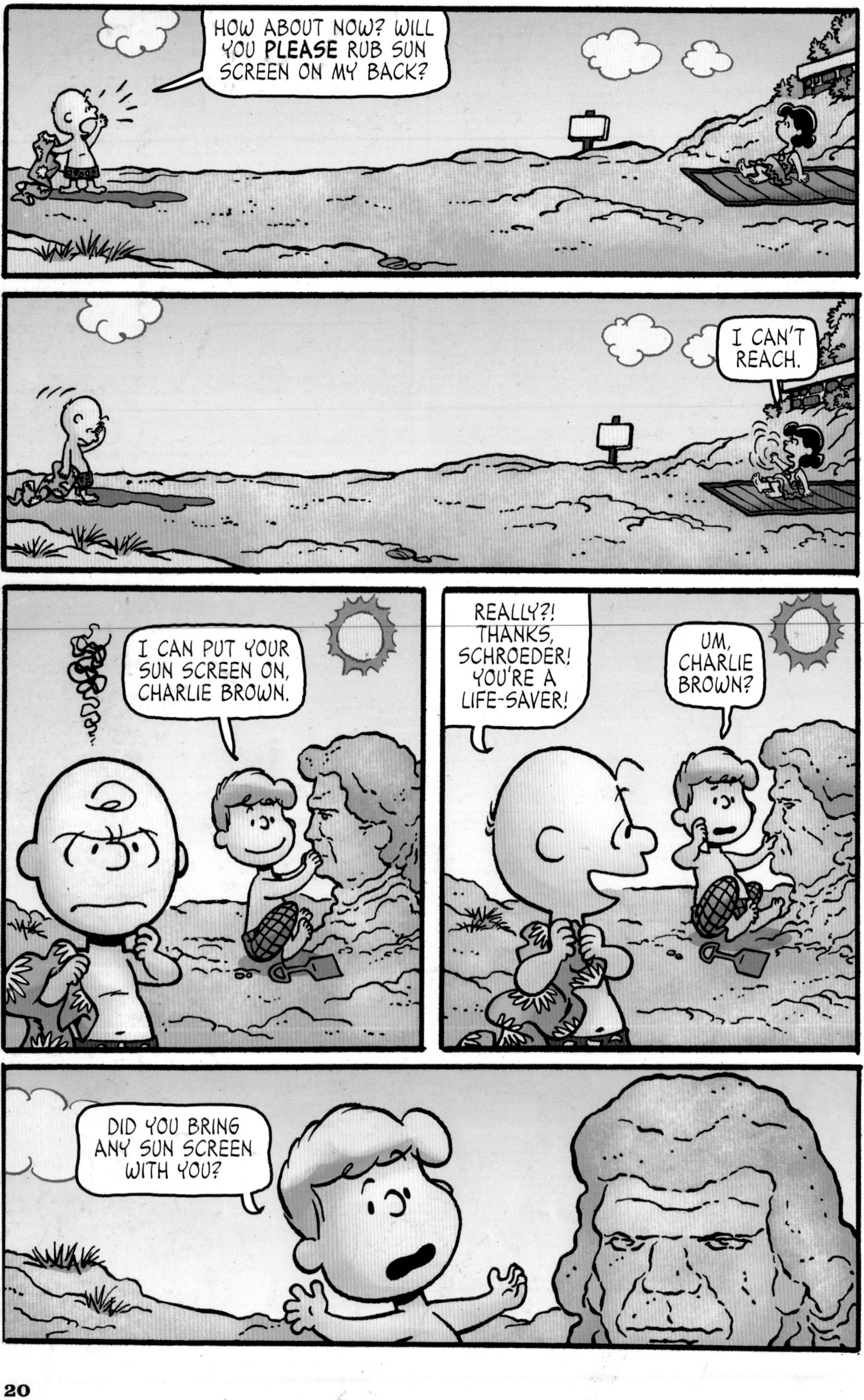
HOW ABOUT NOW? WILL YOU PLEASE RUB SUN SCREEN ON MY BACK?
I CAN'T REACH.
I CAN PUT YOUR SUN SCREEN ON, CHARLIE BROWN.
REALLY?! THANKS, SCHROEDER! YOU'RE A LIFE-SAVER!
UM, CHARLIE BROWN?
DID YOU BRING ANY SUN SCREEN WITH YOU?

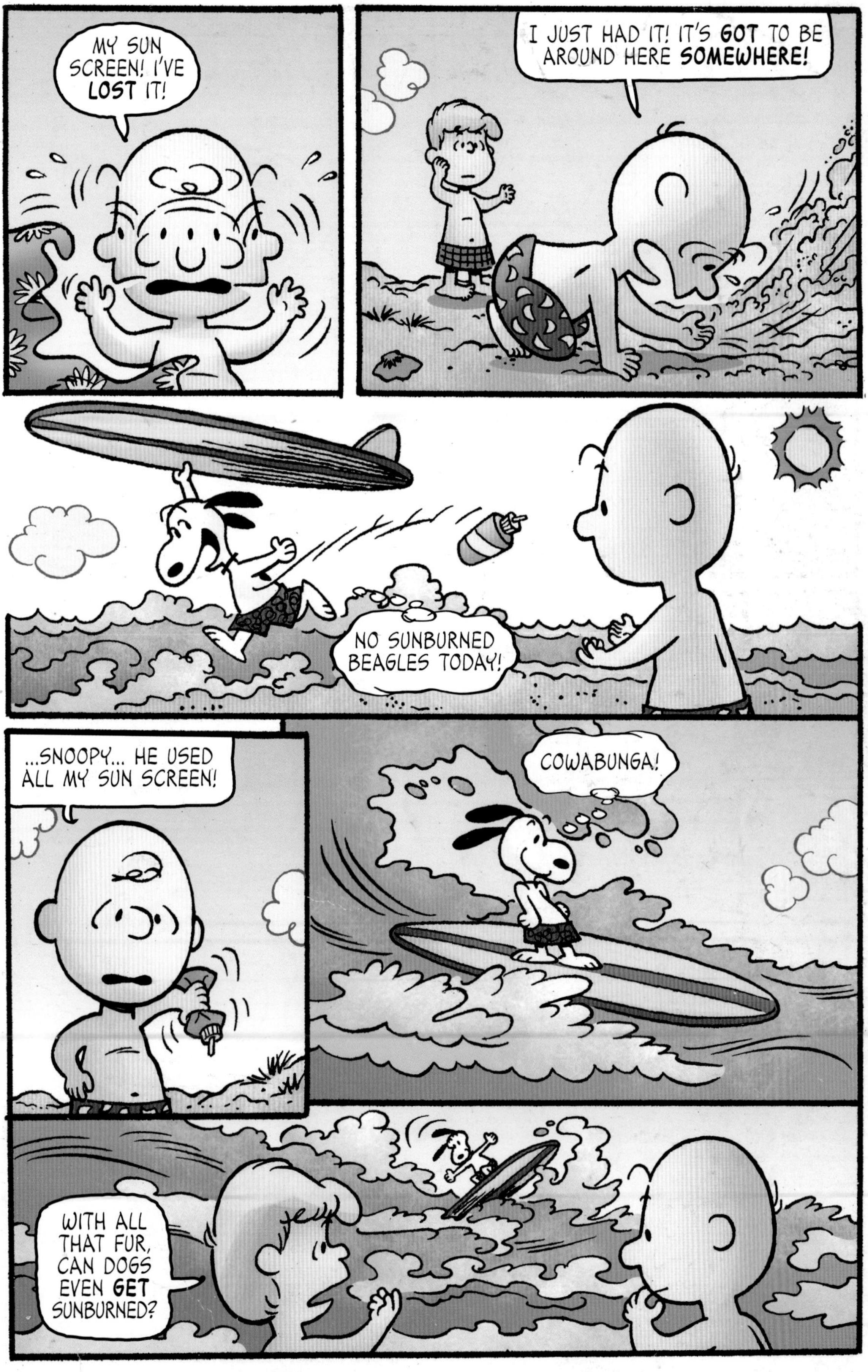
MY SUN SCREEN! I'VE LOST IT!
I JUST HAD IT! IT'S GOT TO BE AROUND HERE SOMEWHERE!
NO SUNBURNED BEAGLES TODAY!
...SNOOPY... HE USED ALL MY SUN SCREEN!
COWABUNGA!
WITH ALL THAT FUR, CAN DOGS EVEN GET SUNBURNED?

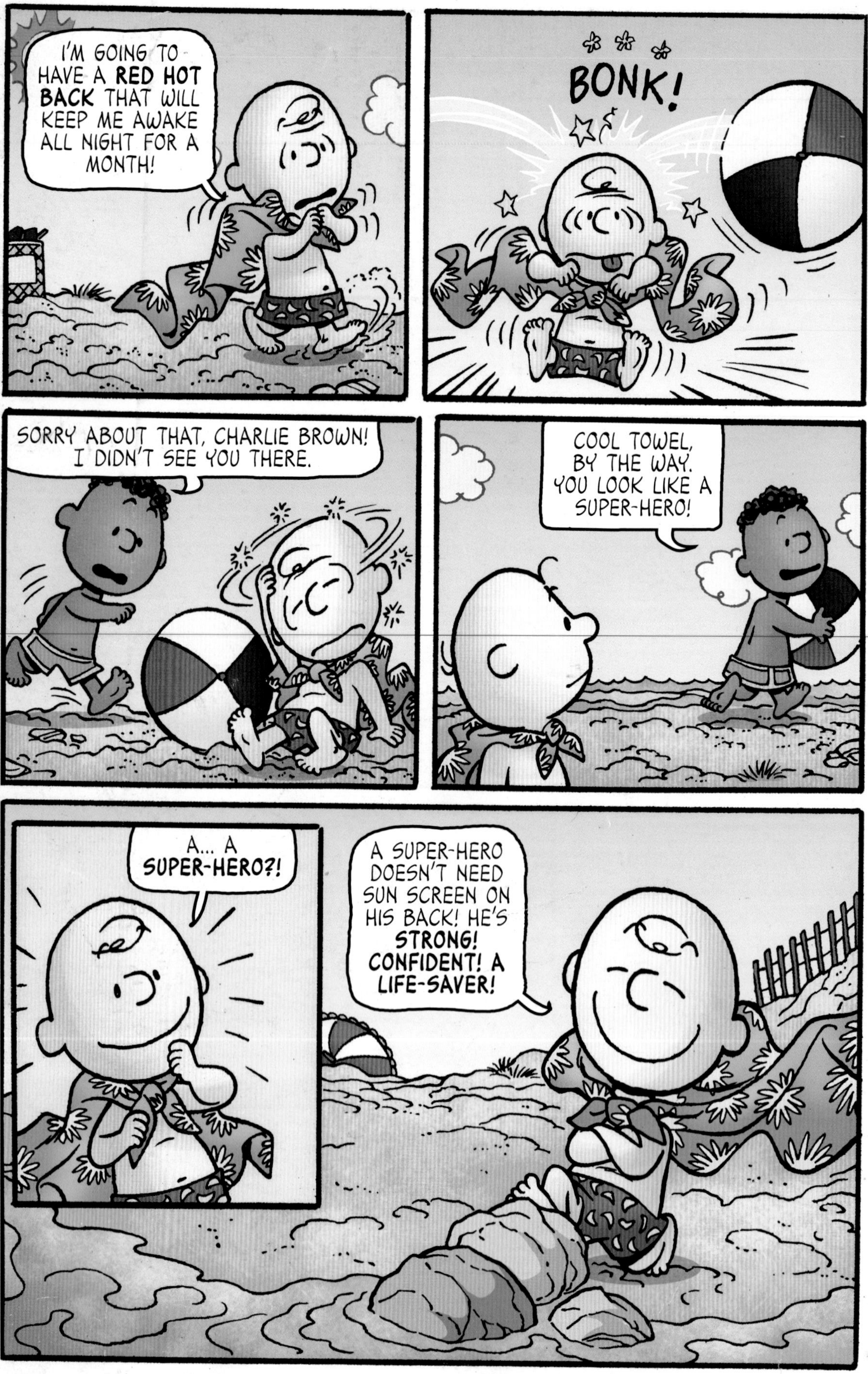
I'M GOING TO HAVE A **RED HOT BACK** THAT WILL KEEP ME AWAKE ALL NIGHT FOR A MONTH!
BONK!
SORRY ABOUT THAT, CHARLIE BROWN! I DIDN'T SEE YOU THERE.
COOL TOWEL, BY THE WAY. YOU LOOK LIKE A SUPER-HERO!
A... A **SUPER-HERO?!**
A SUPER-HERO DOESN'T NEED SUN SCREEN ON HIS BACK! HE'S **STRONG! CONFIDENT! A LIFE-SAVER!**

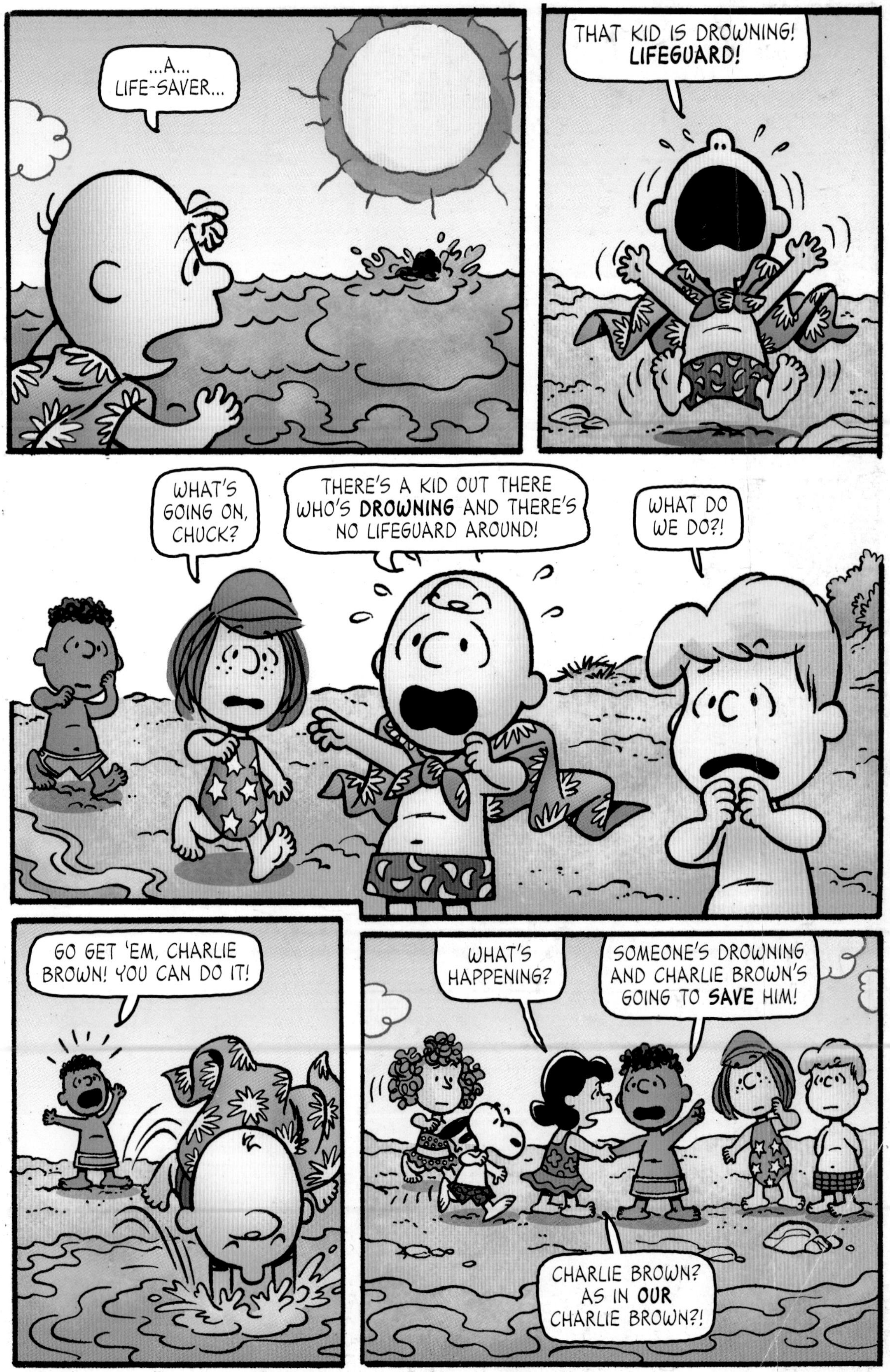

...A... LIFE-SAVER...
THAT KID IS DROWNING! **LIFEGUARD!**
WHAT'S GOING ON, CHUCK?
THERE'S A KID OUT THERE WHO'S **DROWNING** AND THERE'S NO LIFEGUARD AROUND!
WHAT DO WE DO?!
GO GET 'EM, CHARLIE BROWN! YOU CAN DO IT!
WHAT'S HAPPENING?
SOMEONE'S DROWNING AND CHARLIE BROWN'S GOING TO **SAVE** HIM!
CHARLIE BROWN? AS IN **OUR** CHARLIE BROWN?!

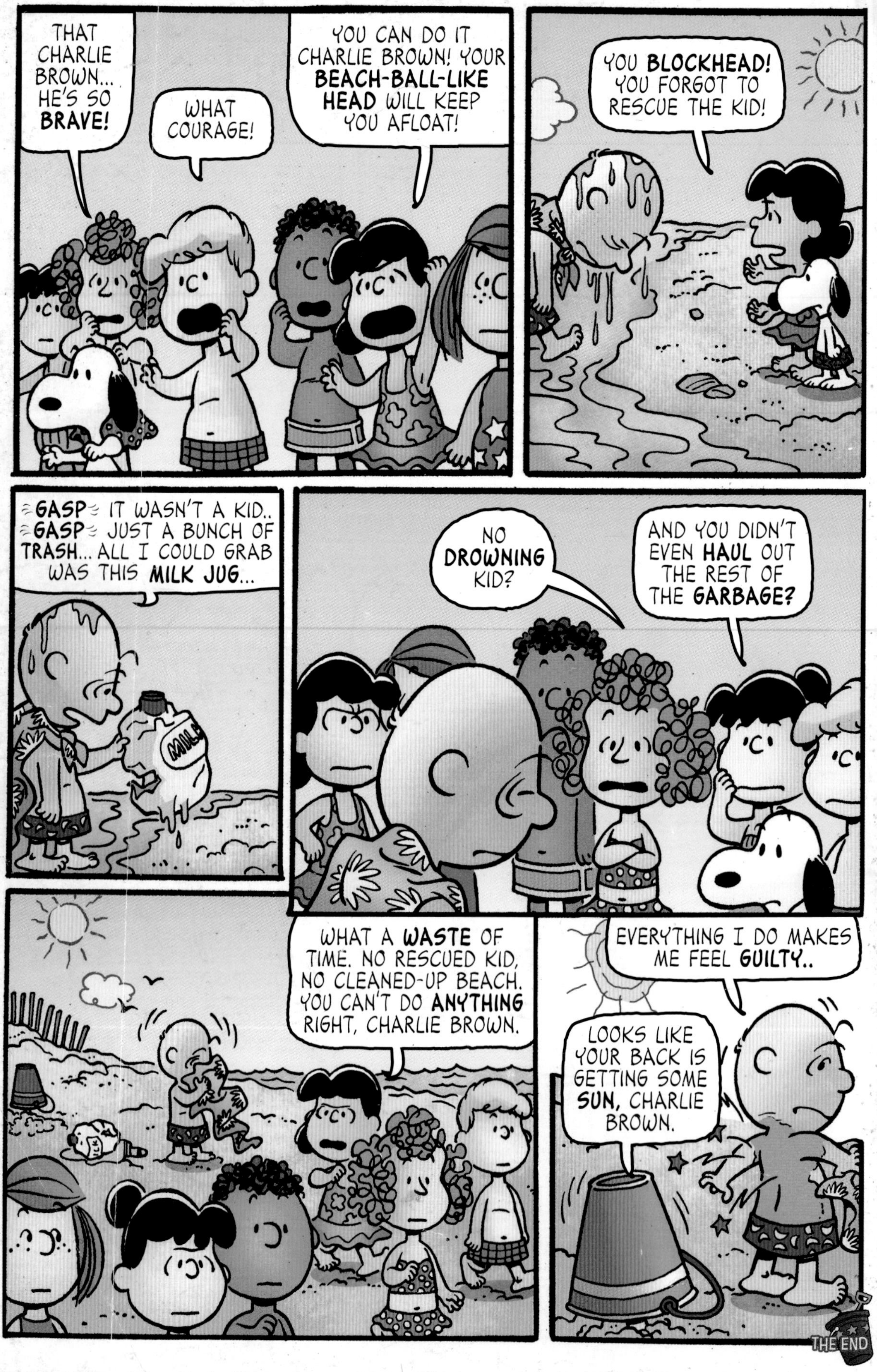
THAT CHARLIE BROWN... HE'S SO BRAVE!
WHAT COURAGE!
YOU CAN DO IT CHARLIE BROWN! YOUR BEACH-BALL-LIKE HEAD WILL KEEP YOU AFLOAT!
YOU BLOCKHEAD! YOU FORGOT TO RESCUE THE KID!
GASP IT WASN'T A KID.. GASP JUST A BUNCH OF TRASH... ALL I COULD GRAB WAS THIS MILK JUG...
MILK
NO DROWNING KID?
AND YOU DIDN'T EVEN HAUL OUT THE REST OF THE GARBAGE?
WHAT A WASTE OF TIME. NO RESCUED KID, NO CLEANED-UP BEACH. YOU CAN'T DO ANYTHING RIGHT, CHARLIE BROWN.
EVERYTHING I DO MAKES ME FEEL GUILTY..
LOOKS LIKE YOUR BACK IS GETTING SOME SUN, CHARLIE BROWN.
THE END

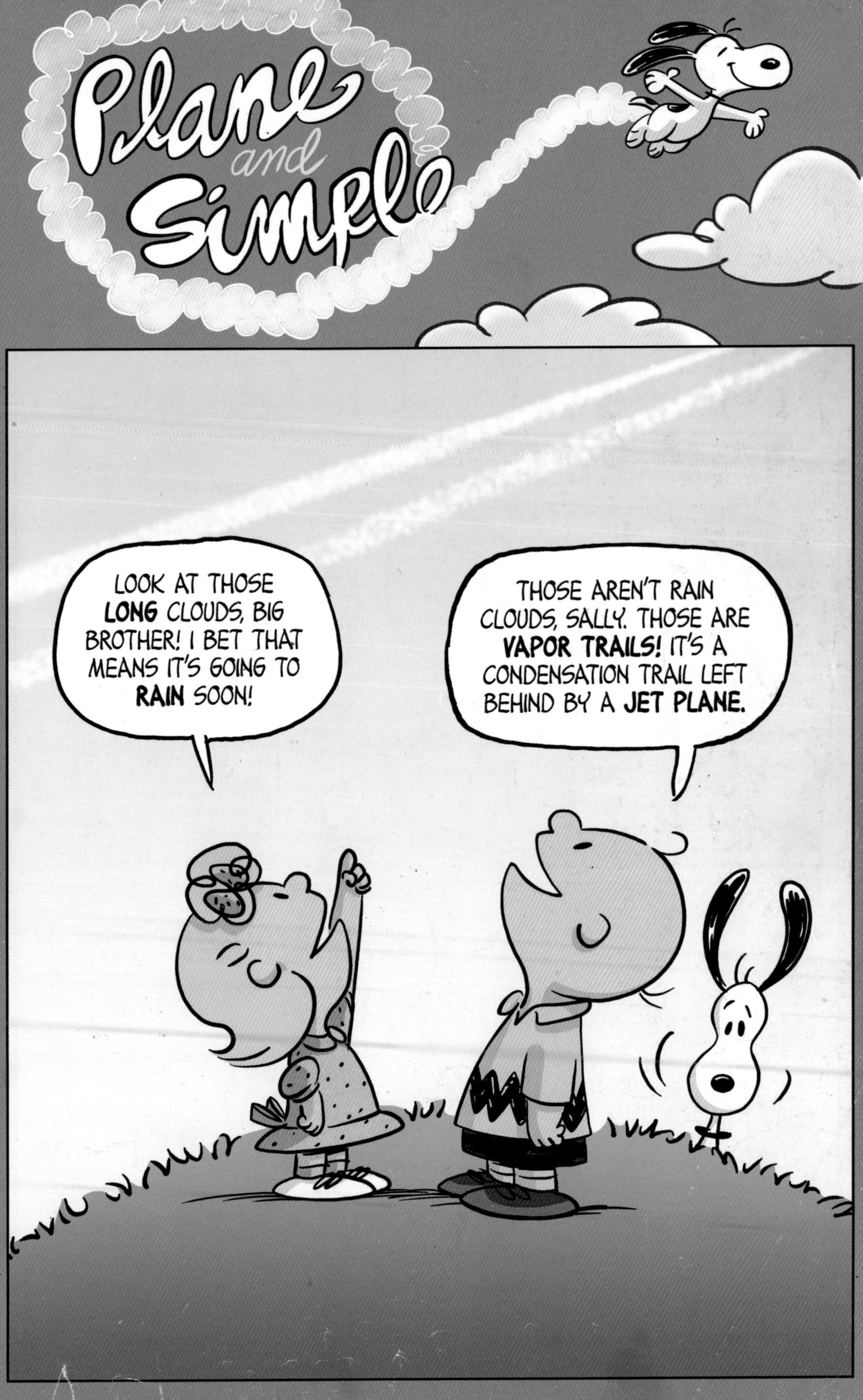
Plane and Simple
LOOK AT THOSE LONG CLOUDS, BIG BROTHER! I BET THAT MEANS IT'S GOING TO RAIN SOON!
THOSE AREN'T RAIN CLOUDS, SALLY. THOSE ARE VAPOR TRAILS! IT'S A CONDENSATION TRAIL LEFT BEHIND BY A JET PLANE.

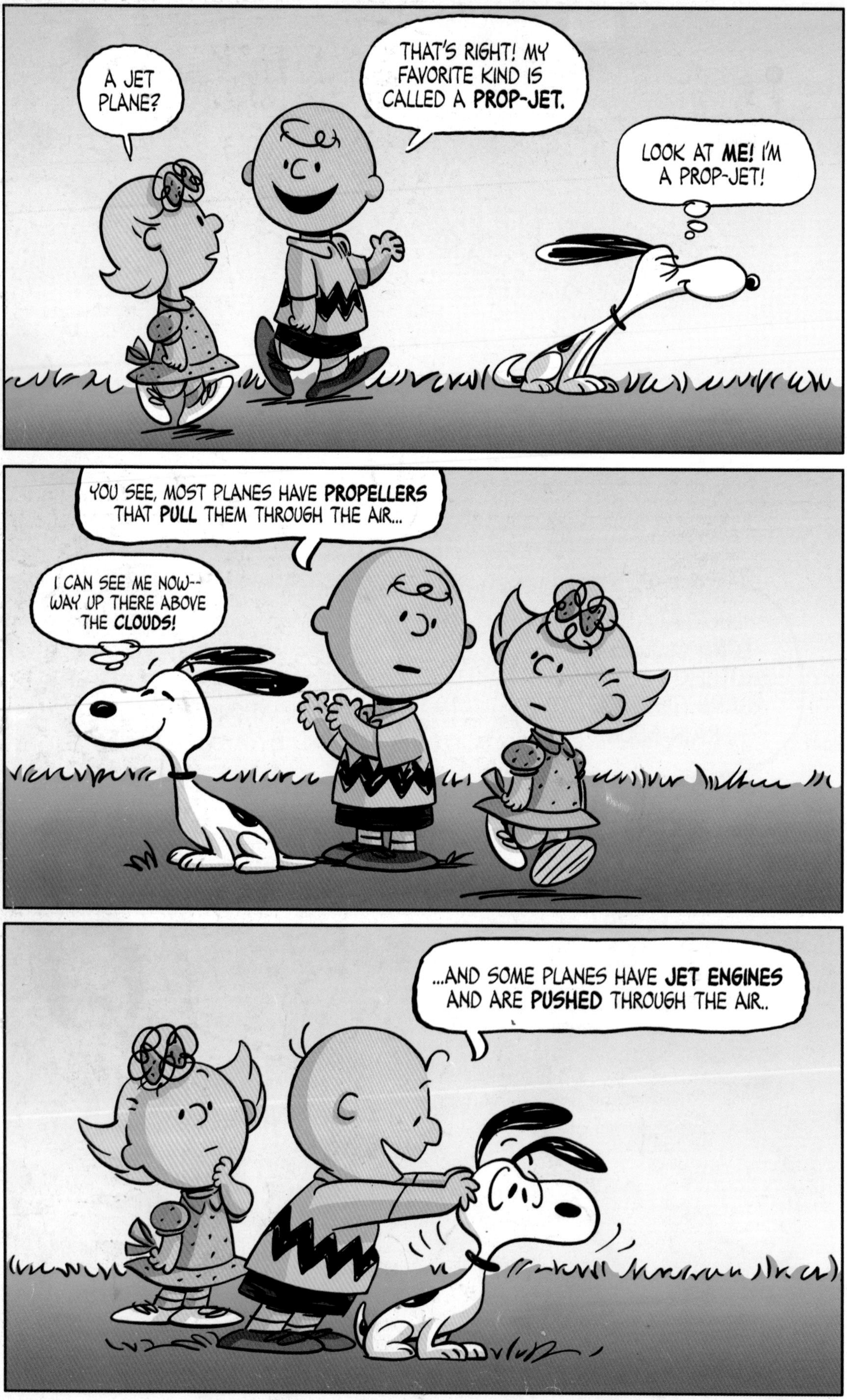
A JET PLANE?
THAT'S RIGHT! MY FAVORITE KIND IS CALLED A **PROP-JET.**
LOOK AT **ME!** I'M A PROP-JET!
YOU SEE, MOST PLANES HAVE **PROPELLERS** THAT **PULL** THEM THROUGH THE AIR...
I CAN SEE ME NOW-- WAY UP THERE ABOVE THE **CLOUDS!**
...AND SOME PLANES HAVE **JET ENGINES** AND ARE **PUSHED** THROUGH THE AIR..

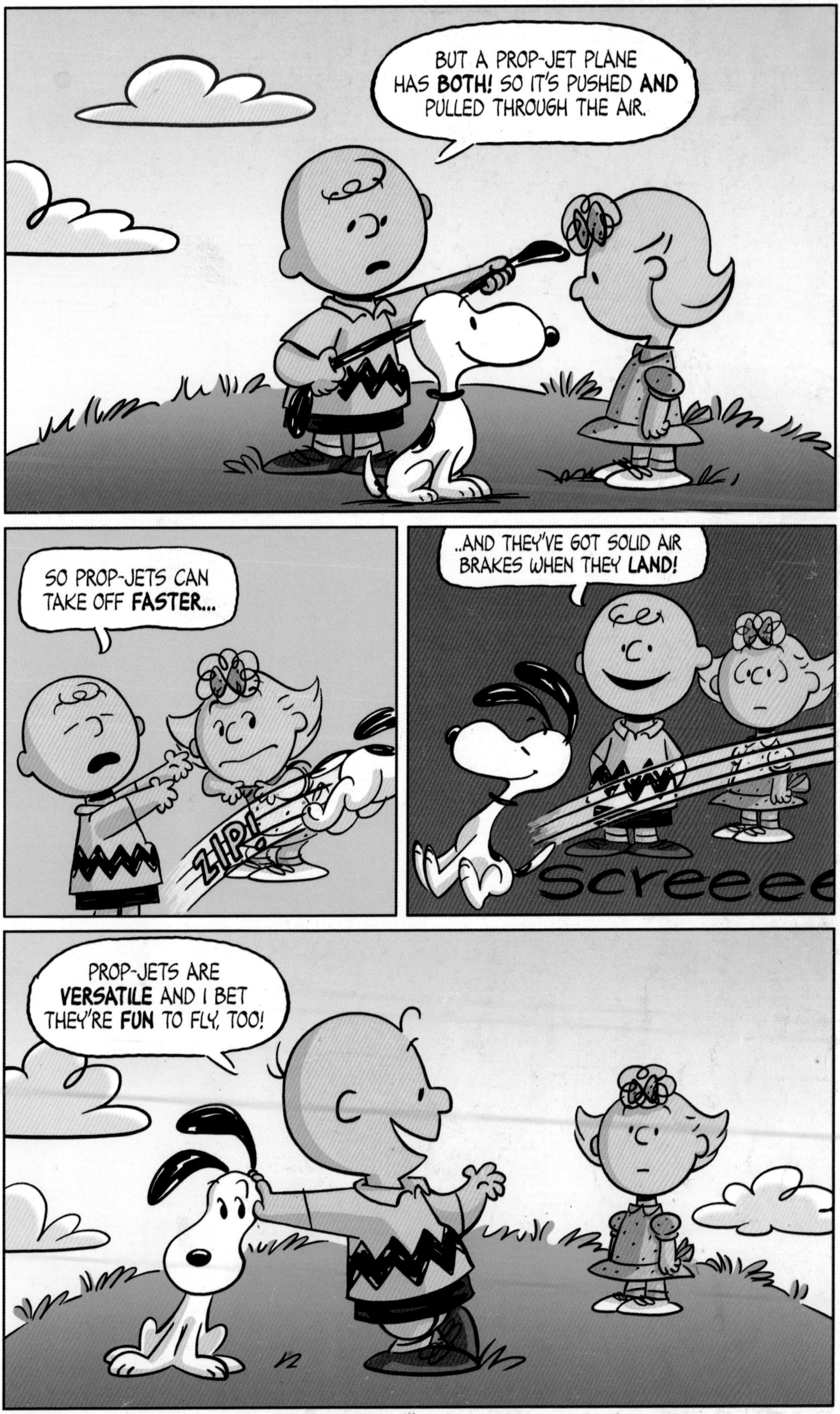
BUT A PROP-JET PLANE HAS BOTH! SO IT'S PUSHED AND PULLED THROUGH THE AIR.
SO PROP-JETS CAN TAKE OFF FASTER...
ZIP!
..AND THEY'VE GOT SOLID AIR BRAKES WHEN THEY LAND!
SCREEEE
PROP-JETS ARE VERSATILE AND I BET THEY'RE FUN TO FLY, TOO!

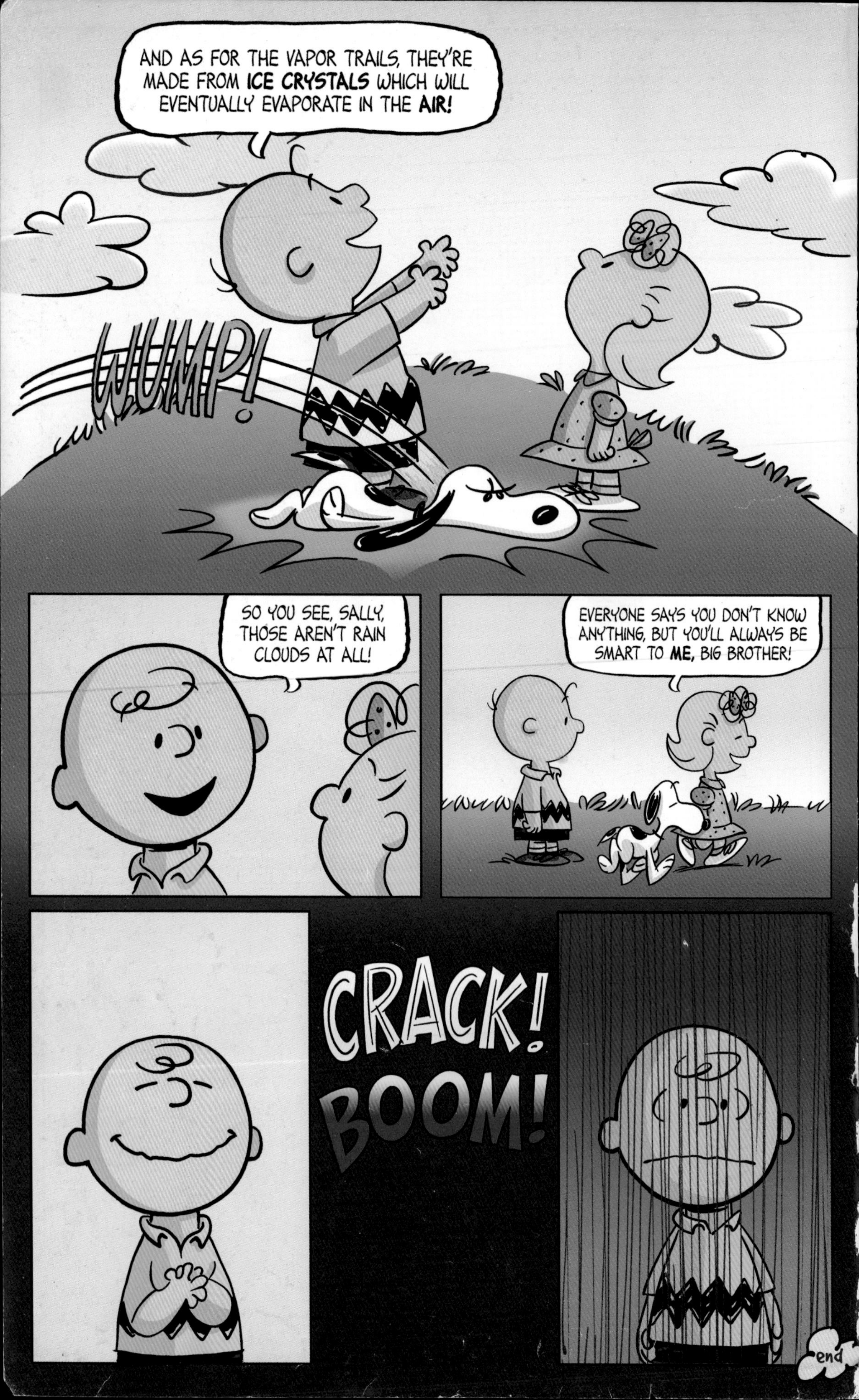
AND AS FOR THE VAPOR TRAILS, THEY'RE MADE FROM ICE CRYSTALS WHICH WILL EVENTUALLY EVAPORATE IN THE AIR!
WUMP!
SO YOU SEE, SALLY, THOSE AREN'T RAIN CLOUDS AT ALL!
EVERYONE SAYS YOU DON'T KNOW ANYTHING, BUT YOU'LL ALWAYS BE SMART TO ME, BIG BROTHER!
CRACK!
BOOM!
end

From the Drawing Board

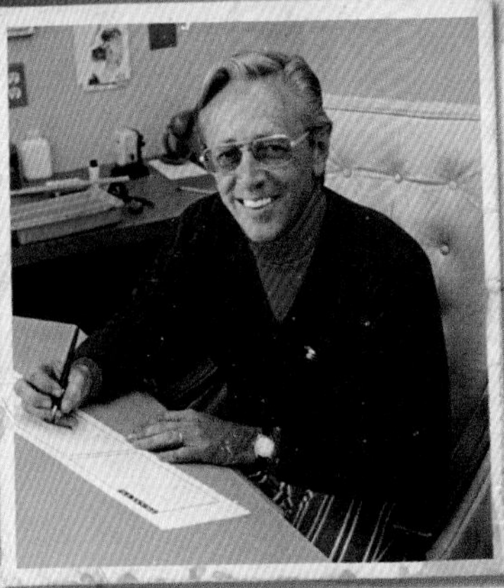

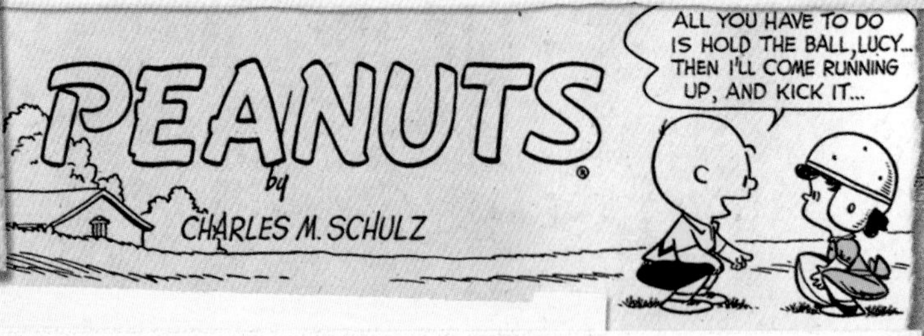
PEANUTS
by
CHARLES M. SCHULZ
ALL YOU HAVE TO DO IS HOLD THE BALL, LUCY... THEN I'LL COME RUNNING UP, AND KICK IT...

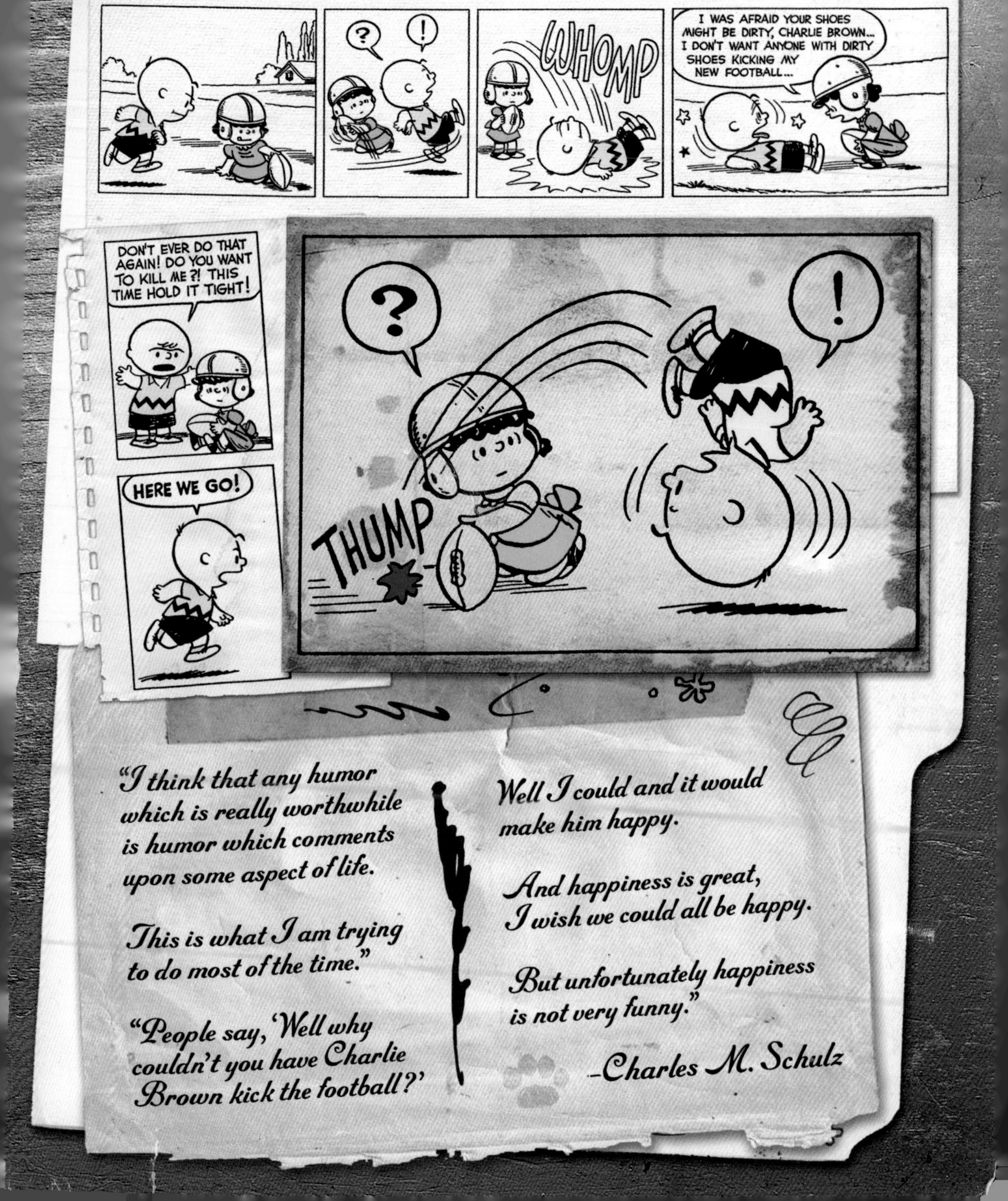
?
!
WHOMP
I WAS AFRAID YOUR SHOES MIGHT BE DIRTY, CHARLIE BROWN... I DON'T WANT ANYONE WITH DIRTY SHOES KICKING MY NEW FOOTBALL...
DON'T EVER DO THAT AGAIN! DO YOU WANT TO KILL ME ?! THIS TIME HOLD IT TIGHT!
HERE WE GO!
?
!
THUMP

"I think that any humor which is really worthwhile is humor which comments upon some aspect of life.

This is what I am trying to do most of the time."

"People say, 'Well why couldn't you have Charlie Brown kick the football?'

Well I could and it would make him happy.

And happiness is great, I wish we could all be happy.

But unfortunately happiness is not very funny."

–Charles M. Schulz

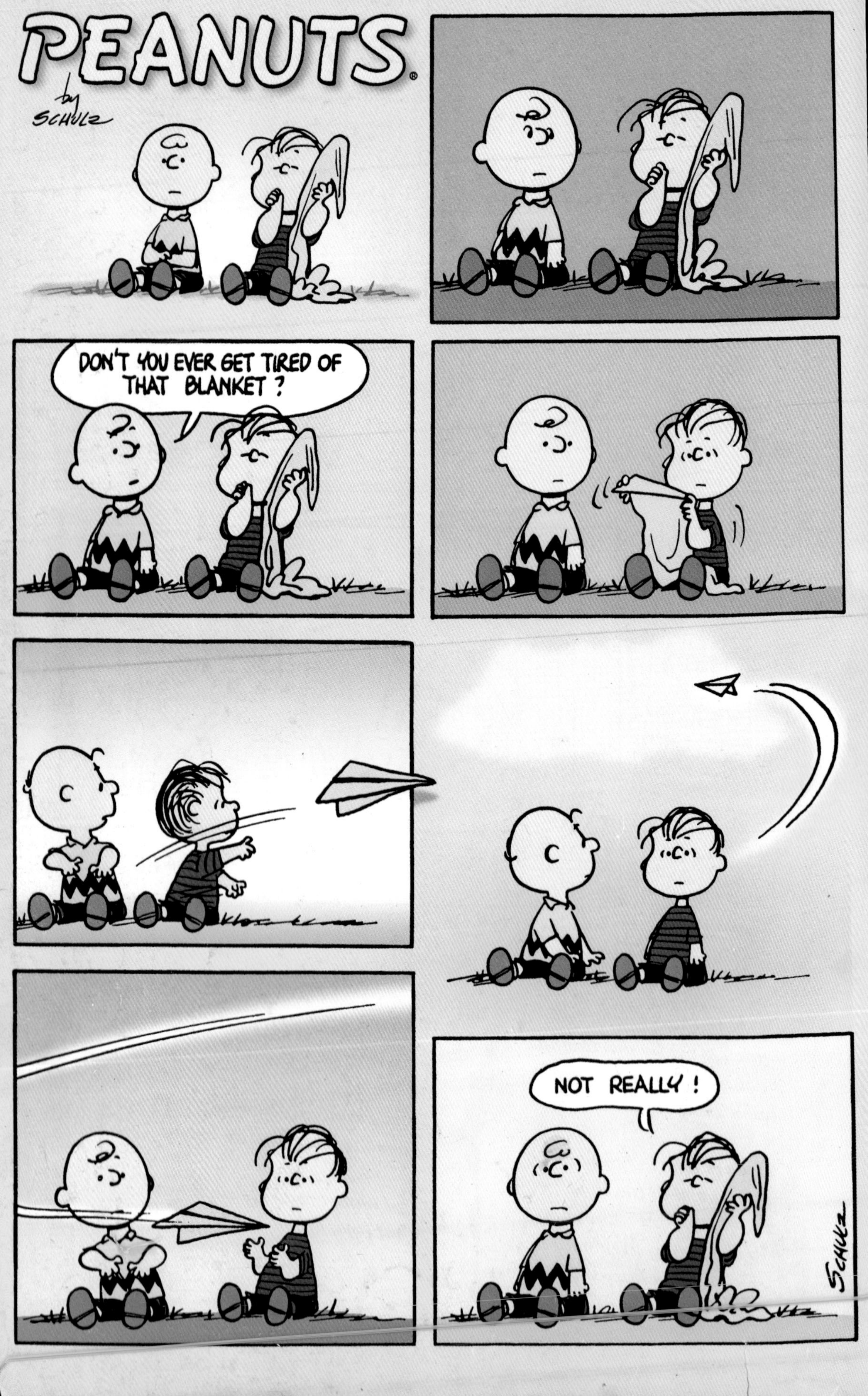
PEANUTS
by SCHULZ
DON'T YOU EVER GET TIRED OF THAT BLANKET?
NOT REALLY!
SCHULZ

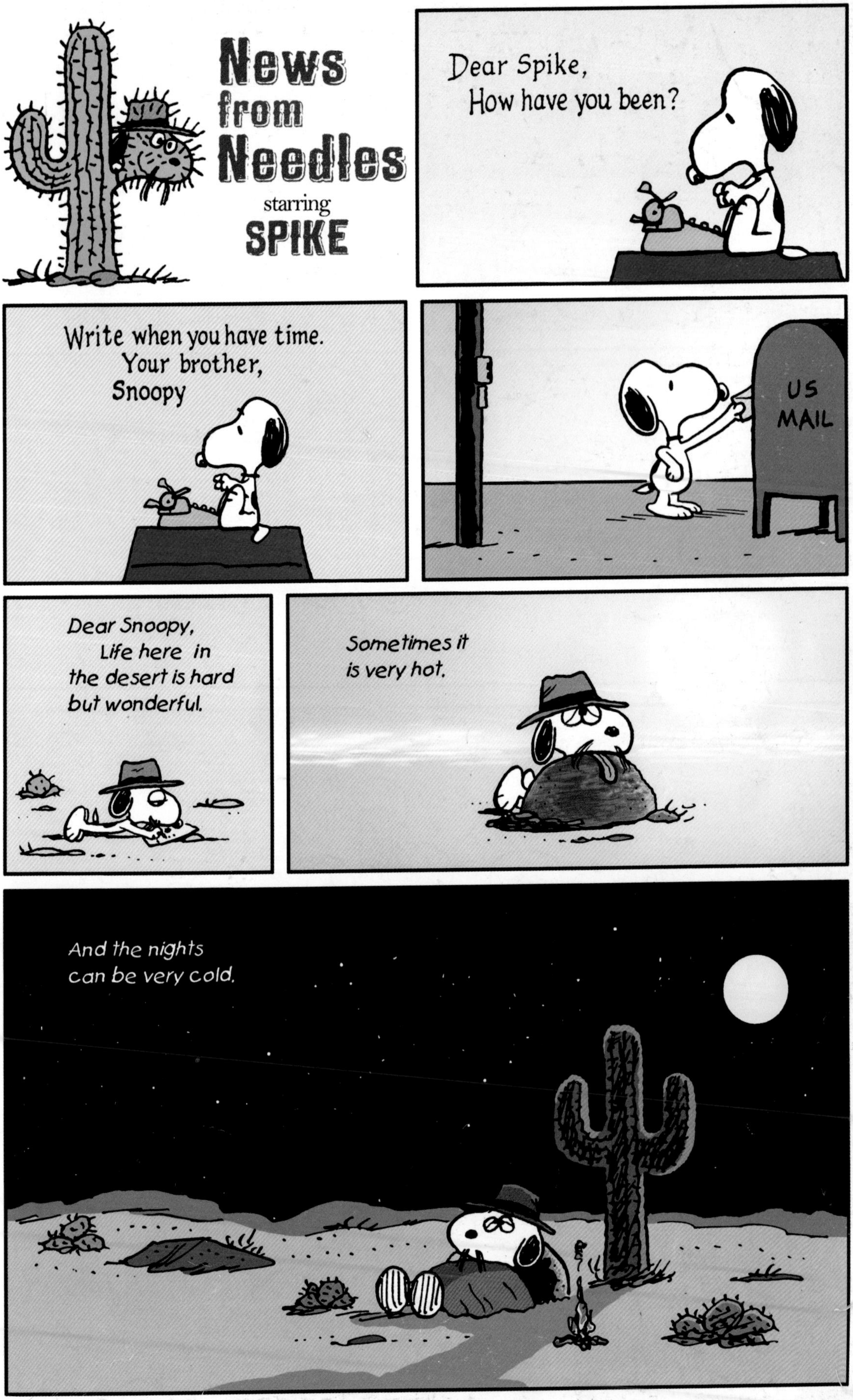
News from Needles
starring
SPIKE
Dear Spike,
How have you been?
Write when you have time.
Your brother,
Snoopy
US MAIL
Dear Snoopy,
Life here in the desert is hard but wonderful.
Sometimes it is very hot.
And the nights can be very cold.

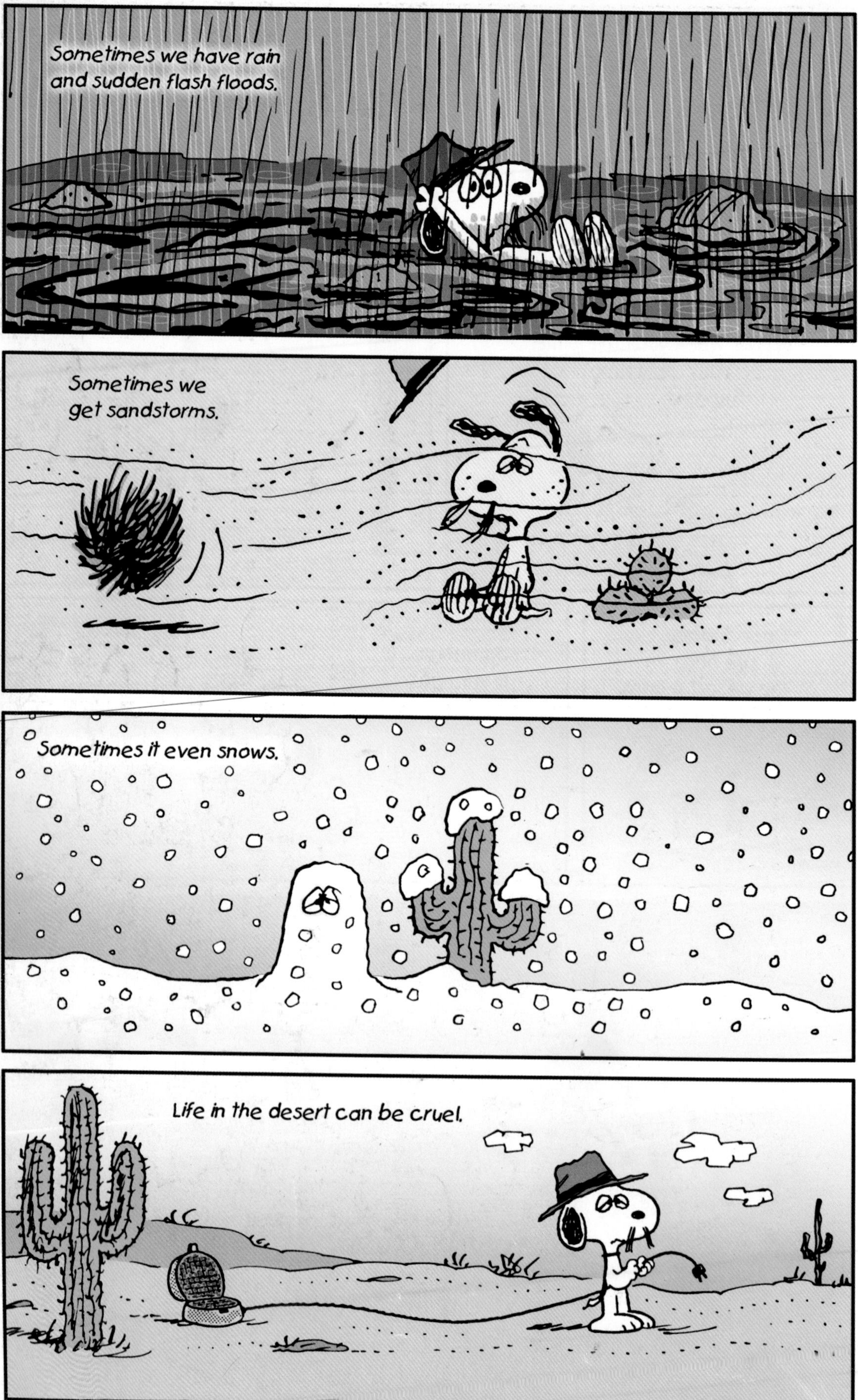
Sometimes we have rain and sudden flash floods.
Sometimes we get sandstorms.
Sometimes it even snows.
Life in the desert can be cruel.

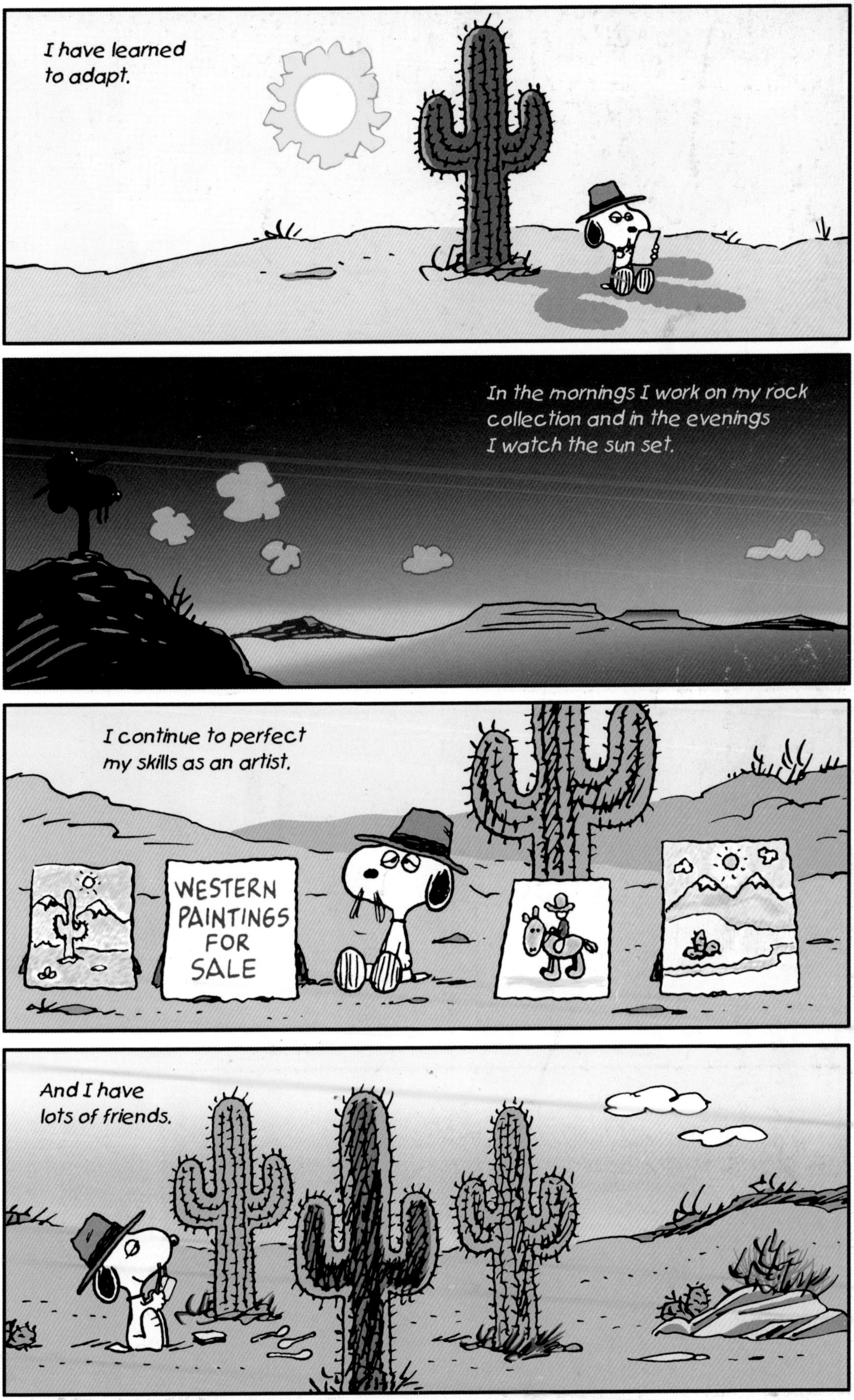
I have learned to adapt.
In the mornings I work on my rock collection and in the evenings I watch the sun set.
I continue to perfect my skills as an artist.
WESTERN PAINTINGS FOR SALE
And I have lots of friends.

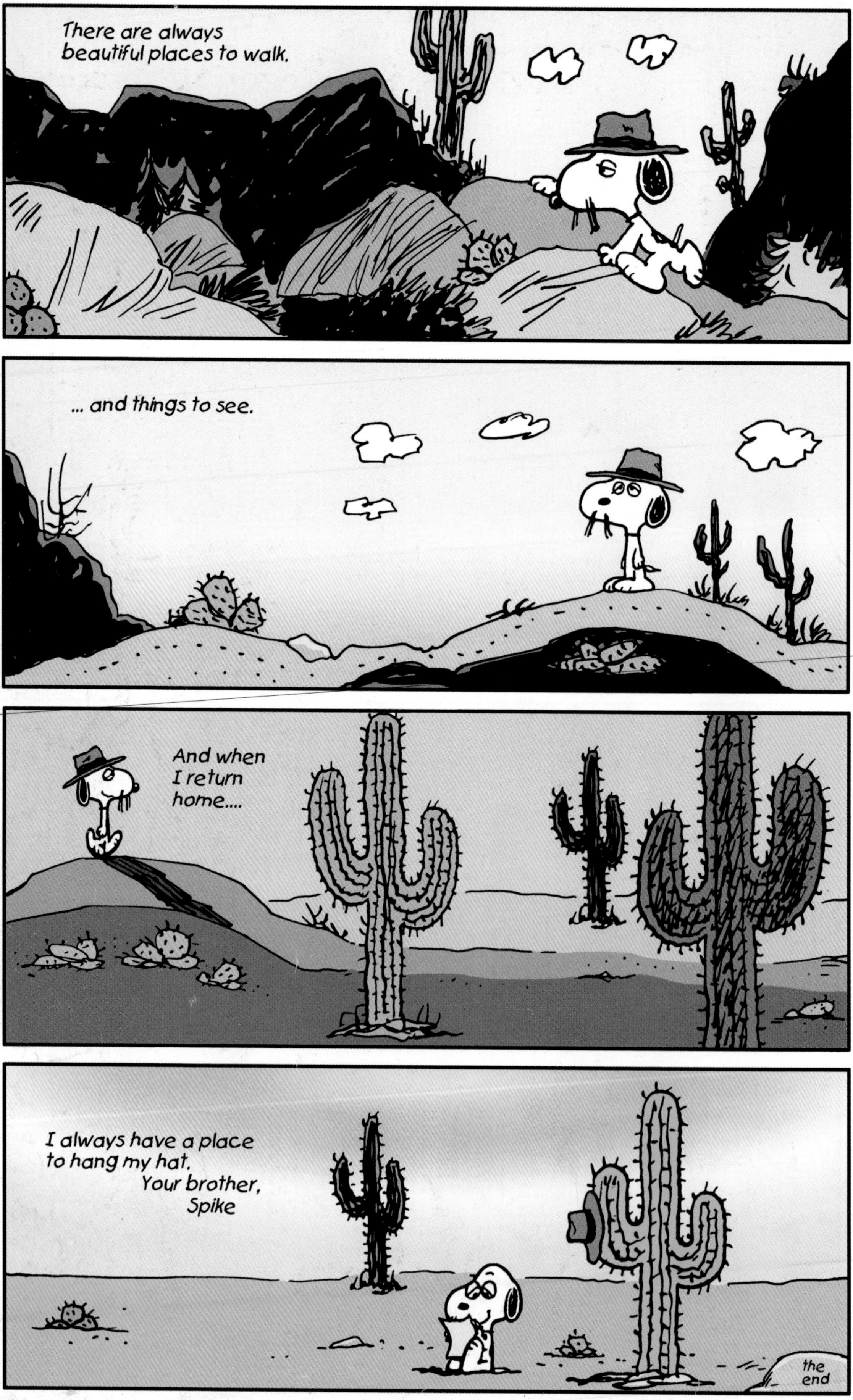
There are always beautiful places to walk.
... and things to see.
And when I return home....
I always have a place to hang my hat.
Your brother, Spike
the end

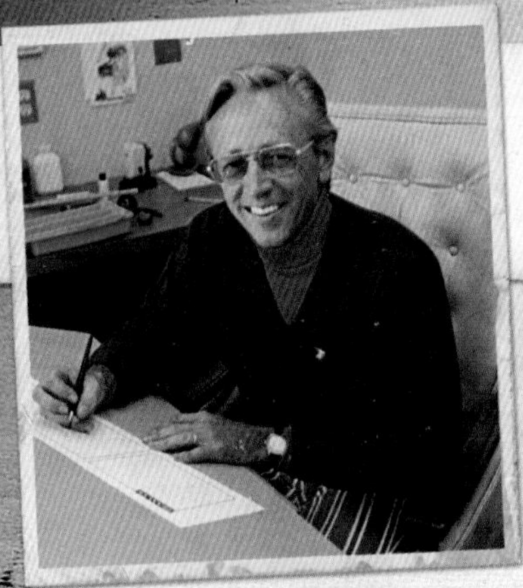

From the Drawing Board

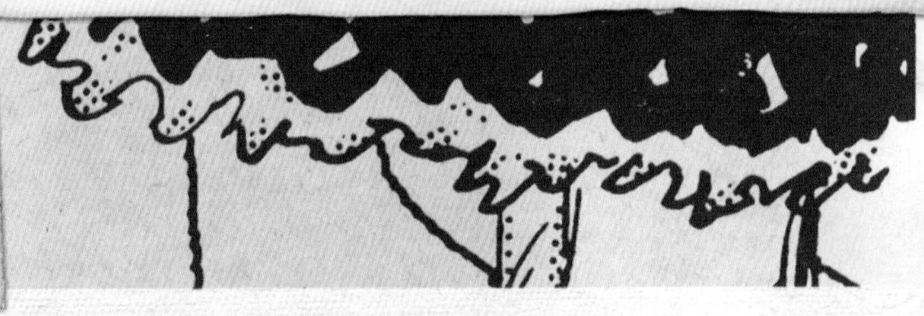

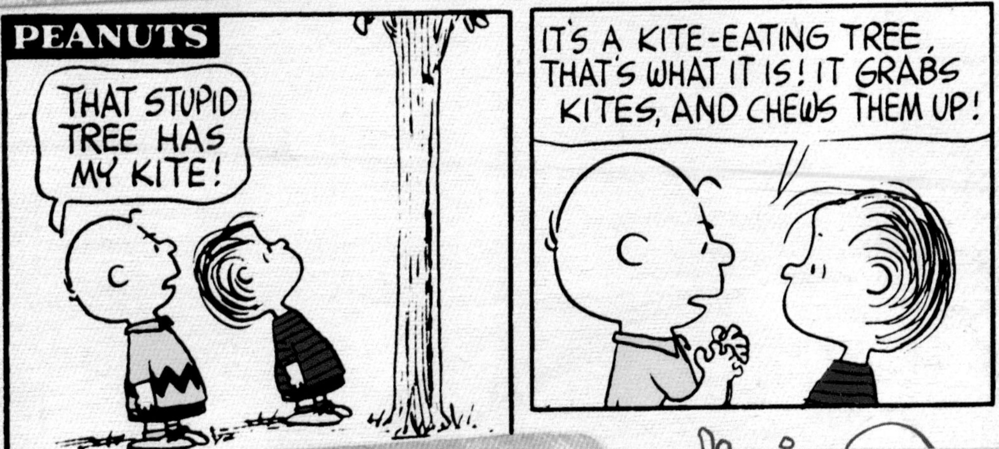
PEANUTS
THAT STUPID TREE HAS MY KITE!
IT'S A KITE-EATING TREE, THAT'S WHAT IT IS! IT GRABS KITES, AND CHEWS THEM UP!

"As a kid, I always tried to fly kites every kite season and they always got caught in the trees.

And then I noticed as the weeks went by, the kite gradually disappeared.

I inevitably came to the conclusion that the tree is eating the kite.

First the paper disappears, it's like eating fried chicken you know, you eat the skin, and then there's nothing left but the bones.

The little sticks.

And then they're gone, so I thought the tree ate the kite."

–Charles M. Schulz

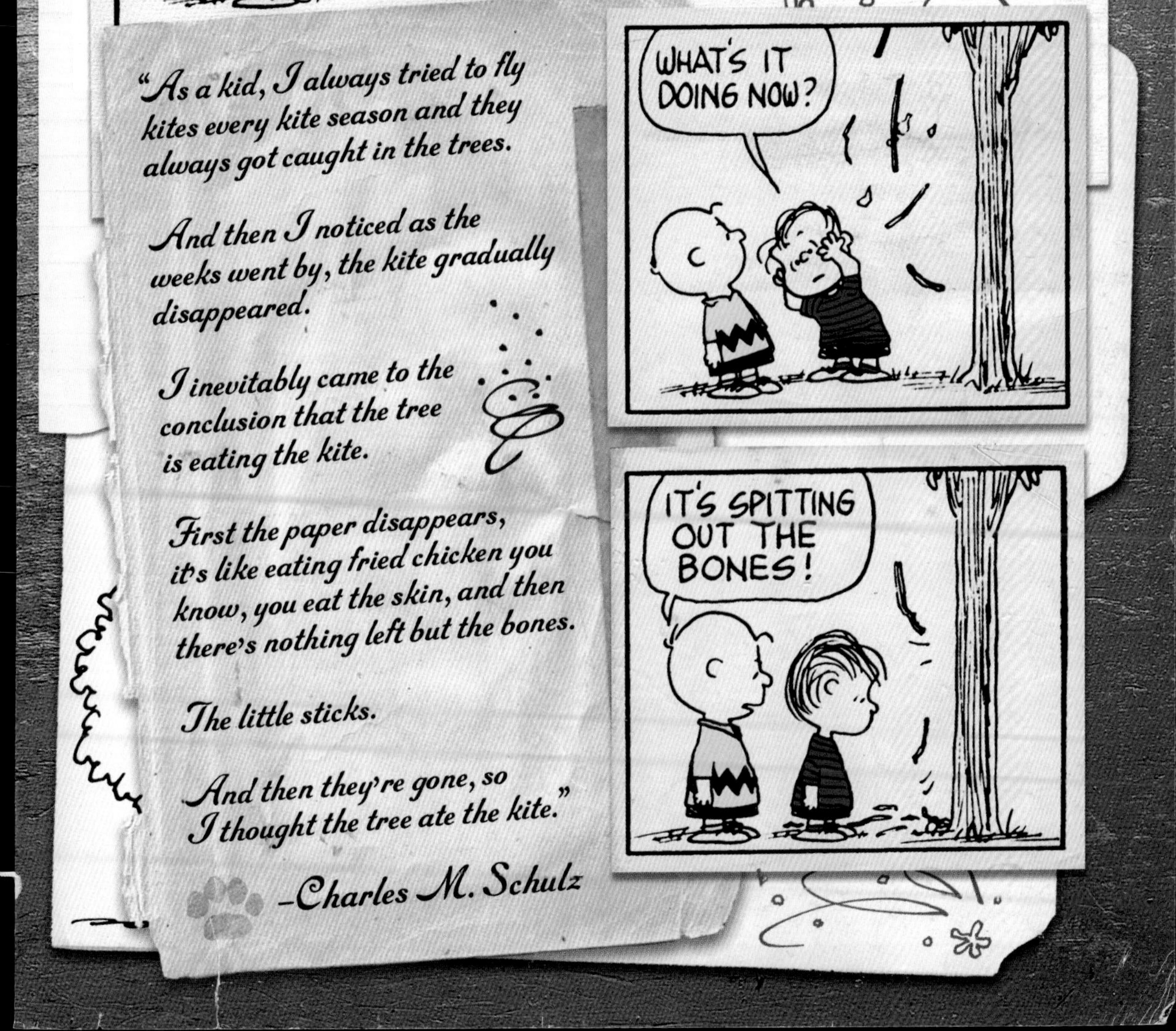
WHAT'S IT DOING NOW?
IT'S SPITTING OUT THE BONES!

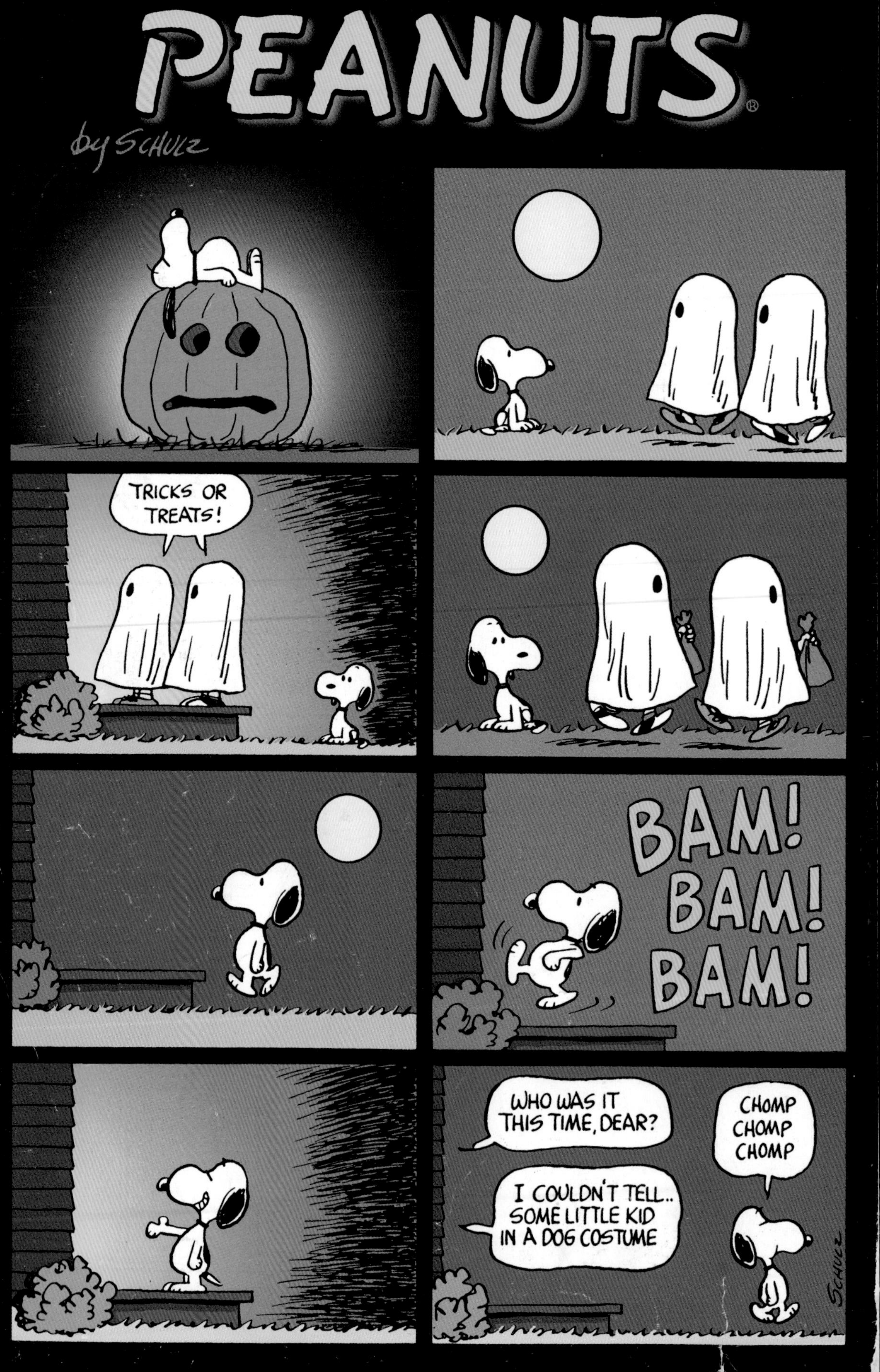
PEANUTS
by SCHULZ
TRICKS OR TREATS!
BAM! BAM! BAM!
WHO WAS IT THIS TIME, DEAR?
I COULDN'T TELL.. SOME LITTLE KID IN A DOG COSTUME
CHOMP CHOMP CHOMP
SCHULZ

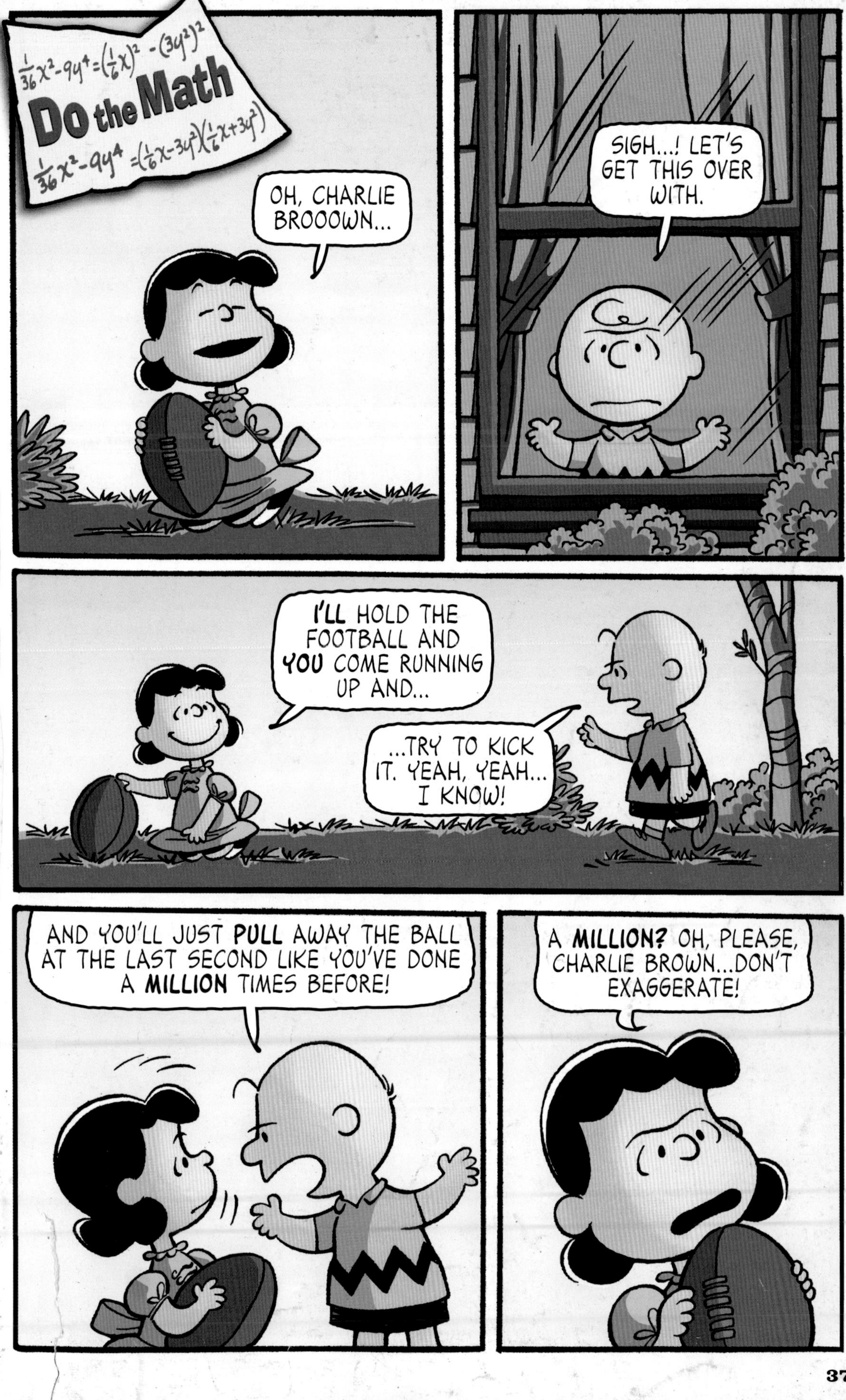
$\frac{1}{36}x^2-9y^4=(\frac{1}{6}x)^2-(3y^2)^2$
Do the Math
$\frac{1}{36}x^2-9y^4=(\frac{1}{6}x-3y^2)(\frac{1}{6}x+3y^2)$
OH, CHARLIE BROOOWN...
SIGH...! LET'S GET THIS OVER WITH.
I'LL HOLD THE FOOTBALL AND YOU COME RUNNING UP AND...
...TRY TO KICK IT. YEAH, YEAH... I KNOW!
AND YOU'LL JUST PULL AWAY THE BALL AT THE LAST SECOND LIKE YOU'VE DONE A MILLION TIMES BEFORE!
A MILLION? OH, PLEASE, CHARLIE BROWN...DON'T EXAGGERATE!

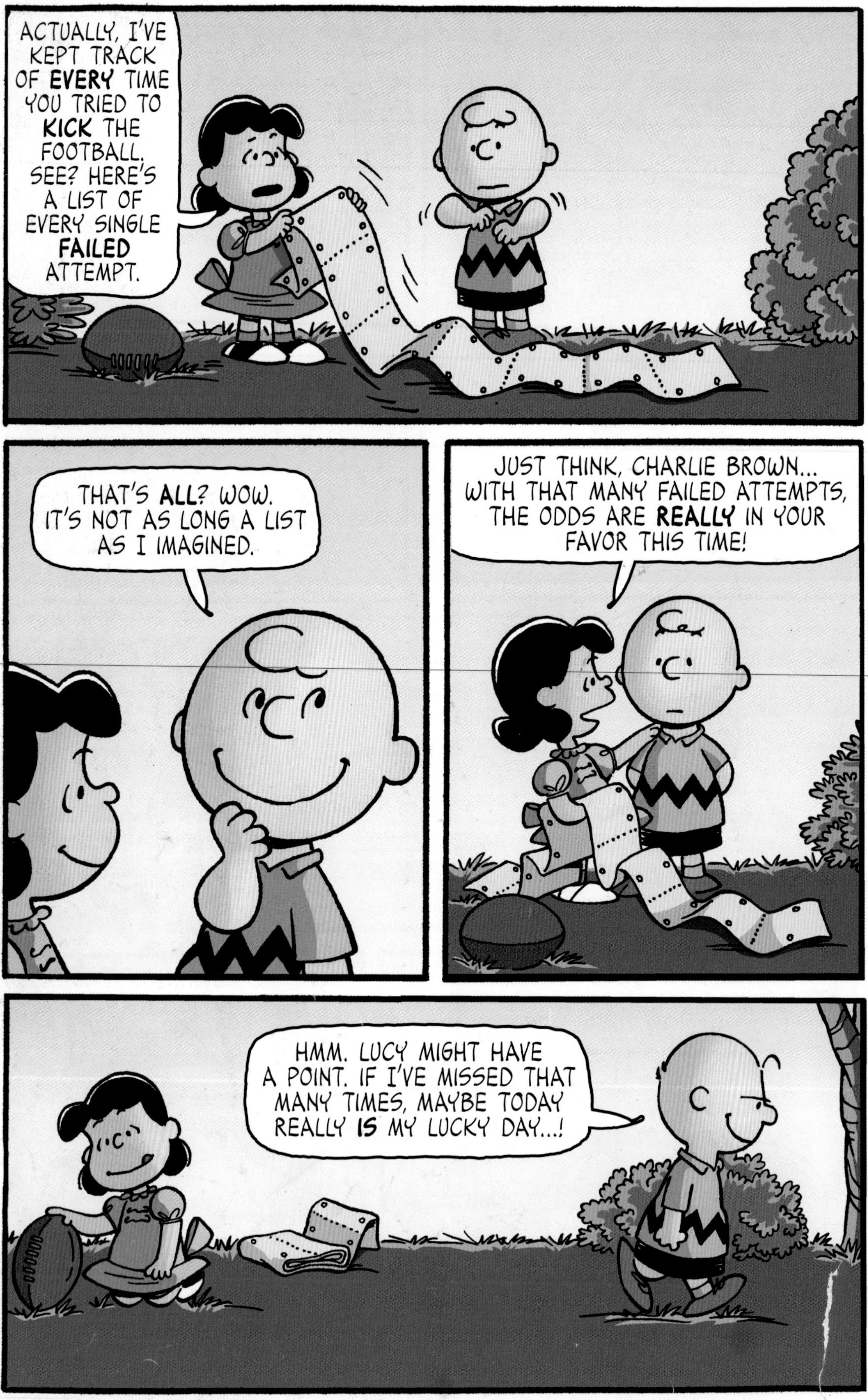
ACTUALLY, I'VE KEPT TRACK OF EVERY TIME YOU TRIED TO KICK THE FOOTBALL. SEE? HERE'S A LIST OF EVERY SINGLE FAILED ATTEMPT.
THAT'S ALL? WOW. IT'S NOT AS LONG A LIST AS I IMAGINED.
JUST THINK, CHARLIE BROWN... WITH THAT MANY FAILED ATTEMPTS, THE ODDS ARE REALLY IN YOUR FAVOR THIS TIME!
HMM. LUCY MIGHT HAVE A POINT. IF I'VE MISSED THAT MANY TIMES, MAYBE TODAY REALLY IS MY LUCKY DAY...!

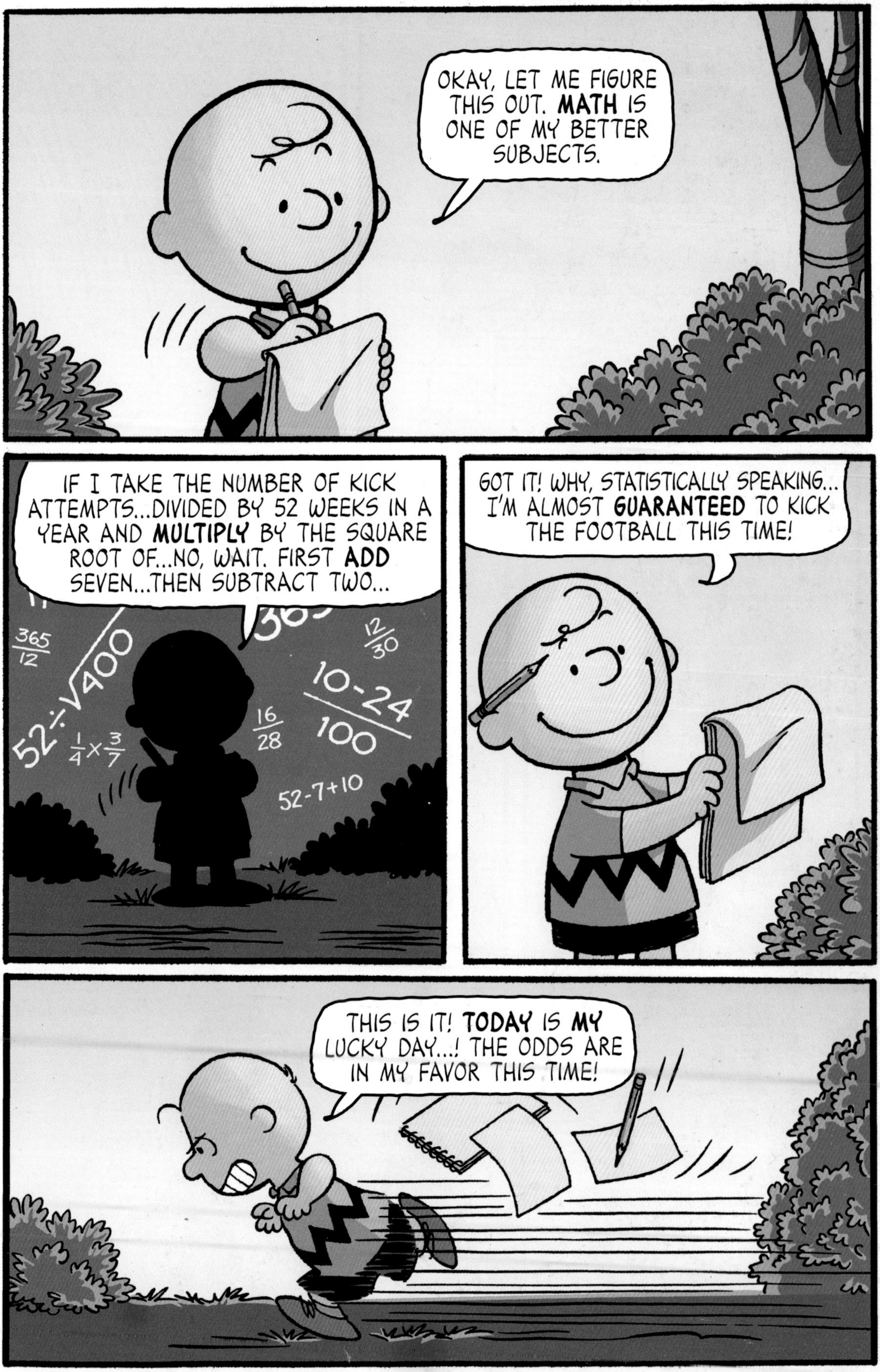
OKAY, LET ME FIGURE THIS OUT. MATH IS ONE OF MY BETTER SUBJECTS.
IF I TAKE THE NUMBER OF KICK ATTEMPTS...DIVIDED BY 52 WEEKS IN A YEAR AND MULTIPLY BY THE SQUARE ROOT OF...NO, WAIT. FIRST ADD SEVEN...THEN SUBTRACT TWO...
365/12
52÷√400
1/4×3/7
16/28
12/30
10-24/100
52-7+10
GOT IT! WHY, STATISTICALLY SPEAKING... I'M ALMOST GUARANTEED TO KICK THE FOOTBALL THIS TIME!
THIS IS IT! TODAY IS MY LUCKY DAY...! THE ODDS ARE IN MY FAVOR THIS TIME!

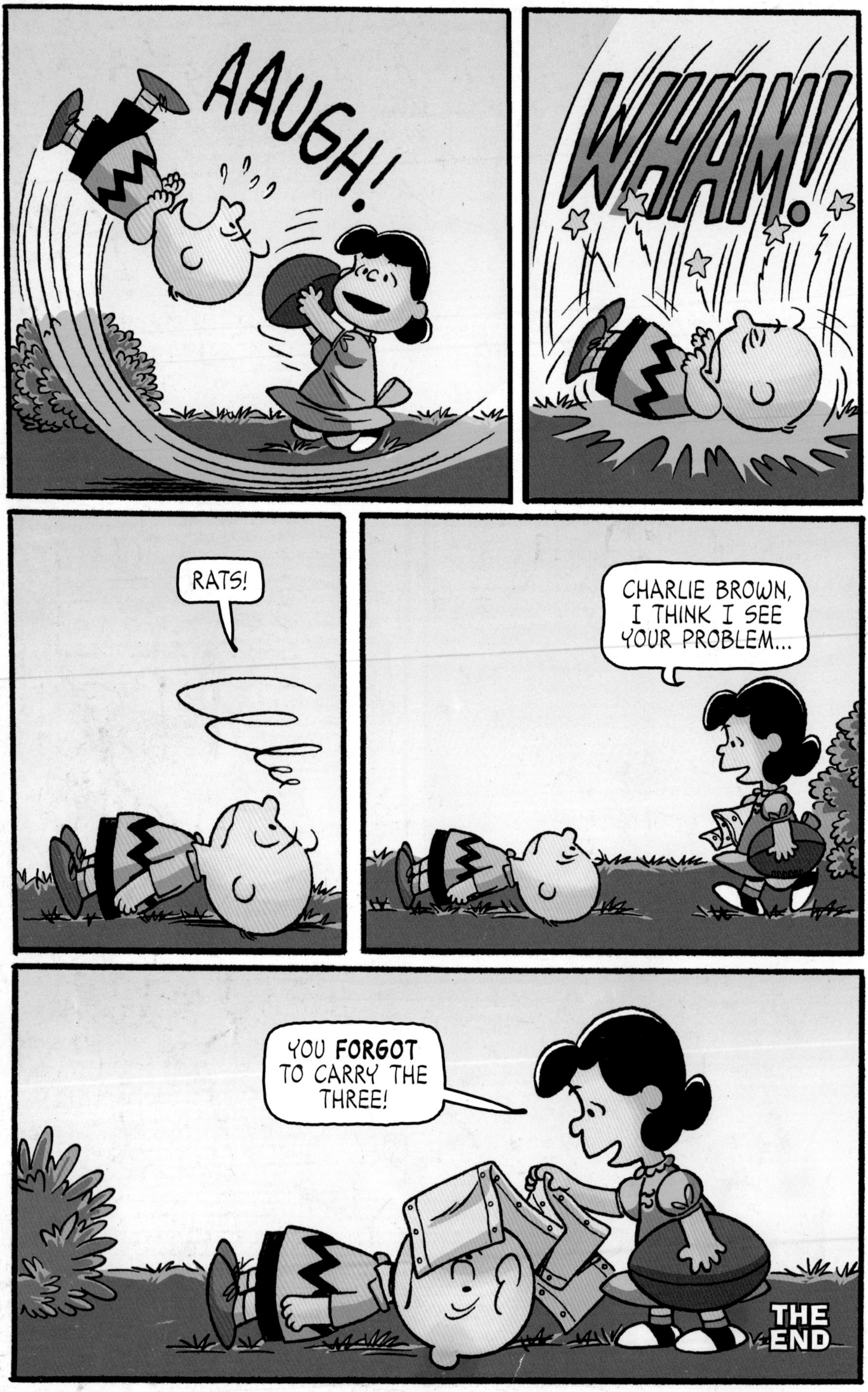
AAUGH!
WHAM!
RATS!
CHARLIE BROWN, I THINK I SEE YOUR PROBLEM...
YOU **FORGOT** TO CARRY THE THREE!
THE END

From the Drawing Board

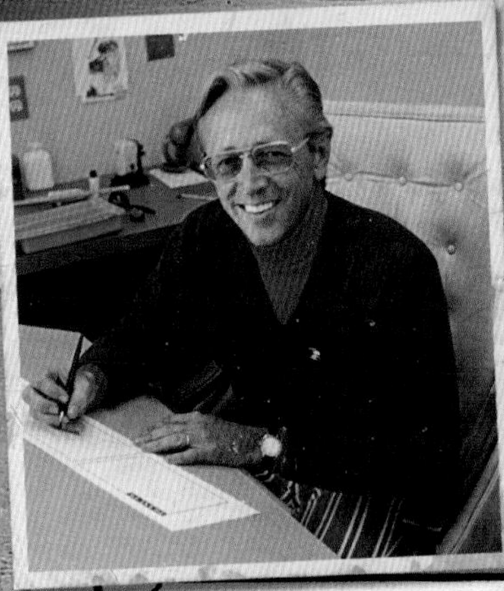

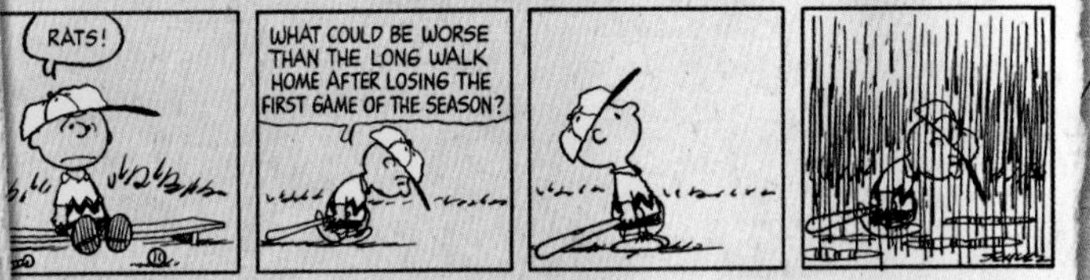

RATS!
WHAT COULD BE WORSE THAN THE LONG WALK HOME AFTER LOSING THE FIRST GAME OF THE SEASON?

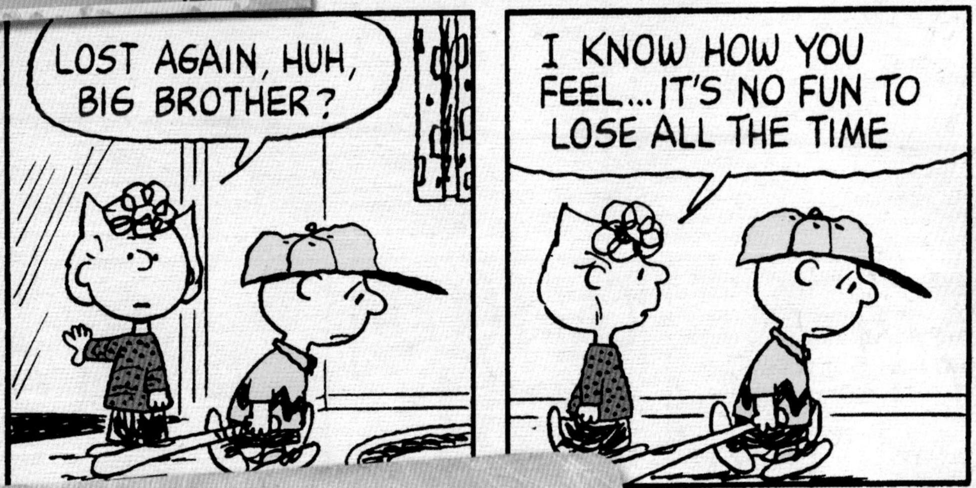

LOST AGAIN, HUH, BIG BROTHER?
I KNOW HOW YOU FEEL...IT'S NO FUN TO LOSE ALL THE TIME

"My strip is filled with life.

And life is filled with sad stories."

"Defeat is a lot funnier than victory.

Most of us know what it is like to lose some kind of contest, and we can identify with that.

How wonderful it must be, thousands of people admire the person who is holding up the trophy.

But we forget also that somebody had to lose and we can all identify much more closely with losing than winning because most of us have lost."

–Charles M. Schulz

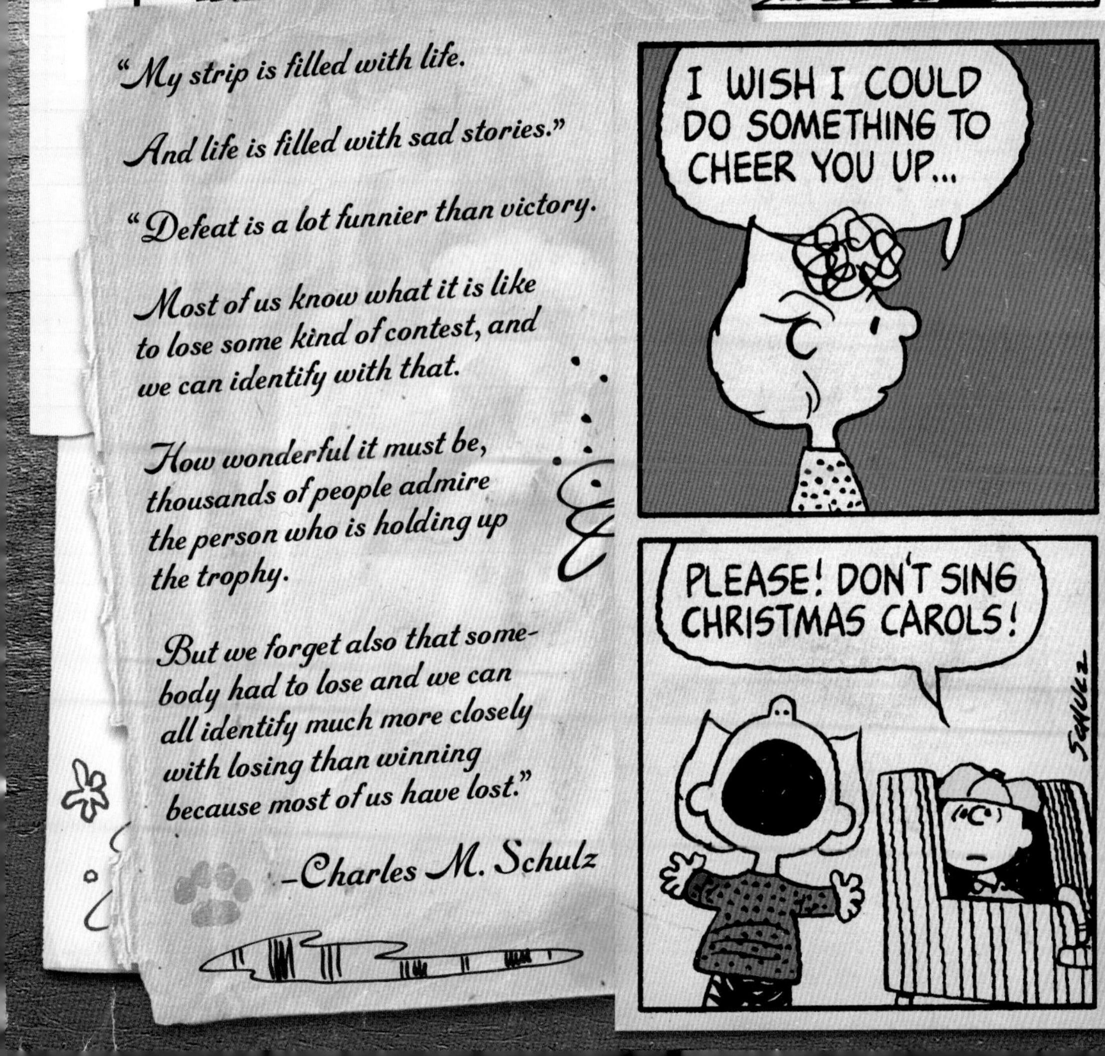

I WISH I COULD DO SOMETHING TO CHEER YOU UP...
PLEASE! DON'T SING CHRISTMAS CAROLS!
SCHULZ

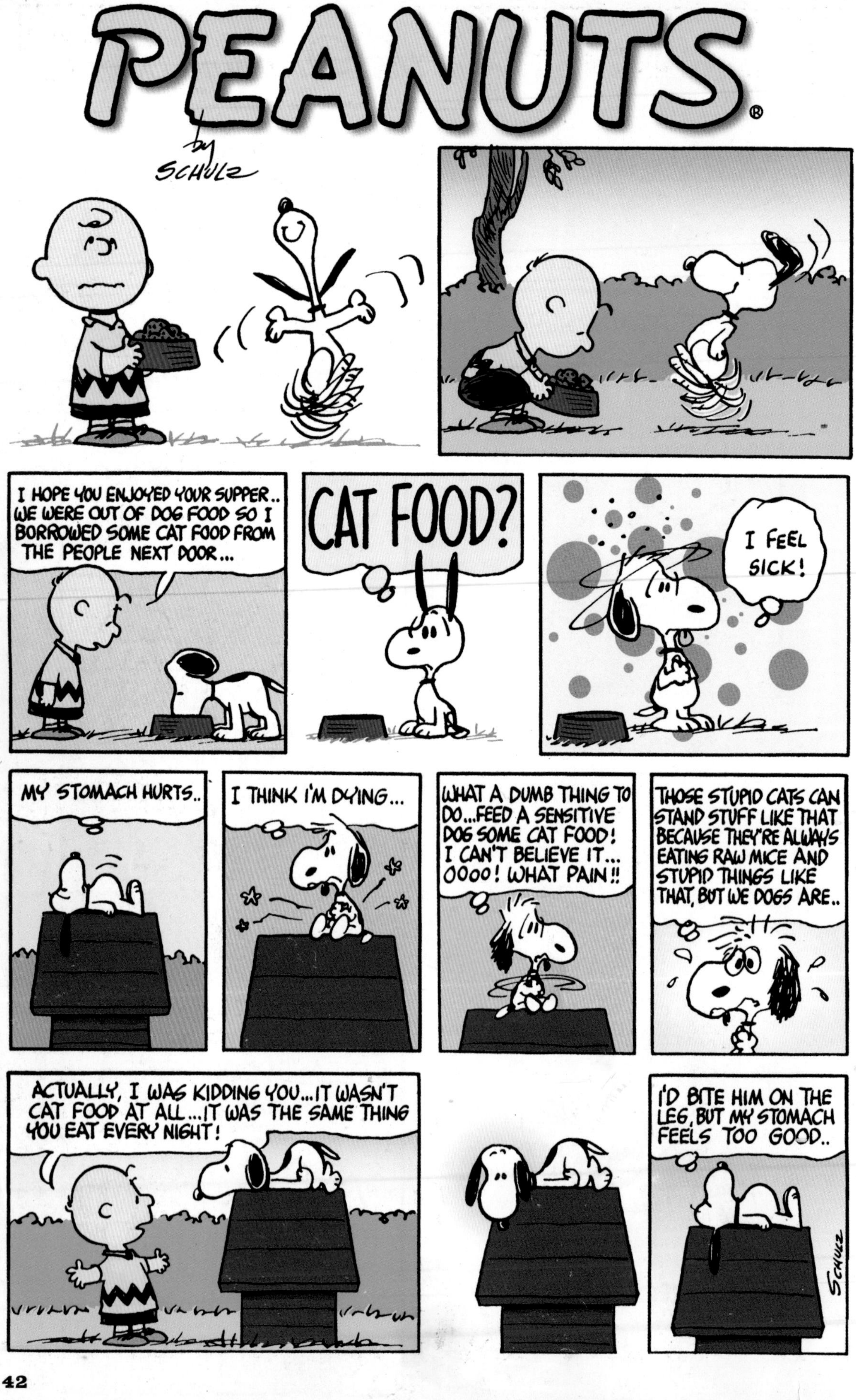
PEANUTS®
by SCHULZ
I HOPE YOU ENJOYED YOUR SUPPER.. WE WERE OUT OF DOG FOOD SO I BORROWED SOME CAT FOOD FROM THE PEOPLE NEXT DOOR...
CAT FOOD?
I FEEL SICK!
MY STOMACH HURTS..
I THINK I'M DYING...
WHAT A DUMB THING TO DO...FEED A SENSITIVE DOG SOME CAT FOOD! I CAN'T BELIEVE IT... OOOO! WHAT PAIN!!
THOSE STUPID CATS CAN STAND STUFF LIKE THAT BECAUSE THEY'RE ALWAYS EATING RAW MICE AND STUPID THINGS LIKE THAT, BUT WE DOGS ARE..
ACTUALLY, I WAS KIDDING YOU...IT WASN'T CAT FOOD AT ALL...IT WAS THE SAME THING YOU EAT EVERY NIGHT!
I'D BITE HIM ON THE LEG, BUT MY STOMACH FEELS TOO GOOD..
SCHULZ

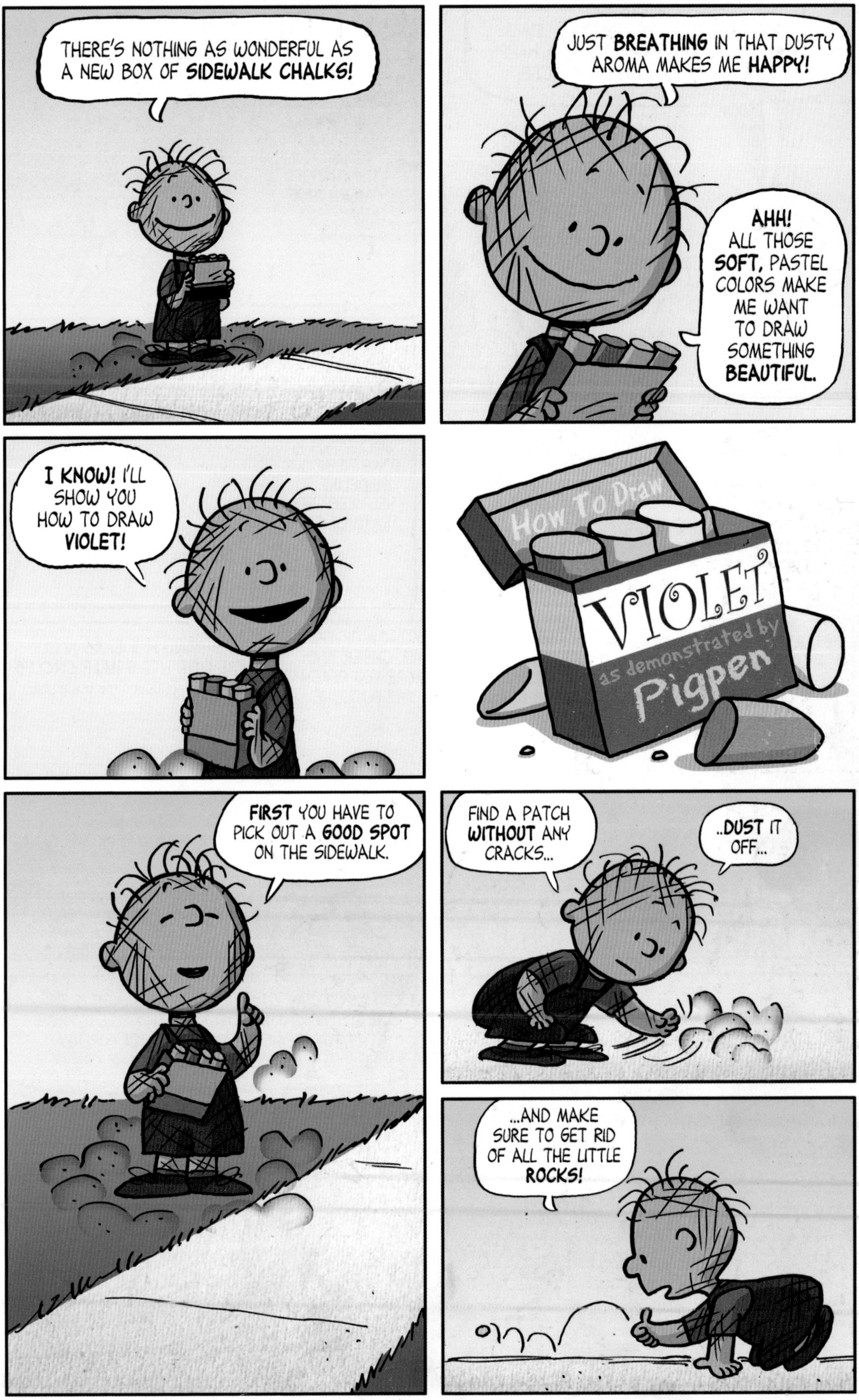
THERE'S NOTHING AS WONDERFUL AS A NEW BOX OF SIDEWALK CHALKS!
JUST BREATHING IN THAT DUSTY AROMA MAKES ME HAPPY!
AHH! ALL THOSE SOFT, PASTEL COLORS MAKE ME WANT TO DRAW SOMETHING BEAUTIFUL.
I KNOW! I'LL SHOW YOU HOW TO DRAW VIOLET!
How To Draw
VIOLET
as demonstrated by
Pigpen
FIRST YOU HAVE TO PICK OUT A GOOD SPOT ON THE SIDEWALK.
FIND A PATCH WITHOUT ANY CRACKS...
..DUST IT OFF...
...AND MAKE SURE TO GET RID OF ALL THE LITTLE ROCKS!

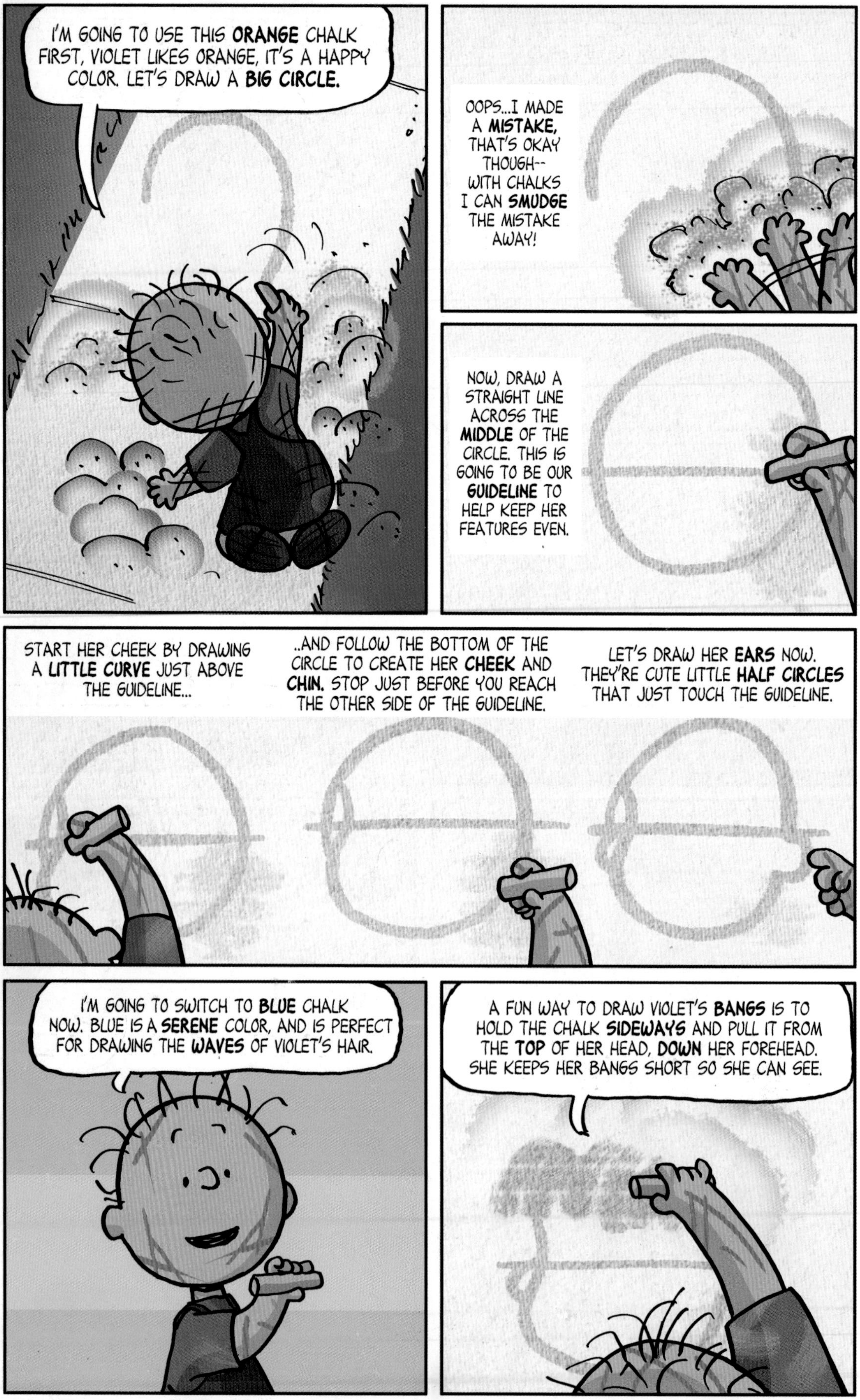
I'M GOING TO USE THIS ORANGE CHALK FIRST, VIOLET LIKES ORANGE, IT'S A HAPPY COLOR. LET'S DRAW A BIG CIRCLE.
OOPS...I MADE A MISTAKE, THAT'S OKAY THOUGH-- WITH CHALKS I CAN SMUDGE THE MISTAKE AWAY!
NOW, DRAW A STRAIGHT LINE ACROSS THE MIDDLE OF THE CIRCLE. THIS IS GOING TO BE OUR GUIDELINE TO HELP KEEP HER FEATURES EVEN.
START HER CHEEK BY DRAWING A LITTLE CURVE JUST ABOVE THE GUIDELINE...
..AND FOLLOW THE BOTTOM OF THE CIRCLE TO CREATE HER CHEEK AND CHIN. STOP JUST BEFORE YOU REACH THE OTHER SIDE OF THE GUIDELINE.
LET'S DRAW HER EARS NOW. THEY'RE CUTE LITTLE HALF CIRCLES THAT JUST TOUCH THE GUIDELINE.
I'M GOING TO SWITCH TO BLUE CHALK NOW. BLUE IS A SERENE COLOR, AND IS PERFECT FOR DRAWING THE WAVES OF VIOLET'S HAIR.
A FUN WAY TO DRAW VIOLET'S BANGS IS TO HOLD THE CHALK SIDEWAYS AND PULL IT FROM THE TOP OF HER HEAD, DOWN HER FOREHEAD. SHE KEEPS HER BANGS SHORT SO SHE CAN SEE.

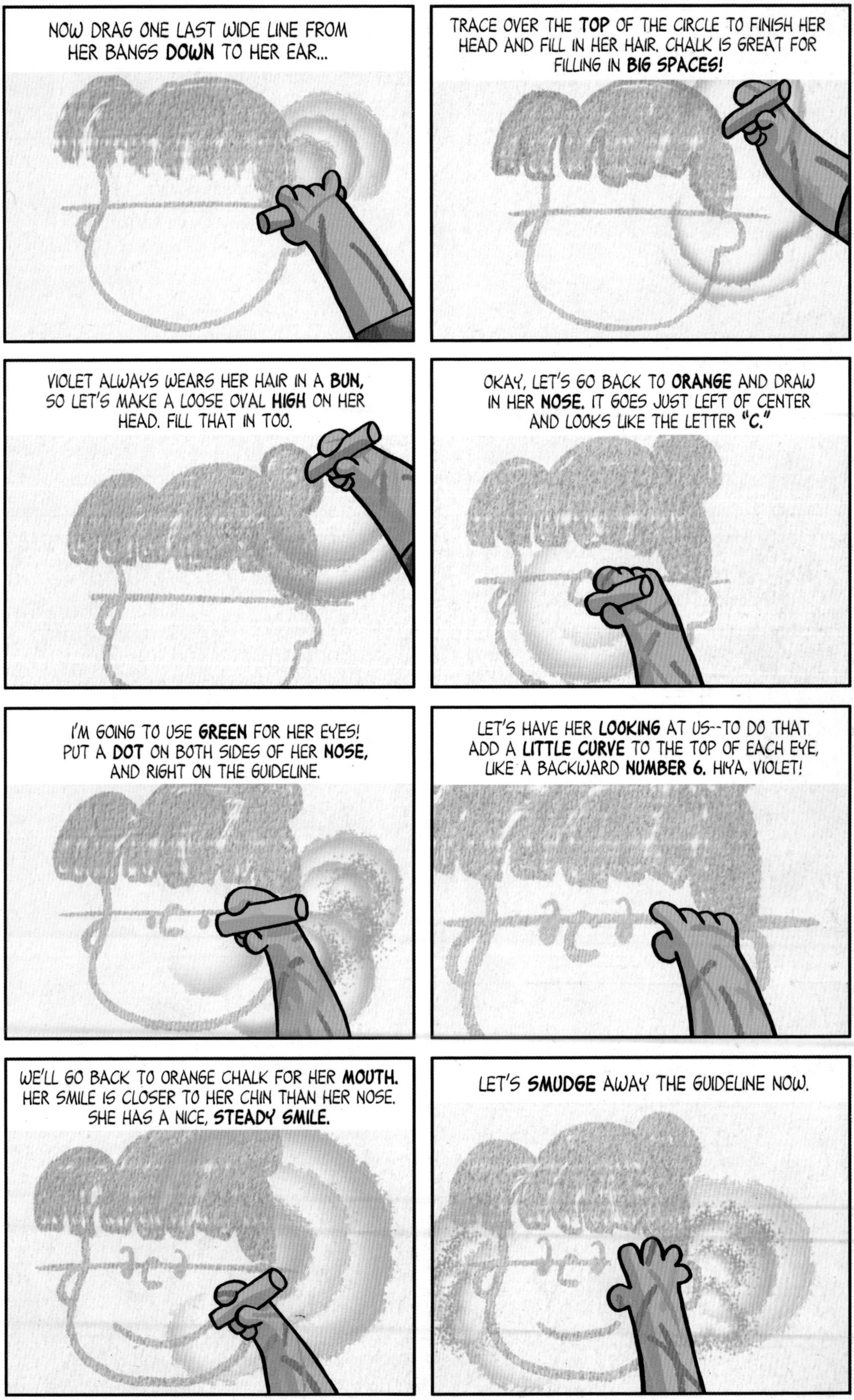
NOW DRAG ONE LAST WIDE LINE FROM HER BANGS **DOWN** TO HER EAR...
TRACE OVER THE **TOP** OF THE CIRCLE TO FINISH HER HEAD AND FILL IN HER HAIR. CHALK IS GREAT FOR FILLING IN **BIG SPACES!**
VIOLET ALWAYS WEARS HER HAIR IN A **BUN,** SO LET'S MAKE A LOOSE OVAL **HIGH** ON HER HEAD. FILL THAT IN TOO.
OKAY, LET'S GO BACK TO **ORANGE** AND DRAW IN HER **NOSE.** IT GOES JUST LEFT OF CENTER AND LOOKS LIKE THE LETTER **"C."**
I'M GOING TO USE **GREEN** FOR HER EYES! PUT A **DOT** ON BOTH SIDES OF HER **NOSE,** AND RIGHT ON THE GUIDELINE.
LET'S HAVE HER **LOOKING** AT US--TO DO THAT ADD A **LITTLE CURVE** TO THE TOP OF EACH EYE, LIKE A BACKWARD **NUMBER 6.** HIYA, VIOLET!
WE'LL GO BACK TO ORANGE CHALK FOR HER **MOUTH.** HER SMILE IS CLOSER TO HER CHIN THAN HER NOSE. SHE HAS A NICE, **STEADY SMILE.**
LET'S **SMUDGE** AWAY THE GUIDELINE NOW.

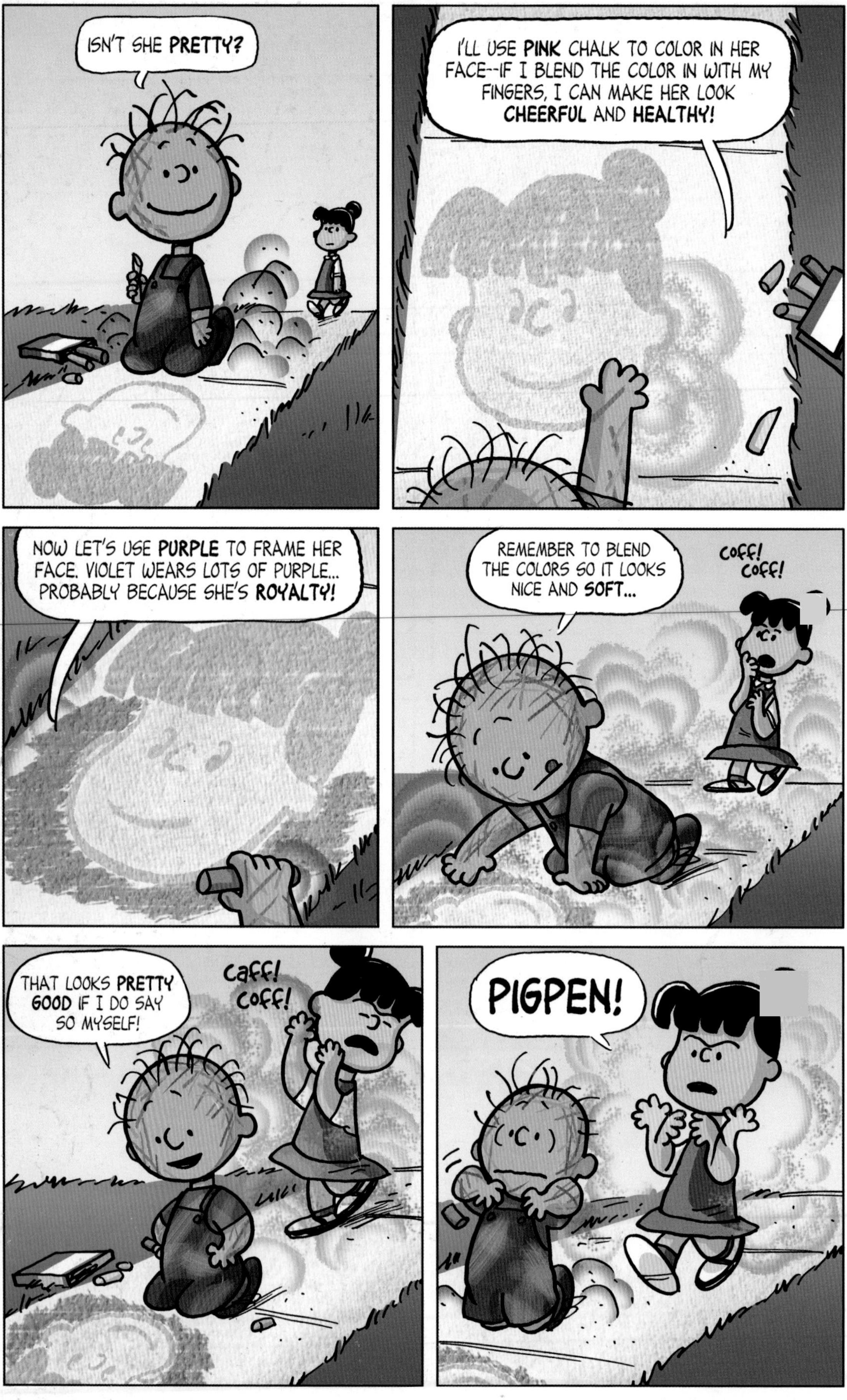
ISN'T SHE PRETTY?
I'LL USE PINK CHALK TO COLOR IN HER FACE--IF I BLEND THE COLOR IN WITH MY FINGERS, I CAN MAKE HER LOOK CHEERFUL AND HEALTHY!
NOW LET'S USE PURPLE TO FRAME HER FACE. VIOLET WEARS LOTS OF PURPLE... PROBABLY BECAUSE SHE'S ROYALTY!
REMEMBER TO BLEND THE COLORS SO IT LOOKS NICE AND SOFT...
COFF! COFF!
THAT LOOKS PRETTY GOOD IF I DO SAY SO MYSELF!
CAFF! COFF!
PIGPEN!

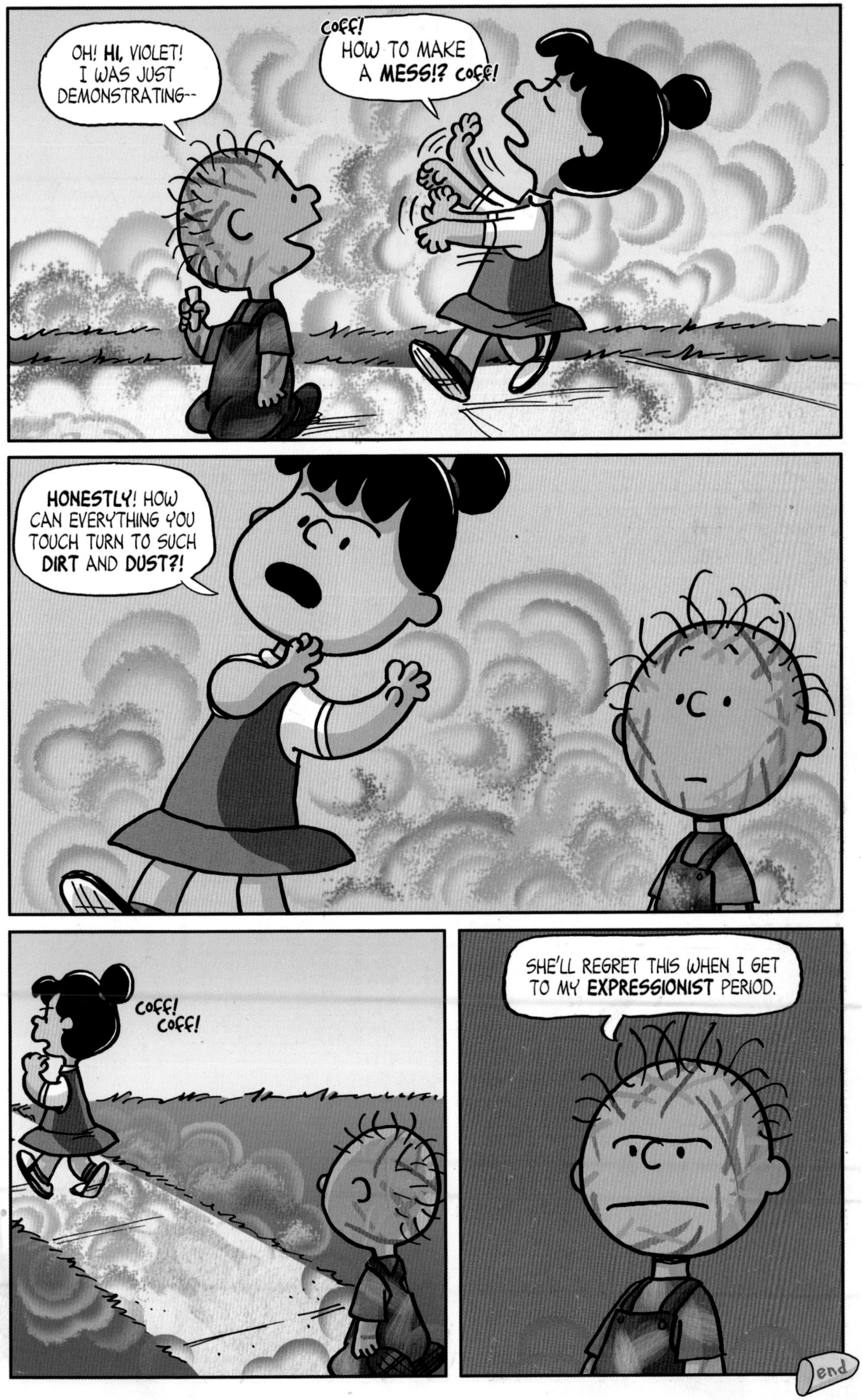
OH! HI, VIOLET! I WAS JUST DEMONSTRATING--
COFF! HOW TO MAKE A MESS!? COFF!
HONESTLY! HOW CAN EVERYTHING YOU TOUCH TURN TO SUCH DIRT AND DUST?!
COFF! COFF!
SHE'LL REGRET THIS WHEN I GET TO MY EXPRESSIONIST PERIOD.
end

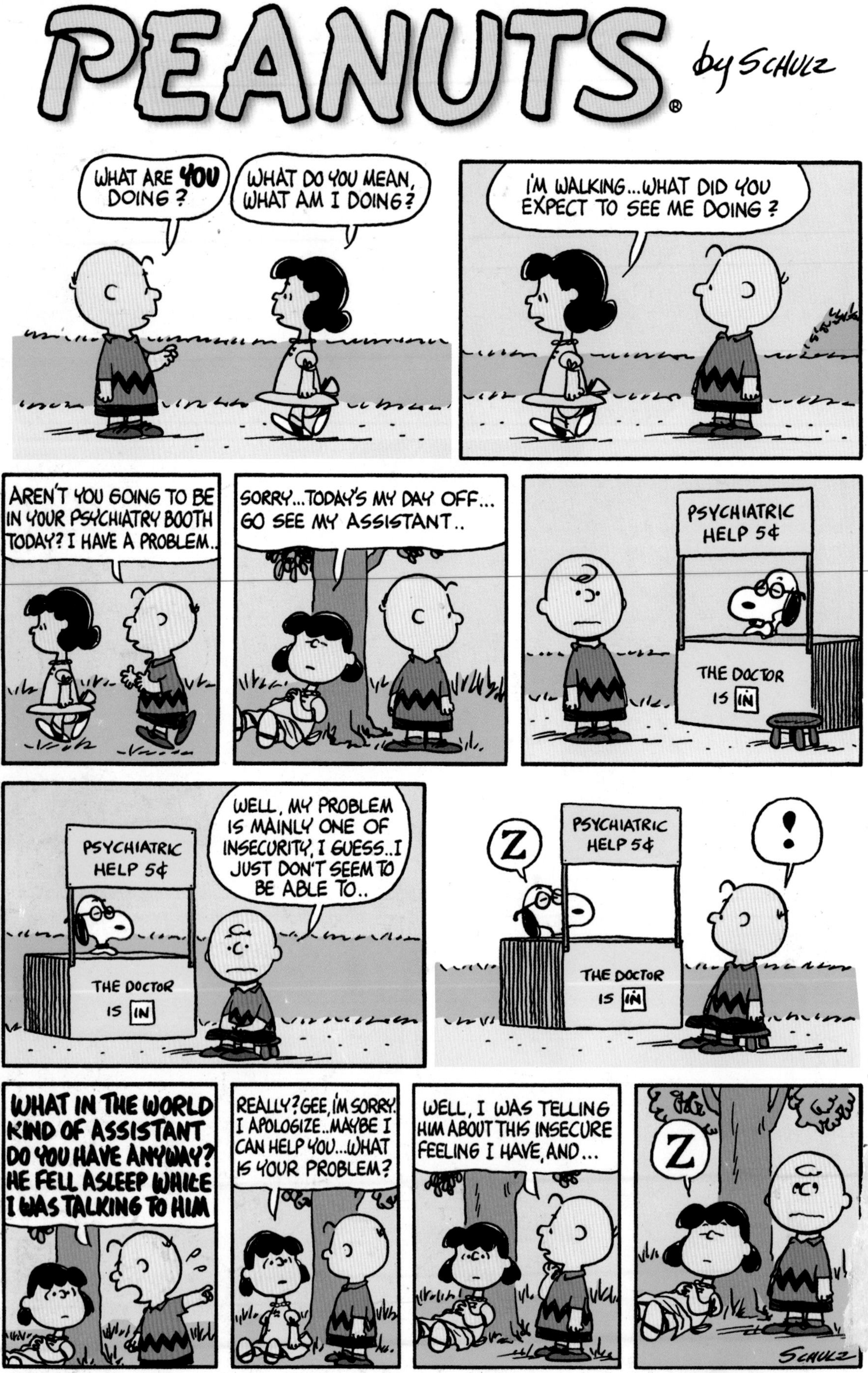
PEANUTS
by SCHULZ
WHAT ARE YOU DOING?
WHAT DO YOU MEAN, WHAT AM I DOING?
I'M WALKING...WHAT DID YOU EXPECT TO SEE ME DOING?
AREN'T YOU GOING TO BE IN YOUR PSYCHIATRY BOOTH TODAY? I HAVE A PROBLEM..
SORRY...TODAY'S MY DAY OFF... GO SEE MY ASSISTANT..
PSYCHIATRIC HELP 5¢
THE DOCTOR IS IN
PSYCHIATRIC HELP 5¢
THE DOCTOR IS IN
WELL, MY PROBLEM IS MAINLY ONE OF INSECURITY, I GUESS..I JUST DON'T SEEM TO BE ABLE TO..
Z
PSYCHIATRIC HELP 5¢
THE DOCTOR IS IN
!
WHAT IN THE WORLD KIND OF ASSISTANT DO YOU HAVE ANYWAY? HE FELL ASLEEP WHILE I WAS TALKING TO HIM
REALLY? GEE, I'M SORRY. I APOLOGIZE..MAYBE I CAN HELP YOU...WHAT IS YOUR PROBLEM?
WELL, I WAS TELLING HIM ABOUT THIS INSECURE FEELING I HAVE, AND...
Z
SCHULZ

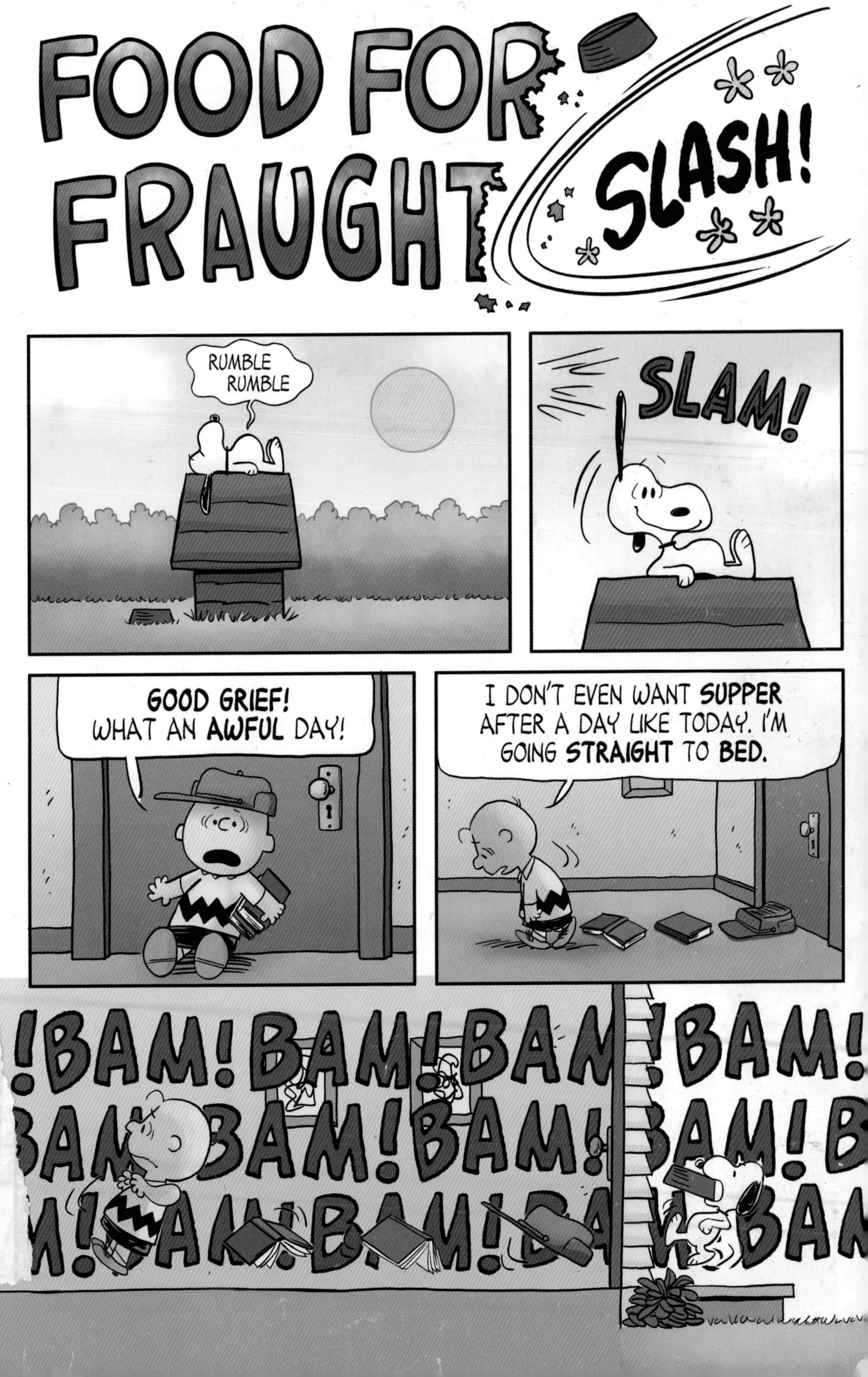
FOOD FOR FRAUGHT
SLASH!
RUMBLE RUMBLE
SLAM!
GOOD GRIEF! WHAT AN **AWFUL** DAY!
I DON'T EVEN WANT **SUPPER** AFTER A DAY LIKE TODAY. I'M GOING **STRAIGHT** TO **BED**.
BAM! BAM! BAM! BAM!
BAM! BAM! BAM! BAM!
BAM! BAM! BAM! BAM!

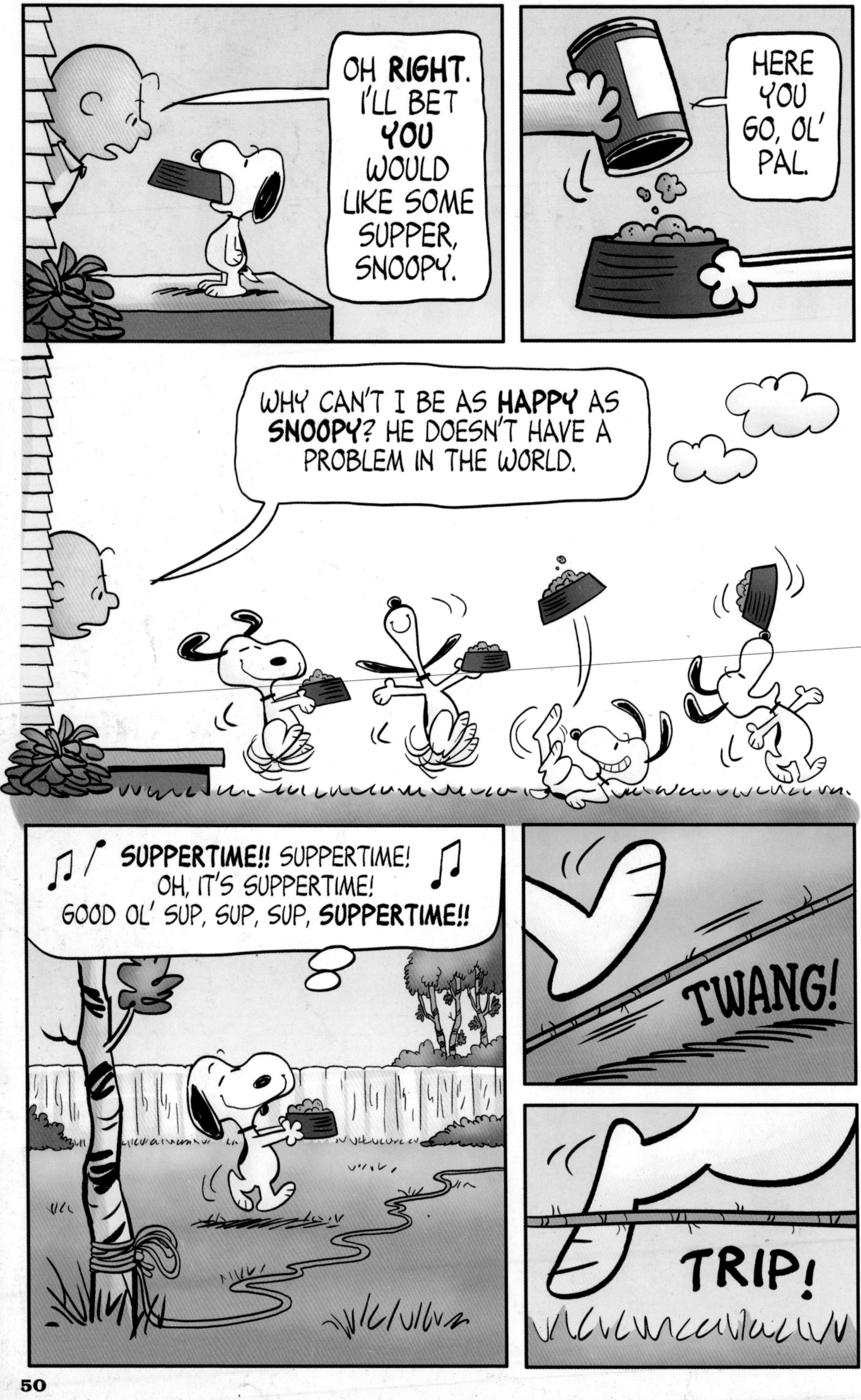
OH RIGHT. I'LL BET YOU WOULD LIKE SOME SUPPER, SNOOPY.
HERE YOU GO, OL' PAL.
WHY CAN'T I BE AS HAPPY AS SNOOPY? HE DOESN'T HAVE A PROBLEM IN THE WORLD.
SUPPERTIME!! SUPPERTIME! OH, IT'S SUPPERTIME! GOOD OL' SUP, SUP, SUP, SUPPERTIME!!
TWANG!
TRIP!

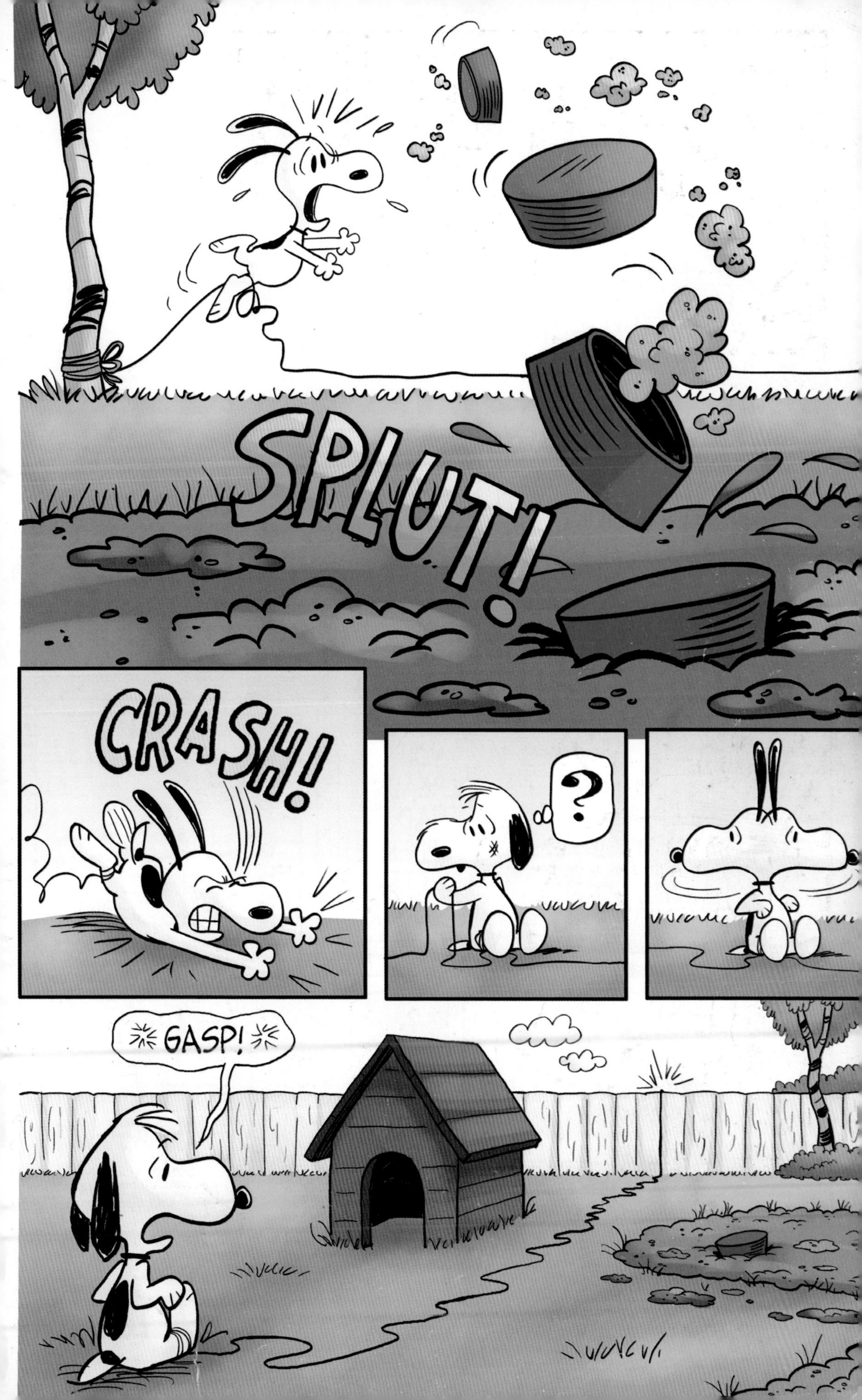
SPLUT!
CRASH!
?
GASP!

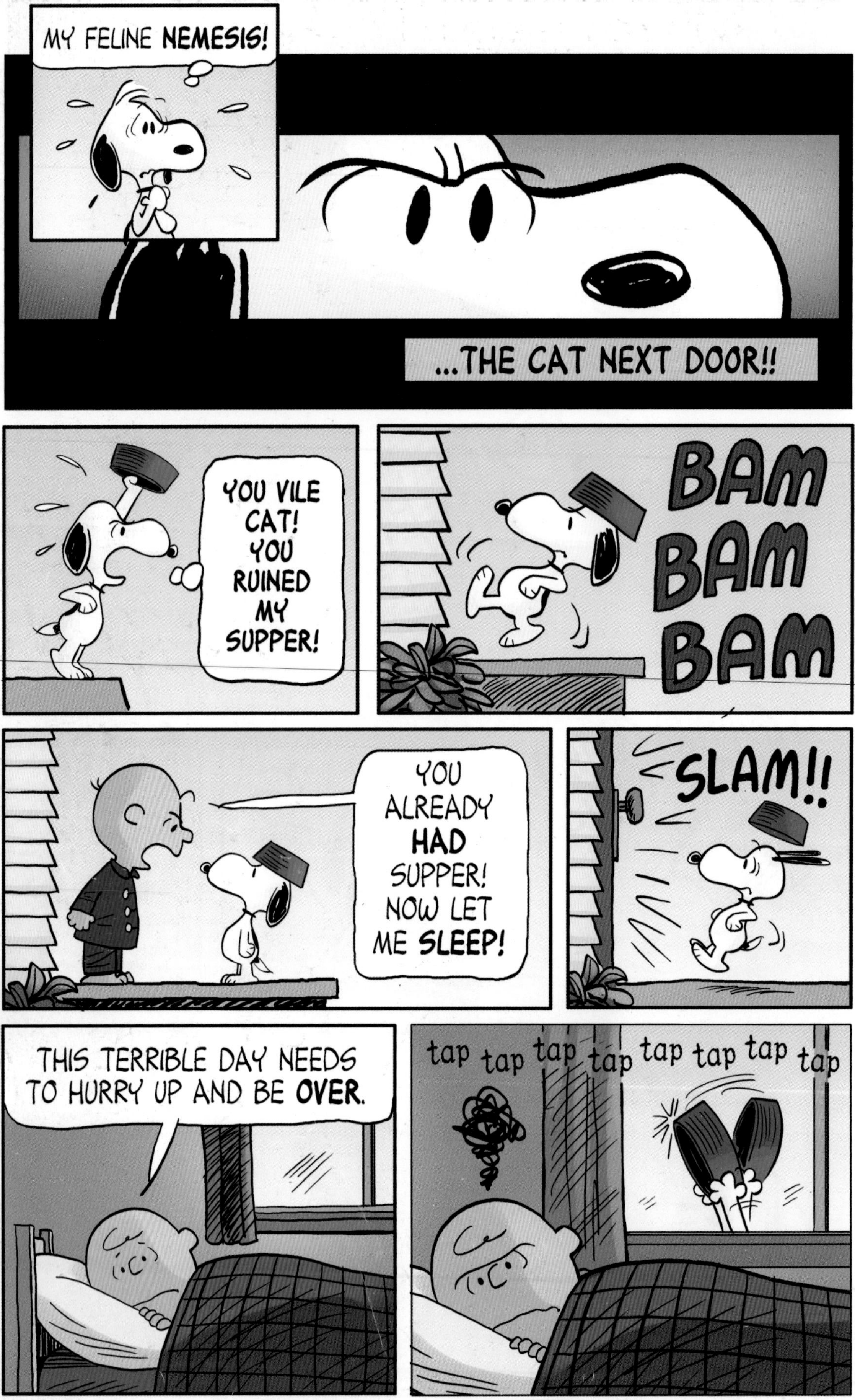
MY FELINE NEMESIS!
...THE CAT NEXT DOOR!!
YOU VILE CAT! YOU RUINED MY SUPPER!
BAM BAM BAM
YOU ALREADY HAD SUPPER! NOW LET ME SLEEP!
SLAM!!
THIS TERRIBLE DAY NEEDS TO HURRY UP AND BE OVER.
tap tap tap tap tap tap tap tap

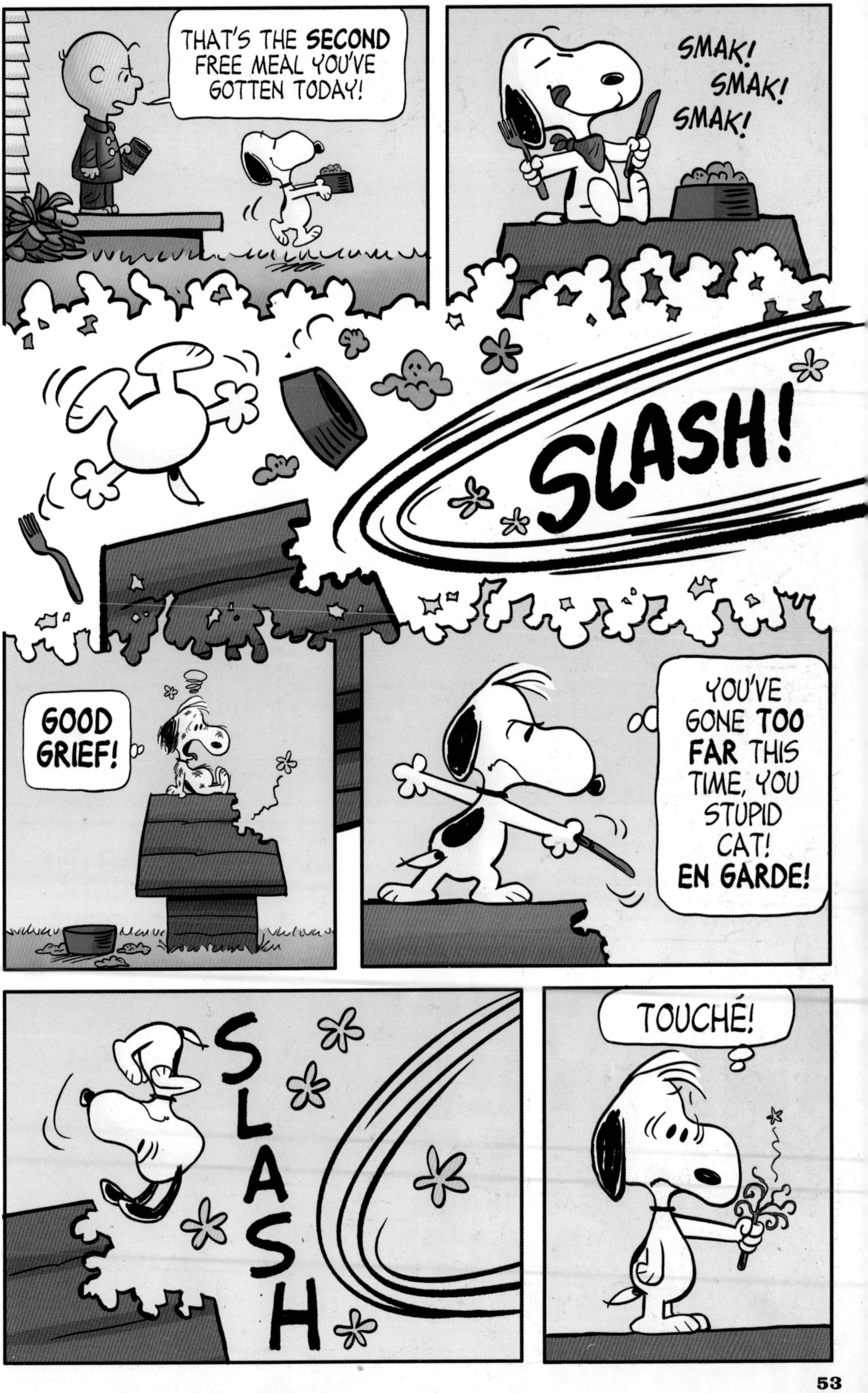
THAT'S THE SECOND FREE MEAL YOU'VE GOTTEN TODAY!
SMAK! SMAK! SMAK!
SLASH!
GOOD GRIEF!
YOU'VE GONE TOO FAR THIS TIME, YOU STUPID CAT! EN GARDE!
SLASH
TOUCHÉ!

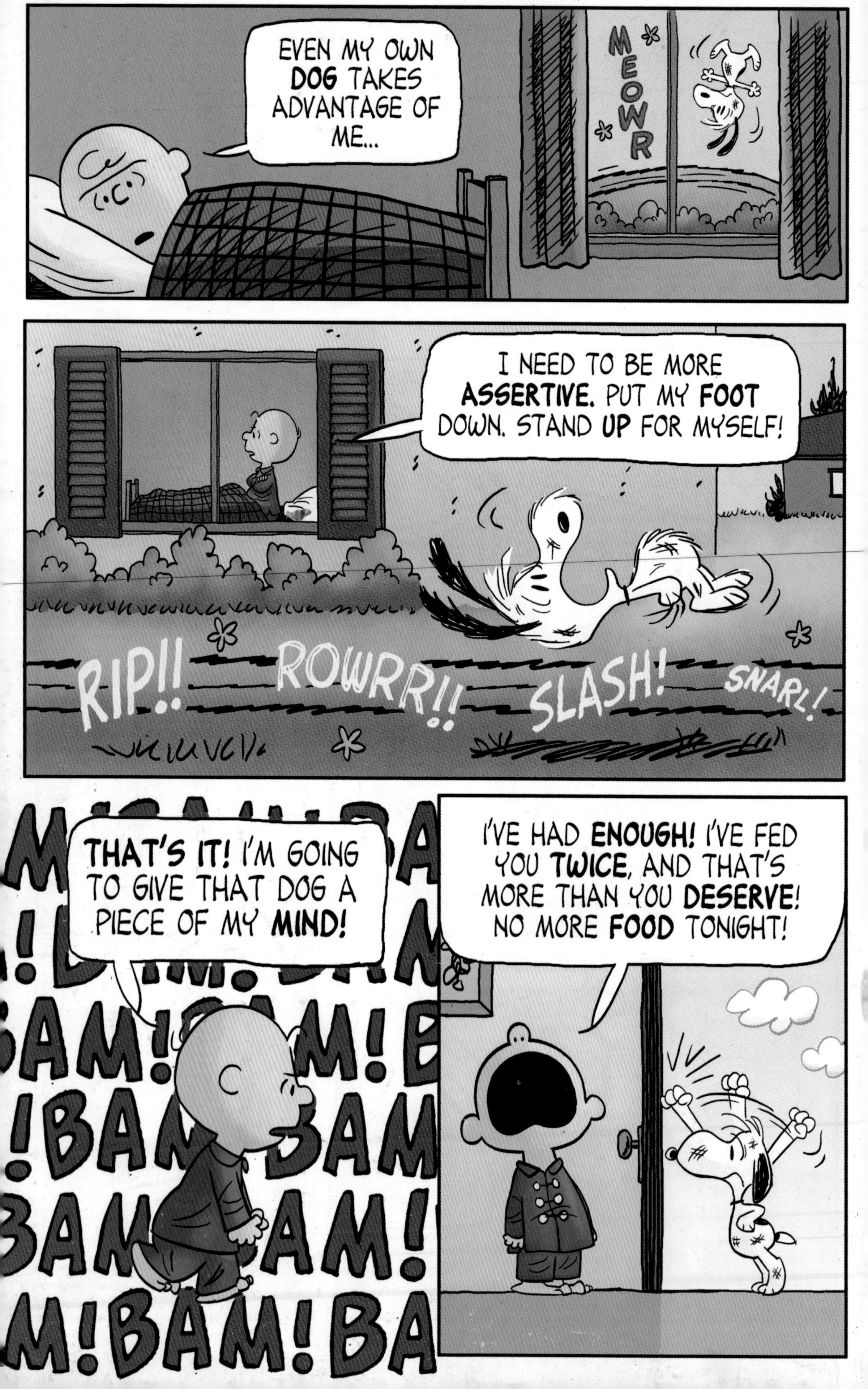
EVEN MY OWN DOG TAKES ADVANTAGE OF ME...
MEOWR
I NEED TO BE MORE ASSERTIVE. PUT MY FOOT DOWN. STAND UP FOR MYSELF!
RIP!!
ROWRR!!
SLASH!
SNARL!
THAT'S IT! I'M GOING TO GIVE THAT DOG A PIECE OF MY MIND!
I'VE HAD ENOUGH! I'VE FED YOU TWICE, AND THAT'S MORE THAN YOU DESERVE! NO MORE FOOD TONIGHT!

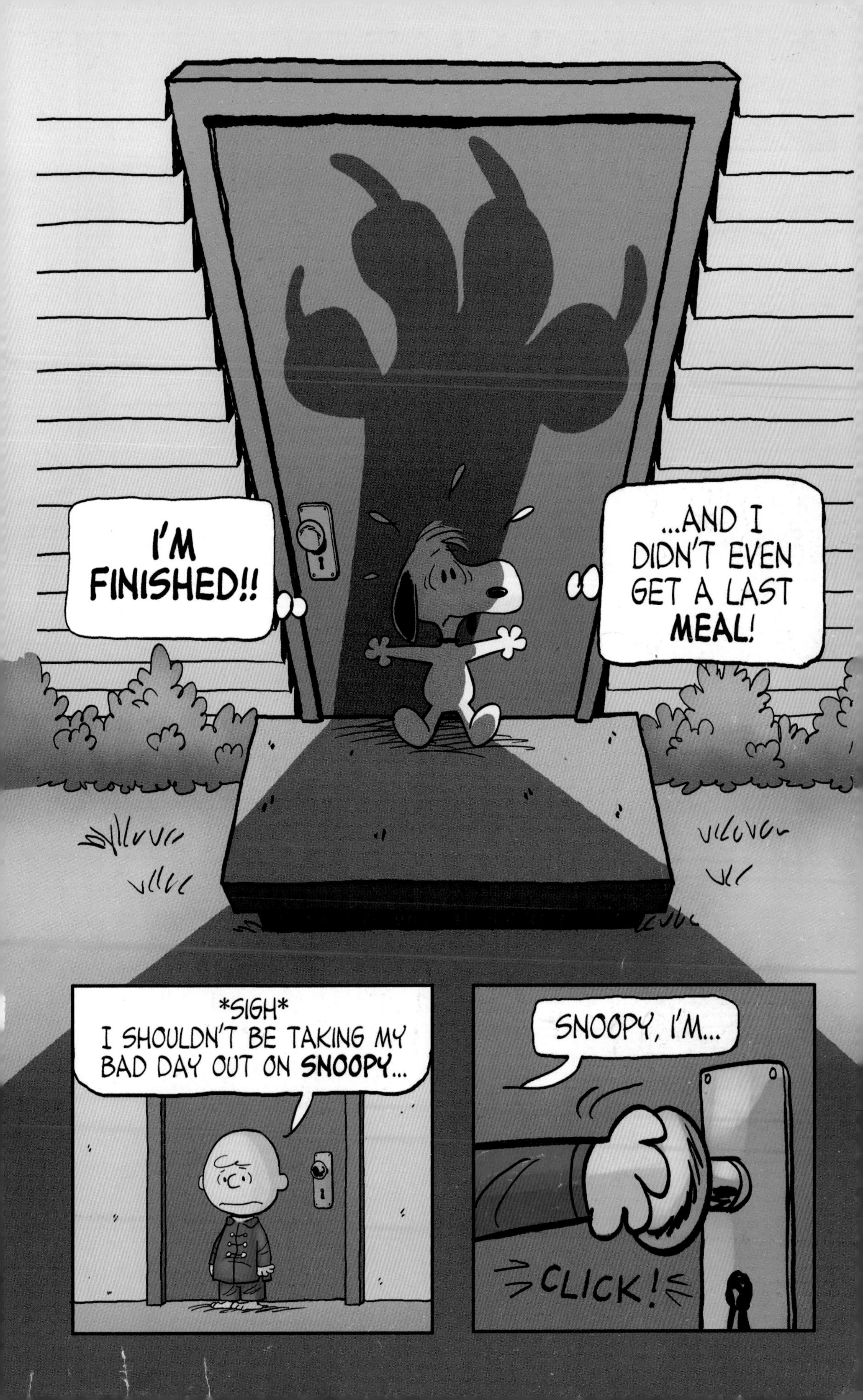
I'M FINISHED!!
...AND I DIDN'T EVEN GET A LAST MEAL!
SIGH I SHOULDN'T BE TAKING MY BAD DAY OUT ON SNOOPY...
SNOOPY, I'M...
CLICK!

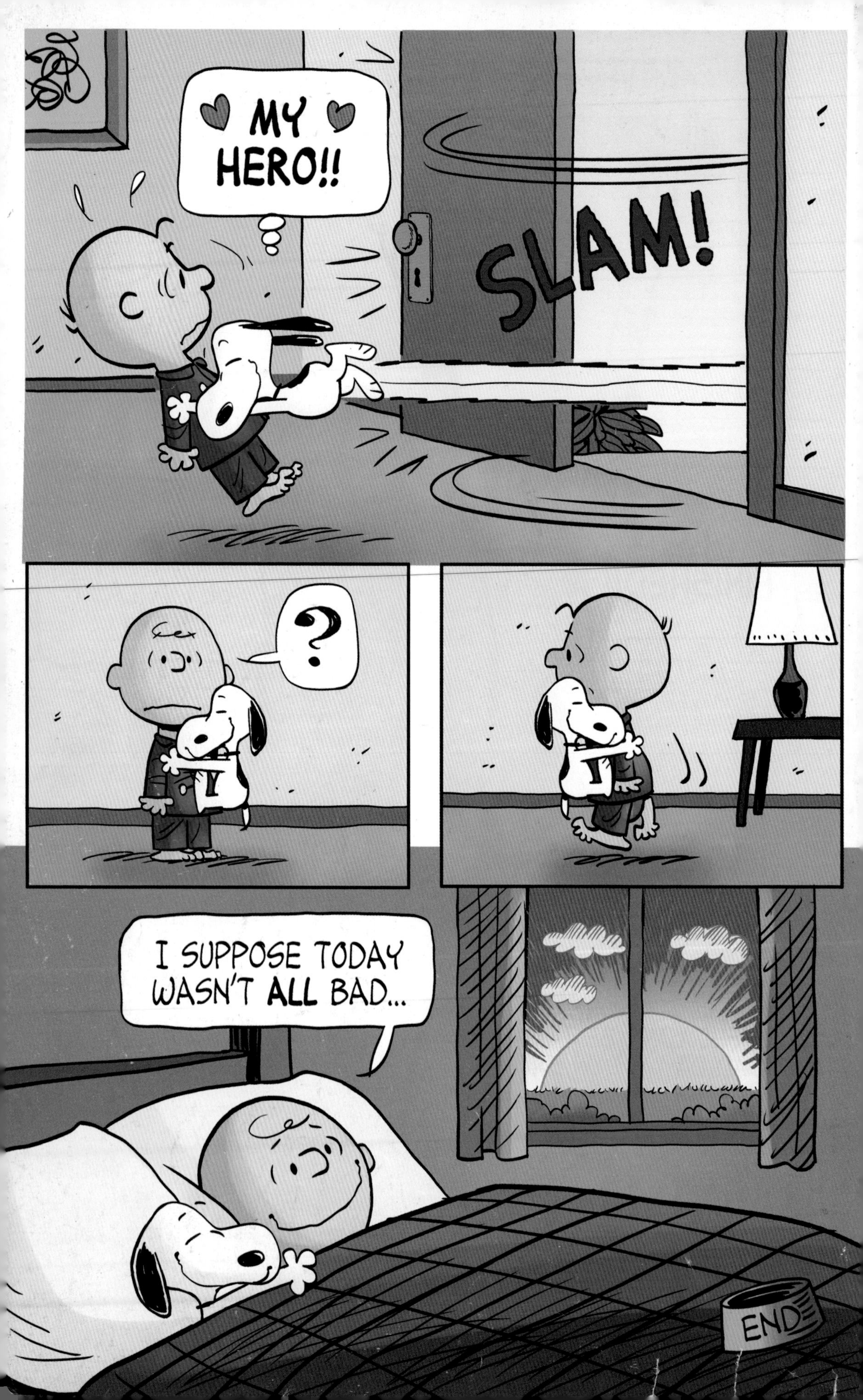

MY HERO!!
SLAM!
?
I SUPPOSE TODAY WASN'T **ALL** BAD...
END

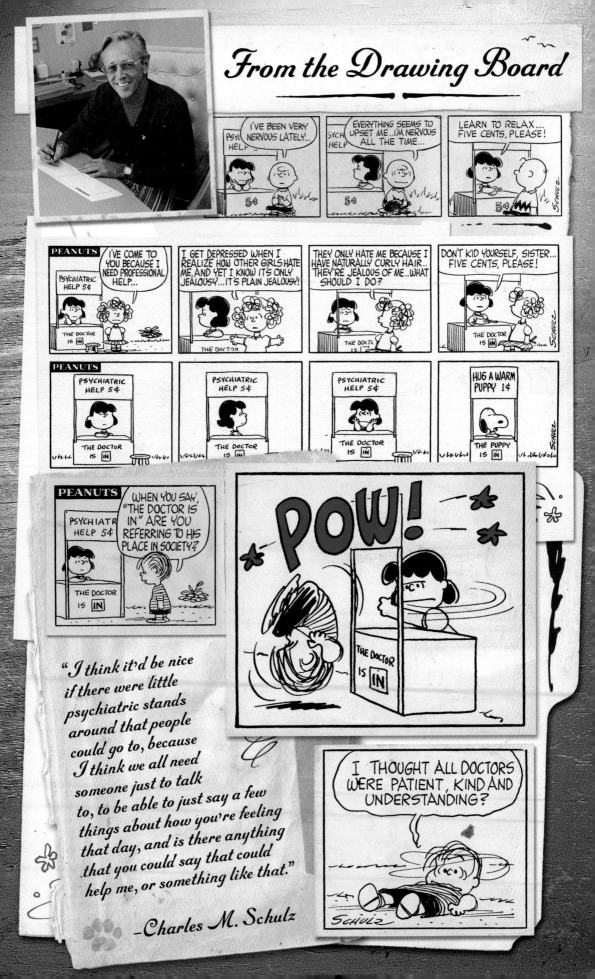

From the Drawing Board

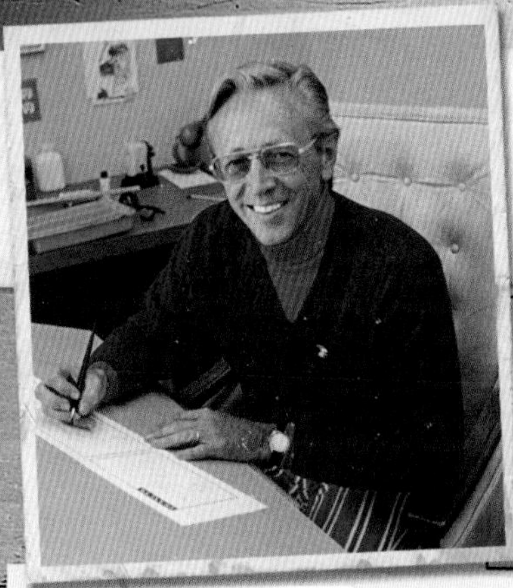

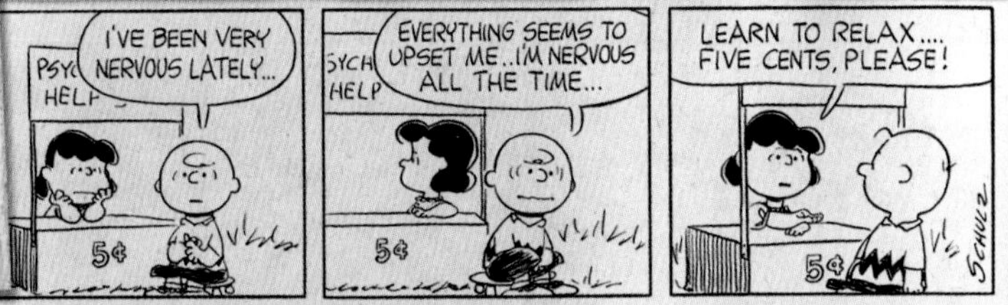
PSYC
HELP
I'VE BEEN VERY NERVOUS LATELY...
5¢
PSYCH
HELP
EVERYTHING SEEMS TO UPSET ME..I'M NERVOUS ALL THE TIME...
5¢
LEARN TO RELAX.... FIVE CENTS, PLEASE!
5¢
SCHULZ

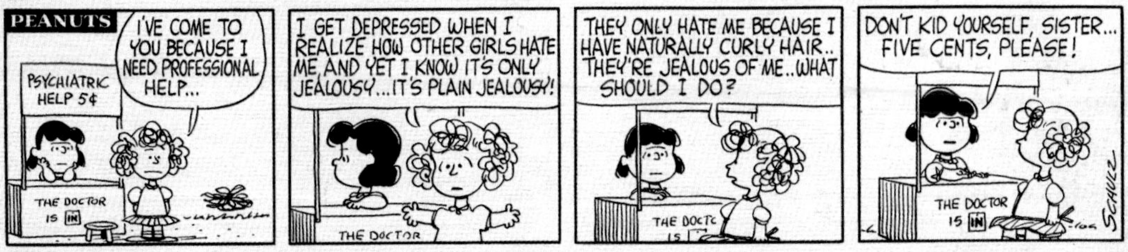
PEANUTS
PSYCHIATRIC HELP 5¢
I'VE COME TO YOU BECAUSE I NEED PROFESSIONAL HELP...
THE DOCTOR IS IN
I GET DEPRESSED WHEN I REALIZE HOW OTHER GIRLS HATE ME, AND YET I KNOW IT'S ONLY JEALOUSY...IT'S PLAIN JEALOUSY!
THE DOCTOR
THEY ONLY HATE ME BECAUSE I HAVE NATURALLY CURLY HAIR.. THEY'RE JEALOUS OF ME..WHAT SHOULD I DO?
THE DOCTC
IS
DON'T KID YOURSELF, SISTER... FIVE CENTS, PLEASE!
THE DOCTOR IS IN
SCHULZ

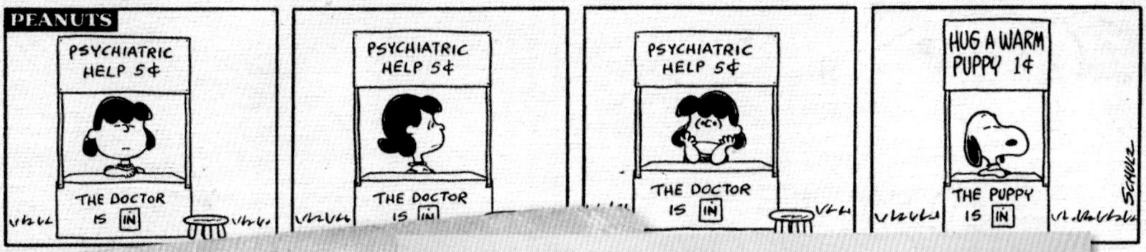
PEANUTS
PSYCHIATRIC HELP 5¢
THE DOCTOR IS IN
PSYCHIATRIC HELP 5¢
THE DOCTOR IS IN
PSYCHIATRIC HELP 5¢
THE DOCTOR IS IN
HUG A WARM PUPPY 1¢
THE PUPPY IS IN
SCHULZ

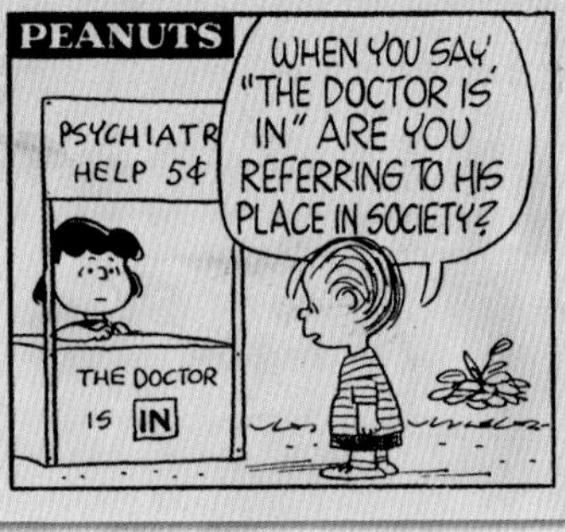
PEANUTS
PSYCHIATR
HELP 5¢
WHEN YOU SAY, "THE DOCTOR IS IN" ARE YOU REFERRING TO HIS PLACE IN SOCIETY?
THE DOCTOR IS IN

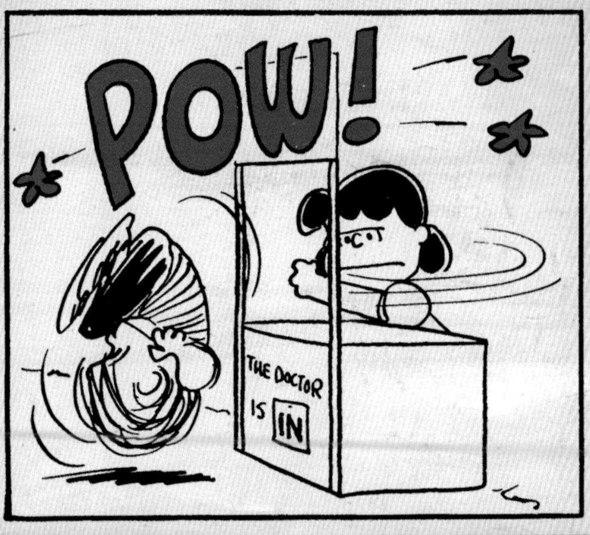
POW!
THE DOCTOR IS IN

"I think it'd be nice if there were little psychiatric stands around that people could go to, because I think we all need someone just to talk to, to be able to just say a few things about how you're feeling that day, and is there anything that you could say that could help me, or something like that."

–Charles M. Schulz

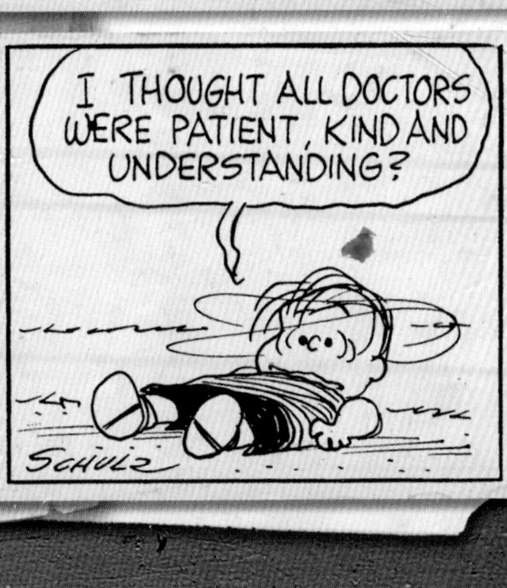
I THOUGHT ALL DOCTORS WERE PATIENT, KIND AND UNDERSTANDING?
SCHULZ

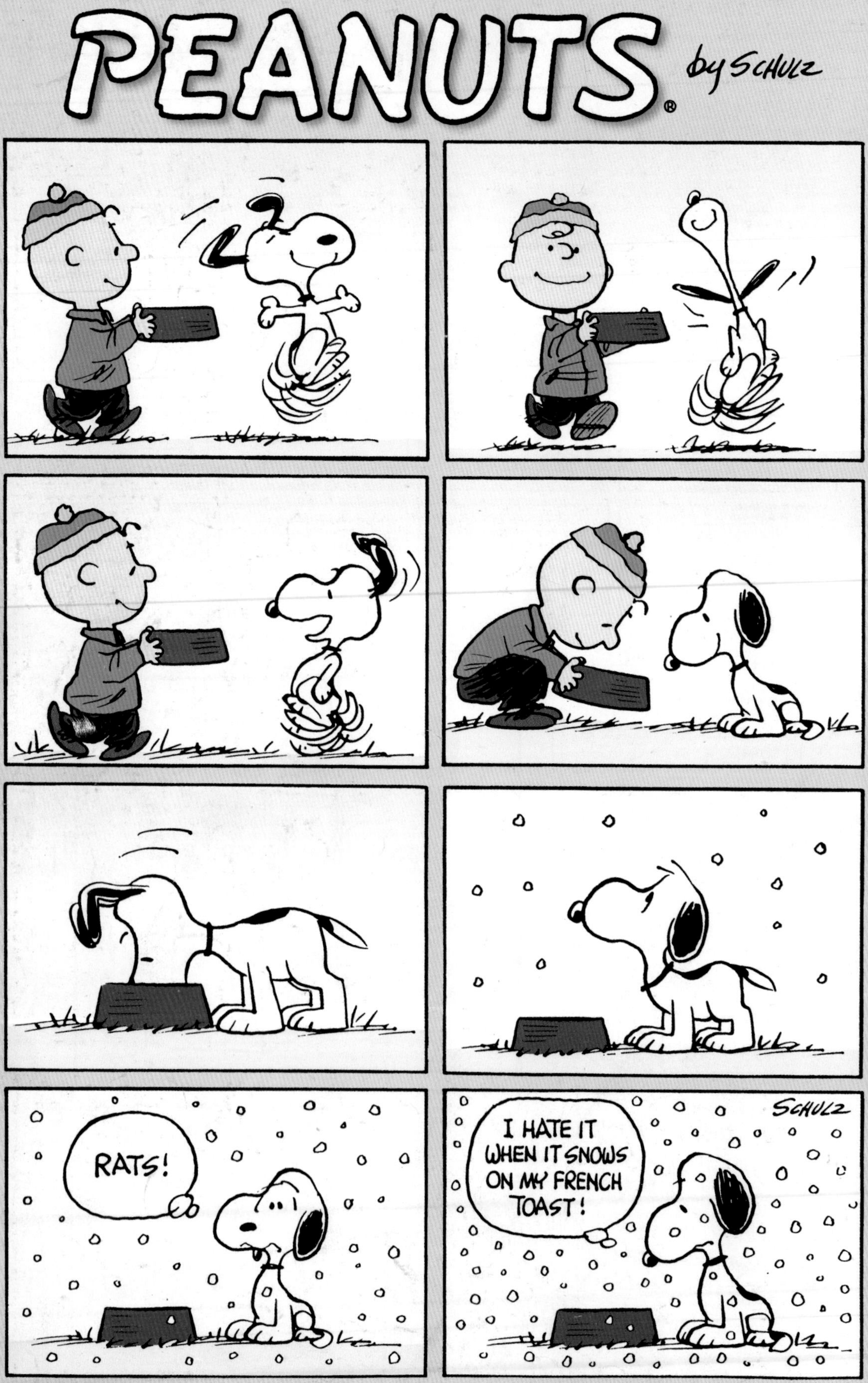
PEANUTS
by SCHULZ
RATS!
SCHULZ
I HATE IT WHEN IT SNOWS ON MY FRENCH TOAST!

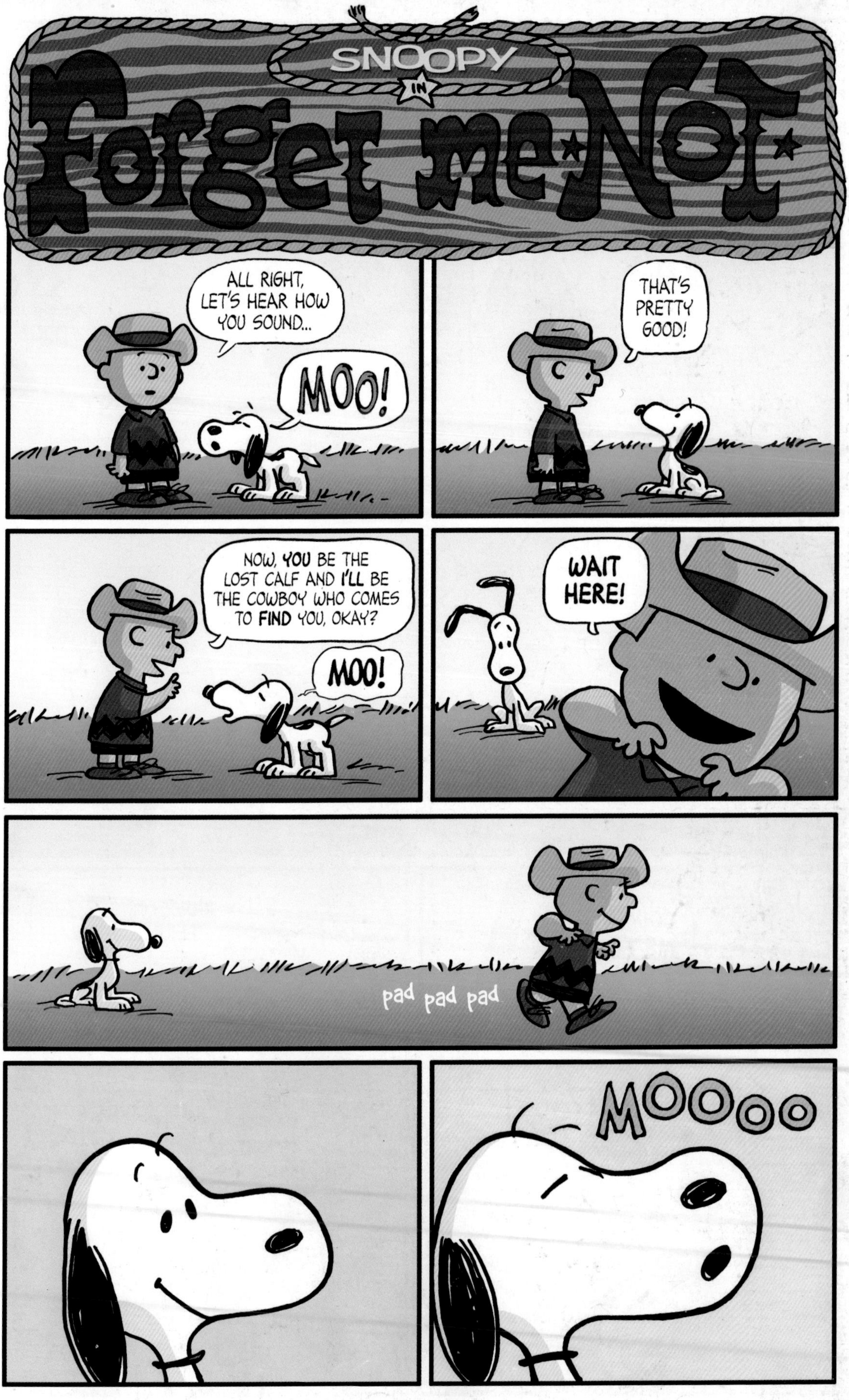
SNOOPY
IN
Forget me Not
ALL RIGHT, LET'S HEAR HOW YOU SOUND...
MOO!
THAT'S PRETTY GOOD!
NOW, YOU BE THE LOST CALF AND I'LL BE THE COWBOY WHO COMES TO FIND YOU, OKAY?
MOO!
WAIT HERE!
pad pad pad
MOOooo

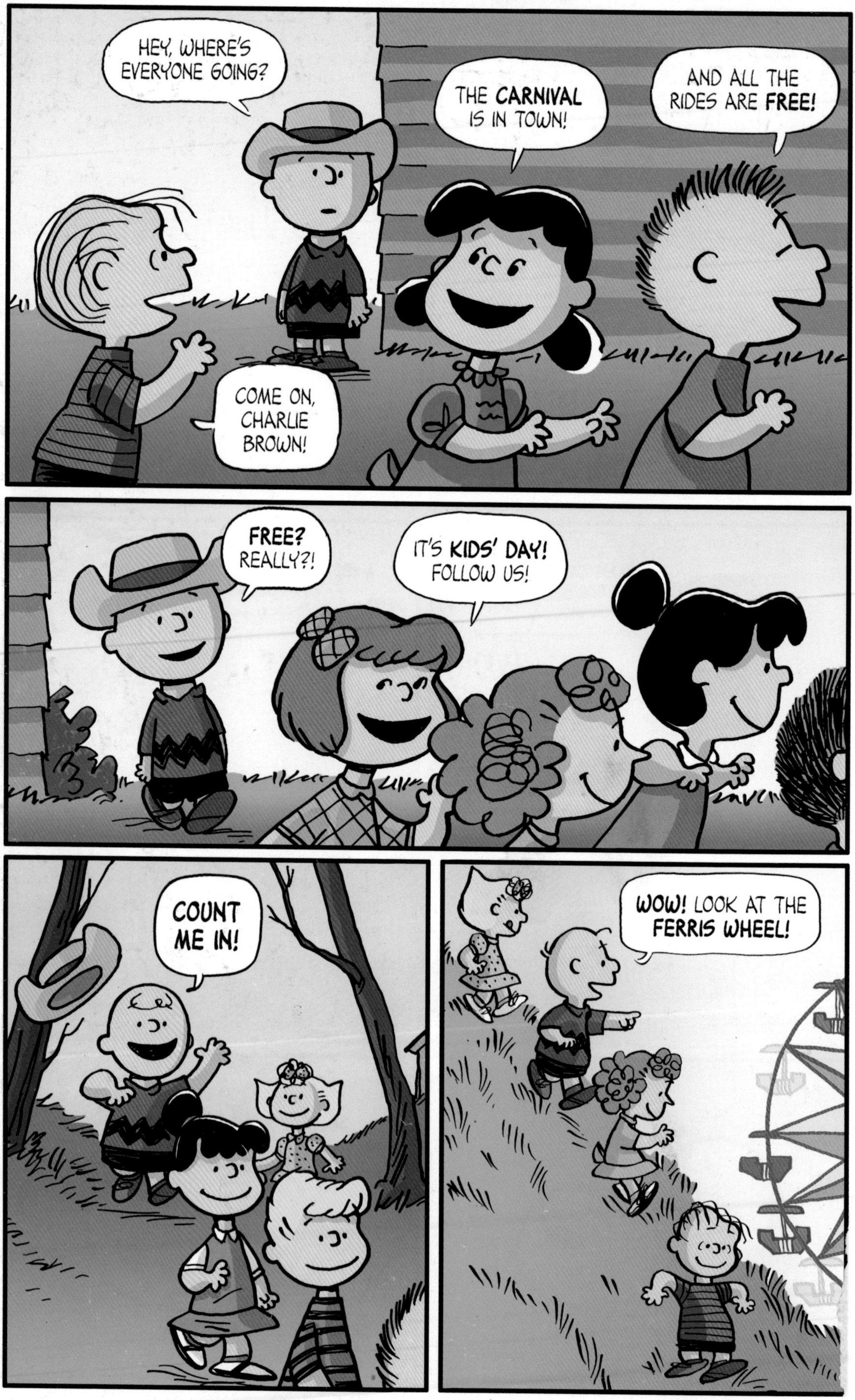
HEY, WHERE'S EVERYONE GOING?
THE CARNIVAL IS IN TOWN!
AND ALL THE RIDES ARE FREE!
COME ON, CHARLIE BROWN!
FREE? REALLY?!
IT'S KIDS' DAY! FOLLOW US!
COUNT ME IN!
WOW! LOOK AT THE FERRIS WHEEL!

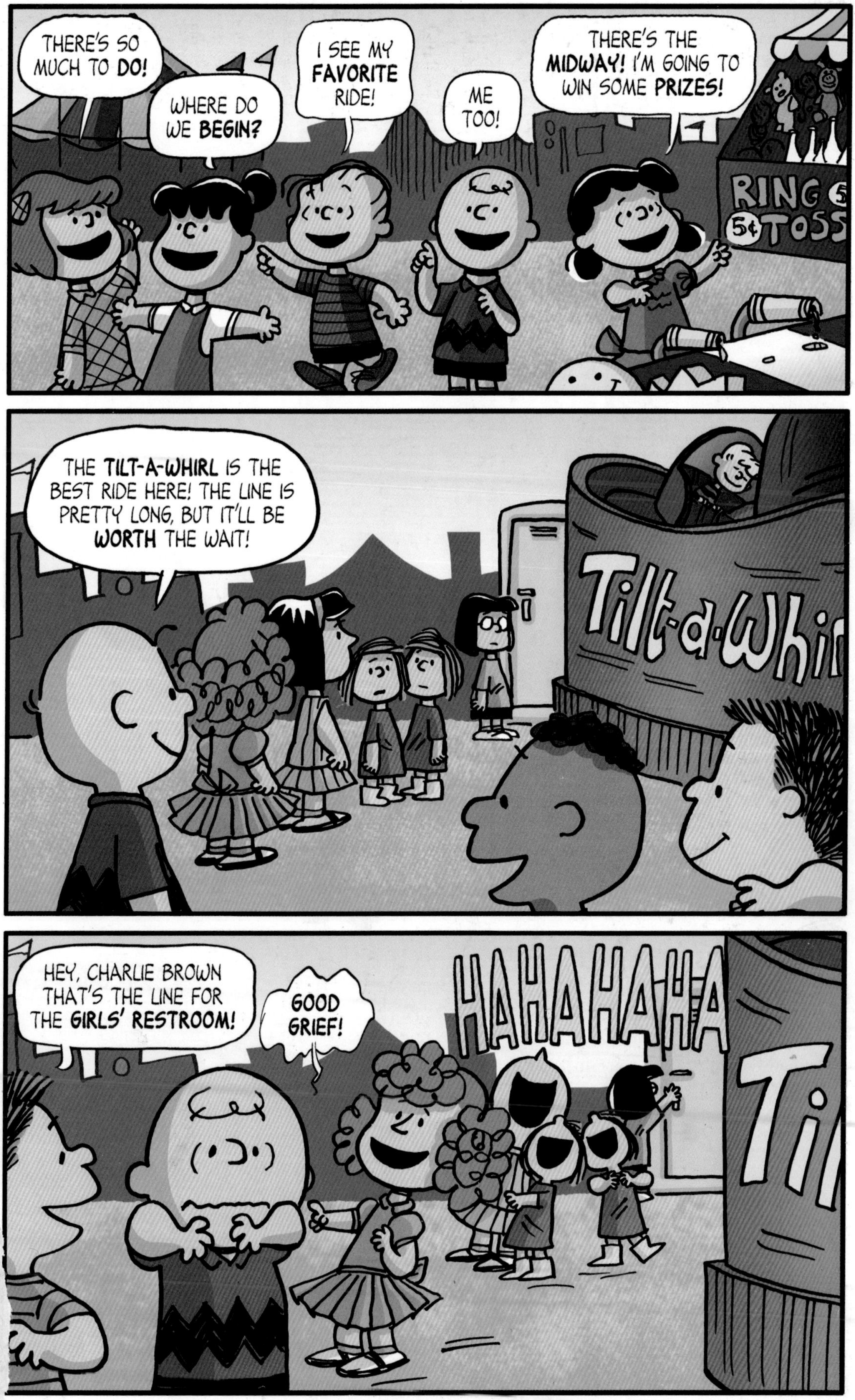
THERE'S SO MUCH TO DO!
WHERE DO WE BEGIN?
I SEE MY FAVORITE RIDE!
ME TOO!
THERE'S THE MIDWAY! I'M GOING TO WIN SOME PRIZES!
RING 5¢ TOSS
THE TILT-A-WHIRL IS THE BEST RIDE HERE! THE LINE IS PRETTY LONG, BUT IT'LL BE WORTH THE WAIT!
Tilt-a-Whirl
HEY, CHARLIE BROWN THAT'S THE LINE FOR THE GIRLS' RESTROOM!
GOOD GRIEF!
HAHAHAHA

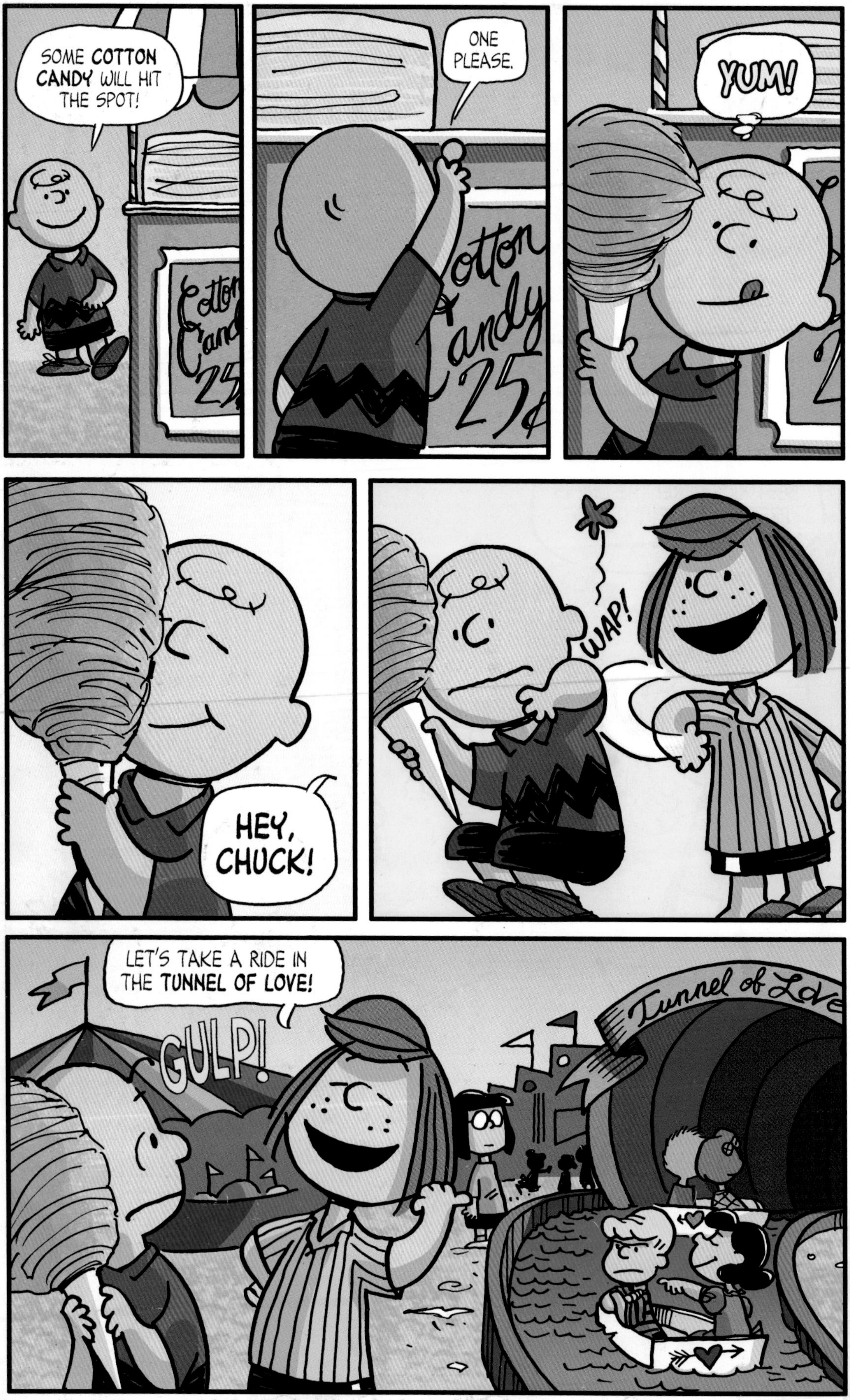
SOME **COTTON CANDY** WILL HIT THE SPOT!
Cotton Candy 25¢
ONE PLEASE.
Cotton Candy 25¢
YUM!
HEY, CHUCK!
WAP!
LET'S TAKE A RIDE IN THE **TUNNEL OF LOVE!**
GULP!
Tunnel of Love

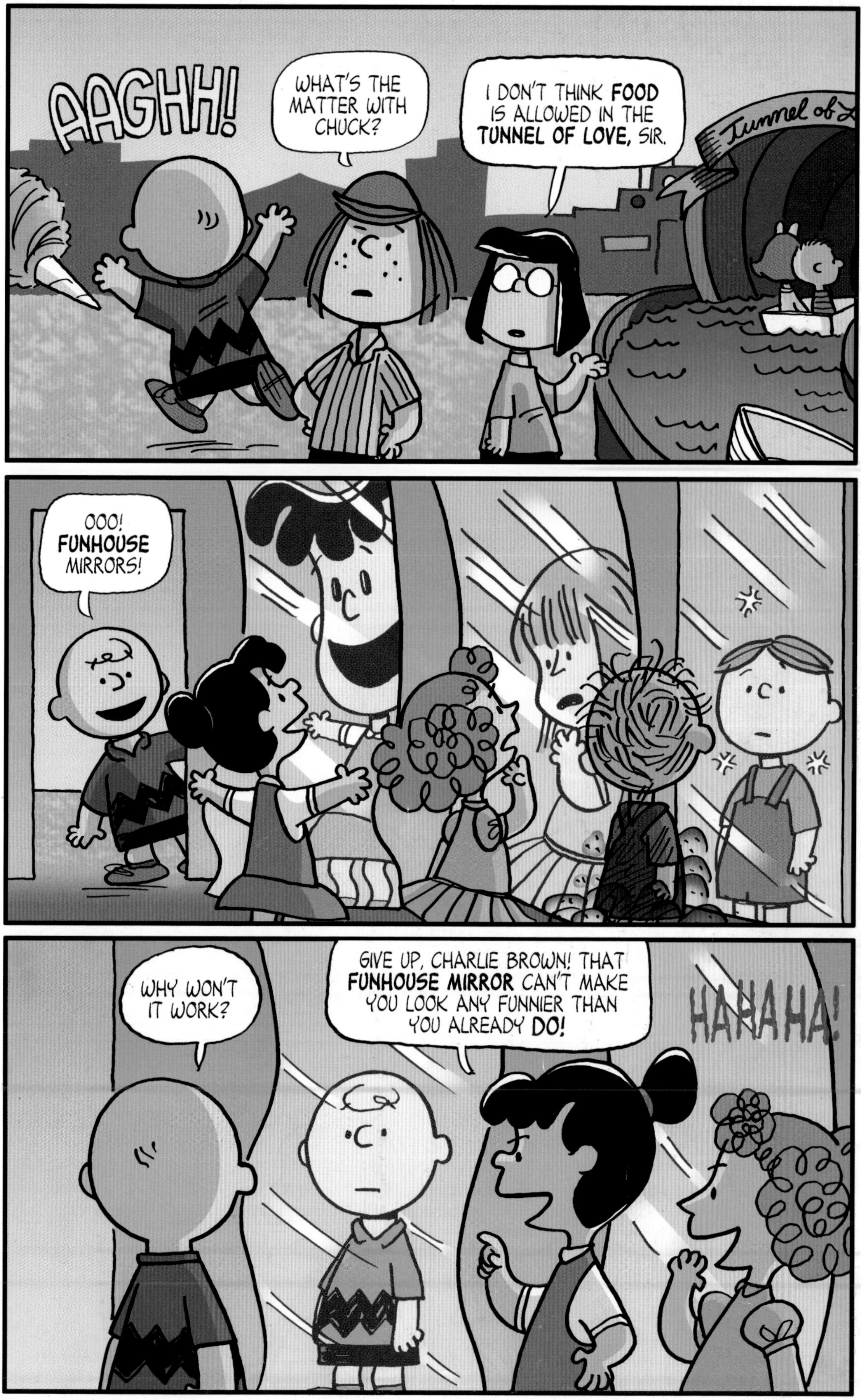
AAGHH!
WHAT'S THE MATTER WITH CHUCK?
I DON'T THINK FOOD IS ALLOWED IN THE TUNNEL OF LOVE, SIR.
OOO! FUNHOUSE MIRRORS!
WHY WON'T IT WORK?
GIVE UP, CHARLIE BROWN! THAT FUNHOUSE MIRROR CAN'T MAKE YOU LOOK ANY FUNNIER THAN YOU ALREADY DO!
HAHAHA!

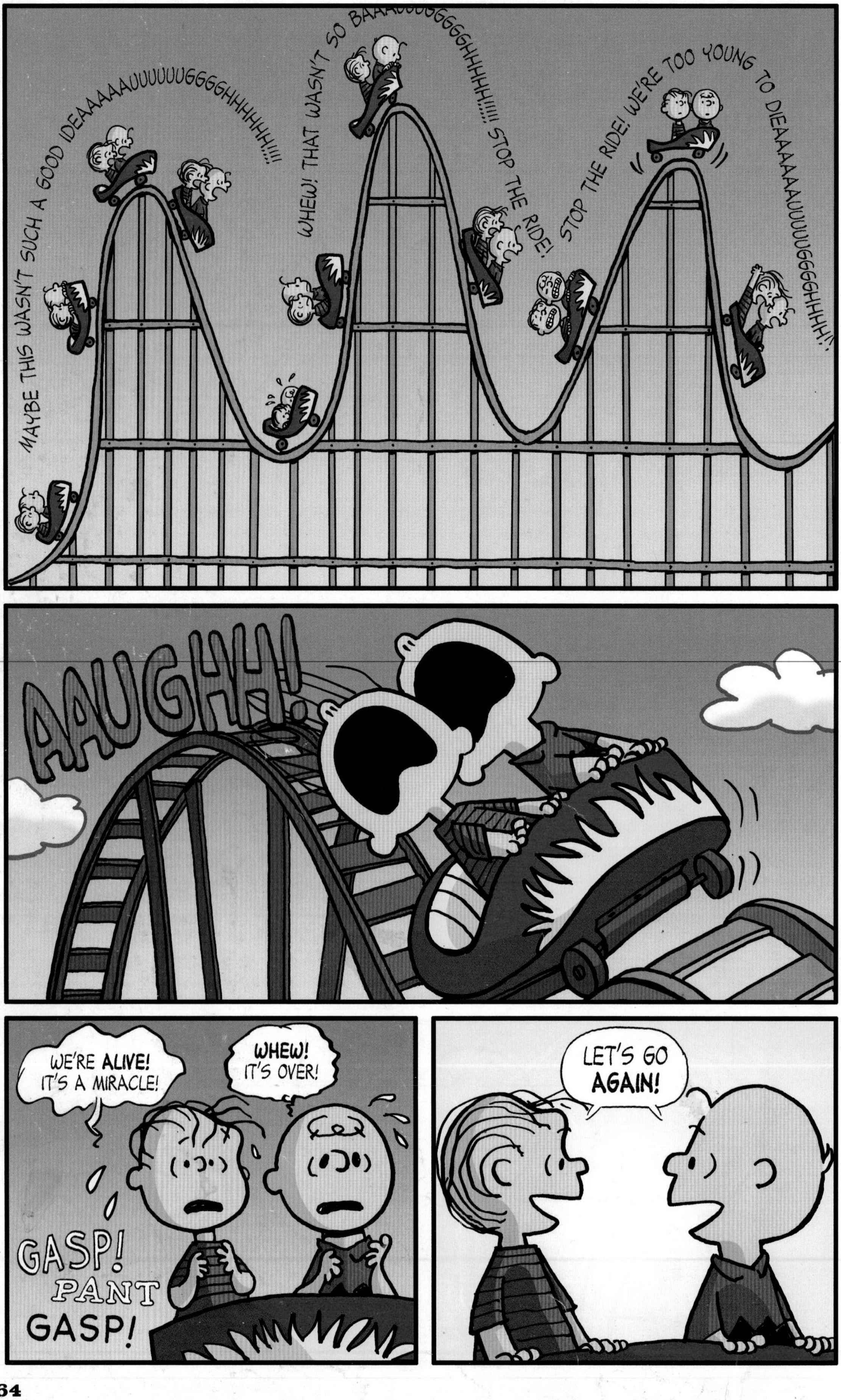
MAYBE THIS WASN'T SUCH A GOOD IDEAAAAAUUUUUUGGGGHHHHHH!!!!!
WHEW! THAT WASN'T SO BAAAUUUUGGGGGHHHHHH!!!!!! STOP THE RIDE!
STOP THE RIDE! WE'RE TOO YOUNG TO DIEAAAAAAUUUUGGGGHHHHH!!!
AAUGHH!
WE'RE ALIVE! IT'S A MIRACLE!
WHEW! IT'S OVER!
GASP!
PANT
GASP!
LET'S GO AGAIN!

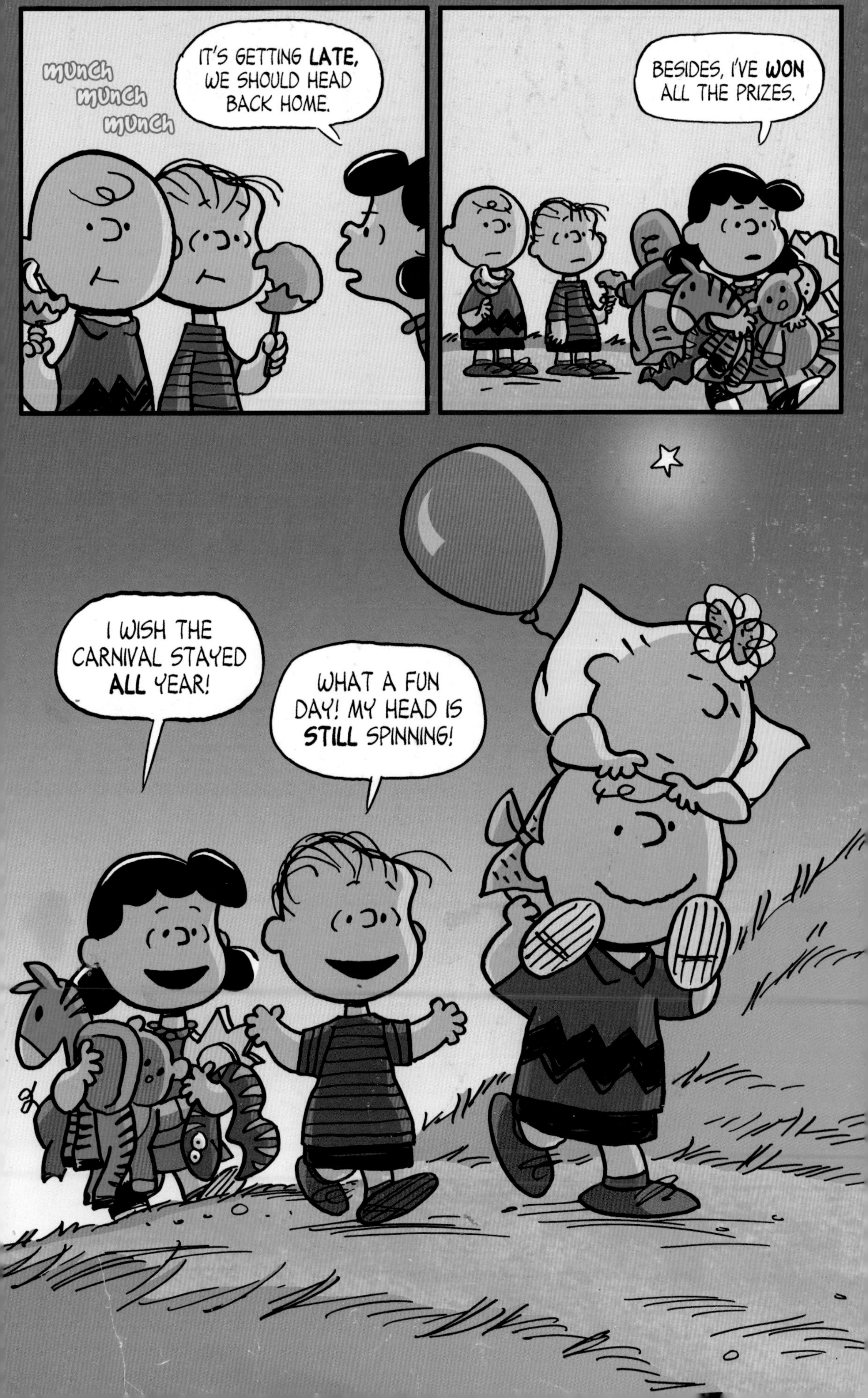
munch munch munch
IT'S GETTING LATE, WE SHOULD HEAD BACK HOME.
BESIDES, I'VE WON ALL THE PRIZES.
I WISH THE CARNIVAL STAYED ALL YEAR!
WHAT A FUN DAY! MY HEAD IS STILL SPINNING!

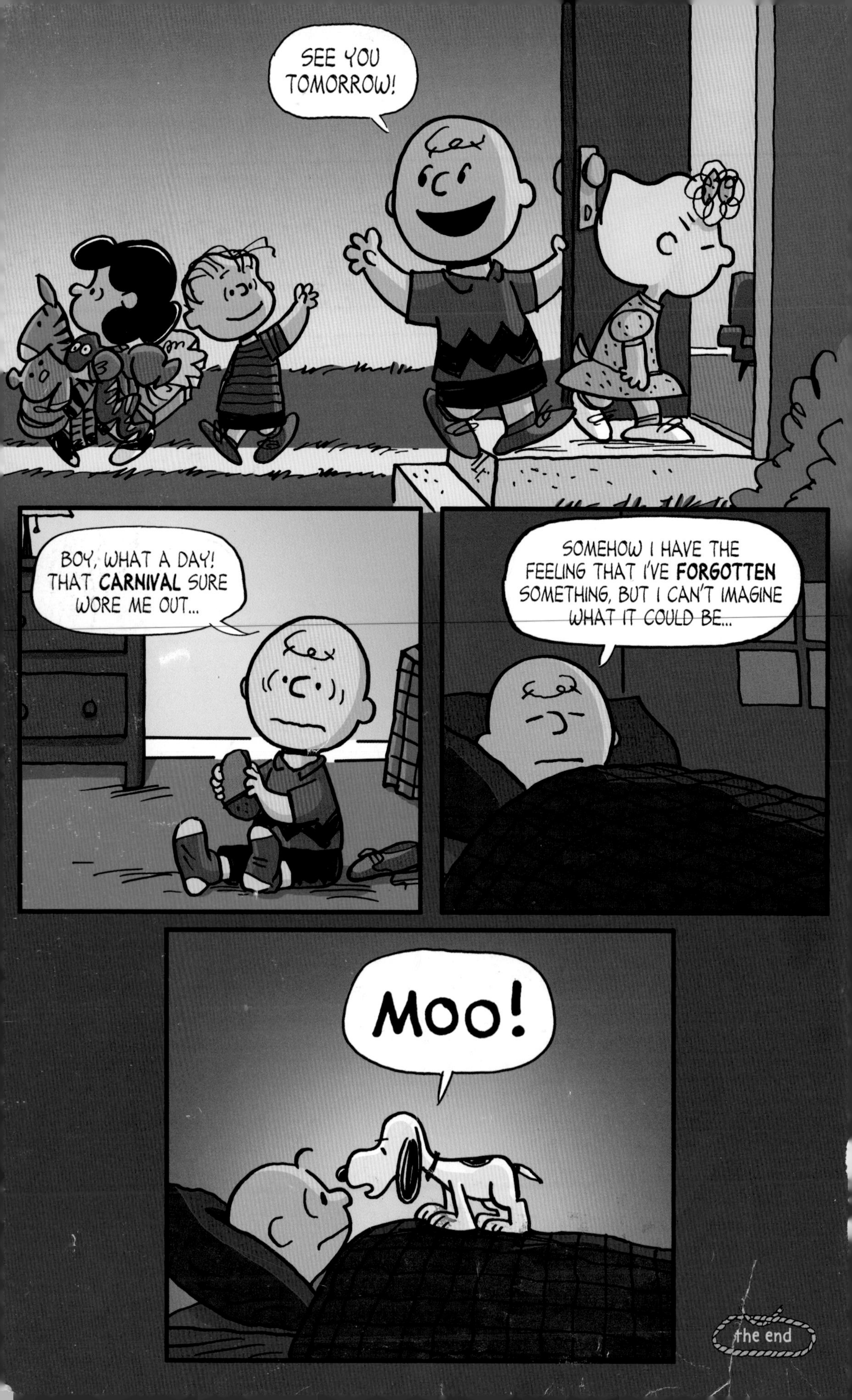
SEE YOU TOMORROW!
BOY, WHAT A DAY! THAT **CARNIVAL** SURE WORE ME OUT...
SOMEHOW I HAVE THE FEELING THAT I'VE **FORGOTTEN** SOMETHING, BUT I CAN'T IMAGINE WHAT IT COULD BE...
MOO!
the end

From the Drawing Board

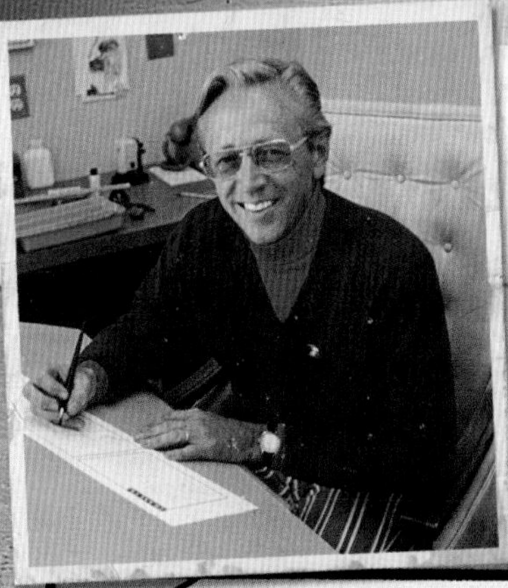

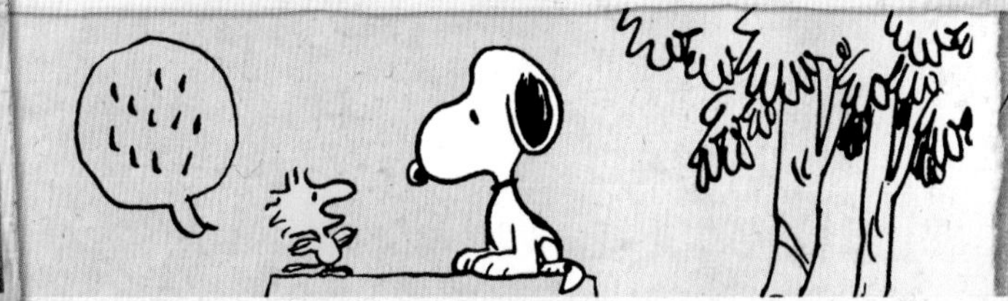

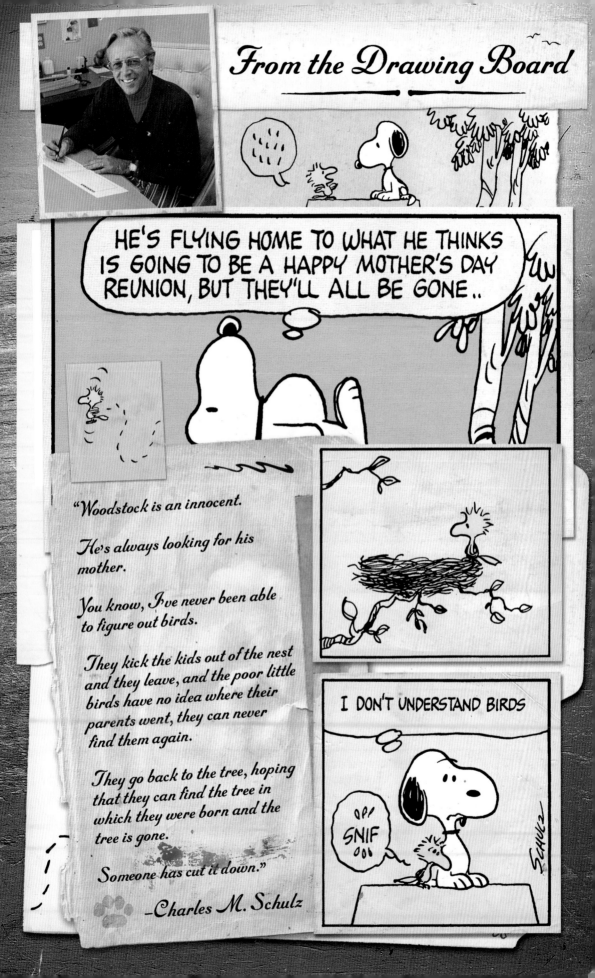

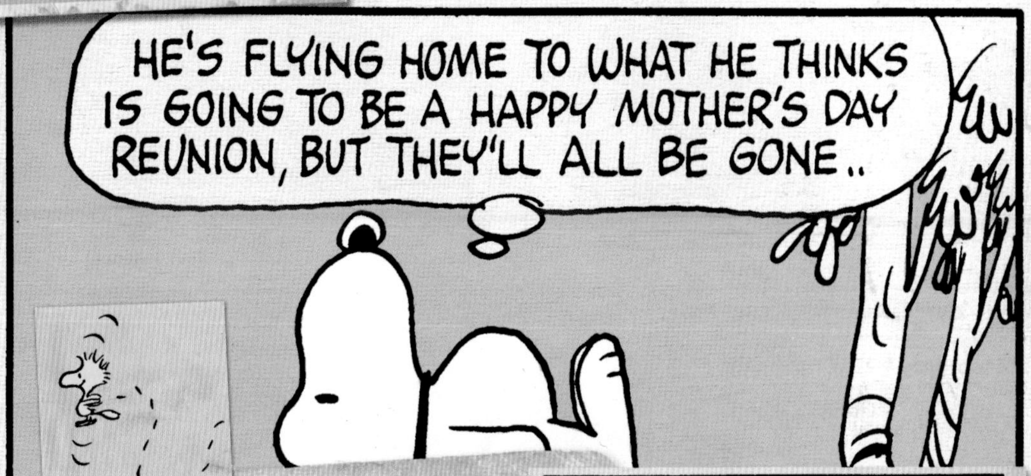
HE'S FLYING HOME TO WHAT HE THINKS IS GOING TO BE A HAPPY MOTHER'S DAY REUNION, BUT THEY'LL ALL BE GONE..

"Woodstock is an innocent.

He's always looking for his mother.

You know, I've never been able to figure out birds.

They kick the kids out of the nest and they leave, and the poor little birds have no idea where their parents went, they can never find them again.

They go back to the tree, hoping that they can find the tree in which they were born and the tree is gone.

Someone has cut it down."

–Charles M. Schulz

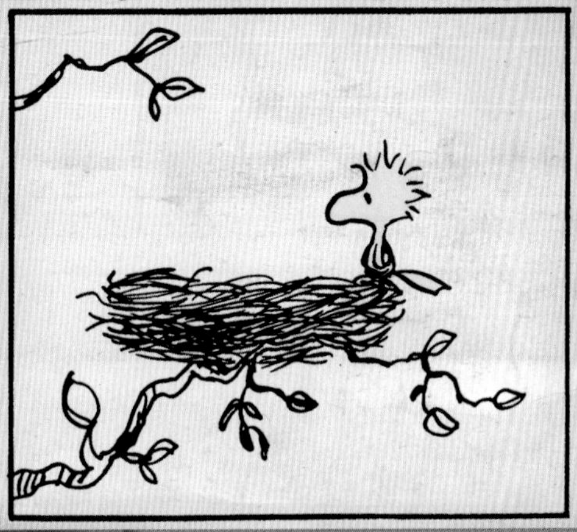

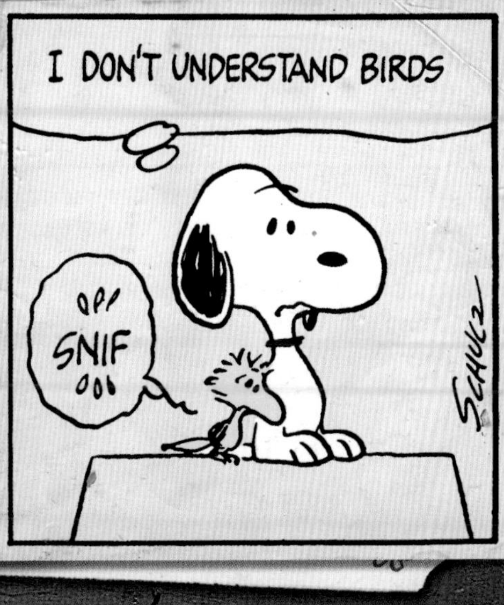
I DON'T UNDERSTAND BIRDS
SNIF
SCHULZ

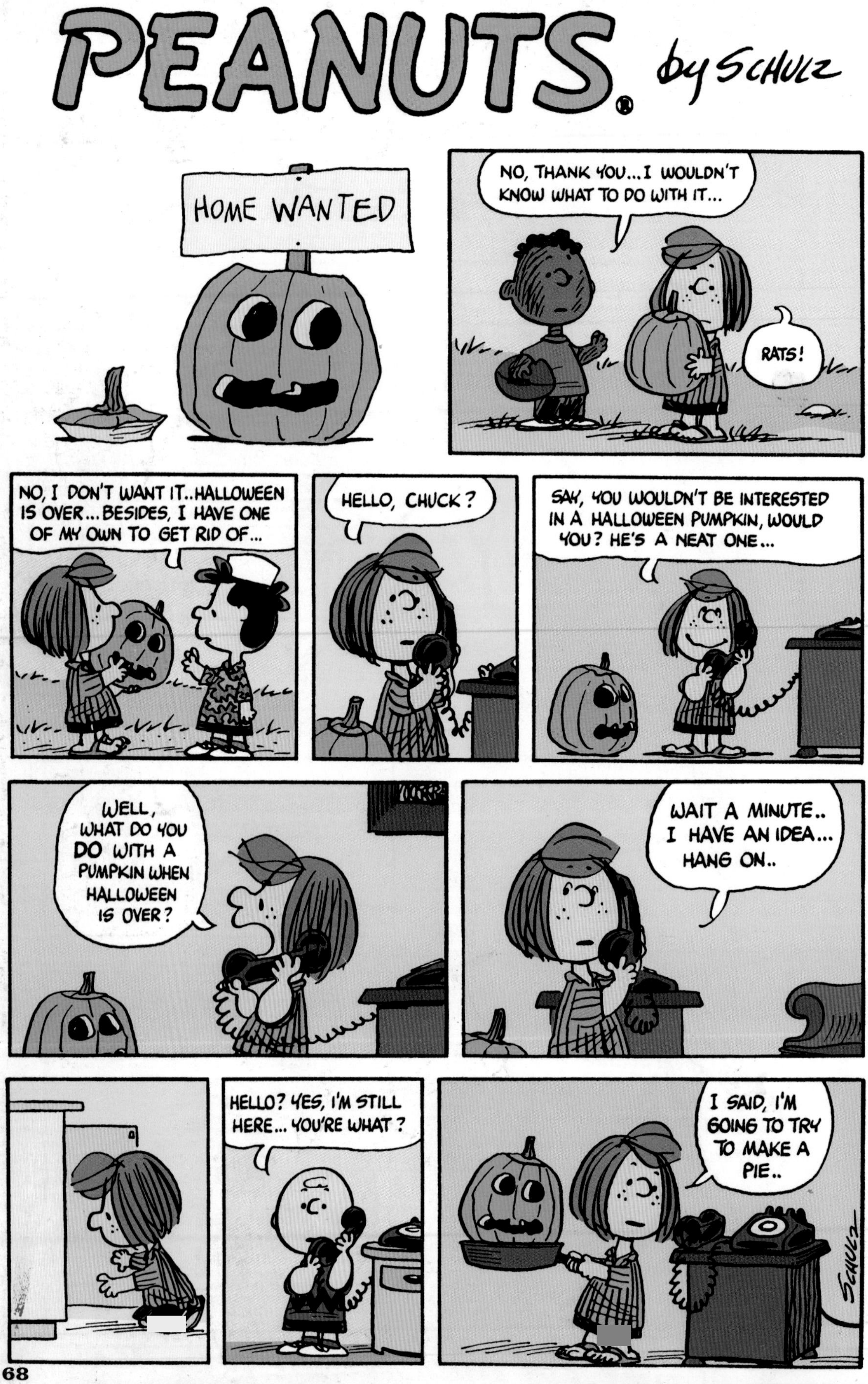
PEANUTS® by SCHULZ
HOME WANTED
NO, THANK YOU... I WOULDN'T KNOW WHAT TO DO WITH IT...
RATS!
NO, I DON'T WANT IT.. HALLOWEEN IS OVER... BESIDES, I HAVE ONE OF MY OWN TO GET RID OF...
HELLO, CHUCK?
SAY, YOU WOULDN'T BE INTERESTED IN A HALLOWEEN PUMPKIN, WOULD YOU? HE'S A NEAT ONE...
WELL, WHAT DO YOU DO WITH A PUMPKIN WHEN HALLOWEEN IS OVER?
WAIT A MINUTE.. I HAVE AN IDEA... HANG ON..
HELLO? YES, I'M STILL HERE... YOU'RE WHAT?
I SAID, I'M GOING TO TRY TO MAKE A PIE..
SCHULZ

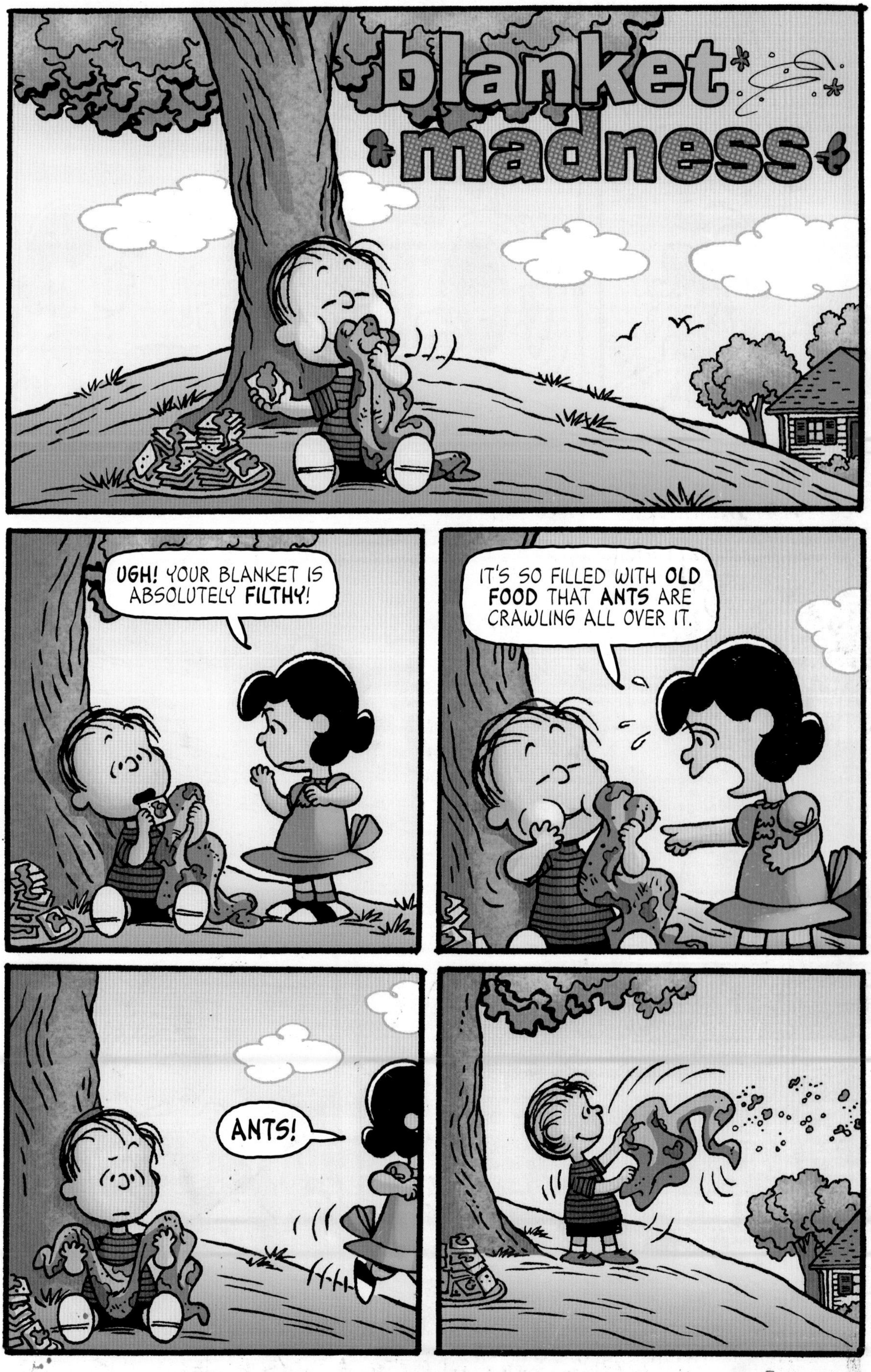
blanket madness
UGH! YOUR BLANKET IS ABSOLUTELY FILTHY!
IT'S SO FILLED WITH OLD FOOD THAT ANTS ARE CRAWLING ALL OVER IT.
ANTS!

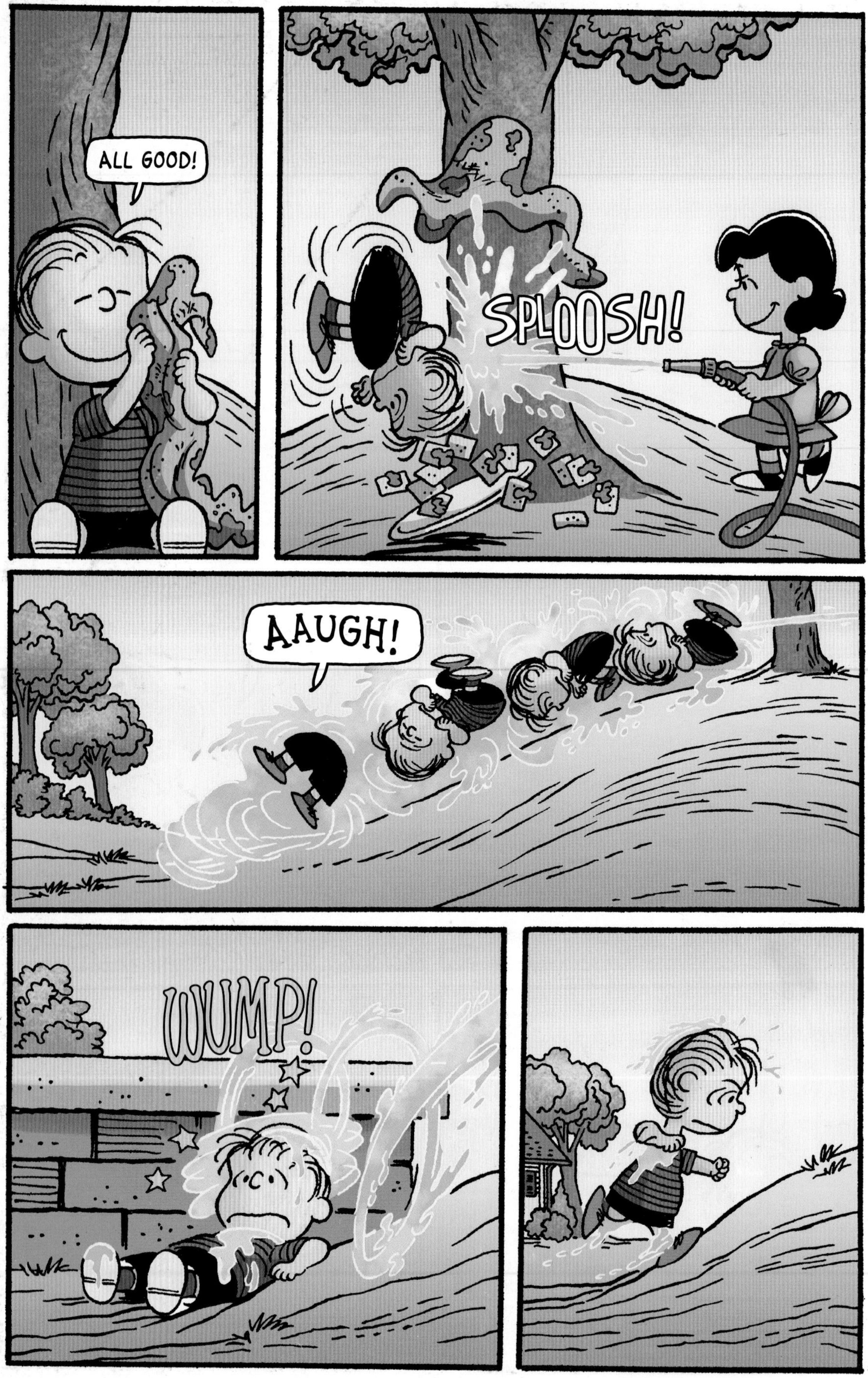

ALL GOOD!
SPLOOSH!
AAUGH!
WUMP!

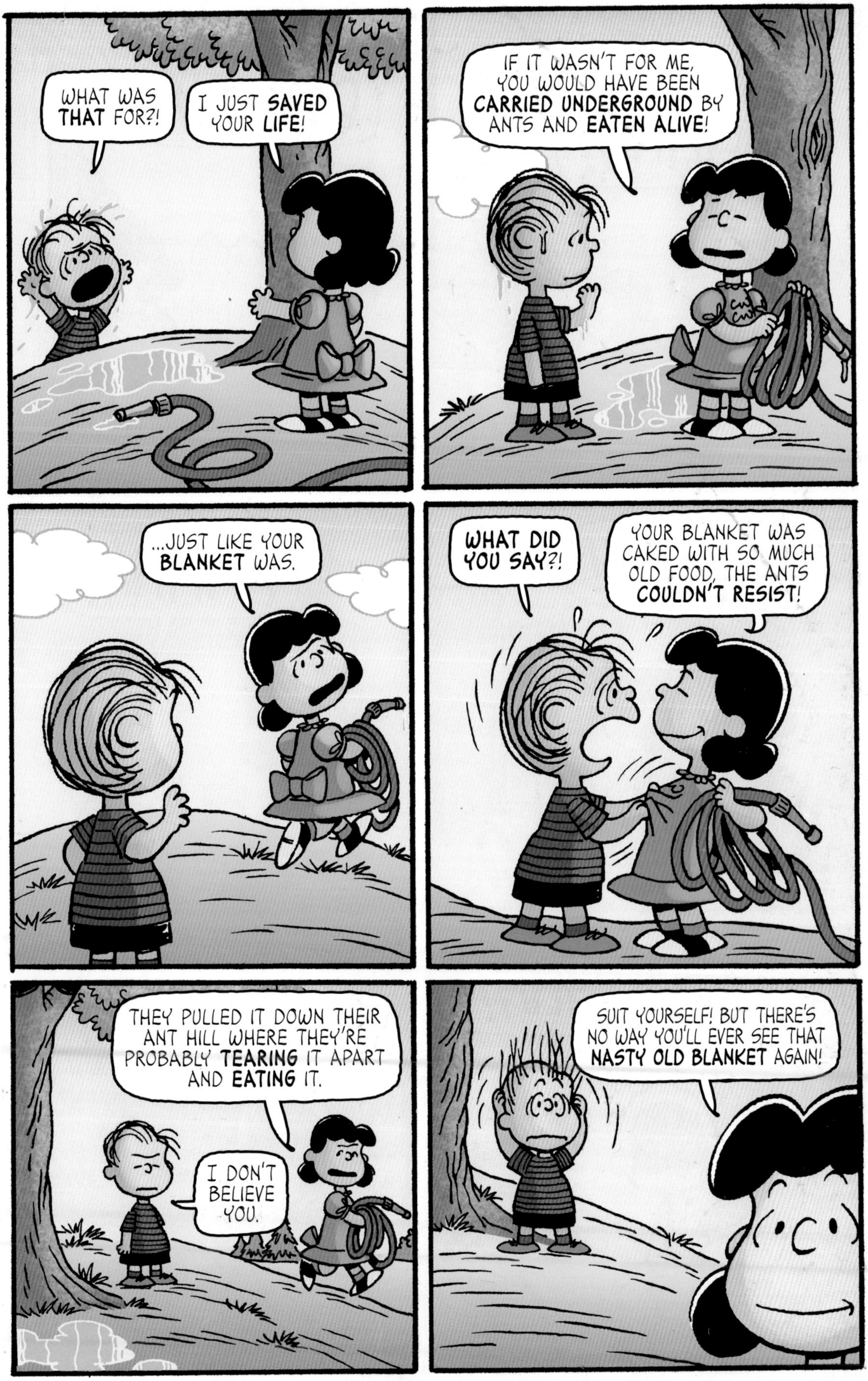
WHAT WAS THAT FOR?!
I JUST SAVED YOUR LIFE!
IF IT WASN'T FOR ME, YOU WOULD HAVE BEEN CARRIED UNDERGROUND BY ANTS AND EATEN ALIVE!
...JUST LIKE YOUR BLANKET WAS.
WHAT DID YOU SAY?!
YOUR BLANKET WAS CAKED WITH SO MUCH OLD FOOD, THE ANTS COULDN'T RESIST!
THEY PULLED IT DOWN THEIR ANT HILL WHERE THEY'RE PROBABLY TEARING IT APART AND EATING IT.
I DON'T BELIEVE YOU.
SUIT YOURSELF! BUT THERE'S NO WAY YOU'LL EVER SEE THAT NASTY OLD BLANKET AGAIN!

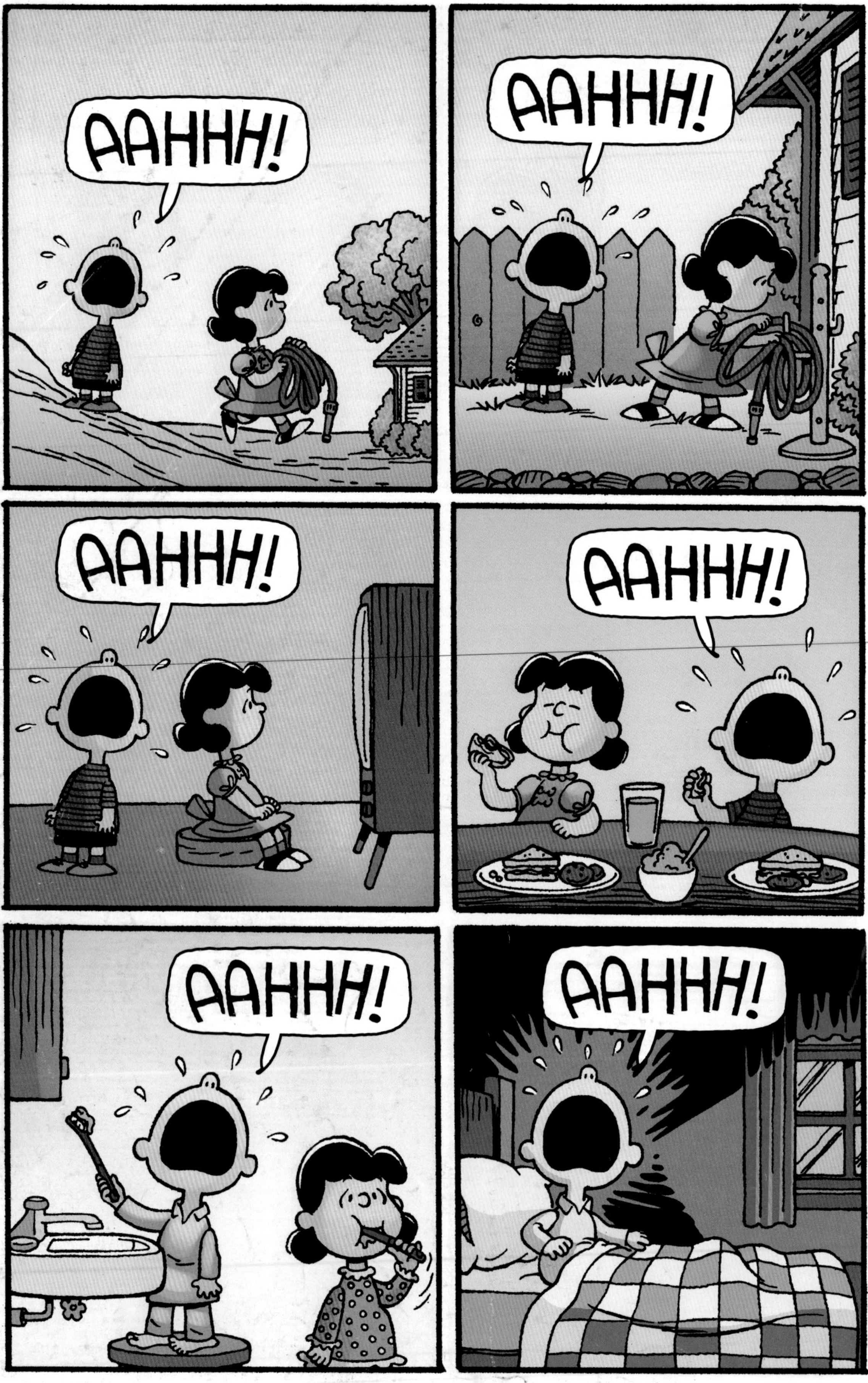
AAHHH!
AAHHH!
AAHHH!
AAHHH!
AAHHH!
AAHHH!

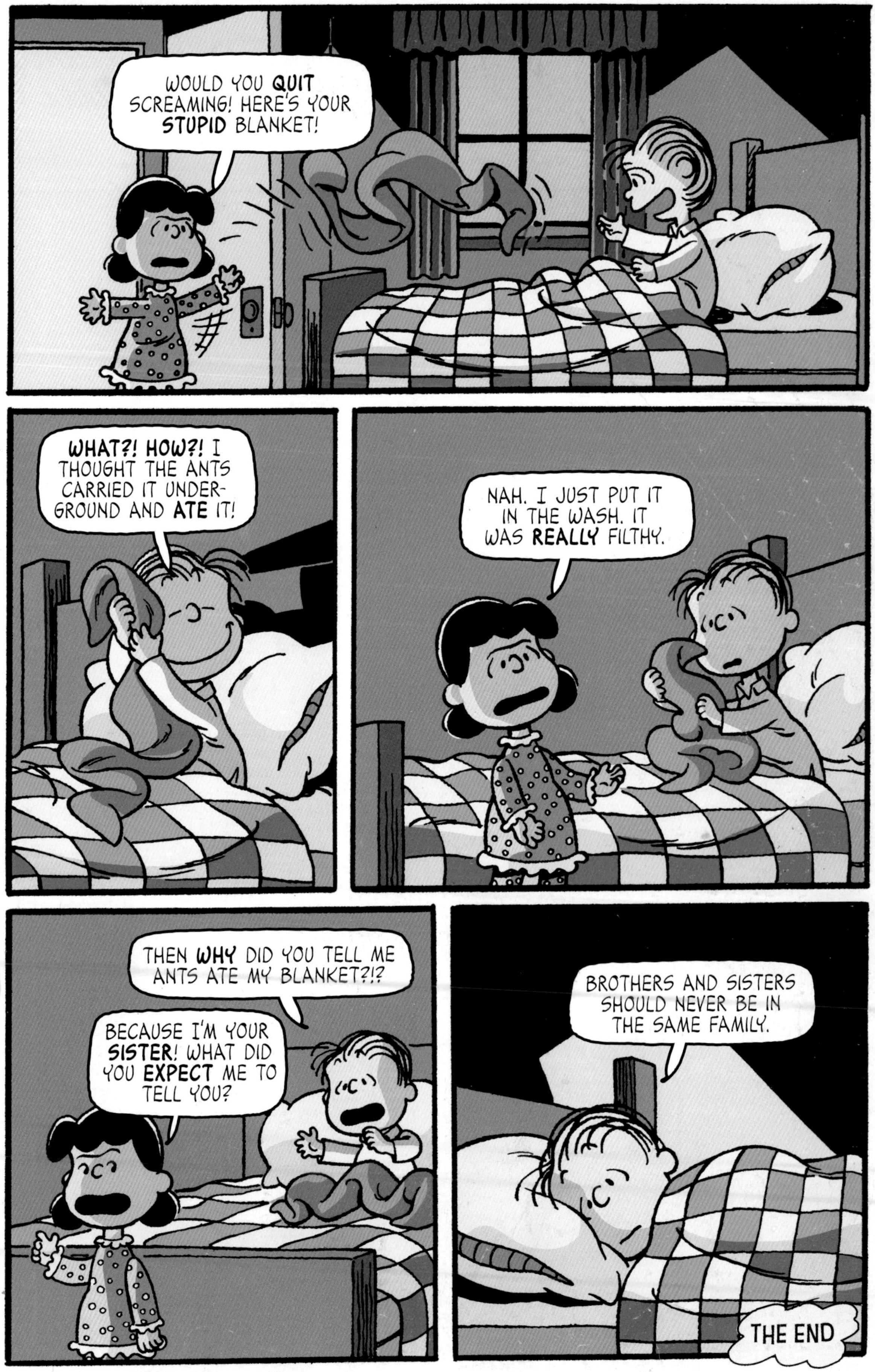
WOULD YOU QUIT SCREAMING! HERE'S YOUR STUPID BLANKET!
WHAT?! HOW?! I THOUGHT THE ANTS CARRIED IT UNDER-GROUND AND ATE IT!
NAH. I JUST PUT IT IN THE WASH. IT WAS REALLY FILTHY.
THEN WHY DID YOU TELL ME ANTS ATE MY BLANKET?!?
BECAUSE I'M YOUR SISTER! WHAT DID YOU EXPECT ME TO TELL YOU?
BROTHERS AND SISTERS SHOULD NEVER BE IN THE SAME FAMILY.
THE END

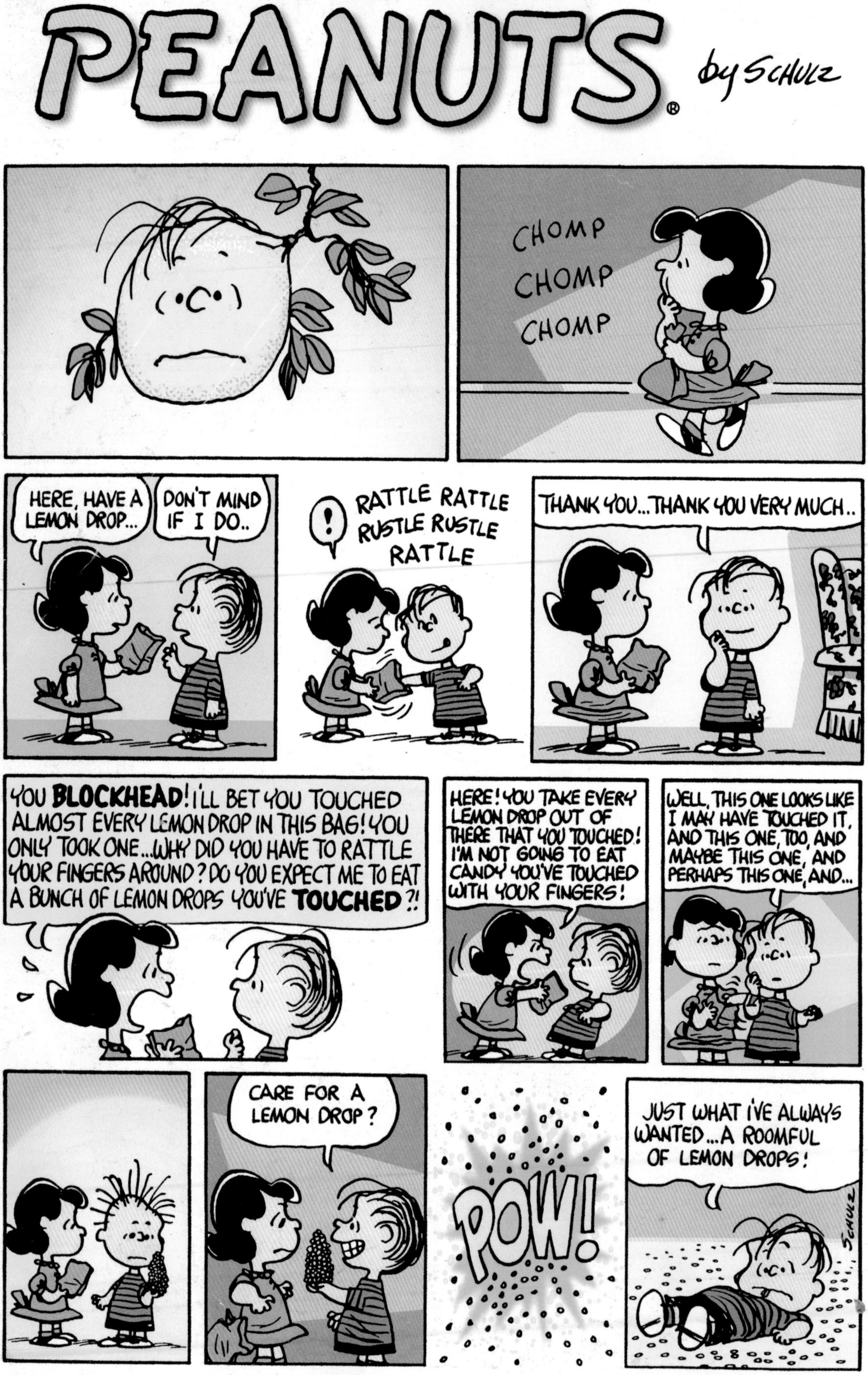
PEANUTS
by SCHULZ
CHOMP CHOMP CHOMP
HERE, HAVE A LEMON DROP...
DON'T MIND IF I DO..
!
RATTLE RATTLE RUSTLE RUSTLE RATTLE
THANK YOU...THANK YOU VERY MUCH..
YOU BLOCKHEAD! I'LL BET YOU TOUCHED ALMOST EVERY LEMON DROP IN THIS BAG! YOU ONLY TOOK ONE...WHY DID YOU HAVE TO RATTLE YOUR FINGERS AROUND? DO YOU EXPECT ME TO EAT A BUNCH OF LEMON DROPS YOU'VE TOUCHED?!
HERE! YOU TAKE EVERY LEMON DROP OUT OF THERE THAT YOU TOUCHED! I'M NOT GOING TO EAT CANDY YOU'VE TOUCHED WITH YOUR FINGERS!
WELL, THIS ONE LOOKS LIKE I MAY HAVE TOUCHED IT, AND THIS ONE, TOO, AND MAYBE THIS ONE, AND PERHAPS THIS ONE, AND...
CARE FOR A LEMON DROP?
POW!
JUST WHAT I'VE ALWAYS WANTED...A ROOMFUL OF LEMON DROPS!
SCHULZ

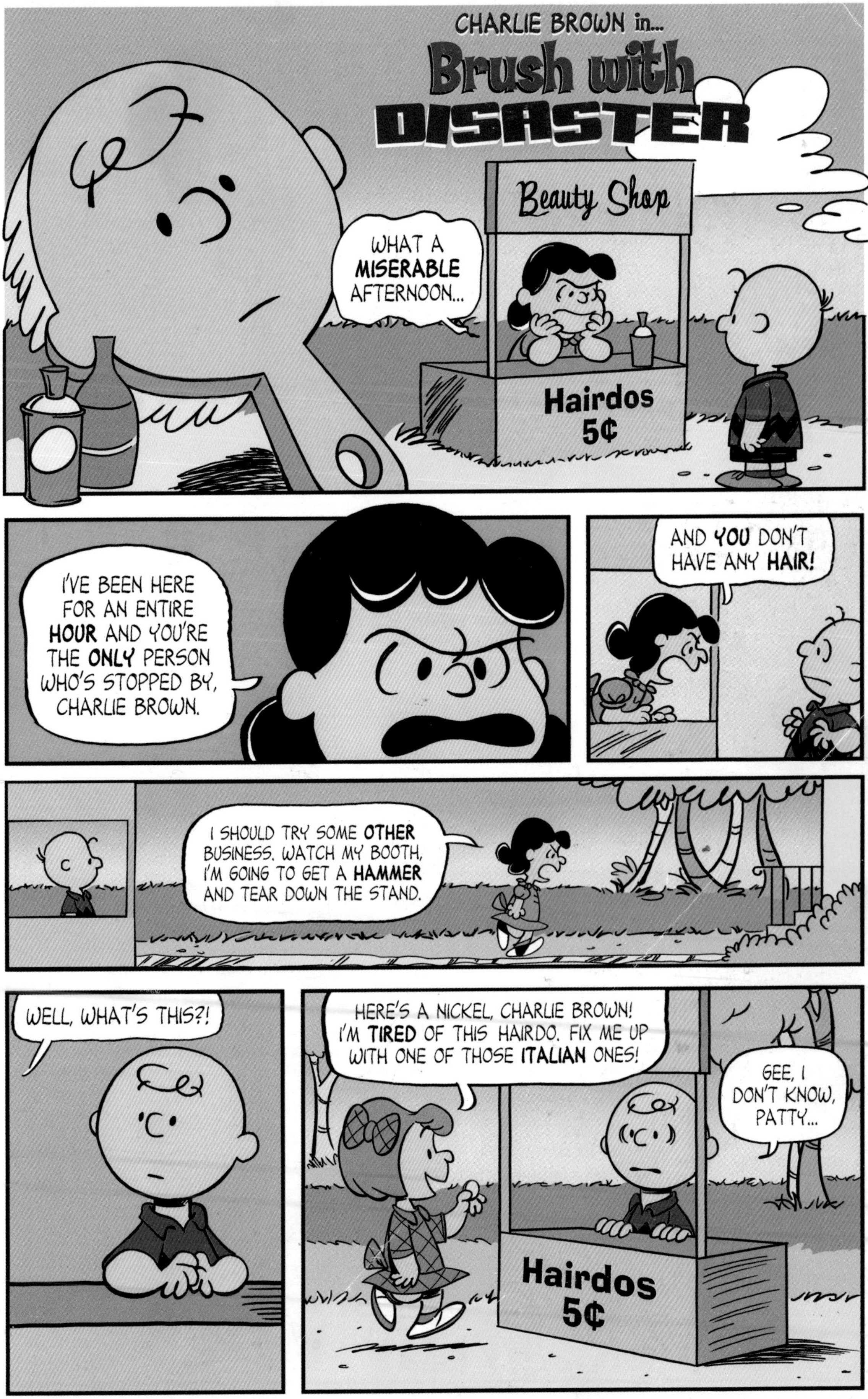
CHARLIE BROWN in...
Brush with DISASTER
Beauty Shop
WHAT A MISERABLE AFTERNOON...
Hairdos 5¢
I'VE BEEN HERE FOR AN ENTIRE HOUR AND YOU'RE THE ONLY PERSON WHO'S STOPPED BY, CHARLIE BROWN.
AND YOU DON'T HAVE ANY HAIR!
I SHOULD TRY SOME OTHER BUSINESS. WATCH MY BOOTH, I'M GOING TO GET A HAMMER AND TEAR DOWN THE STAND.
WELL, WHAT'S THIS?!
HERE'S A NICKEL, CHARLIE BROWN! I'M TIRED OF THIS HAIRDO. FIX ME UP WITH ONE OF THOSE ITALIAN ONES!
GEE, I DON'T KNOW, PATTY...
Hairdos 5¢

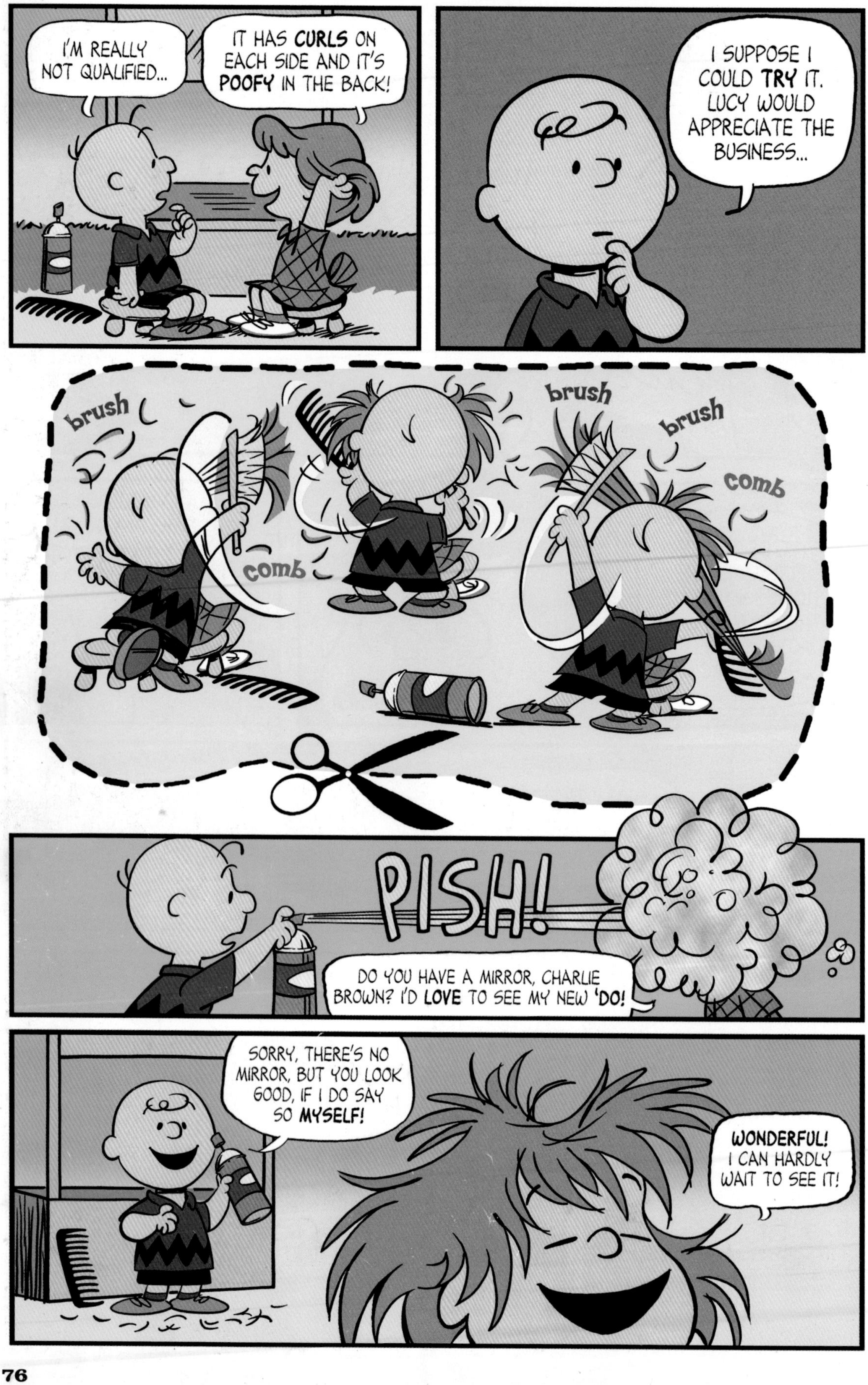
I'M REALLY NOT QUALIFIED...
IT HAS CURLS ON EACH SIDE AND IT'S POOFY IN THE BACK!
I SUPPOSE I COULD TRY IT. LUCY WOULD APPRECIATE THE BUSINESS...
brush
comb
brush
brush
comb
PISH!
DO YOU HAVE A MIRROR, CHARLIE BROWN? I'D LOVE TO SEE MY NEW 'DO!
SORRY, THERE'S NO MIRROR, BUT YOU LOOK GOOD, IF I DO SAY SO MYSELF!
WONDERFUL! I CAN HARDLY WAIT TO SEE IT!

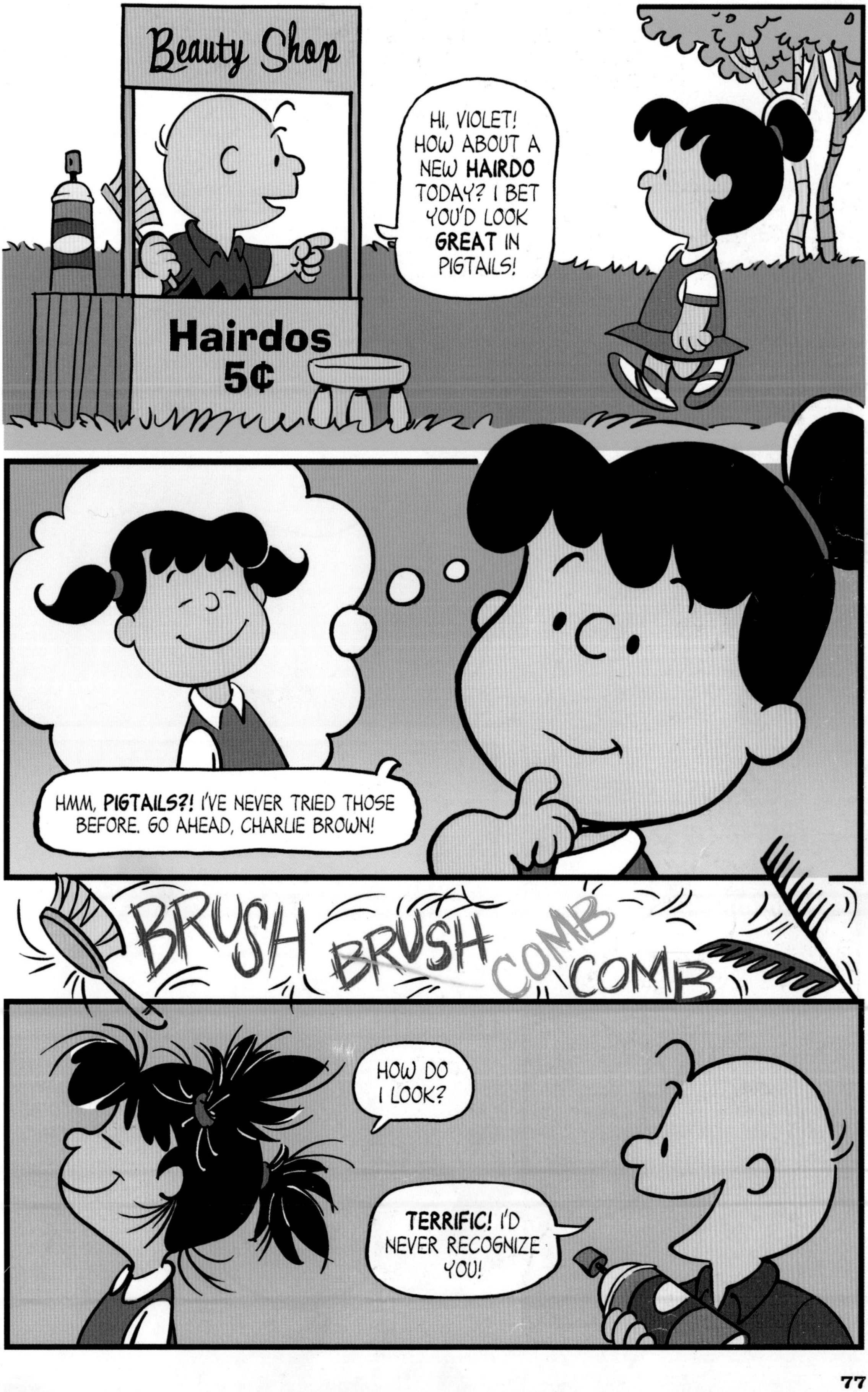
Beauty Shop
HI, VIOLET! HOW ABOUT A NEW **HAIRDO** TODAY? I BET YOU'D LOOK **GREAT** IN PIGTAILS!
Hairdos 5¢
HMM, **PIGTAILS?!** I'VE NEVER TRIED THOSE BEFORE. GO AHEAD, CHARLIE BROWN!
BRUSH BRUSH COMB COMB
HOW DO I LOOK?
TERRIFIC! I'D NEVER RECOGNIZE YOU!

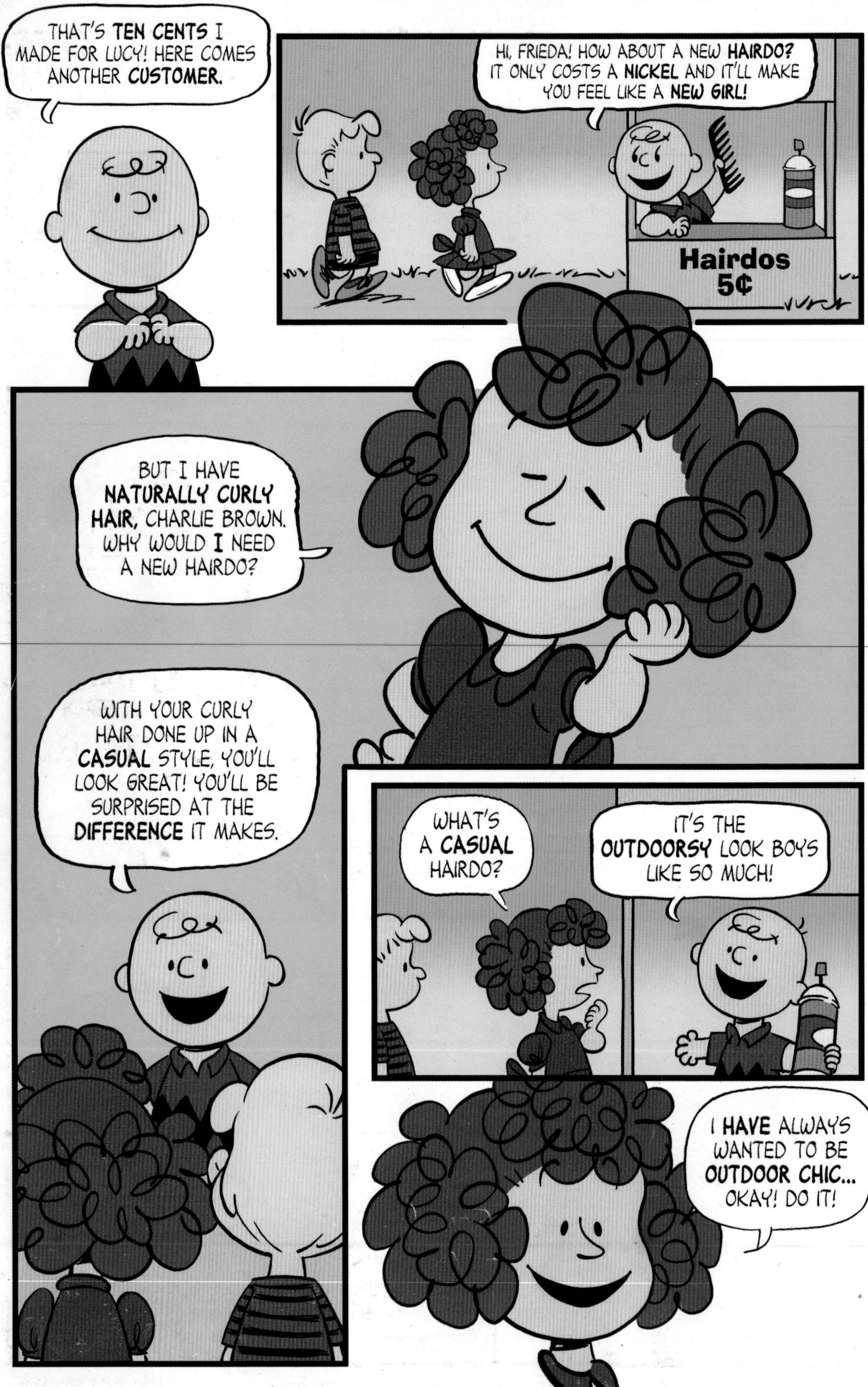
THAT'S TEN CENTS I MADE FOR LUCY! HERE COMES ANOTHER CUSTOMER.
HI, FRIEDA! HOW ABOUT A NEW HAIRDO? IT ONLY COSTS A NICKEL AND IT'LL MAKE YOU FEEL LIKE A NEW GIRL!
Hairdos 5¢
BUT I HAVE NATURALLY CURLY HAIR, CHARLIE BROWN. WHY WOULD I NEED A NEW HAIRDO?
WITH YOUR CURLY HAIR DONE UP IN A CASUAL STYLE, YOU'LL LOOK GREAT! YOU'LL BE SURPRISED AT THE DIFFERENCE IT MAKES.
WHAT'S A CASUAL HAIRDO?
IT'S THE OUTDOORSY LOOK BOYS LIKE SO MUCH!
I HAVE ALWAYS WANTED TO BE OUTDOOR CHIC... OKAY! DO IT!

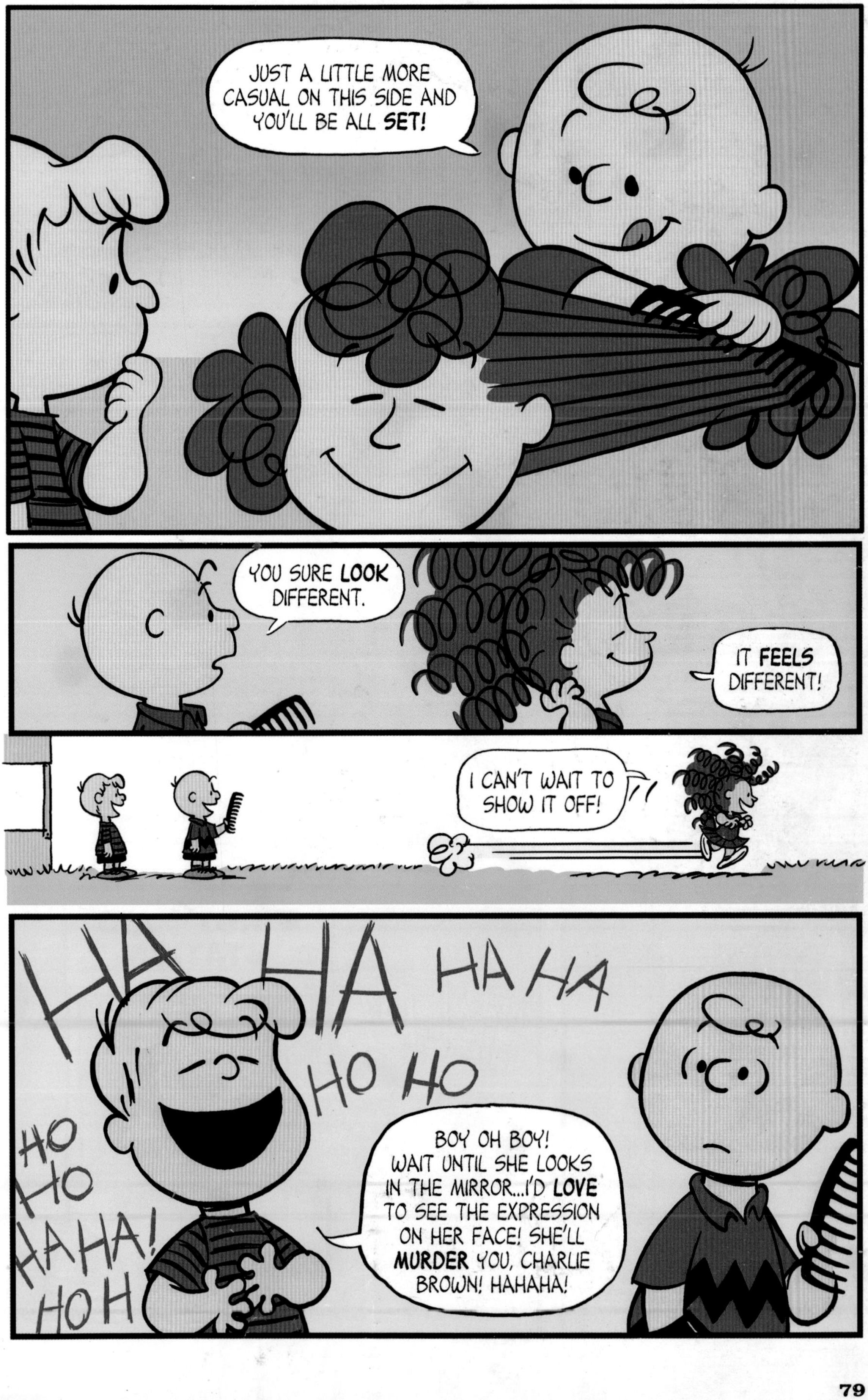
JUST A LITTLE MORE CASUAL ON THIS SIDE AND YOU'LL BE ALL **SET!**
YOU SURE **LOOK** DIFFERENT.
IT **FEELS** DIFFERENT!
I CAN'T WAIT TO SHOW IT OFF!
HA HA HA HA
HO HO
HO HO HAHA! HO H
BOY OH BOY! WAIT UNTIL SHE LOOKS IN THE MIRROR...I'D **LOVE** TO SEE THE EXPRESSION ON HER FACE! SHE'LL **MURDER** YOU, CHARLIE BROWN! HAHAHA!

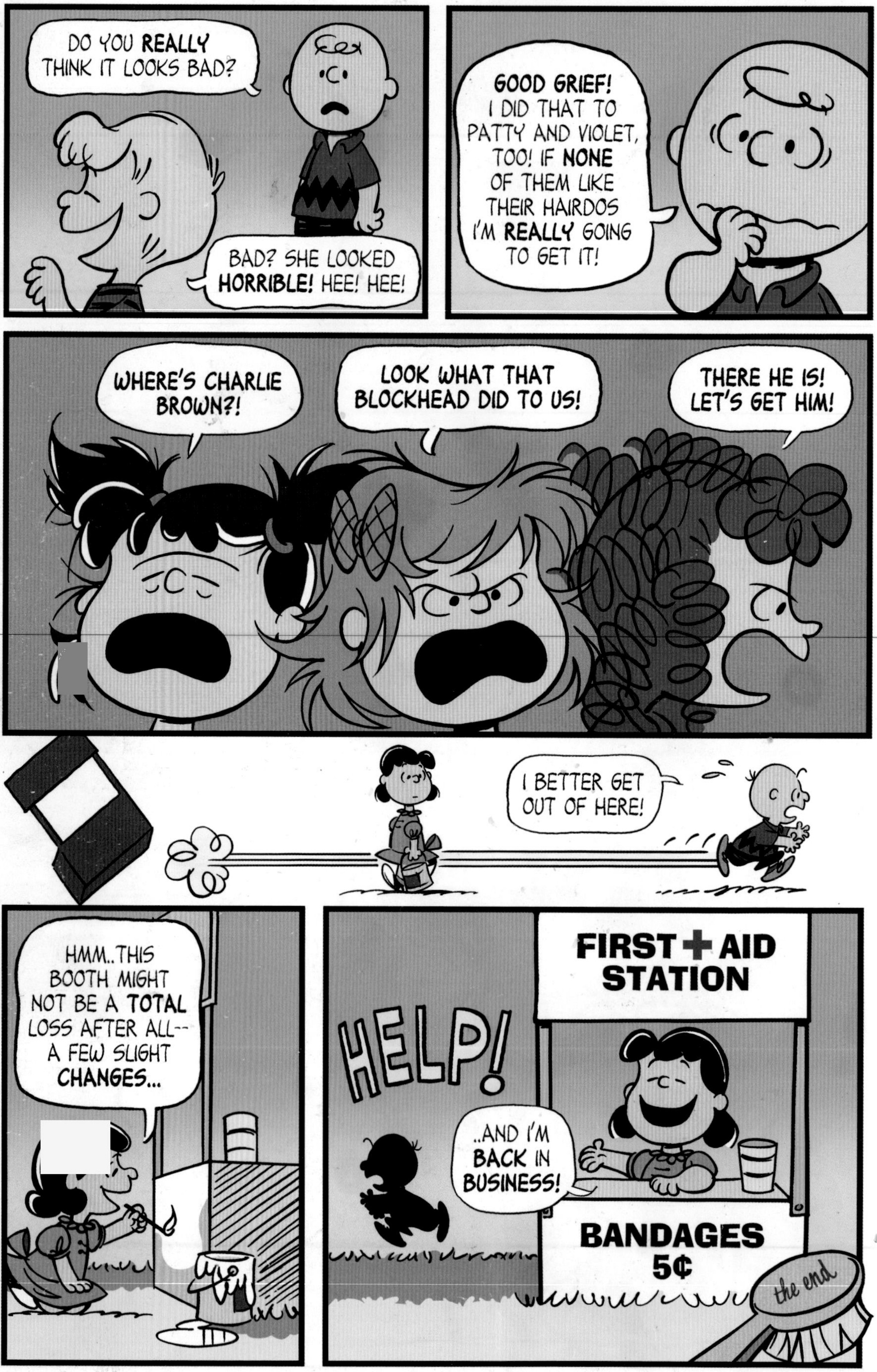
DO YOU REALLY THINK IT LOOKS BAD?
BAD? SHE LOOKED HORRIBLE! HEE! HEE!
GOOD GRIEF! I DID THAT TO PATTY AND VIOLET, TOO! IF NONE OF THEM LIKE THEIR HAIRDOS I'M REALLY GOING TO GET IT!
WHERE'S CHARLIE BROWN?!
LOOK WHAT THAT BLOCKHEAD DID TO US!
THERE HE IS! LET'S GET HIM!
I BETTER GET OUT OF HERE!
HMM..THIS BOOTH MIGHT NOT BE A TOTAL LOSS AFTER ALL-- A FEW SLIGHT CHANGES...
FIRST AID STATION
HELP!
..AND I'M BACK IN BUSINESS!
BANDAGES 5¢
the end

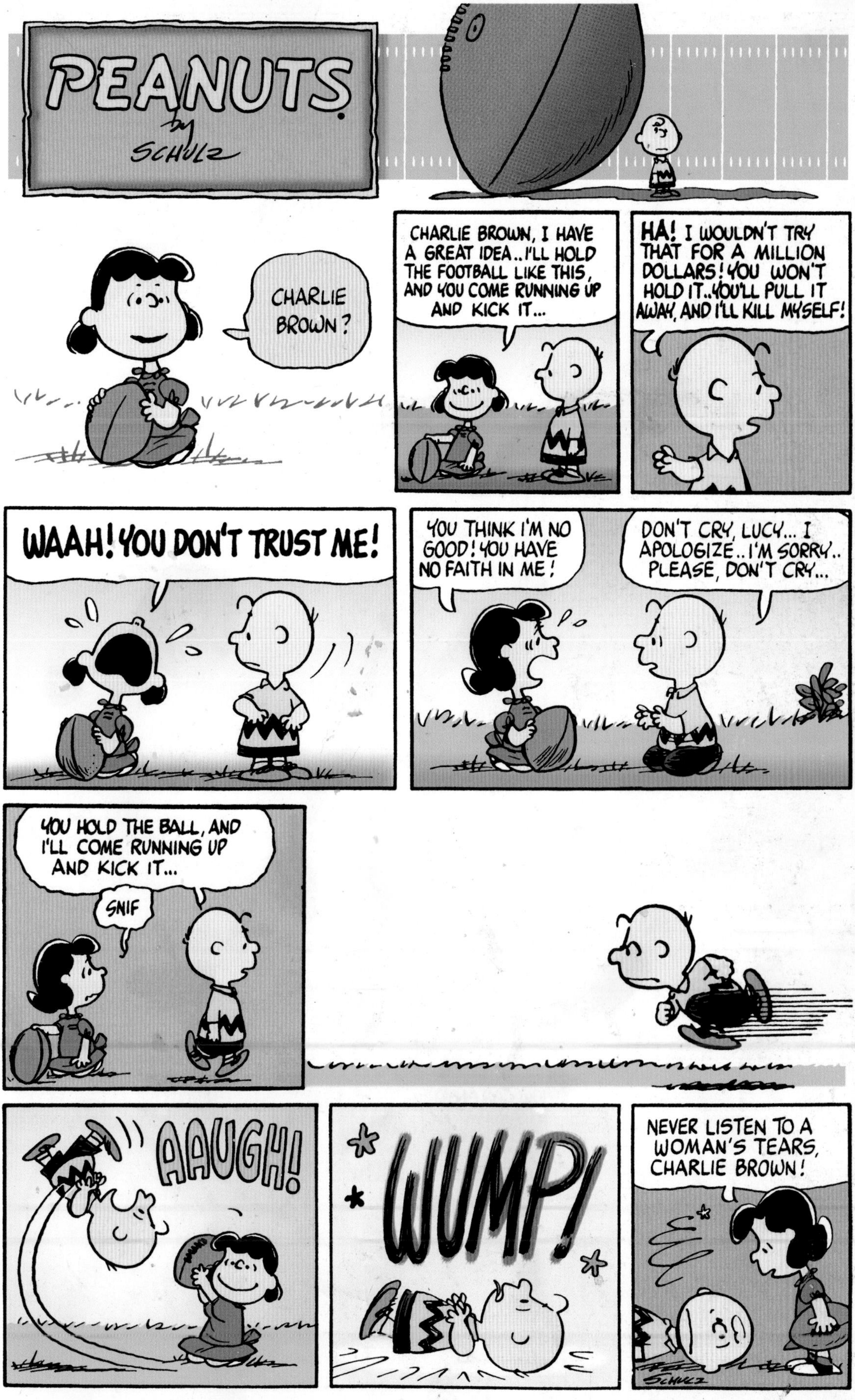
PEANUTS
by SCHULZ
CHARLIE BROWN?
CHARLIE BROWN, I HAVE A GREAT IDEA..I'LL HOLD THE FOOTBALL LIKE THIS, AND YOU COME RUNNING UP AND KICK IT...
HA! I WOULDN'T TRY THAT FOR A MILLION DOLLARS! YOU WON'T HOLD IT..YOU'LL PULL IT AWAY, AND I'LL KILL MYSELF!
WAAH! YOU DON'T TRUST ME!
YOU THINK I'M NO GOOD! YOU HAVE NO FAITH IN ME!
DON'T CRY, LUCY... I APOLOGIZE..I'M SORRY.. PLEASE, DON'T CRY...
YOU HOLD THE BALL, AND I'LL COME RUNNING UP AND KICK IT...
SNIF
AAUGH!
WUMP!
NEVER LISTEN TO A WOMAN'S TEARS, CHARLIE BROWN!
SCHULZ

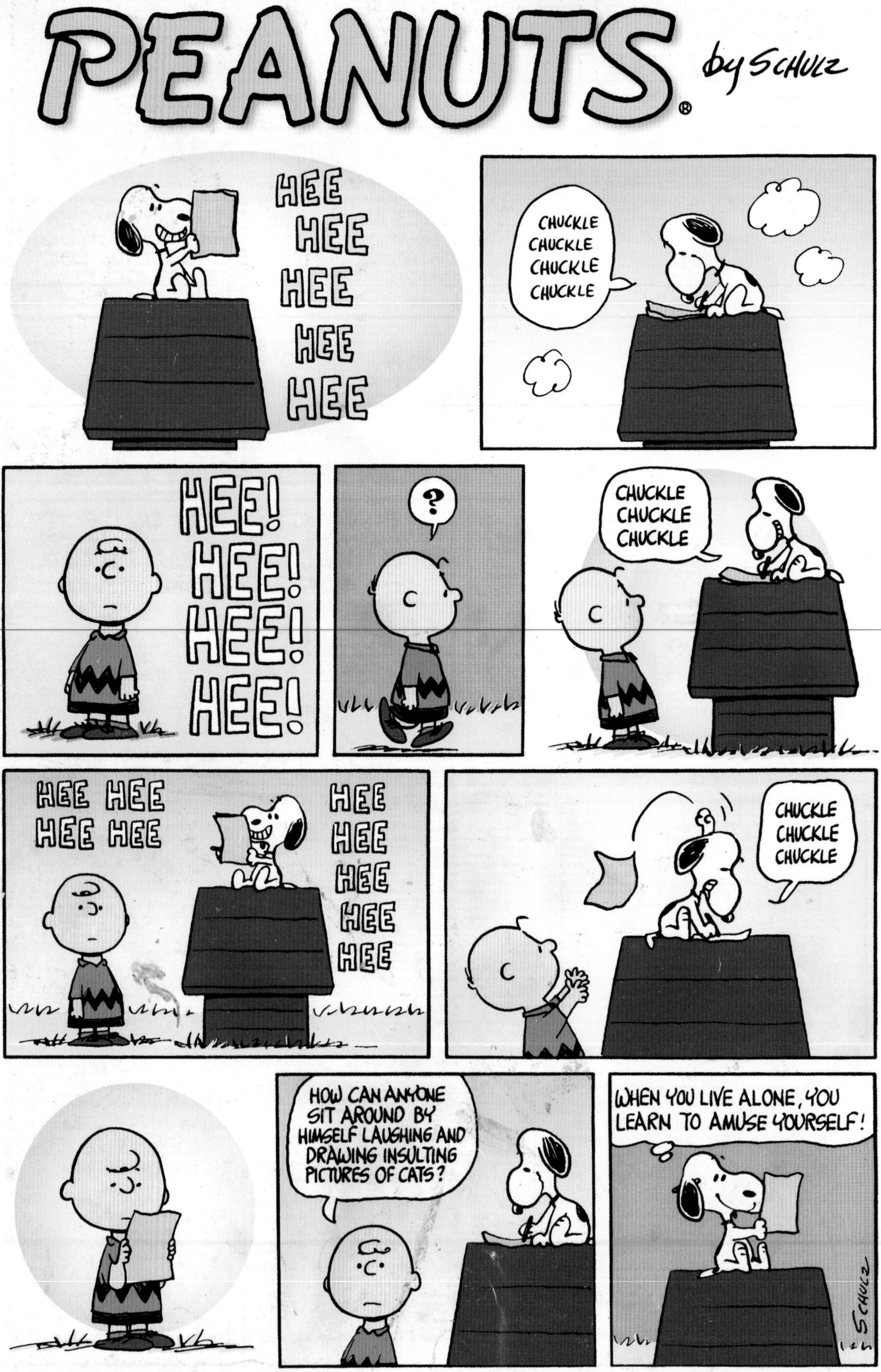
PEANUTS
by SCHULZ
HEE HEE HEE HEE HEE
CHUCKLE CHUCKLE CHUCKLE CHUCKLE
HEE! HEE! HEE! HEE!
?
CHUCKLE CHUCKLE CHUCKLE
HEE HEE HEE HEE
HEE HEE HEE HEE HEE
CHUCKLE CHUCKLE CHUCKLE
HOW CAN ANYONE SIT AROUND BY HIMSELF LAUGHING AND DRAWING INSULTING PICTURES OF CATS?
WHEN YOU LIVE ALONE, YOU LEARN TO AMUSE YOURSELF!
SCHULZ

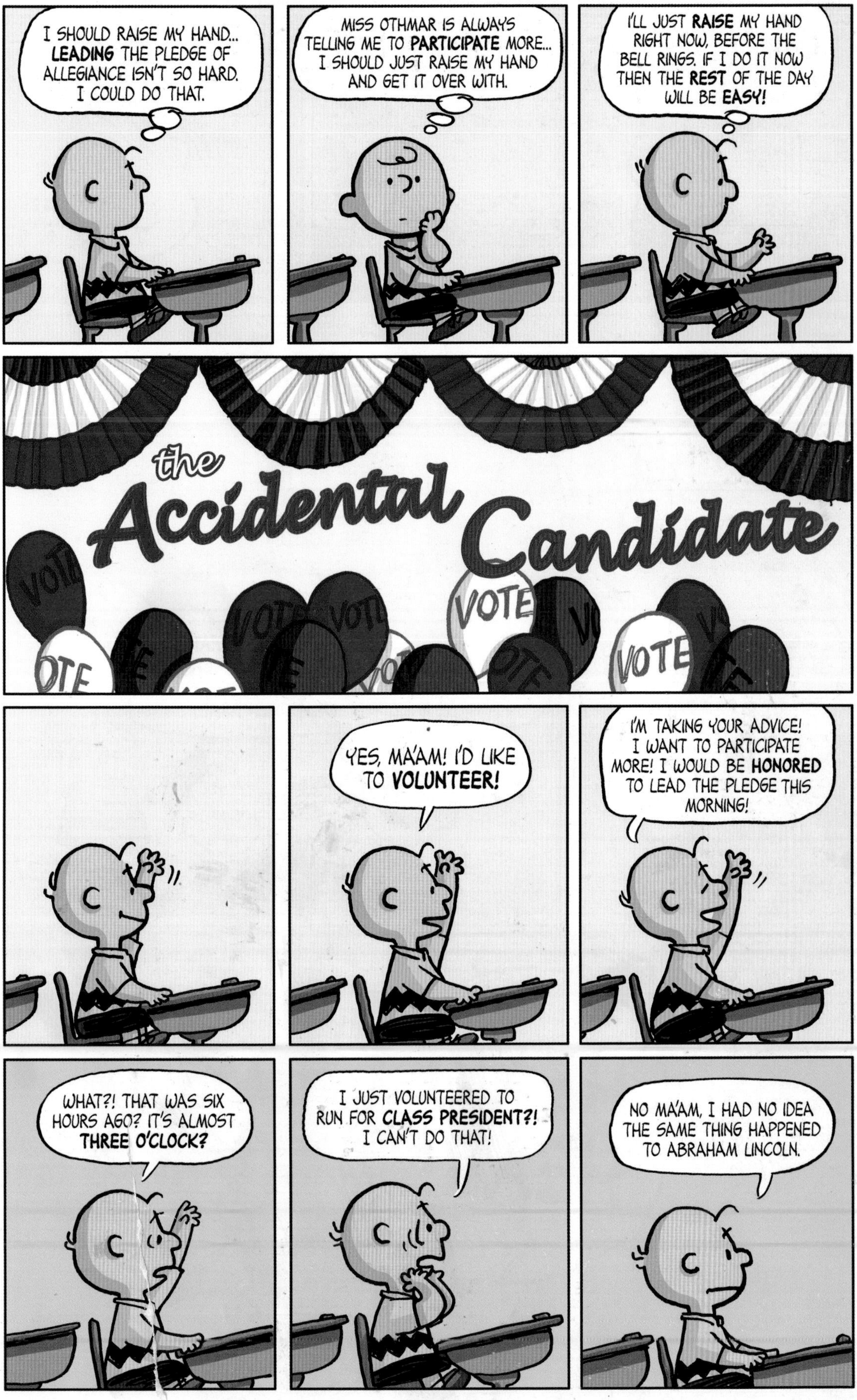
I SHOULD RAISE MY HAND... LEADING THE PLEDGE OF ALLEGIANCE ISN'T SO HARD. I COULD DO THAT.
MISS OTHMAR IS ALWAYS TELLING ME TO PARTICIPATE MORE... I SHOULD JUST RAISE MY HAND AND GET IT OVER WITH.
I'LL JUST RAISE MY HAND RIGHT NOW, BEFORE THE BELL RINGS. IF I DO IT NOW THEN THE REST OF THE DAY WILL BE EASY!
the Accidental Candidate
YES, MA'AM! I'D LIKE TO VOLUNTEER!
I'M TAKING YOUR ADVICE! I WANT TO PARTICIPATE MORE! I WOULD BE HONORED TO LEAD THE PLEDGE THIS MORNING!
WHAT?! THAT WAS SIX HOURS AGO? IT'S ALMOST THREE O'CLOCK?
I JUST VOLUNTEERED TO RUN FOR CLASS PRESIDENT?! I CAN'T DO THAT!
NO MA'AM, I HAD NO IDEA THE SAME THING HAPPENED TO ABRAHAM LINCOLN.

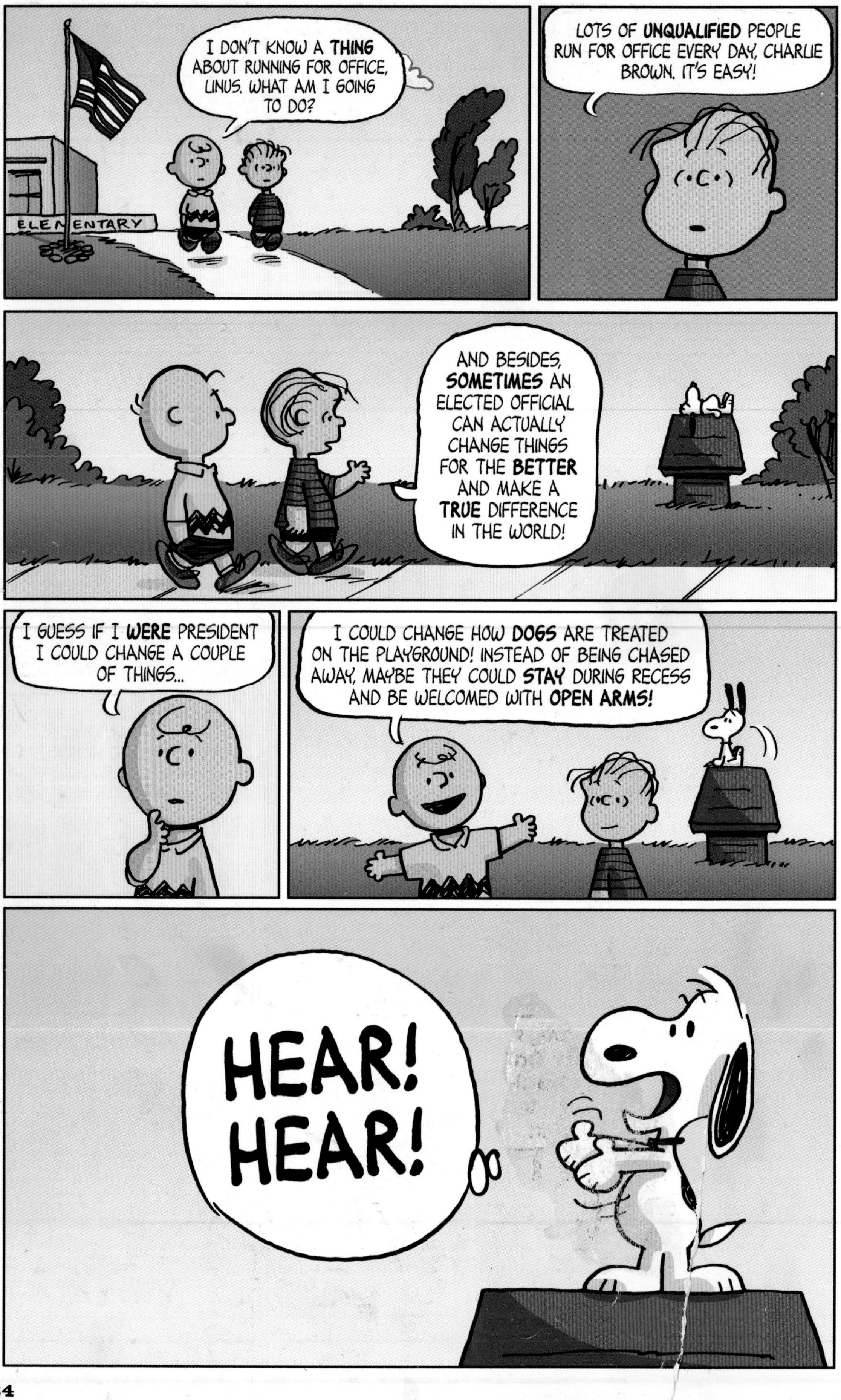

ELEMENTARY
I DON'T KNOW A THING ABOUT RUNNING FOR OFFICE, LINUS. WHAT AM I GOING TO DO?
LOTS OF UNQUALIFIED PEOPLE RUN FOR OFFICE EVERY DAY, CHARLIE BROWN. IT'S EASY!
AND BESIDES, SOMETIMES AN ELECTED OFFICIAL CAN ACTUALLY CHANGE THINGS FOR THE BETTER AND MAKE A TRUE DIFFERENCE IN THE WORLD!
I GUESS IF I WERE PRESIDENT I COULD CHANGE A COUPLE OF THINGS...
I COULD CHANGE HOW DOGS ARE TREATED ON THE PLAYGROUND! INSTEAD OF BEING CHASED AWAY, MAYBE THEY COULD STAY DURING RECESS AND BE WELCOMED WITH OPEN ARMS!
HEAR! HEAR!

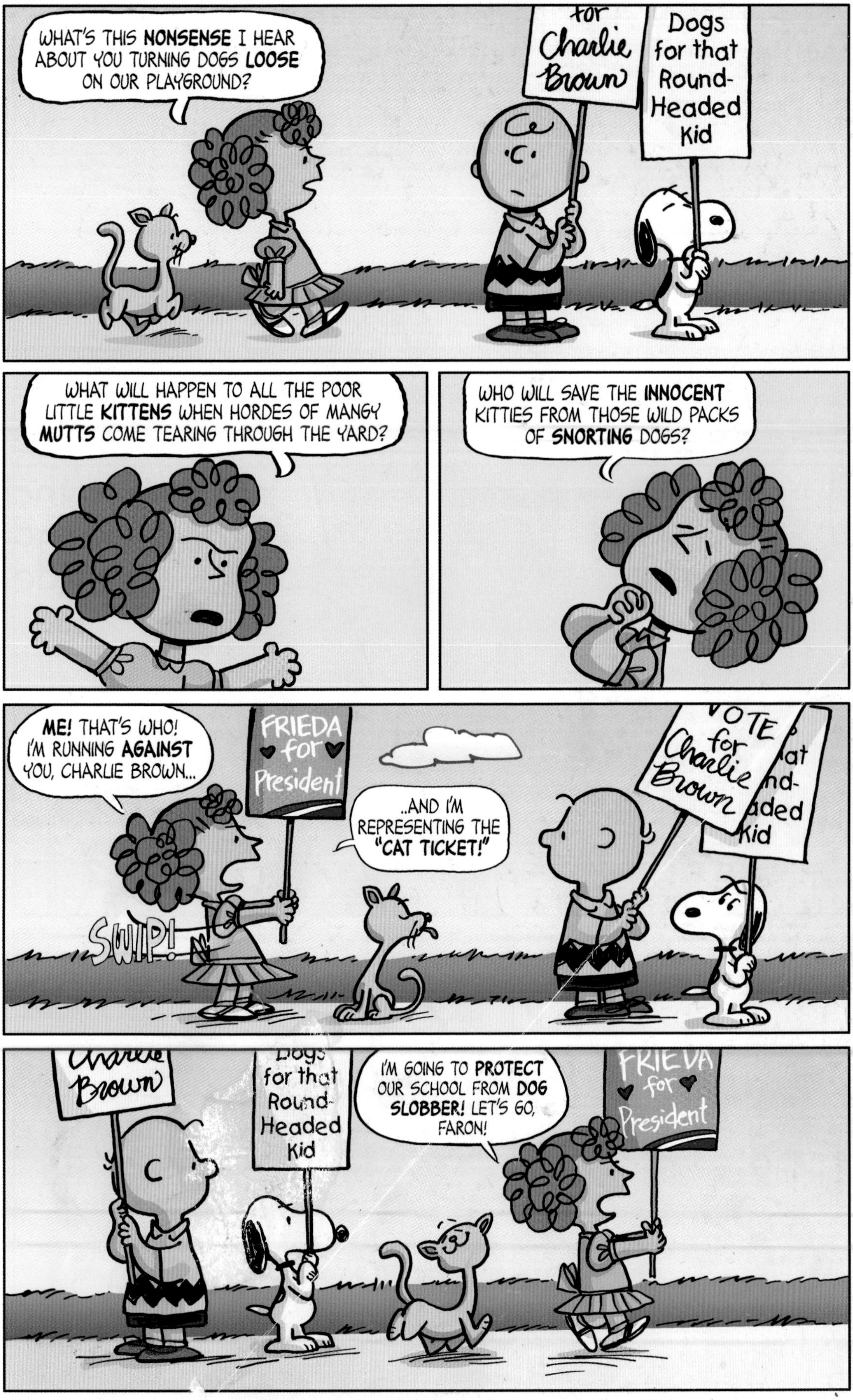
WHAT'S THIS NONSENSE I HEAR ABOUT YOU TURNING DOGS LOOSE ON OUR PLAYGROUND?
for Charlie Brown
Dogs for that Round-Headed Kid
WHAT WILL HAPPEN TO ALL THE POOR LITTLE KITTENS WHEN HORDES OF MANGY MUTTS COME TEARING THROUGH THE YARD?
WHO WILL SAVE THE INNOCENT KITTIES FROM THOSE WILD PACKS OF SNORTING DOGS?
ME! THAT'S WHO! I'M RUNNING AGAINST YOU, CHARLIE BROWN...
FRIEDA for President
SWIP!
..AND I'M REPRESENTING THE "CAT TICKET!"
VOTE for Charlie Brown
Brown
Dogs for that Round-Headed Kid
I'M GOING TO PROTECT OUR SCHOOL FROM DOG SLOBBER! LET'S GO, FARON!
FRIEDA for President

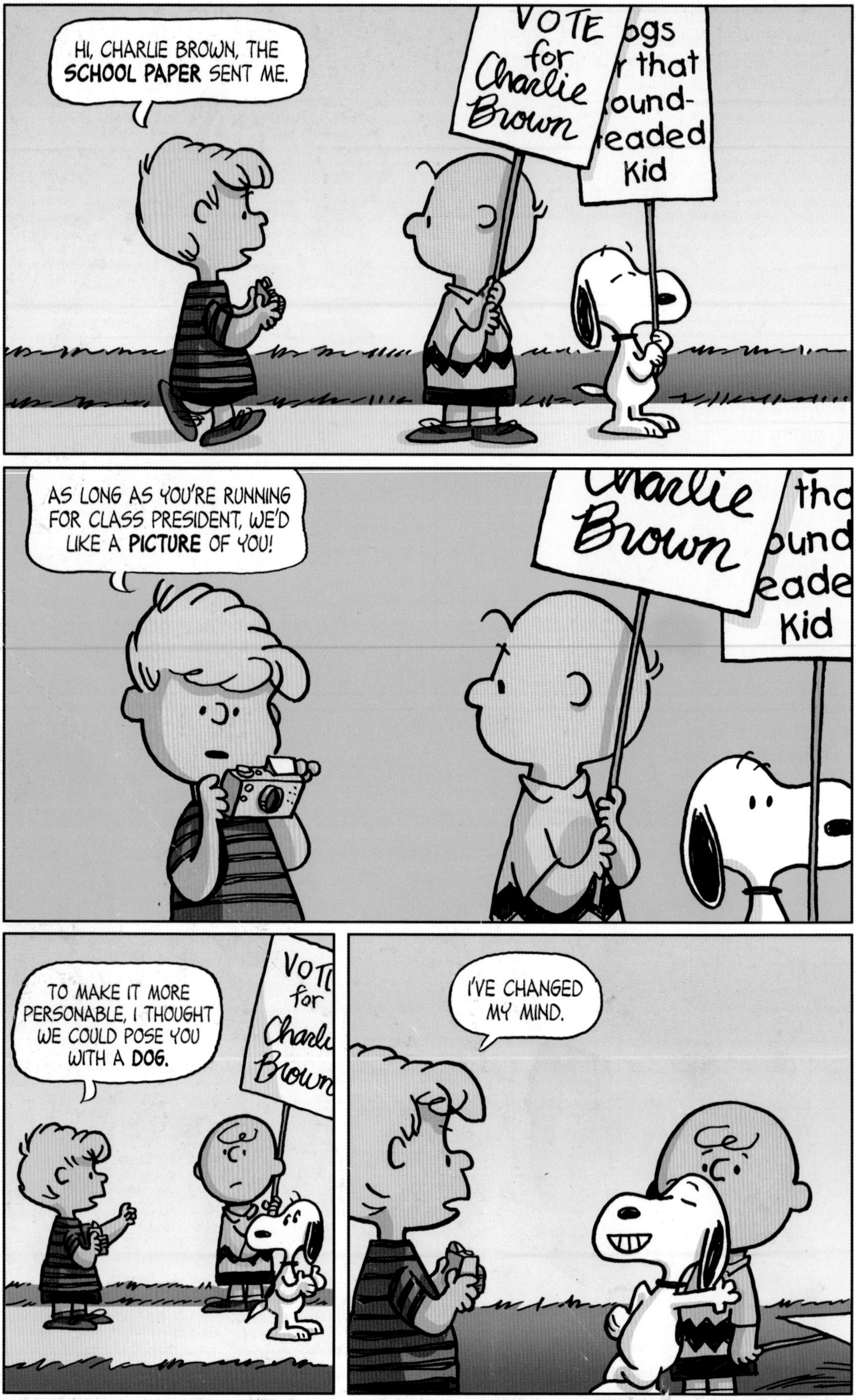
HI, CHARLIE BROWN, THE SCHOOL PAPER SENT ME.
VOTE for Charlie Brown
Kid
AS LONG AS YOU'RE RUNNING FOR CLASS PRESIDENT, WE'D LIKE A PICTURE OF YOU!
TO MAKE IT MORE PERSONABLE, I THOUGHT WE COULD POSE YOU WITH A DOG.
I'VE CHANGED MY MIND.

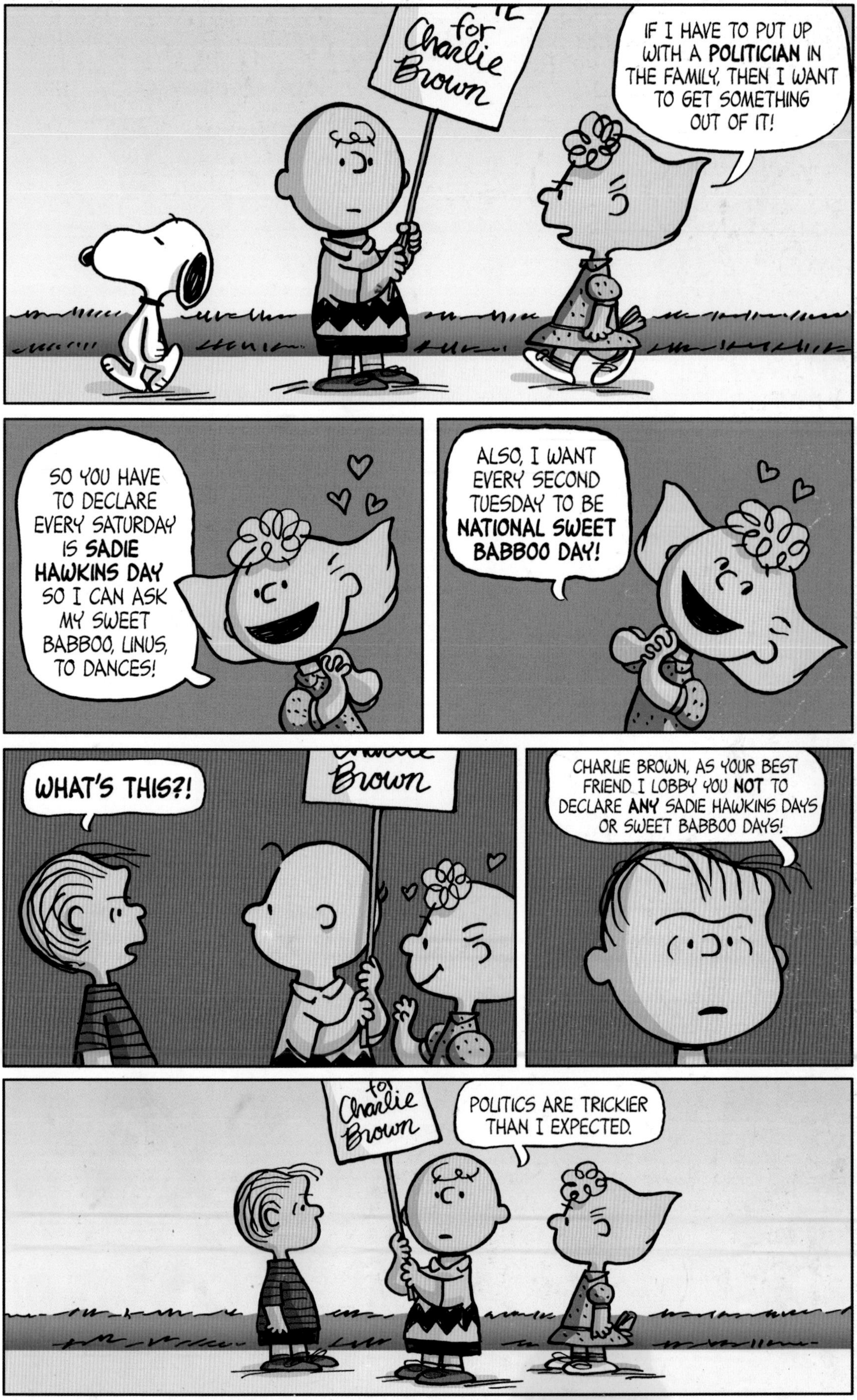
for Charlie Brown
IF I HAVE TO PUT UP WITH A **POLITICIAN** IN THE FAMILY, THEN I WANT TO GET SOMETHING OUT OF IT!
SO YOU HAVE TO DECLARE EVERY SATURDAY IS **SADIE HAWKINS DAY** SO I CAN ASK MY SWEET BABBOO, LINUS, TO DANCES!
ALSO, I WANT EVERY SECOND TUESDAY TO BE **NATIONAL SWEET BABBOO DAY!**
WHAT'S THIS?!
Brown
CHARLIE BROWN, AS YOUR BEST FRIEND I LOBBY YOU **NOT** TO DECLARE **ANY** SADIE HAWKINS DAYS OR SWEET BABBOO DAYS!
for Charlie Brown
POLITICS ARE TRICKIER THAN I EXPECTED.

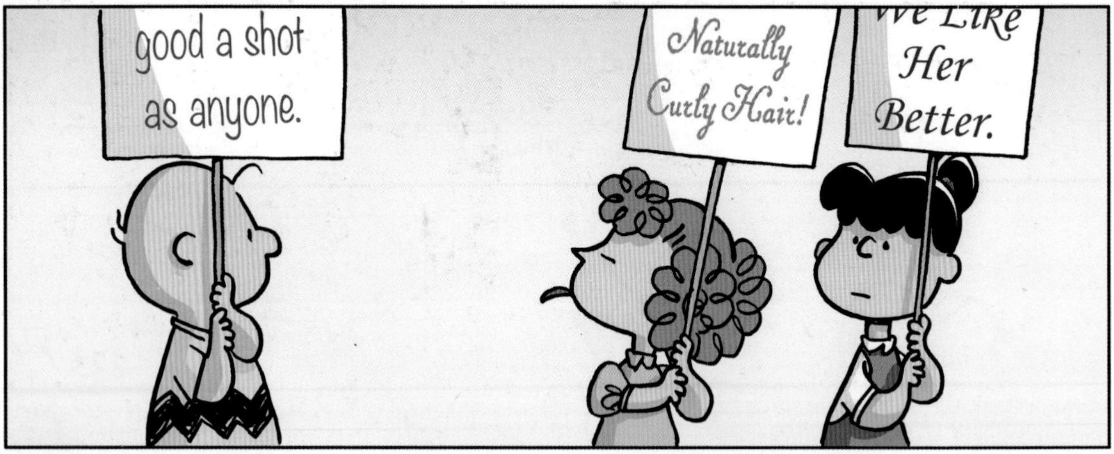
good a shot as anyone.
Naturally Curly Hair!
Her Better.

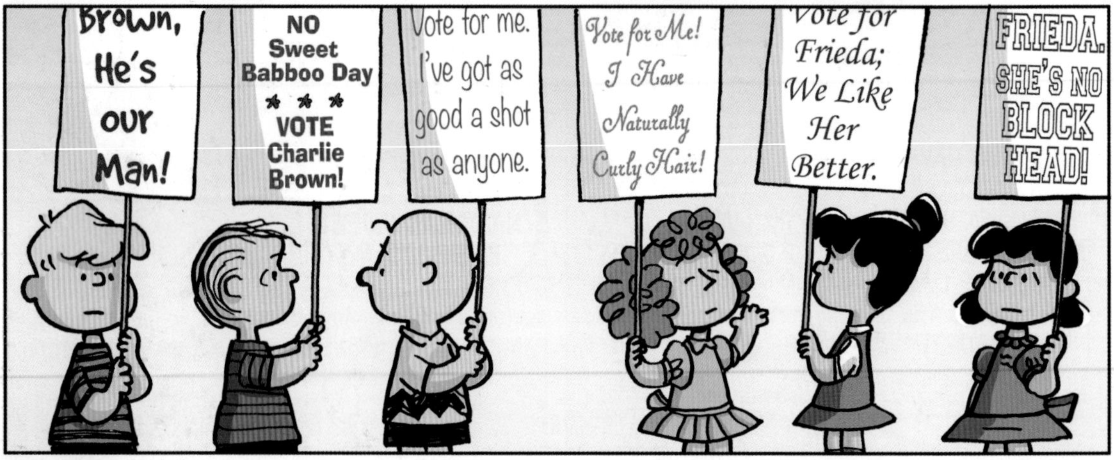
Brown, He's our Man!
NO Sweet Babboo Day
VOTE Charlie Brown!
Vote for me. I've got as good a shot as anyone.
Vote for Me! I Have Naturally Curly Hair!
Vote for Frieda; We Like Her Better.
FRIEDA. SHE'S NO BLOCK HEAD!

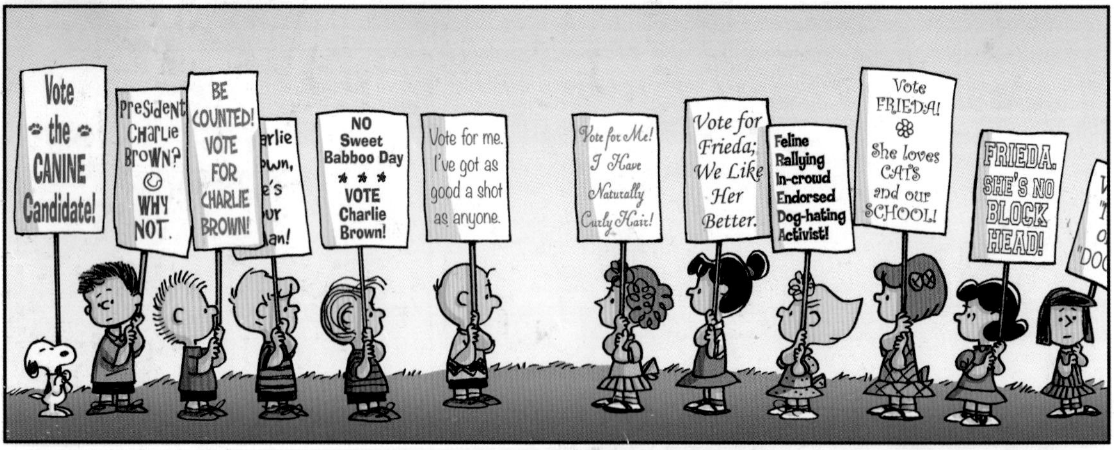
Vote the CANINE Candidate!
President Charlie Brown? WHY NOT.
BE COUNTED! VOTE FOR CHARLIE BROWN!
NO Sweet Babboo Day
VOTE Charlie Brown!
Vote for me. I've got as good a shot as anyone.
Vote for Me! I Have Naturally Curly Hair!
Vote for Frieda; We Like Her Better.
Feline Rallying In-crowd Endorsed Dog-hating Activist!
Vote FRIEDA! She loves CATS and our SCHOOL!
FRIEDA. SHE'S NO BLOCK HEAD!

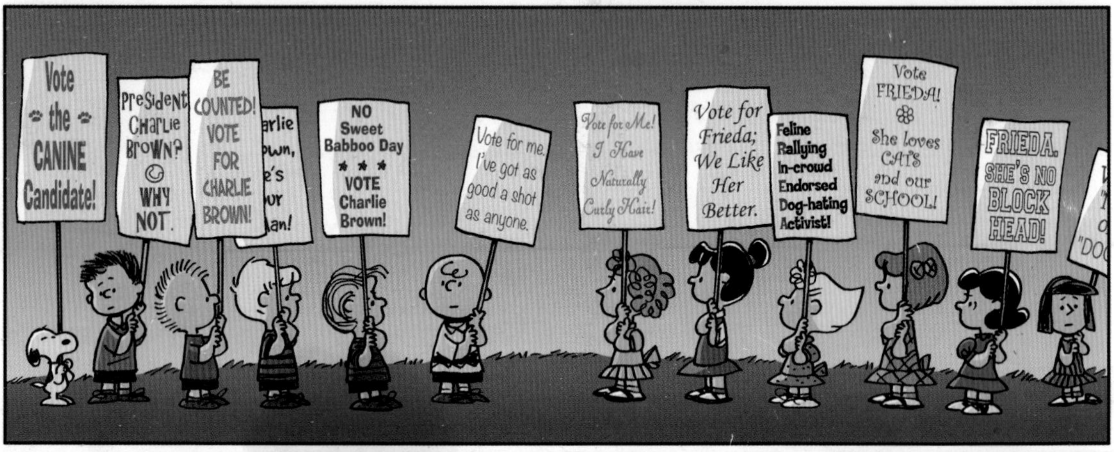
Vote the CANINE Candidate!
President Charlie Brown? WHY NOT.
BE COUNTED! VOTE FOR CHARLIE BROWN!
NO Sweet Babboo Day
VOTE Charlie Brown!
Vote for me. I've got as good a shot as anyone.
Vote for Me! I Have Naturally Curly Hair!
Vote for Frieda; We Like Her Better.
Feline Rallying In-crowd Endorsed Dog-hating Activist!
Vote FRIEDA! She loves CATS and our SCHOOL!
FRIEDA. SHE'S NO BLOCK HEAD!

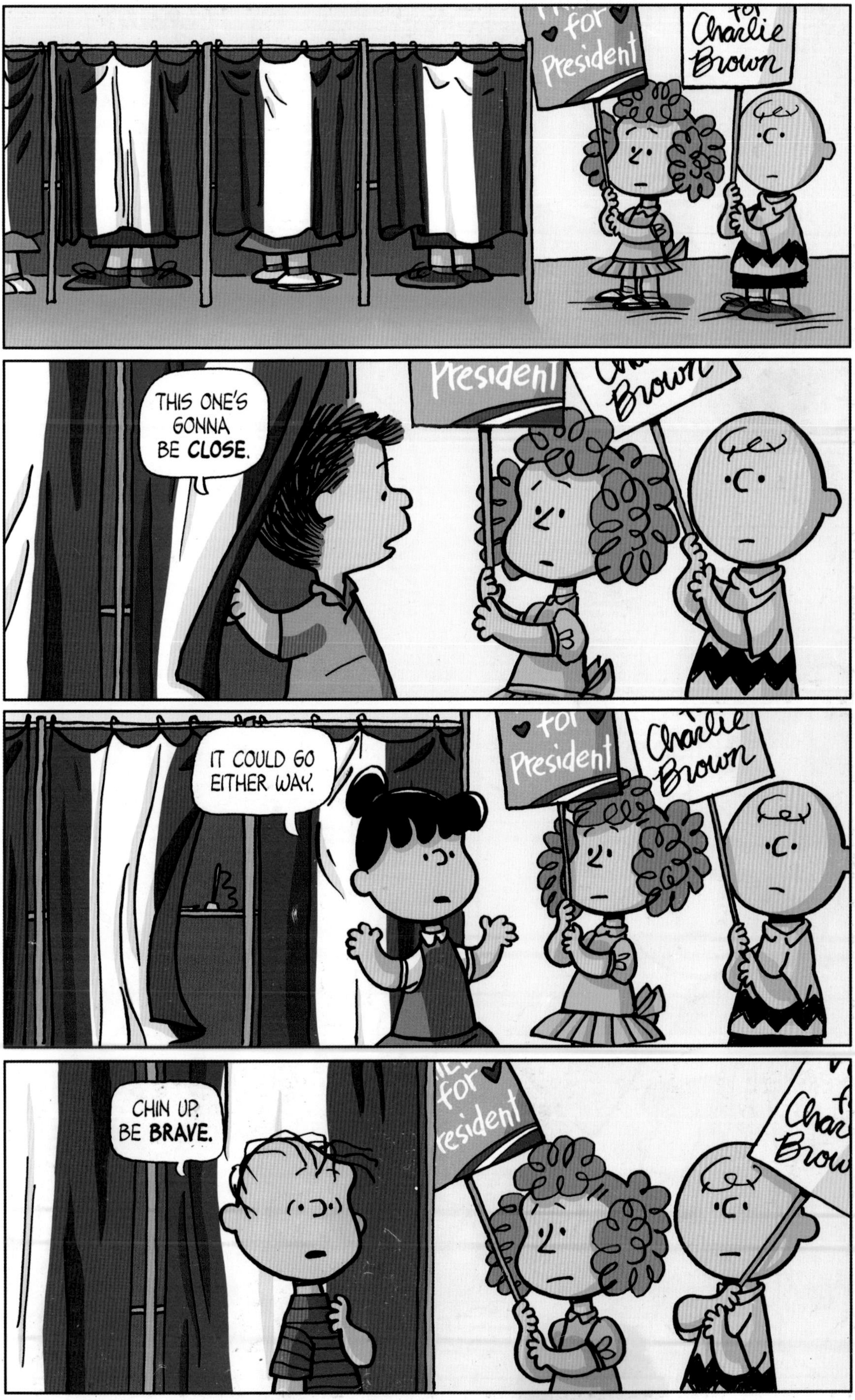
for President
for Charlie Brown
THIS ONE'S GONNA BE **CLOSE**.
IT COULD GO EITHER WAY.
CHIN UP. BE **BRAVE**.

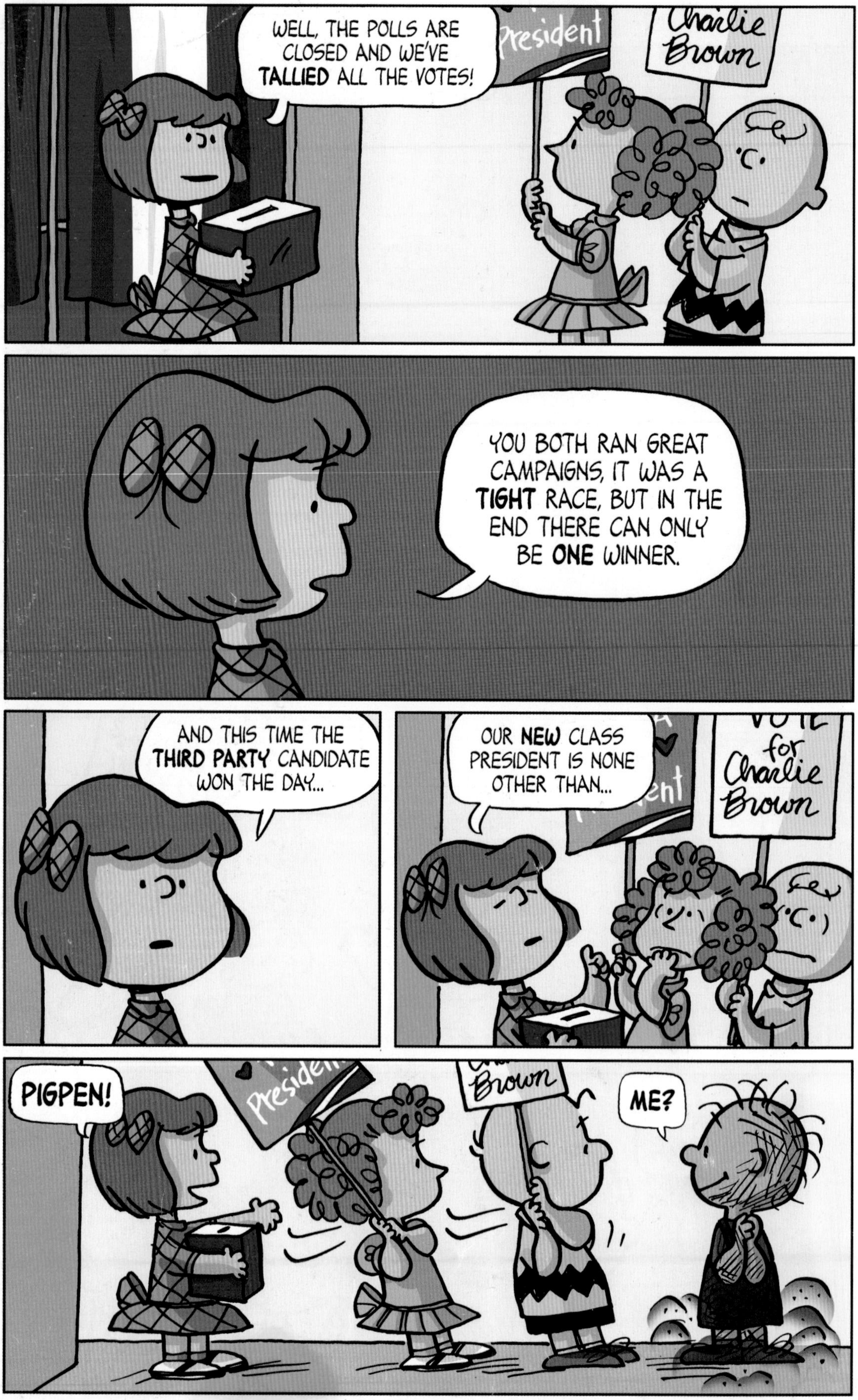

WELL, THE POLLS ARE CLOSED AND WE'VE TALLIED ALL THE VOTES!
President
Charlie Brown
YOU BOTH RAN GREAT CAMPAIGNS, IT WAS A TIGHT RACE, BUT IN THE END THERE CAN ONLY BE ONE WINNER.
AND THIS TIME THE THIRD PARTY CANDIDATE WON THE DAY...
OUR NEW CLASS PRESIDENT IS NONE OTHER THAN...
for Charlie Brown
PIGPEN!
Brown
ME?

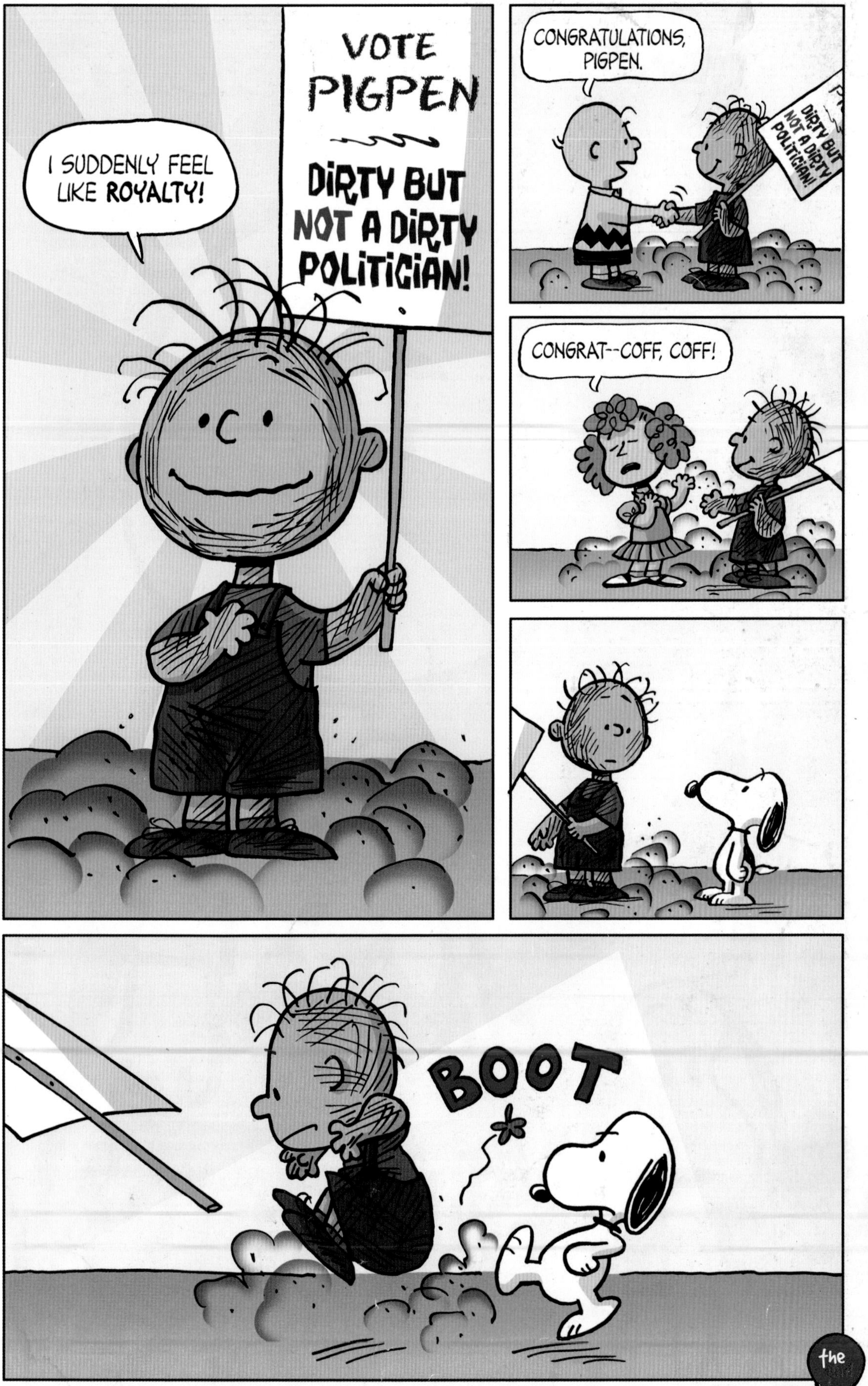
I SUDDENLY FEEL LIKE ROYALTY!
VOTE PIGPEN
DIRTY BUT NOT A DIRTY POLITICIAN!
CONGRATULATIONS, PIGPEN.
DIRTY BUT NOT A DIRTY POLITICIAN!
CONGRAT--COFF, COFF!
BOOT
the

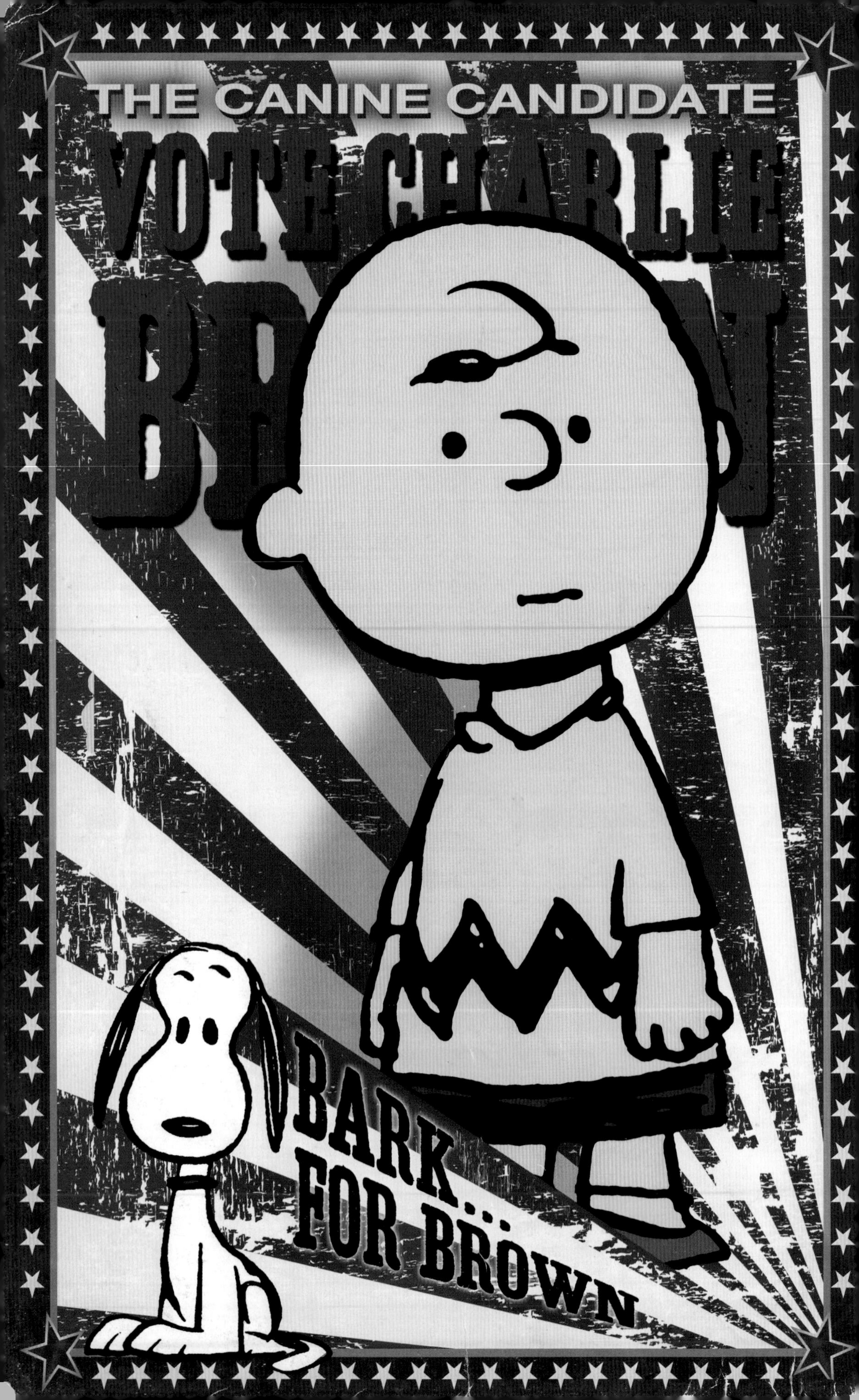
THE CANINE CANDIDATE
VOTE CHARLIE
BARK...
FOR BROWN

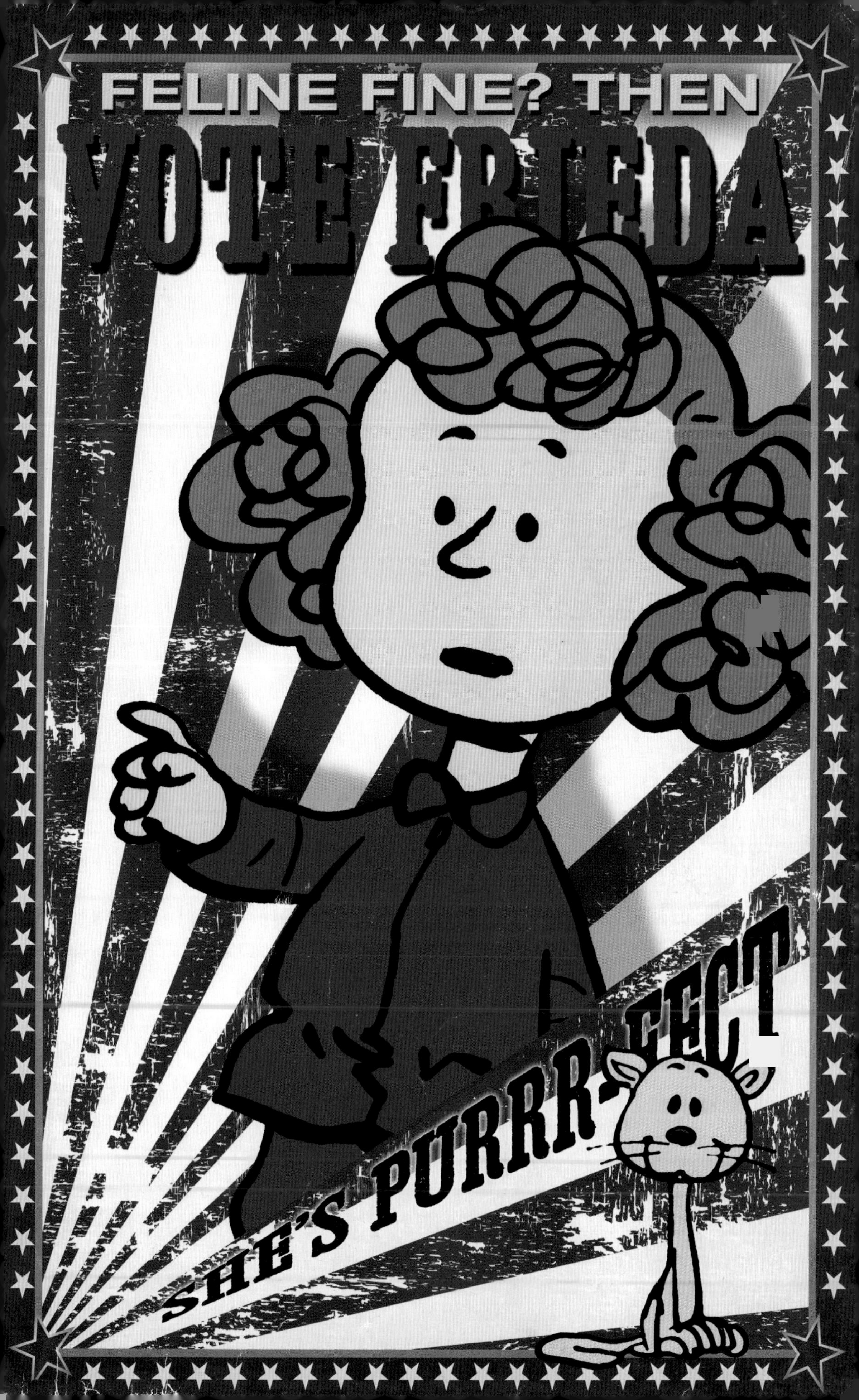
FELINE FINE? THEN
VOTE FRIEDA
SHE'S PURRR-FECT

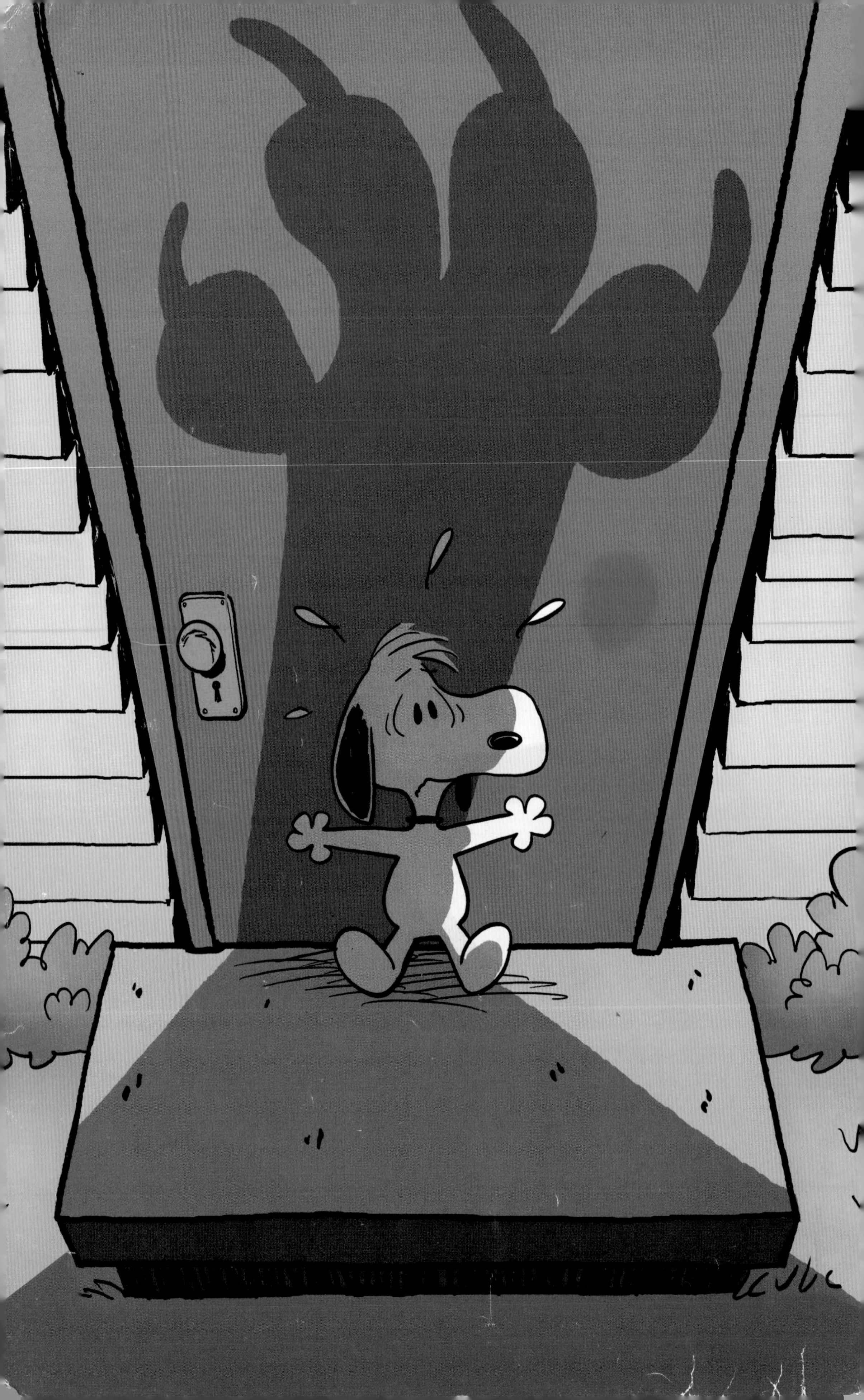

COVER GALLERY

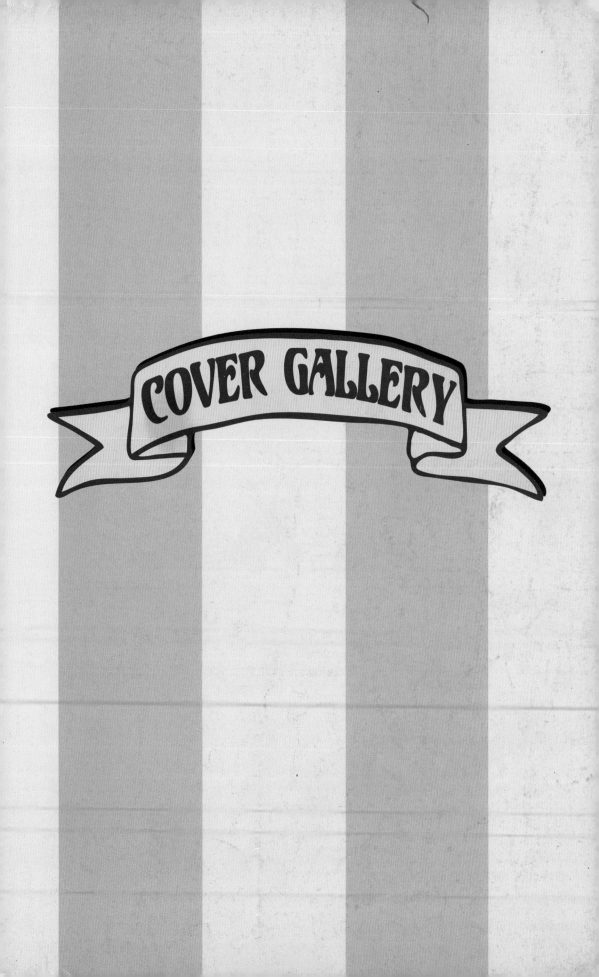

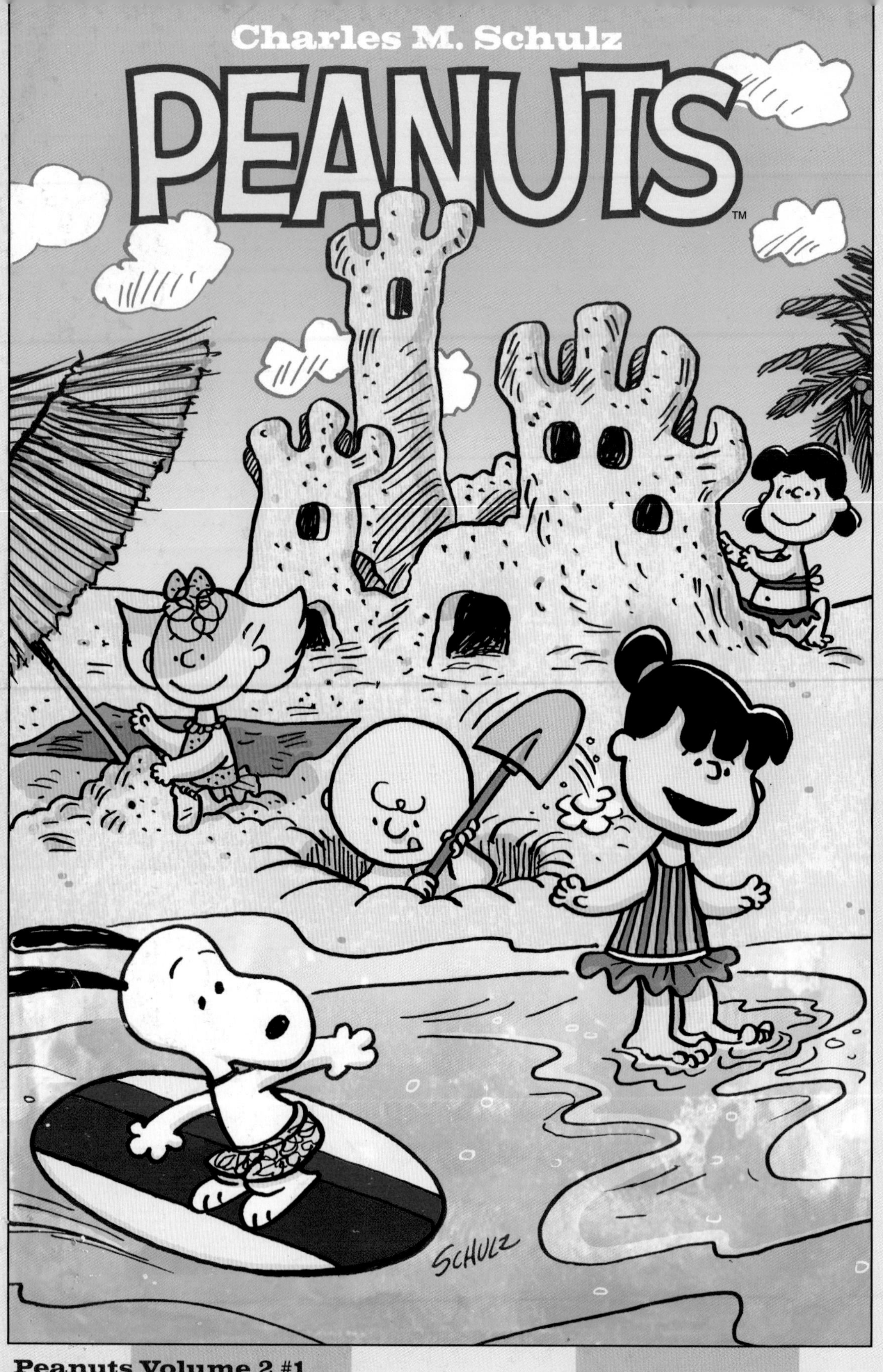
Charles M. Schulz
PEANUTS
SCHULZ

Peanuts Volume 2 #1

Pencils by Vicki Scott
Inks by Paige Braddock
Colors by Art Roche
Design by Iain R. Morris

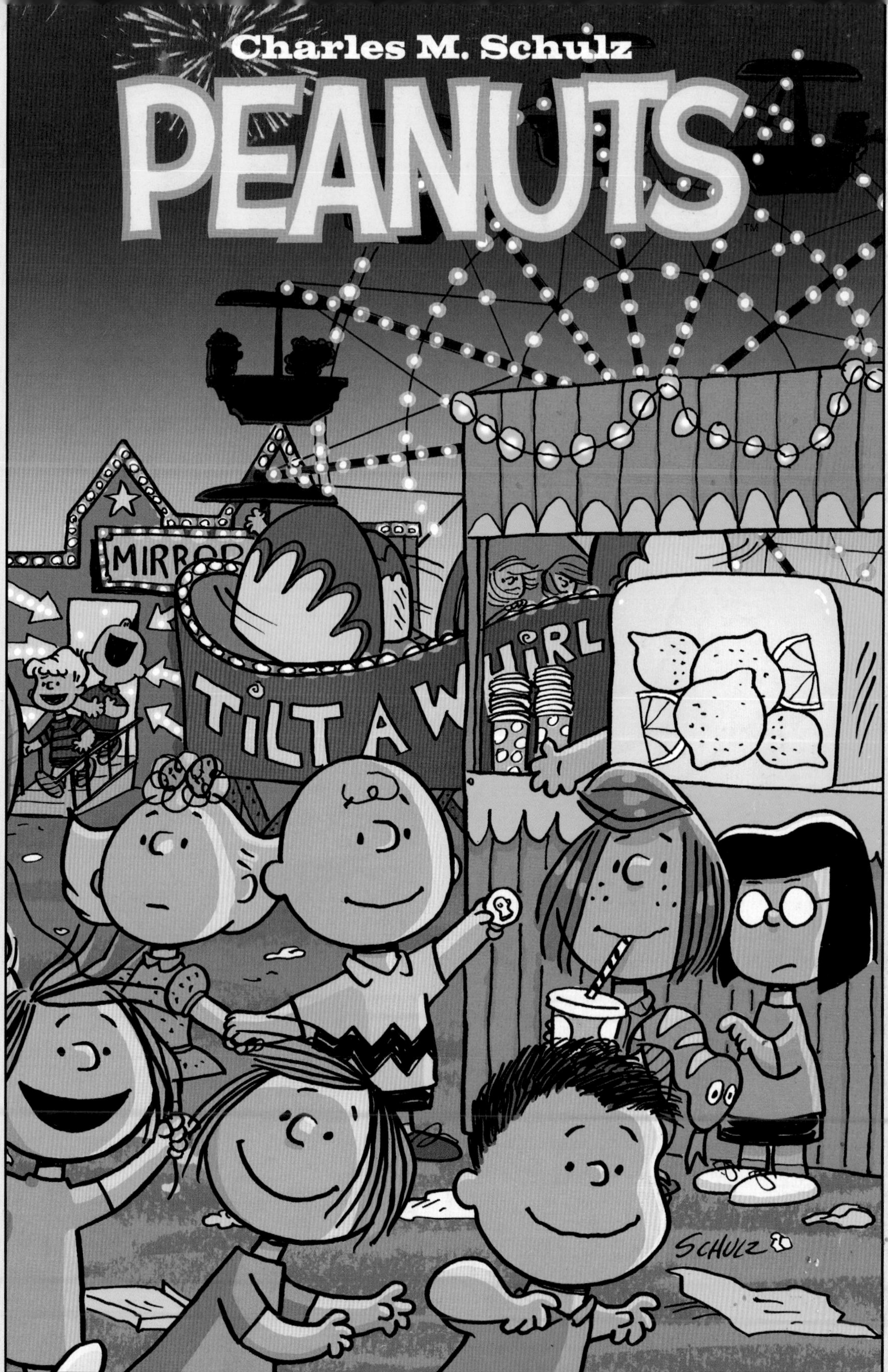
Charles M. Schulz
PEANUTS
SCHULZ

Peanuts Volume 2 #2
Pencils by Vicki Scott
Inks by Paige Braddock
Colors by Art Roche
Design by Iain R. Morris

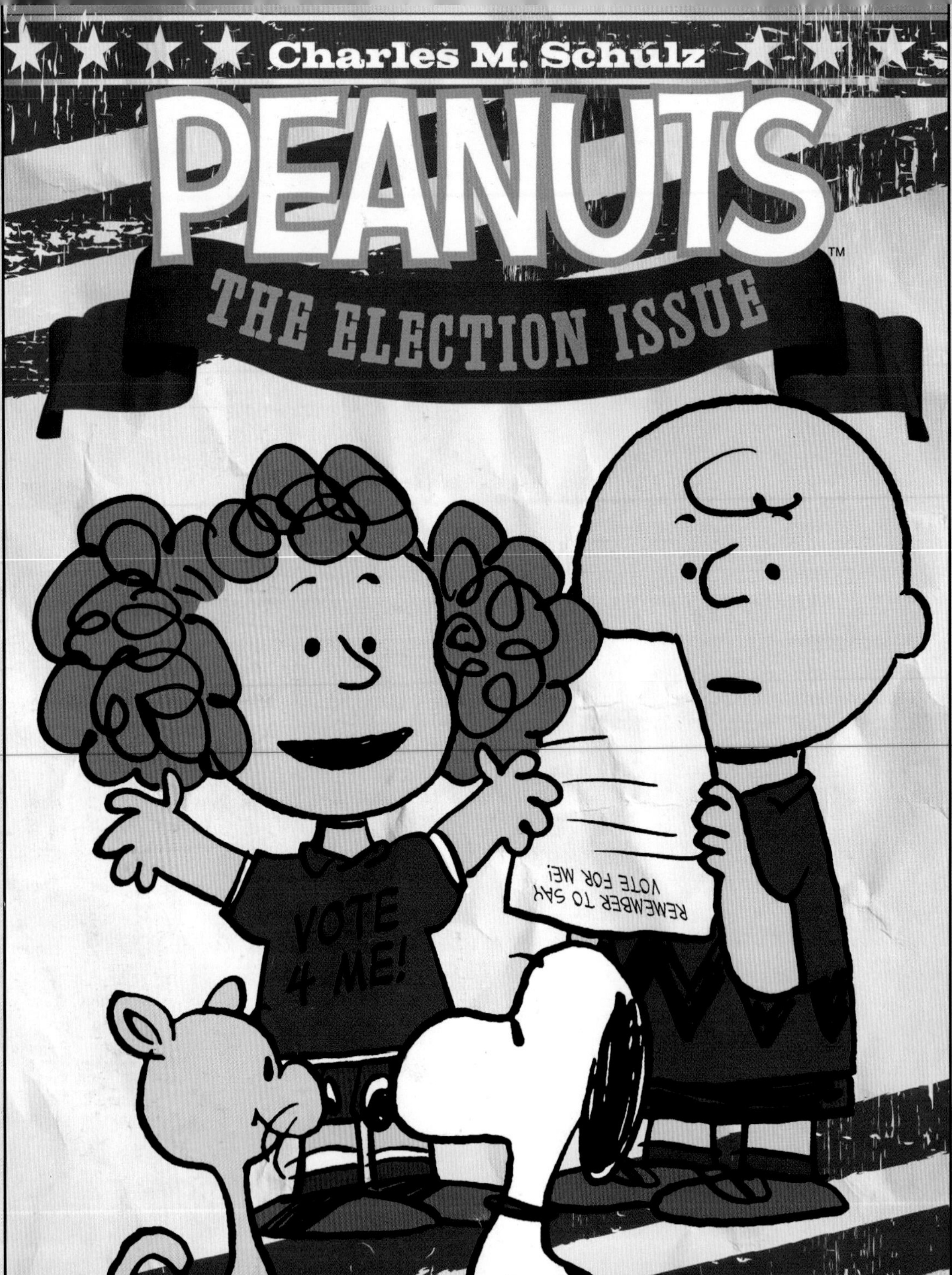
Charles M. Schulz
PEANUTS
THE ELECTION ISSUE
VOTE 4 ME!
REMEMBER TO SAY VOTE FOR ME!
SCHULZ

Peanuts Volume 2 #3
by Charles M. Schulz
Designed by Iain R. Morris

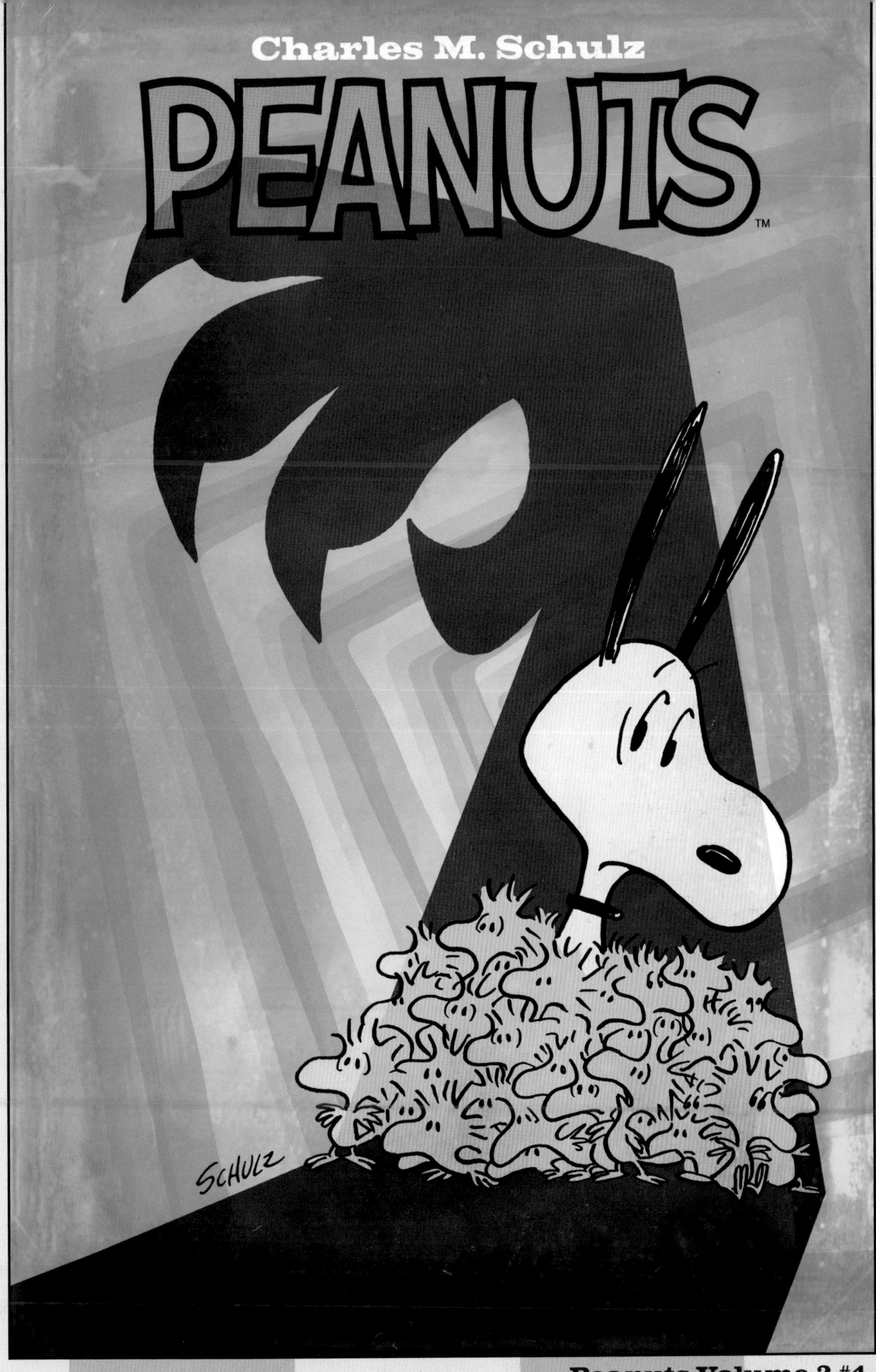
Charles M. Schulz
PEANUTS
TM
SCHULZ

Peanuts Volume 2 #4

Pencils by **Bob Scott**
Inks and Colors by **Paige Braddock**
Design by **Iain R. Morris**

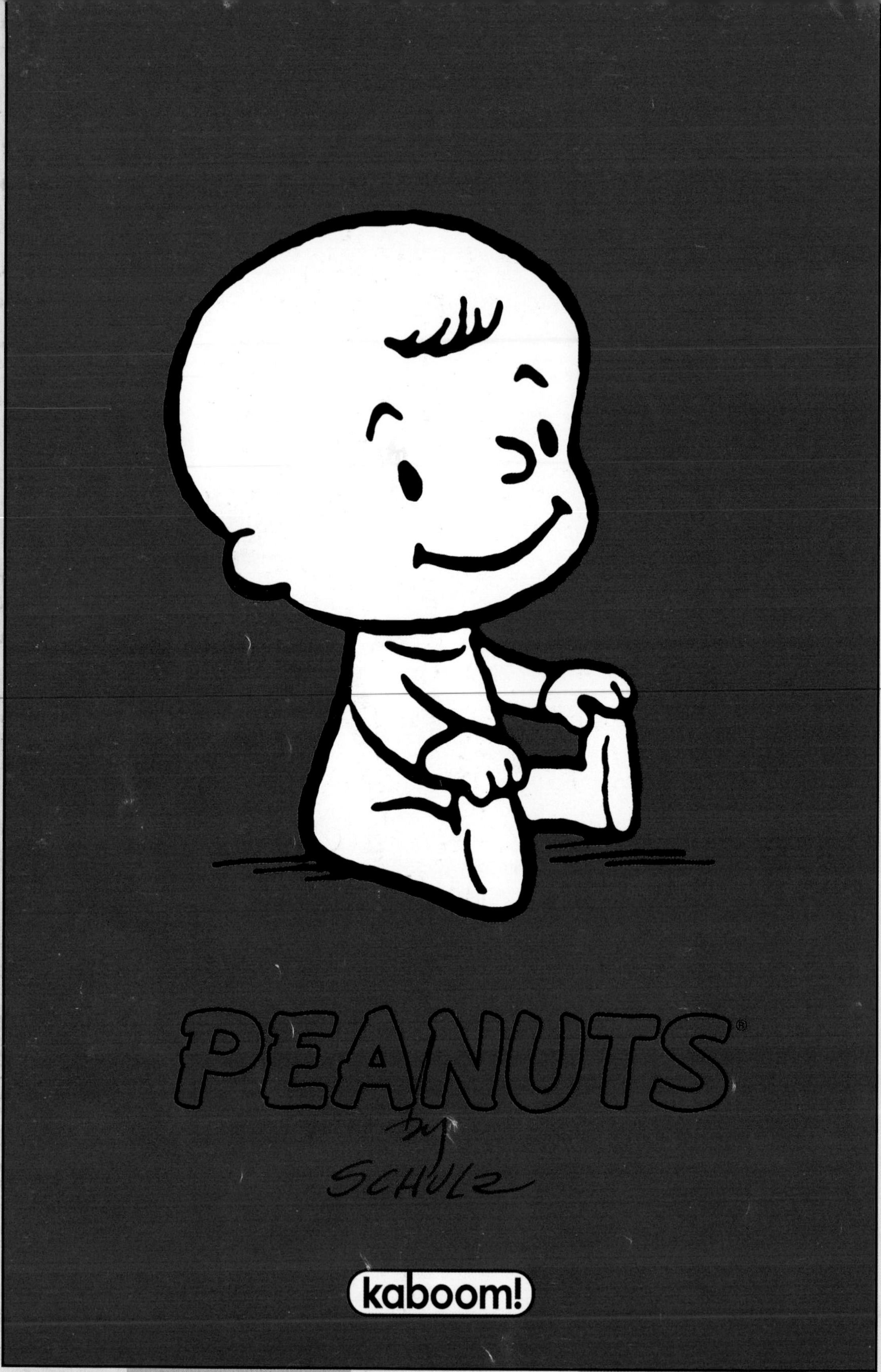
PEANUTS
by
SCHULZ
kaboom!

Peanuts Volume 2 #1 Schroeder First Appearance Cover

Art by **Charles M. Schulz**

Design by **Emily Chang**

PEANUTS

by SCHULZ

"PEANUTS"
HAVE YOU MET SCHROEDER YET, CHARLIE BROWN?
SCHROEDER?! WHO'S HE?
HE LIVES NEXT DOOR...C'MON, I'LL INTRODUCE YOU
HERE HE IS! SAY SOMETHING TO HIM
I DON'T KNOW WHAT TO SAY...
I ALWAYS FEEL SO UNCOMFORTABLE NEAR CHILDREN!
SCHULZ
5/30
Copr. 1951 by United Feature Syndicate, Inc.

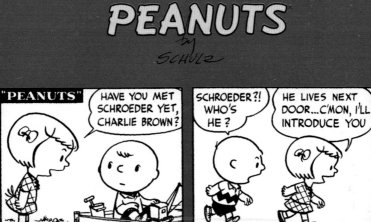

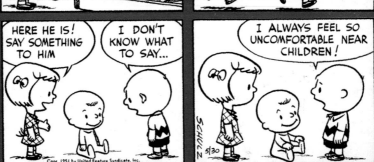

SCHROEDER
FIRST APPEARANCE
MAY 30, 1951

kaboom!

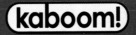

SELECT SERIES II
ISSUE ONE

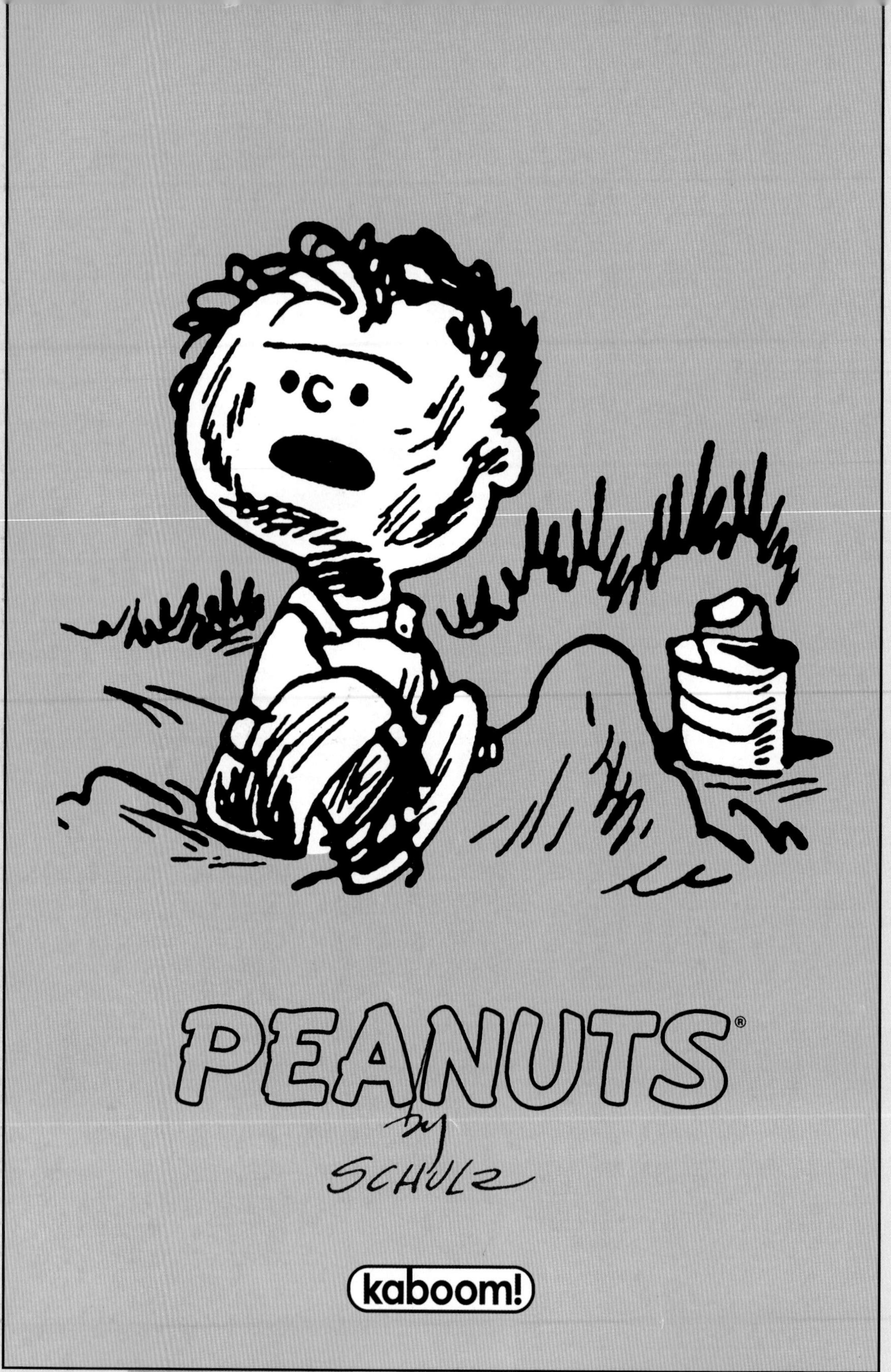
PEANUTS®
by
SCHULZ
kaboom!

Peanuts Volume 2 #2 Pig-Pen First Appearance Cover
Art by Charles M. Schulz
Design by Emily Chang

PEANUTS

by SCHULZ

"PEANUTS"
HELLO, THERE.. WHAT'S **YOUR** NAME?
I HAVEN'T GOT A NAME..PEOPLE JUST CALL ME THINGS.. REAL INSULTING THINGS...
WHAT DO THEY CALL YOU **MOST** OF THE TIME?
I'LL TELL YOU IF YOU WON'T LAUGH...
'PIG-PEN'
7-13
SCHULZ
Tm. Reg. U. S. Pat Off.—All rights reserved
Copr. 1954 by United Feature Syndicate, Inc.

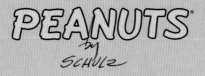

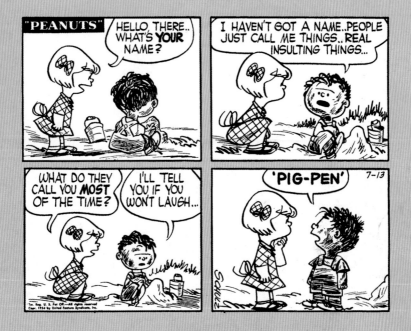

Pig-Pen

First appearance

July 13, 1954

kaboom!

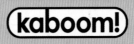

SELECT SERIES II

ISSUE TWO

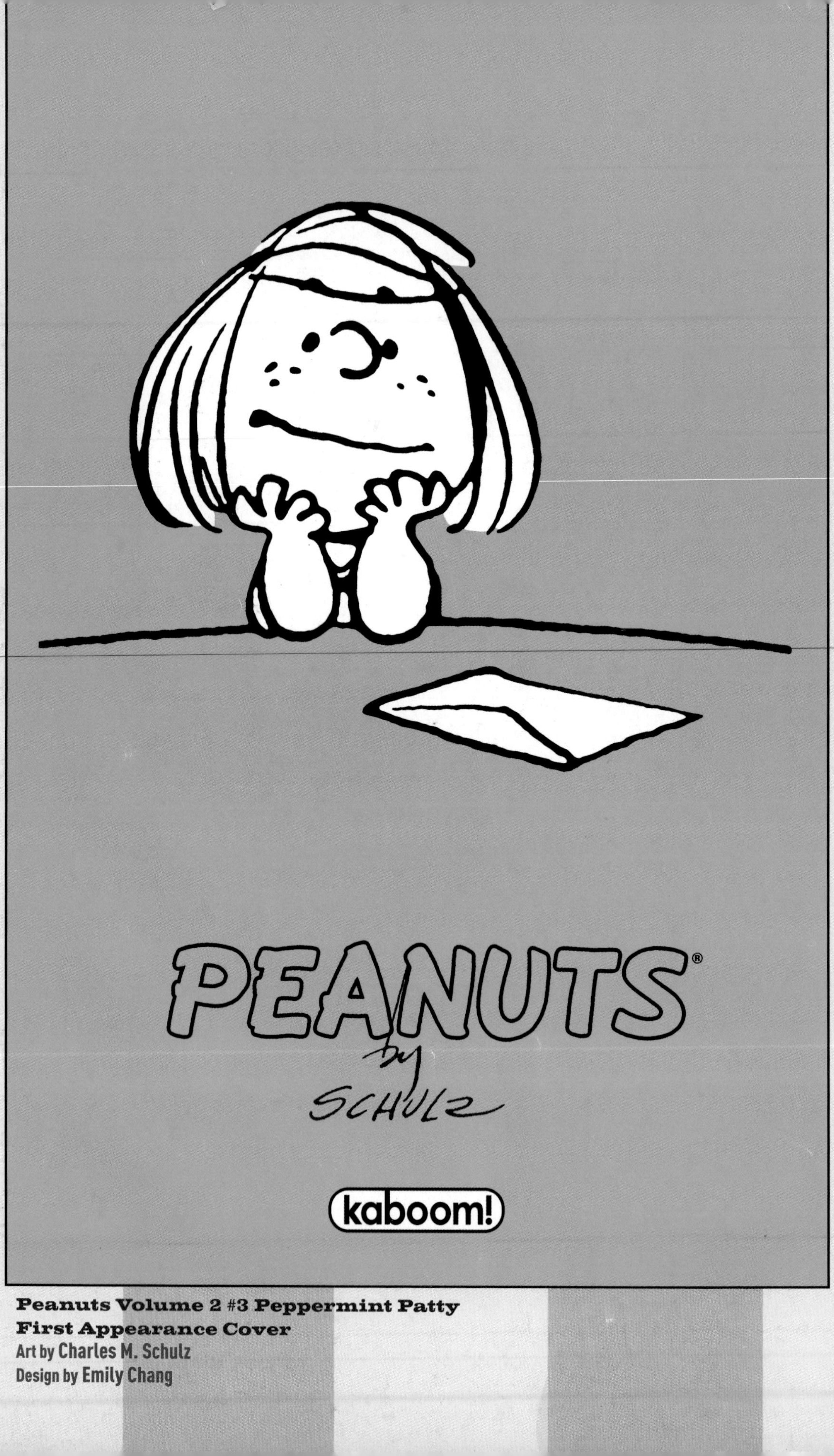
PEANUTS®
by SCHULZ
kaboom!

Peanuts Volume 2 #3 Peppermint Patty First Appearance Cover
Art by Charles M. Schulz
Design by Emily Chang

PEANUTS

by SCHULZ

PEANUTS
HI, ROY... WHO YOU WRITIN' TO?
I'M WRITING TO A LITTLE KID NAMED LINUS THAT I MET AT CAMP SEVERAL WEEKS AGO
IS HE CUTE? IF HE IS, TELL HIM YOUR VERY GOOD FRIEND, "PEPPERMINT" PATTY SAYS, "HELLO"
TELL HIM WHAT A REAL SWINGER I AM...
Tm. Reg. U.S. Pat. Off.—All rights reserved ©1966 by United Feature Syndicate, Inc.
8-22
PUT IN A GOOD WORD FOR ME, ROY, AND THE NEXT TIME WE INDIAN WRESTLE I'LL TRY NOT TO CLOBBER YOU!
SCHULZ

Peppermint Patty
First appearance
August 22, 1966

kaboom!

SELECT SERIES II
ISSUE THREE

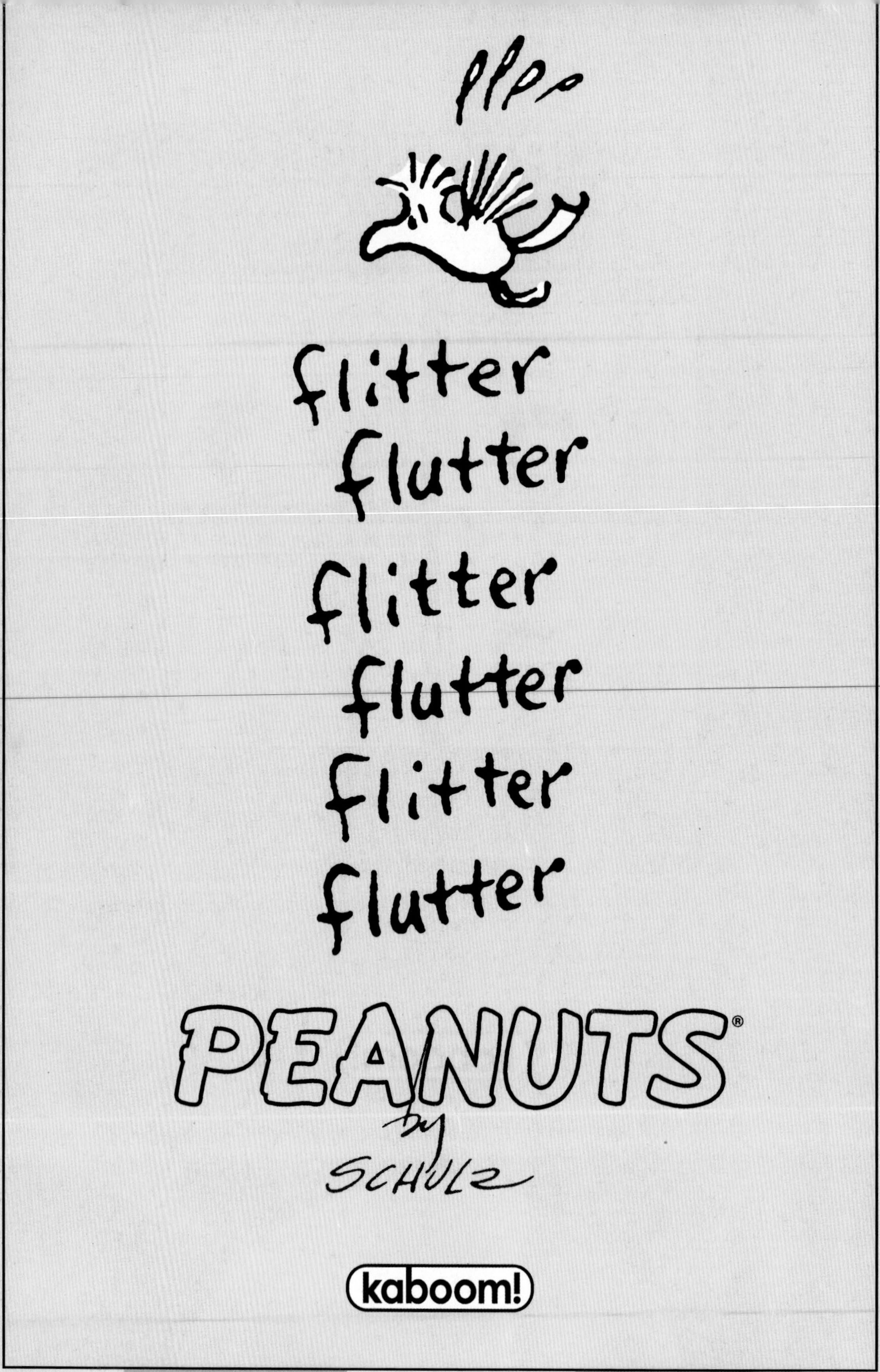
flitter
flutter
flitter
flutter
flitter
flutter
PEANUTS®
by SCHULZ
kaboom!

Peanuts Volume 2 #4 Woodstock First Appearance Cover
Art by Charles M. Schulz
Design by Emily Chang

PEANUTS by SCHULZ

PEANUTS
!
flitter flutter flitter flutter flitter flutter
whew!
GASP GASP
4-4
Z
MUST HAVE BEEN A ROUGH FLIGHT
SCHULZ

Woodstock
First appearance
April 4, 1967

kaboom!

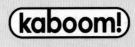

SELECT SERIES II
ISSUE FOUR

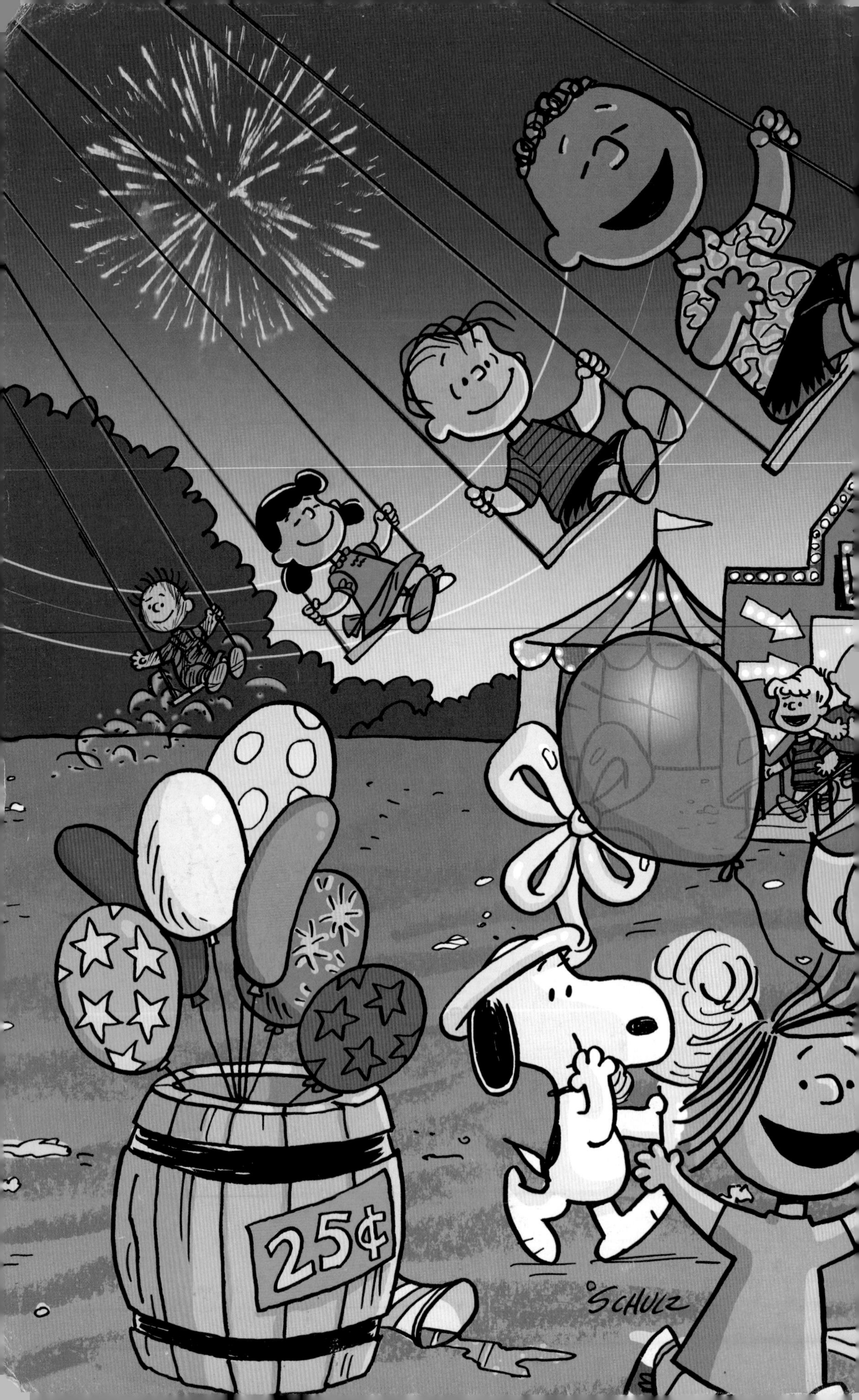
25¢
SCHULZ

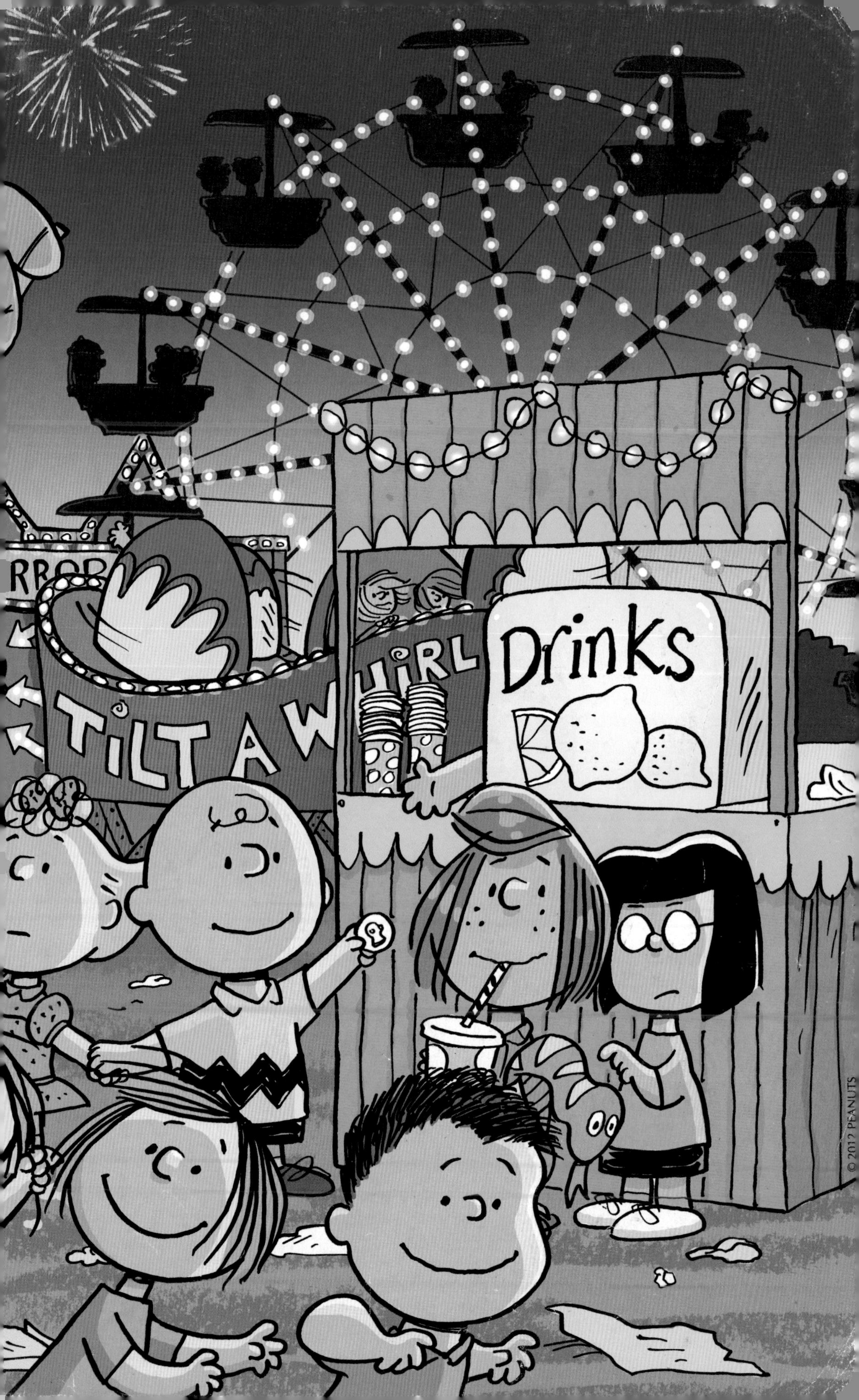

RROR
TILT A W
HIRL
Drinks

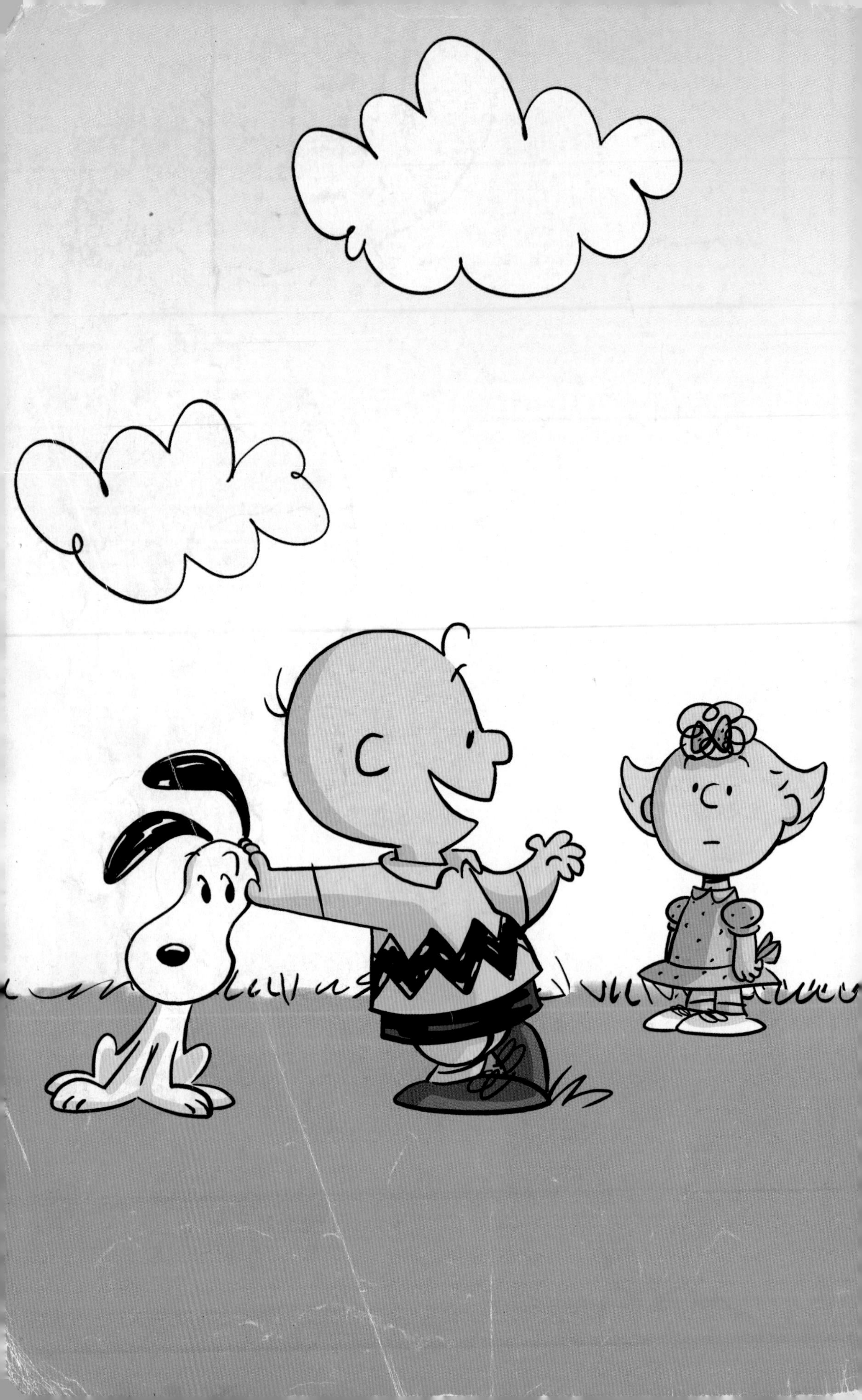

Charles M. Schulz once described himself as "born to draw comic strips." Born in Minneapolis, at just two days old, an uncle nicknamed him "Sparky" after the horse Spark Plug from the Barney Google comic strip, and throughout his youth, he and his father shared a Sunday morning ritual reading the funnies. After serving in the Army during World War II, Schulz's first big break came in 1947 when he sold a cartoon feature called "Li'l Folks" to the *St. Paul Pioneer Press.* In 1950, Schulz met with United Feature Syndicate, and on October 2 of that year, PEANUTS, named by the syndicate, debuted in seven newspapers. Charles Schulz died in Santa Rosa, California, in February 2000—just hours before his last original strip was to appear in Sunday papers.

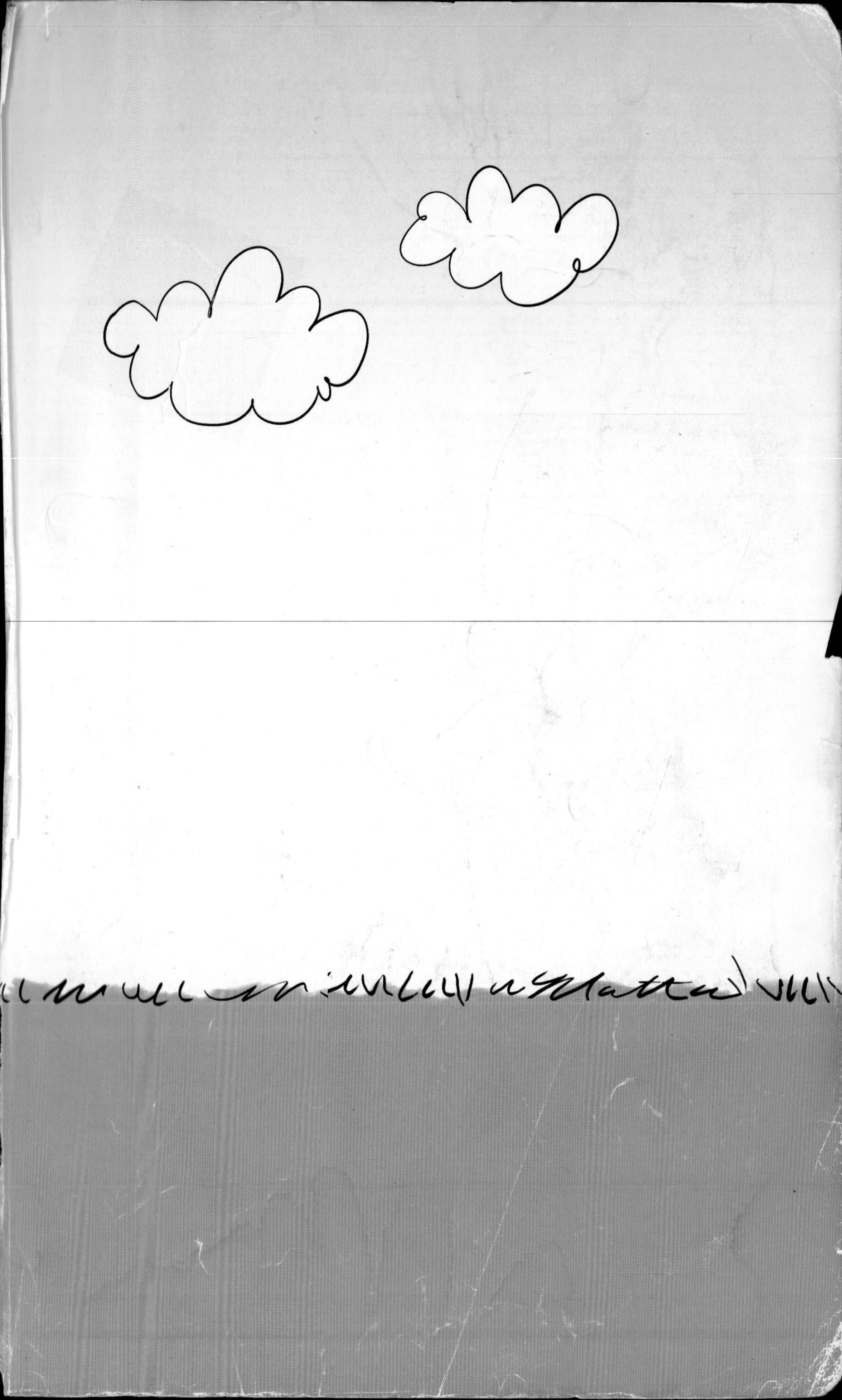